Acknowledgments

Good things happen with great people.

I'd like to thank my good friend, and fellow author, Jessica Barksdale Inclán, for pushing me across the finish line. Since we were seven years old, Jodi Fung King always believed I was a writer and never doubted I would get published—thanks for always being in my creative corner. My inner circle—Christina Liang Wong, Cynthia Schroeder, and Nancy Sue Martin—what would I do without you? Dr. Wynnshang Sun, who chose to write about his best friend (me!) in eighth grade for a class report while I chose to write about myself—this book is dedicated to you, so now we're even.

To my agent, Jean Naggar, and my editor at Berkley Books, Christine Zika, thank you for bringing *Good Things* to bookshelves everywhere. A big *mahalo* to Tina Anderson, senior publicist at Berkley. I'm forever grateful to Leona Nevler, who first said yes.

To my parents, Dr. I-Chi and Priscilla Hsu, who bravely walk their own paths and gifted me with a desire to write and create, and to my in-laws, Arthur and Betty Gee, who gave me support and watched the kids so I could meet deadlines and finally get my hair cut. A huge hug and flurry of thankful kisses go to my brother, Lawrence Hsu, who morphs from sibling to good friend to web guru to design kingpin while somehow managing to have a life and family of his own.

And a heartfelt thanks to my beautiful family—to my two children, Maya and Eric, who remind me every day that I already have it all, and to my husband, business partner, and fellow author, Darrin Gee, who is my soulmate in the truest sense of the word.

Praise for Mia King's *Good Things*

"*Good Things* is a funny, true look at a woman's quest for taste in life whether in men or in food. Mia King writes with style and verve, making you laugh and cry along with Deidre. You'll enjoy every morsel of this book."

—Jessica Barksdale Inclán,
author of *The Matter of Grace* and *Her Daughter's Eyes*

"Mia King writes with originality and freshness. She skillfully spins her story, infusing it with memorable characters, sparkling dialogue, humor, emotion, and passion."

—Catherine Spangler,
national bestselling author of *Touched by Darkness*

"Thank heaven and Mia King for this delightful debut novel to remind us of what's important. Save *Good Things* for one of those weeks where nothing is going right, because this book is sure to rescue you."

—Justina Chen Headley,
author of *Nothing But the Truth (and a Few White Lies)*

GOOD THINGS

MIA KING

BERKLEY BOOKS, NEW YORK

THE BERKLEY PUBLISHING GROUP
Published by the Penguin Group
Penguin Group (USA) Inc.
375 Hudson Street, New York, New York 10014, USA
Penguin Group (Canada), 90 Eglinton Avenue East, Suite 700, Toronto, Ontario M4P 2Y3, Canada (a division of Pearson Penguin Canada Inc.)
Penguin Books Ltd., 80 Strand, London WC2R 0RL, England
Penguin Group Ireland, 25 St. Stephen's Green, Dublin 2, Ireland (a division of Penguin Books Ltd.)
Penguin Group (Australia), 250 Camberwell Road, Camberwell, Victoria 3124, Australia (a division of Pearson Australia Group Pty. Ltd.)
Penguin Books India Pvt. Ltd., 11 Community Centre, Panchsheel Park, New Delhi—110 017, India
Penguin Books (NZ), Cnr. Airborne and Rosedale Roads, Albany, Auckland 1310, New Zealand (a division of Pearson New Zealand Ltd.)
Penguin Books (South Africa) (Pty.) Ltd., 24 Sturdee Avenue, Rosebank, Johannesburg 2196, South Africa

Penguin Books Ltd., Registered Offices: 80 Strand, London WC2R 0RL, England

Cover design by Rita Frangie
Cover photo by Digital Vision / Getty Images
Book design by Kristin del Rosario

PRINTING HISTORY
Berkley trade paperback edition / February 2007

Library of Congress Cataloging-in-Publication Data

King, Mia.
Good things : a novel / Mia King.
p. cm.
ISBN-13: 978-0-425-21371-1 (alk. paper)
1. Television personalities—Fiction. 2. Single women—Fiction. I. Title.

PS3611.I5834G66 2007
813'.6—dc22 2006048506

PRINTED IN THE UNITED STATES OF AMERICA

10 9 8 7 6 5 4 3 2 1

To Wynnshang,
the real William Sen,
who always knows a good thing or two

Good Things

CHAPTER 1

Illusion is the first of all pleasures.

—OSCAR WILDE

"THESE CORN FRITTERS are simply orgasmic!"

Deidre McIntosh blushed modestly and tried not to look too startled as her guest, Manuela Jamison, heiress to Jamison Cookies and Confections, took another bite of the corn fritter Deidre had just prepared. Manuela chewed slowly, her eyes rolled to the back of her head, little bits of cooked egg at the corners of her mouth. Deidre resisted the temptation to offer her a napkin or brush it away—after all, they were on television, and live.

Deidre kept her smile on and waited politely as Manuela finished the last of the corn fritter, smacking her lips with great satisfaction. She sighed and opened her eyes, then draped an arm over Deidre's shoulders. Deidre stumbled slightly; she couldn't help it, her five-foot six-inch, 125-pound frame was no match against Manuela's five-foot ten-inch, two-hundred-plus pounds of womanly oomph.

"You are a genius," Manuela pronounced before planting a greasy kiss on Deidre's cheek, leaving a perfect red imprint. "I've always preferred the sweet to the savory, but this is enough to make me cross over." She gave Deidre a wink, and Deidre almost dropped the empty platter.

Catching herself, Deidre turned back to the camera, broadened her smile, and said, "Thank you for joining us today. I'm Deidre McIntosh, reminding you always to . . ."

"Live Simple, and Simply Live!" her audience chorused obediently. The applause began, followed by the closing music. The minute the camera's red light turned off, Deidre released her smile, dropped her shoulders, and put the platter on the counter.

"Oh, Deidre honey, I got lipstick all over you," Manuela exclaimed. She took her balled-up napkin and tried to dab at Deidre's cheeks, standing a little too close for Deidre's comfort.

"It's all right, Manuela, I'll take care of it in a little bit. Thank you so much for being on the show, it was truly an honor to have you here." Deidre began to edge away but Manuela followed in quick pursuit.

"Honey, if I had known you could cook like this, I would have been here years ago."

Deidre forced another broad smile and patted Manuela's arm before turning to head to the dressing room. "It was good to see you. Take care and please give my regards to Frank."

Manuela waved away the flock of personal assistants who were asking questions and trying to move her out of the studio. She leaned in toward Deidre. "Frank is off on some hunting trip in western Canada for Labor Day Weekend, in between touring a few factories. I have some free time this week, if you'd like to get together and, you know, talk shop. I think we have a lot in common." She gave Deidre a knowing look.

Deidre almost choked. She pointed to her throat and took a safe step backward. "Excuse me, Manuela. I need to get a glass of water. So good to see you—take care!" Deidre feigned a cough, then turned the corner quickly, walking down the hallway as fast as she could.

Once inside her office, Deidre looked in the large mirror over her credenza and groaned. She *did* have lipstick all over her cheek, and Manuela's attempts to clean it up had only resulted in a smeared mess. Deidre dabbed some makeup remover on a cotton ball and rubbed her cheek intently while picking up the telephone and dialing the extension for the producer of *Live Simple*, Len Stevens. Len picked up immediately.

"Deidre, good show. It was really orgasmic!" His English accent was even more exaggerated. She could hear laughing in the background—the boys in the sound room were probably making obscene gestures.

"All right, all right. I'm glad everyone got their kicks." Deidre tossed the stained cotton ball into the trash. "At least she said *simply* orgasmic. Was the lipstick kiss obvious?"

"Scarily so, but Dan had good coverage from four so we switched the angle. No worries, pet. Your million-dollar smile was all the audience noticed."

Her million-dollar smile. Len was confident that smile would one day get them syndication.

"Good. I'll see you in a bit."

Deidre hung up the phone, kicked off her Cole Haan slingbacks and stretched out her feet. Common sense told her to get comfortable shoes—the camera never went below the table, but Deidre's fashion sense wouldn't permit it.

Deidre's cell phone rang. It was William Sen, her best friend and roommate.

"*Oh my God*, was she hitting on you or what?"

Deidre smiled, rolling her eyes to the ceiling. "You saw the show?"

"Just the last ten minutes. I said I had to check a cadaver in the morgue and that bought me a little time."

Deidre shuddered. William was a surgeon at King County General.

"Did you put the crème fraîche in the fritter?"

"Of course."

"And the sherry?"

"Doubled the serving. I think that may have been responsible for Manuela's, uh, enthusiastic response."

William gave a snicker. "No, *mon cherie*, it's not the sherry. Did you forget about our secret ingredient?"

Deidre racked her brain—she couldn't remember anything anymore. She dug into her pocket and pulled out the scrap of paper she had scribbled the recipe on the night before. It was one of William's old family recipes, one of the many that he knew by heart. She scanned the list quickly.

"The Chinese peppercorn," she said with a smile. It was illegal in the U.S., but William had jars full of them. They left a tingle on your tongue that was practically sensual.

"God, I love that stuff," he said, sighing. "Okay, I've got to go. See you at six?"

"Probably seven. See you then. Love you."

"Love you, too. Bye." They hung up.

Deidre sighed happily, staring contentedly at her reflection in the mirror until a knock on the door interrupted her reverie. The show's program supervisor, Anne Ross, walked in before Deidre could answer.

"Here's the program format for the 'Everything's Coming Up Roses' segment," Anne announced, dropping an armful of paperwork and a basket overflowing with pink and red ribbons, wax envelopes, and tissue flowers onto Deidre's desk.

"Anne, have you ever heard of knocking?"

"I *did* knock."

"Have you ever heard of waiting?"

Anne looked at her impatiently. "June over at Avalon Gardens wants to know if we want to use her heirloom roses for the show. We promised we'd get back to her a week ago."

"So what are we waiting for?" Deidre pushed the papers and basket aside.

"You," Anne said. "We're waiting for you to sign off on the program. I did a checklist—here." She pushed a clipboard and pen toward Deidre. "Just check and initial."

"Ooh, you even put the little boxes in," Deidre said with admiration.

"I do what I can. Now will you please sign off on this so I can move onto the next show? We are two weeks behind and I'm a little stressed out. Len has been breathing down my neck, which to say the least, is a little freaky."

"Hey, what you do on your own time is your business," Deidre said with a smile, but, at Anne's frown, began ticking through the list. "Sorry. I was just kidding, Anne." Deidre hesitated at one of the boxes. "Rose tea? With what, rose hips?"

"No, this would be with actual dried rose petals."

"A rose sauce with linguine? That seems a little too much, don't you think?"

"Deidre, it was *your* idea. Six months ago, remember?"

"Oh, right," Deidre lied. She had no recollection—she had been surfing the Web for last minute ideas and apparently this was one of them.

"Do you want me to find a substitute recipe?"

"No, let's just use it."

Anne looked at her, slightly suspicious. "You've cooked it before, right?"

Deidre tried to look offended. Anne just rolled her eyes.

"Are these the paper roses for the 'Craft Corner'?" Deidre held up a huge pink tissue bouquet. She wrinkled her nose in distaste. Tacky.

"Not exactly—Tom thought the tissue would be easier. We could scale it down so we can put them on top of presents, make napkin rings, etc. The paper roses you proposed were a little complicated. Do they even sell nail scissors anymore?"

Deidre glanced at Anne's nails. Never had a manicure. She made a mental note and hoped she'd remember to get Anne a manicure set for Christmas. "Yes, Anne, they do."

"Tom also wanted to paper a wall using some of that New England rose wallpaper you found last year. It's classic, still popular, a nice look for the traditional set."

"Good. What else?"

"Here are the proposed color swatches . . ." Anne taped up different shades of pink and red. "I like one hundred eighteen and one hundred twenty-three. We can work on variations of those two colors."

"Okay, great." Deidre initialed the last page and handed the clipboard back to Anne. "Are we done?"

"No, we need to talk about the 'Fabulous at Forty' segment . . ."

Deidre looked irritated. "Whose idea was that, anyway?"

"Len's. A celebration of things in their forties. Like . . ." Anne pointed her chin imperceptibly toward Deidre.

"I'll pretend I didn't see that," Deidre said curtly. She didn't mind being forty, in fact she loved it, but that didn't mean she wanted to broadcast it live across Seattle.

Anne hugged the clipboard against her chest. "Deidre, you're amazing at forty! I would kill to be like you when I'm that old."

Deidre gave her an exasperated look. Anne was in her early thirties, still young and tactless. "Try to find a non-profit, something to do with kids or the arts, that might be celebrating their fortieth anniversary this year. We could do a little spotlight on them as well. Can you get something together by next week?"

"I'll have it ready by the end of this week." Anne gave Deidre a smug, confident look.

Deidre rolled her eyes. Young, tactless, *and* a super achiever. "While you're at it, add a 'Personality Type' segment."

Anne gasped and instantly brightened. "I just took the Myers-Briggs Type Indicator! That would be so great, we could . . ."

"Focus, Anne, focus! Just add it to the list and we'll talk about it at our next editorial meeting, okay?"

There was another knock on the door and her administrative assistant, Karen Donnelly, stuck her head in. "I have mail and need some autographs." She waved a small stack of black-and-white headshots.

Tom came in behind Karen holding a bolt of pink satin and a roll of wallpaper under his arm. "I love this wall paper, Deidre. And look what I found in the basement—I think it's ours." He shrugged. "Well, it is now." He began draping it over her chair. "I thought we could brighten up the set a bit for the show. Where are those buttons?" He fished through Anne's basket, eventually producing a medium-sized tin that he shook happily like a castanet. "Got 'em." He beamed at Deidre and she sighed. Tom was so easy to please.

Len was whistling as he strolled in. "I think we might have Nissan. They really want our audience to drive their new Altimas."

"I have an Altima," Tom said absently, milling through the buttons. "I love mine."

Len raised an eyebrow. "The target market for the Altima is professional women in their thirties and forties, Tom."

"I got a good deal," Tom said defiantly.

"Don't listen to Len," Anne advised. "He just said that to rattle you."

"Facts are facts," Len said. He sat down in a chair and smiled. "But don't worry, Tom. We won't tell anyone."

"Very funny."

Karen handed Deidre the photos and placed a small stack of mail on her desk. "You also had a few phone calls—I put them right into your voice mail."

"Thanks, Karen. Also, make sure my office fridge is stocked. I have a meeting on Thursday with the people from Calypso Papers and it could take a while. Len, are you here for any reason in particular or just to bother me?"

"To bother you. And how come you didn't save any fritters for the rest of the crew?"

"Second oven's broken. Waiting for someone to get it fixed." Deidre stared at him accusingly as she gestured for the pen in his shirt pocket.

"That's Karen's job," he said, and Karen immediately protested. Len handed Deidre the pen without moving from his comfortable position, and in doing so accidentally knocked over Anne's basket. The spools of pink and red ribbon began to unravel as they traveled across the floor. Anne began yelling at Len who was half-heartedly apologizing while randomly shoving things back into the basket.

As Deidre wrote, *"Live Simple, and Simply Live! Deidre McIntosh"* with flourish across each photograph, she caught another glimpse of herself in the mirror, surrounded by the creative chaos, and felt that no one could love their life more than she did in this moment.

IT WAS ALMOST 7:00 P.M. by the time Deidre got home to the apartment she shared with William. They had been best friends for almost twenty years, ever since sophomore year at Washington University.

They had both signed up for an elective culinary arts class, Cooking Around the World. While arguing over whether or not to use cream of tartar in a meringue they would be making for dessert, William and Deidre had forgotten to watch their shared pot of gnocchi. The entire batch burned and was now permanently solidified to the pot, but their instructor was resolute in her demand that the pot be scrubbed anyway. Two futile hours later, they threw the pot in the trash and left a check. They went out for a latté and their friendship was born.

Deidre turned the key with a smile and stepped into the apartment. Familiar sounds and smells were coming from the kitchen—it was William's night to cook. She dropped her keys into the pewter bowl by the door and breathed an audible sigh of relief as she kicked off her shoes.

"I'm home," she called to William. Gratefully, she let her feet sink into the plush carpet. "I'll change and be right out to help."

"No rush," came the reply. "I'm about to take out the chicken and the rice is already done. Drink's on the buffet, though it might not be chilled anymore. I can make another."

Deidre eagerly crossed the room and plucked the martini glass out of the bed of ice. She took a sip, suppressing a grin. It was William's infamous sake martini with colossal green Spanish olives soaked in fresh ginger and chili peppers. It was perfect, as Deidre suspected he knew it would be. "It's amazing," she called to him, before heading to her bedroom.

After a quick glance through her closet, Deidre chose a pair of black Eileen Fisher stretch crepe crop pants and a matching top. It was her latest find after her big shopping spree in Vancouver last week. She had a definite weakness for clothes. And shoes. And any kind of accessory. Fortunately, when she moved in with William, he offered her the master suite with the huge walk-in closet after watching the endless parade of wardrobe boxes. There had been twenty-four in all.

Deidre was the victim of good luck and timing, and she knew it. After graduation she had bade William a teary good-bye and returned to Denver to be with her boyfriend, Stephen, who was just finishing law school. She floated from job to job doing whatever seemed interesting and helped pay the rent—baker's assistant, florist, event planner. Stephen, on the other hand, was steadily moving up the ladder at his law firm. He broke up with Deidre on the eve of his promotion to partner, which happened to coincide with her thirtieth birthday. He told her he needed someone with a serious career, someone who could relate to the demands of his job. A month later, he was engaged to his twenty-four-year-old legal assistant.

She had called William, sobbing on the phone, but couldn't understand him because he was sobbing, too, crushed by his recent breakup with his live-in boyfriend, Kenny, who suddenly realized that maybe he wasn't gay and wanted to start seeing other people. Like women.

So Deidre moved to Seattle and into the gorgeous apartment William rented. That had been almost ten years ago. Deidre moved in and never left.

She found a job at Nordstrom the next day. The restaurant had just lost their assistant chef and although Deidre didn't have as much professional experience as they would have preferred, they hired her. Six months later, bored in the kitchen, Deidre moved to the sales floor and reveled in her new job as a personal shopper. She loved helping people acquire new and beautiful things, herself included. She spent her paycheck and commission on whatever came through the women's department, as well as the kitchen and home departments. Wüsthof chef knives,

Le Creuset omelette pans, Silpat baking mats, Nambé candlesticks . . . she wanted, and bought, them all.

Then came that fateful day, the consequence of being in the right place at the right time. Deidre was helping one of her favorite clients, sixty-four-year-old Eleanor Graves, into an Albert Nippon mélange suit.

"I was so thrilled to find the set," Eleanor was saying, referring to the thirteen-piece antique dining room set she had found at a flea market. "We had one just like it when I was growing up. And it was such a deal, I just couldn't believe it."

"Sounds wonderful," Deidre said. She smoothed the pick-stitch detail on the jacket. "You're lucky to have found something in such good condition."

"Well, that's just it. The table and chairs are in excellent condition, but I need to reupholster the chairs. When I got the quote, I almost fell over. It was more than the price of the entire set! I mean, what is the point of getting a good deal if I have to pay more to get it reupholstered?" Eleanor was indignant.

"That is a shame," Deidre agreed, frowning at the back besom pockets, which seemed to draw a little too much attention to her client's generous behind. "You know, it's really not that hard to reupholster chairs. You could probably do it yourself, Eleanor."

"Me?" Eleanor laughed. "I have two left hands."

"Well, I'd be happy to come over and take a look. I could show you how to do it."

"Really?"

"Sure. It'll be fun."

So that weekend, Deidre, Eleanor, and her three college-aged grandchildren reupholstered twelve dining room chairs in a charming Astor Rose pattern. In between chairs, Deidre took a quick look into Eleanor's closet and helped put some outfits together, then made a pit stop in the kitchen where she showed one of the granddaughters how to make buttermilk-thyme drop biscuits to go with the simple chopped salad Deidre had brought to share.

"It's amazing," said Eleanor as she accompanied Deidre to her car. "You're amazing! You just saved me a couple thousand dollars. Plus my grandkids learned a thing or two."

"It was my pleasure," Deidre said, and it was. She gave a weary but satisfied smile.

Eleanor invited Deidre to tea the following weekend, where several of Eleanor's friends gathered around to ask Deidre's advice on everything from how to organize a baby scrapbook to polishing copper and painting wicker. Deidre's strawberry shortcake with vanilla whipped cream was a hit, and just before Deidre was about to leave, Eleanor's neighbor, Rosalind Buford, pulled her to the side.

"Eleanor's told me all about you," Rosalind said approvingly, placing a confiding hand on Deidre's arm. "And from what I saw today, I think she's right."

Deidre gave a polite but perplexed look. "Right about what?"

"We need a show for Seattle women, and you're the person to host it."

Deidre was speechless. When she finally found her voice, she stammered, "Me? But I don't know anything about running a show, much less being on TV."

Rosalind dismissed Deidre's protest with a wave of the hand. "Nonsense. You're Seattle's own Martha Stewart, except cuter and much simpler. Seattle women need good, simple tips for everyday living. Nothing too complicated or intimidating."

Deidre found herself agreeing. "Tools for living simply," she said slowly.

"Exactly," Rosalind said briskly. " Now my husband, John, owns Channel Five. He always complains about how hard it is to find quality programming. I'm going to talk to him tonight. What do you think?"

"Well, to be honest . . ."

"Great. No more discussion. Eleanor has your number, I'll get in touch with you next week." She gave Deidre a peck on the cheek and was gone.

John Buford, a humorless, burly man in his sixties, clearly did not share his wife's enthusiasm for the proposed show or for Deidre. But apparently Rosalind didn't allow him to have much say about it either, because Buford grudgingly agreed to give the show—and Deidre—a chance. Suddenly, Deidre found a way for all of her many job experiences to come together in one place. Learning to run, much less host, a television show was the ultimate crash course, but Deidre wouldn't have it any other way.

Managing the show's budget was the most challenging, and she hired Len to help her take care of the money side of things. They tended to go over budget in order to increase the show's appeal, convinced the payoff wouldn't be too far down the road. "Creative necessity," was what Len called it. Buford grumbled but the show and its audience continued to grow, as did Deidre's paycheck.

Deidre glanced back at the closet, her hand on the light switch. After a childhood of feeling like she never had enough, a full closet was strangely satisfying. She was finally making good money with her show, and despite the lectures from her financially-astute cousin, Caroline, Deidre still hadn't kicked the habit of spending almost all of her paycheck. It was actually a relief not to have a mortgage, because keeping up her image wasn't cheap.

William was calling from the kitchen. "Deidre, the food's getting cold."

"Be right there," she said, taking one last look at her perfect closet before turning off the light and closing the doors carefully behind her.

"ROSE WATER," WILLIAM was saying.

"What?" Deidre finished loading the dishwasher and turned back to face him.

He walked into the living room with his coffee mug. "Focus on rose water, toilet water, lavender water, eau de toilette. Freshen sheets, linen closets, lingerie drawers . . ." He took a sip of coffee and settled back on the couch. "It's very French, your audience will eat it up."

Deidre gasped. "That's brilliant." She grabbed a pen and started scribbling on the notepad by the phone.

William was nonchalant. "I know."

Deidre tore the sheet of paper from the pad and tucked it in her purse, then walked over to the couch and sat next to William. He reached for one of Deidre's shortbread cookies, neatly stacked in a porcelain cookie jar, and took a bite. "These cookies are amazing, Deidre. The almonds and brown sugar go well together."

Deidre reached for a cookie as well. "The recipe's so easy, I need to find a way to get it on the show."

"The French love vanilla."

Deidre frowned, chewing slowly. That was another off-the-cuff, totally unrelated reference to France William had made this evening, and she was starting to notice a theme. It had been going on all week, but she had chosen to ignore it in case it proved to be something serious. Deidre wasn't ready for anything serious.

She waited for a few minutes, and then asked casually, "Um, William, I've noticed that you've been talking a lot about France and things that are French. Is there anything going on that I should maybe know about?"

William looked apprehensive and his face turned crimson.

"No," he said flatly. He rubbed his neck and then took another sip of his latté.

"Excuse me, but are you blushing?"

"No."

"Are you sure?" she teased. She grabbed his hands. "You swear?"

William looked away and Deidre felt a prickly sense of dread.

"Well," he finally said. "There's a new doctor, an oncologist, at the hospital. Well, not so new anymore, he's been there, oh, maybe six months and one week."

Deidre released his hands slowly.

"He's French, born and raised in Provence, but got his citizenship when he married a few years ago." William hesitated. "He's not married anymore, because it turned out that he's gay."

Deidre waited, not comprehending. "So . . ."

"So . . . we've been spending some time together at the hospital."

"Oh my God," Deidre said, feeling happy, sick, and envious at the same time. "What's his name?"

"Alain Rousseau." William's high school French was sounding strangely advanced.

"Why didn't you tell me?"

He shrugged. "I don't know. I didn't know how you'd . . . react."

"React? What, are you worried I would flip out or something?" The laugh that came from her was high-pitched and unnatural.

William was watching her nervously. "It's just that you and I have kind of created this little . . . nest, and we've pretty much been spending all of our free time together for the past few years . . ."

"William, don't be ridiculous. I mean, it's not like we're married." Her voice sounded hollow. "I think this is great. Really."

"Really?"

"Really." Deidre smiled and tried to remember to breathe. "I just wasn't expecting it but it was bound to happen. You're a great catch. I just didn't think you were looking, after what you went through with Kenny. You said it wasn't worth it."

"Did I say that?" William gave a wry smile. "Maybe I did. I wasn't exactly looking, Dee. It just sort of happened."

They sat next to each other quietly, lost in their own thoughts.

"Is it serious?" Deidre finally asked. She played with her watch.

William looked guilty.

"If this is so serious, how come you haven't been playing sleepover?"

William looked even more guilty. "We have. Just, um, not at night."

"Oh." Deidre feigned another smile, suddenly feeling matronly and frumpy. Deidre played with the clasp of her watch. "Well, I'd like to meet him. Can we have him over for dinner on Friday?"

William looked relieved. "I would love that. I'll check with Alain, but I'm sure he can do it. We'll help cook."

"No, no." Deidre waved the thought away. "Let me take care of it."

William looked doubtful so she took his hand. "I want to. It'll be fun." She gave his hand a squeeze. "Don't worry, I'm fine."

"Are you sure?"

"Sure I'm sure. I'm Deidre McIntosh of *Live Simple.* This is what I do." She forced her million-dollar smile, then started to clear their coffee cups. "I'm going to bed. I have a long day tomorrow."

"Dee . . ." William took her hand. "Thanks, honey." His eyes were bright, and he looked happy. "Alain's amazing, you'll love him."

"I'm sure I will." She resisted the urge to panic. Their life together was comfortable, so comfortable in fact that she hadn't found anyone worth getting involved with and hadn't expected he would, either. All her future plans relied on their unique relationship, made acceptable and trendy by eight seasons of *Will & Grace*, and she was content. Even with her doctor's warnings that the window of opportunity was closing if she ever wanted children, Deidre wasn't worried. She could see herself adopting with William if it came down to that. When Caroline pressed her to own her own place, Deidre just laughed. She was living in one of the most exclusive neighborhoods in Seattle, with a man who was a better cook than she was and who made her laugh. Come on. Deidre had an answer to everything. Everything except this. Even though William was sitting next to her, she felt suddenly alone.

"Don't worry, Deidre," William said kindly, as if reading her mind. "It'll happen to you, too. When you least expect it."

"That'll be anytime, then," Deidre said, managing a small smile.

CHAPTER 2

One must be thrust out of a finished cycle in life,
and that leap is the most difficult to make.

—ANAÏS NIN

DEIDRE'S CELL PHONE kept ringing. It was in her purse, which was resting on the table next to her bed, and the vibrating feature meant that her purse was skittishly edging its way to the side of the nightstand until it fell onto the floor, spilling all of its contents.

Half-asleep, Deidre reached down and picked up her phone. The display read 5:16 A.M., and she had missed five calls. There were five messages. Deidre sat up in bed, still sleepy, but perplexed.

The phone rang again and she answered it. It was Len, who sounded agitated. "Deidre, I've been ringing for almost half an hour."

Deidre propped herself up on her elbow. "What? Is everything okay?"

"Channel Two is launching a competitive show, *At Home with Marla Banks*."

"Marla Banks, the socialite?" Deidre was confused.

"Yes. Very similar format to *Live Simple*, and they are going to run it during the same time slot."

Deidre fell back against the pillows, relieved, and let out a small laugh. "Oh my God, Len. Is that it?" She yawned.

"What do you mean, is that it? Buford isn't happy, Deidre. I think this is serious."

Deidre got out of bed and walked into her closet, looking for something to wear. "I can't control what other stations want to do. It won't last, Len. They never do. There's been, what, *Seattle Living*; *The Janine Glasser Show*—that bombed; *Karen and Dave* . . . The only one with any staying power has been *Live Simple*. Buford should know that. Besides, Channel Two thrives on new programming, and most of them crash and burn. They'll give anyone a chance. I'm sure Marla's program isn't anything more than that."

"Don't be so sure, Deidre." Len was acting strangely paranoid, which was unlike him. If anything, Len was the consummate Boy Scout, always prepared.

Deidre tried to reassure him. "We've brought so many new viewers to Channel Five—Buford won't want to lose them. *Live Simple* fans are loyal." She said this with a touch of pride.

"The man is all about numbers. You know that."

"Len, you worry about everything," Deidre chided. She chose a taupe Elie Tahari pantsuit and held it against herself, looking in the mirror.

"It's my job to worry about everything."

Deidre spotted a stray gray hair and pulled it. She saw another, pulled it, then turned her attention back to the phone. "I'll be there at eight. I have to go. Don't worry, Len," she said firmly. "It's all under control."

"Fine, you're the boss." There was a bitterness about his tone. "Bye."

In the bathroom mirror, Deidre studied her face as she put her makeup on.

"I'm getting old," she said to her reflection. Her skin still looked great but she was definitely getting wrinkles around her eyes. She sighed. Marla Banks was in her late forties but had gone through at least two face-lifts and a tummy tuck, which meant that she looked youthful and gorgeous and, of course, wrinkle-free. Marla Banks was the quintessential poster child for cosmetic surgery and travel-size shots of BOTOX, and she was proud of it.

Deidre didn't know Marla personally. They saw each other at different functions and events around town but didn't have enough in common to hold a conversation. Marla Banks, known in many circles as "The Tigress" for her catty yet ferocious demeanor, had spoken to Deidre only once, at the Willow Bend Charity Auction for Autism. Marla was exactly as Deidre had expected: snobby, aristocratic, athletic, and slender with perfect arms—she had a famous trainer, another fact she was happy to share.

That was four years ago, barely a year after *Live Simple* had launched. Deidre felt mousy and lanky in comparison, but Marla's date didn't think so. He bumped into Deidre at the bar and they talked for almost an hour as Marla made her way around the room, laughing, glittering, kissing the air. Deidre didn't even remember his name, James or Jonathan maybe, their conversation abruptly coming to an end when Marla appeared.

"This is Deidre McIntosh," he had said. "She hosts the show, *Live Simple*. You watch that show."

Marla gave both of them a haughty look. "Hardly." She turned to Deidre. "No offense. Home economics just isn't high on my agenda."

"I understand," Deidre said. It may have been the wine because she really didn't mind: Marla wasn't exactly her target market. "No offense taken."

Marla gave her a frosty smile before draping a perfect arm over James-Jonathan's shoulders and steered him away, never looking back. James-Jonathan managed to look over his shoulder and give Deidre an apologetic shrug, but then turned and put his arm around Marla's waist. Deidre felt a twinge of betrayal then shrugged it off, something she was good at. She avoided looking in his direction for the rest of the evening.

Now, as Deidre applied her mascara, she found herself hesitating for a moment. She gazed at her reflection, perplexed. Why would Marla Banks want to spend her time hosting a home living show? She didn't need the money, she didn't need the attention (attention was never a problem for Marla Banks), and while it had its high points, it was hardly more glamorous than the life Marla was already leading. It didn't make sense.

In the living room, William was reading the paper with the morning news on the television. He nodded to a fresh pot of coffee.

"Smells great," Deidre said as she put on her favorite pair of Mikimoto pearl earrings. She poured herself a cup and sat down to make a shopping list for Friday's dinner.

The news cut to a commercial. Out of the corner of her eye, Deidre saw a flash of hot pink and looked up.

It was Marla Banks, outlandishly and expensively dressed, a fuchsia feather boa wrapped around her neck and trailing behind her as she walked down a street in downtown Seattle. She stopped in front of a grocery store and approached a woman who was leaving the store.

"Hi, I'm Marla Banks, and you're on national television."

The woman, in her mid-fifties, looked startled. She was dressed in sweats, was overweight, and had a lot of gray in her hair that was outgrowing a perm. "I, uh . . ."

"We'd like to make you an offer you can't refuse. What's your name?"

"Marsha. Marsha Friedman."

"Well, Marsha, you are our first Marla Makeover. We are going to make you over, all expenses paid by my new show, *At Home with Marla Banks*, airing this month on Channel Two at four P.M. . . ."

"I watch *Live Simple* at four o'clock."

William looked up, glancing between the television and Deidre's face, which was growing pale.

Marla continued, unfazed, "And, as a bonus, we are going to walk into whatever place you call home and make it as beautiful as you. That's the Marla Makeover, what do you think?"

Marsha's eyes popped. "My house?"

"Your entire house, Marsha, and you. Think we can do it?"

"I don't know. I hope so!"

Marla looked straight at the camera, her arm looped through Marsha who had overcome her shyness in front of the camera and was beaming. "Tune in and see me, and

Marsha, in *At Home with Marla Banks*, weekday afternoons at four o'clock starting September sixteenth. You might be our next lucky guest." Marla gave a big wink and blew a kiss to the camera.

An enthusiastic male voice-over boomed, "Join Seattle's own Marla Banks, weekday afternoons at four o'clock." There was the sound of a kiss and then Marla's voice, "Why thank you, dahling!"

William muted the volume and turned to Deidre. "What the hell was that?"

Deidre had been gripping her coffee cup until her knuckles turned white. She closed her eyes, unable to speak. "That," she finally managed to say, "is not a good thing."

DEIDRE WAITED IMPATIENTLY in her car for the light to turn green. Beside her, a city bus pulled up. A familiar face caught her eye and Deidre turned. The banner on the bus read:

> *Who would you rather be in bed with?* At Home with Marla Banks, *4:00 P.M. weekdays, Channel 2. Premiering September 16th.*

The image to the right showed Marla, fully dressed with martini in hand, sitting up in bed and winking.

Deidre's mouth dropped open as the bus pulled away. Behind it, a billboard with Marla's mouth in an *O*, shrugging her shoulders, this time with a martini in one hand and dog in the other. It read:

A complicated creature in a complicated world. What's a girl to do? Tune in weekdays starting September 16, 4:00 P.M., Channel 2.

The cars behind her honked repeatedly, but Deidre couldn't hear them.

AT THE STATION, there was an anxious buzz that filled the hallways and seemed to permeate throughout the entire building. Deidre walked straight into Len's office. It was empty. She spotted an almost-full cup of coffee on his desk.

Odd, she thought as she walked to her office. She passed Karen's desk and handed her a Tupperware of walnut-cranberry-orange muffins from her bag. "Good morning. New recipe, I snuck in some lemon zest. Baked them the other day but they should still be good. You can warm them up in the oven on the set."

"Oh. Thanks." Karen looked distressed and stared at the Tupperware timidly.

Deidre raised an eyebrow. It wasn't like Karen to refuse food. "Not hungry?" she asked.

Karen managed a smile before gingerly taking a muffin and placing it on a napkin. She handed Deidre a clipboard.

Deidre tried to look calm as she previewed the program manifest for the day. *Live Simple* had a rerun scheduled, so the set would be relatively quiet in preparation for Friday's live show, "Just Be Me."

"Is there, uh, anything going on?" Karen finally asked, picking at her muffin.

"No. Why?"

"Just wondering." Karen hesitated, then lowered her voice. "There's talk about *Live Simple* being canceled. Is it true?"

The word *canceled* made Deidre shiver but she looked through her calendar, nonchalant. "Don't be ridiculous, Karen. Who said that?"

Karen shrugged meekly. "I don't know. Everyone."

"Well, it's the first I've heard of it," Deidre said, a little sharply. She looked at Karen, who seemed startled. "Sorry. Look, I'll find out what's going on. I'm sure it's nothing to worry about. A little competition is healthy."

"What competition?"

Deidre stopped looking through her papers and gave Karen a tight smile. "Never mind. Can you please check on whether or not those shoji screens are going to be available for the 'Now and Zen' segment?"

"Sure, Deidre."

Deidre watched Karen hurry away and then walked toward the conference room.

She knocked on the door and walked in.

John Buford, Len, Anne, and Tom sat around the conference table. The atmosphere was somber.

Deidre forced a bright smile. "Good morning," she said.

Buford glanced at the clock on the wall and Deidre followed his eyes. She was five minutes late.

"Sorry," she said, keeping her voice breezy. "Traffic. What did I miss?"

Buford was not amused. "We were just discussing Channel Two's new show, *At Home with Marla Banks*."

Deidre glanced around the room. Anne and Tom were looking at the table, like two children who had been reprimanded. Len was studying something intently on the wall behind her head. Heart pounding, Deidre kept her composure. "Yes, I saw, uh, some advertising and a trailer for the makeover show this morning."

"She stole our 'Just Be Me' idea," Anne muttered.

"More like, 'Just Be Someone Else,'" Tom added darkly.

Deidre shot them warning looks. "I'm just surprised we hadn't heard about this before," she said. "It seems very sudden."

Len coughed. "Apparently Channel Two was planning to run their *Autumn in Seattle* show but there were some legal complications so that got canceled at the last minute. Marla volunteered to come to the rescue."

"Why? Why should she care?"

"Her family owns sixty percent of the station. She's a pinch hitter program for them." Buford sounded bored, as if the entire conversation were a waste of his time.

"Oh, so it's a temporary thing," Deidre said, smiling. "It won't affect *Live Simple.*"

There was silence around the table. Len coughed and finally spoke up.

"Mr. Buford believes that Channel Two, with Marla's new show, may attract a lot of new viewers."

Deidre gave Len an odd look. Why was he speaking on behalf of Buford? "I still don't see how this has anything to do with our show. Marla can do whatever she wants, as far as I'm concerned."

Buford shifted in his chair, the leather rubbing against his suit. The sound grated Deidre's nerves. "Deidre, there's been talk for some time about picking up a syndicated show for the *Live Simple* time slot. With the debut of Marla's show, we're looking at introducing that possibility now."

Deidre stared at him, dumbfounded. "Are you serious? You're seriously considering canceling *Live Simple?*"

Buford was unaffected. "Since the show's launch, you've been over budget . . ."

"Well, yes, but it takes a while for these things to take off. We'll be in good shape by next season . . ."

Buford cut her off. "I've always been candid about my position on *Live Simple.* I don't think it fits in with the rest of our lineup."

Deidre glanced at Len, waiting for him to jump in and say something, to turn on that English charm that always seemed to work on her. But he didn't say anything. She turned back to Buford and tried to focus on the facts. "*Live Simple* has a steady following of almost thirty thousand unique viewers. That's huge for a non-syndicated show."

"And multifold for one that is. We can pull in stronger advertisers—yours can't even cover the costs for the show." He laced his fingers together and rested them on the table with an unsettling air of finality.

"We're getting those stronger advertisers," Deidre said, a little desperately. "Len just landed Nissan, right?"

Len shook his head. "Uh, not yet."

"Well, he will," Deidre said firmly. "And in the meantime, we're putting Seattle on the map—we feature local purveyors and businesses, they all tell us how their business doubles after being on our show."

"Great. Then you should have had them buying some advertising instead of getting it for free." Buford's expression was deadpan.

Deidre looked at him, furious. He clearly had no idea how important *Live Simple* was to Seattle, that she had letters from fans saying they loved her show more than *Oprah*. *Live Simple* had become *the* touchstone for local programming. "Please tell me you are not seriously thinking about canceling the show."

Buford was starting to look irate, which made Tom and Anne shrink in their chairs. "I think considering other options might be in the best interest of the station."

Deidre sat there, stunned. "You're not going to give the show a chance to go up against Marla? We have some great segments planned . . ."

Buford ignored her. "You've been running past shows three times a week, and yet your production costs have risen exponentially."

"I'm not sure how that's happened," Deidre said, casting an uncertain look in Len's direction. He was in charge of helping her manage the budget. "But I would be happy to look at everything again. Like I was saying, we have some truly fantastic shows lined up. Okay, we might have to abandon the 'Just Be Me' segment since it has some of the same elements as Marla's premier, but there's what . . . 'Everything's Coming Up Roses,' 'Fabulous at Forty,' 'Now and Zen' . . ." She looked to Anne for help.

"Uh, 'Just Right For Your Type,' based on personality testing," Anne said.

Tom joined in ". . . 'Seattle's Best Spas' . . ."

". . . 'Home for the Holidays' . . ."

". . . 'Dream Big' . . ."

". . . 'Marriage Sabbaticals' . . ."

Deidre could sense that this was it: she had to make it happen now or she would lose the show forever.

"We can do this, Mr. Buford. We can take on Marla Banks—advertisers will love it, our audience will love it—and we will cut back on costs, restructure our approach. You have too much invested to let it go . . . the *Seattle Tribune* said we were the voice of Seattle's Everywoman. When was that, March?"

Anne and Tom nodded their heads vehemently. Len was still uncharacteristically mute.

Buford didn't look convinced.

Desperate, Deidre pulled her trump card. "And Rosalind. Rosalind dropped me a note the other month, telling me how much she loved our 'Stitch in Time' program, the one that focused on antique quilts and making your own family keepsake. We also did a short feature on the use of comfort quilts at the cancer center . . ."

Buford had walked over to the window, looking at the view of downtown Seattle. Deidre wasn't even sure if he had heard them. She cast a furtive glance in Len's direction, who finally acknowledged her by returning a guilty smile. Deidre felt the blood rushing to head. *Don't worry*, she told herself. *He would be crazy to cut us off.*

After what seemed like forever, Buford turned around. "I've made my decision," he said. They all looked at him, expectantly. He walked over to Len, clapped him on the shoulder and gave them all a broad smile. It was the first time Deidre had ever seen him smile. She smiled back, relieved.

"I'm pulling the show."

CHAPTER 3

Left to themselves, things tend to go from bad to worse.
—MURPHY'S LAW

"IT'S A TRAGEDY, an absolute tragedy!" Deidre's hairdresser, Stella, was washing Deidre's hair in the sink and looking truly devastated. "They have no idea what they've done to the city of Seattle!" She slammed the shampoo bottle back onto the shelf indignantly.

"All good things must come to an end," Deidre said, somewhat unconvincingly.

Stella's expert fingers raked through Deidre's hair. "You were a godsend to the women of Seattle; we all know it." Stella massaged Deidre's scalp ferociously, which felt good. "Marla's all fluff and fancy," she huffed.

Deidre closed her eyes, trying not to think about the past week. Everything had moved in fast forward. Deidre's contract was terminated immediately and she was expected to be out by the end of the day. Everyone else on the *Live Simple* crew had until Friday, since Buford wanted to pare down payroll costs as well. Everyone except for Len.

"What?" Deidre was dumbfounded when she found out. "The entire *Live Simple* crew has been thrown out, but you get to stay?"

Len gave an uneasy shrug. "Luck of the Irish, I guess."

"Except that you're not Irish." She gave him a long look before slamming some more things into boxes. She was still seething. "God, he was practically gloating. He looked like the cat that swallowed the canary. You really could have backed me up in there, Len."

"Well, quite frankly, I didn't think it would help."

"You didn't think it would help?" She spun around to give him a flabbergasted look. "That's why I hired you, Len. Remember? To *help* me. To *help* me manage the budget, to *help* me with production. You told me when I hired you that you would take care of these things so I could focus on the creative aspects of the show. You told me everything would be fine. I stood by you when accounting kept questioning the numbers, even that time Buford questioned your salary. I would have liked it if you could have stood by me just now."

Len shook his head and feigned helplessness. "I did what I could, Deidre."

Deidre gave a little snort. "Oh, really? How? Telepathically? Because I didn't hear you say a word in there in my defense."

Anne stormed in. Her eyes were rimmed red from crying, but she was livid.

"Guess what I found out?" she demanded, throwing Len an insolent look.

Deidre resumed angrily packing her boxes, not really in the mood. "Anne . . ."

Len glanced uneasily between the two women. "Well, I should leave you to it. I'll call you for lunch next week, when everything cools down a bit."

"Are you sure you'll have time?" Anne asked sarcastically. "What with your new promotion and all?"

Deidre felt the hairs on the back of her neck at attention. "What?" she asked. Len instantly reddened. "What new position?"

"Senior Producer for the entire studio," Anne said. "Isn't that nice? With the power to accept or reject new shows. He's going to be reporting directly to Buford." She crossed her arms in front of her chest and glared at him.

"It's very complicated," Len began and coughed.

Deidre turned to face him. "When were you going to tell me this?"

"I was just about to, actually . . ."

"Out," she said, pointing to the door. "It's still my office, at least for the next three and a half hours, and I want you out."

"Oh, come on, Deidre. It's just business . . ."

"Good-bye, Len." Deidre turned her back and slammed more things into the box.

Anne pointedly held the door open, a satisfied smirk on her face.

Len was about to protest when Deidre shot him another look.

"Fine," he said and left. Anne slammed the door behind him. The two women stared at each other, the bravado gone.

Deidre shook her head. "God, Anne, I am so sorry about all of this. I just can't believe it. Is Tom okay? What about Karen and the rest of the team?" She willed herself not to cry.

"They're all fine," Anne reassured her, reaching for a tissue. "Tom's already posted his resume on monster.com. This is TV. It happens. Don't blame yourself."

Deidre blinked back tears as she continued to pack. "How can I not? I let everyone down."

"The only one who could have done anything, did nothing," Anne said somewhat vehemently. "Len could have convinced Buford to give us another chance, but he gave us up to further his career. Len knew that Buford was getting divorced and didn't tell us."

Deidre froze. "Buford divorced Rosalind?"

Anne nodded. "It was final yesterday. Karen found out from Linda, his secretary. And you know how Rosalind was always a major supporter and insisted Buford take on the show . . ."

"Oh my God." She slumped against the desk.

"Like I said, don't blame yourself. As for *him* . . ." Anne was referring to Len and stared hard at the closed door. "He made the suggestion to Buford to cut *Live Simple*. Looking out for the greater interests of the studio, or some bullshit like that."

Deidre's office, stripped of all her personal effects, no longer felt welcoming. It had been her sanctuary for five years and in a matter of hours, had become just another room with four walls. "What are you going to do?" she asked Anne. She sealed the final box.

Anne shrugged, then tossed her tissue into the trash. "I hear Starbucks is hiring," she said. "I wouldn't mind free frappuccinos and stock options. Anyway, the vision plan here sucks and I need LASIK." Then she sniffed, and

Deidre saw that she was on the verge of crying. "Thanks, Deidre. I really learned a lot." She gave Deidre a hasty hug then hurried out the door.

The rest of the team came by to say good-bye, and when it was finally time to leave, the security guard checked her boxes before escorting her to her car.

"My wife will miss your show," he said, handing her the last box. "What are you going to do now?"

Deidre opened her mouth to answer but nothing came out.

THE NEXT DAY, Deidre met her cousin, Caroline, for lunch at the Uptown Bistro. Caroline had her own boutique brokerage firm and was Deidre's financial advisor.

"God, Deidre," Caroline was saying as she took a bite of her spinach and Roquefort cheese salad. "I can't believe it. I thought you'd get a couple more years out of it, maybe go national."

Deidre took a sip of water and didn't say anything.

Caroline leaned forward confidentially. "Marla's spending a lot of her own cash to fund the show. Family money," she said in hushed tones, waving her fork in the air. "Everyone's going to be watching to see what happens there, that's for sure."

Discretion was never one of Caroline's strong points. Deidre tried not to stress too much about what was just said. "Look, Caroline, I just need to know how my portfolio looks right now. I'm going to need some cash to get me through the next few months."

Caroline took another bite, followed by a swig of mineral water. "Aren't you getting your statements?"

"Yes, but . . ." Deidre pictured her desk at home, the unopened envelopes from Caroline's office piled in one of her drawers. "Can't you just summarize it for me?"

Caroline sighed. "Okay, hold on." She took a quick bite of salad and then fumbled through her bag for her cell phone. She called the office, tearing off chunks of bread and slathering them with butter as she waited. She nodded at Deidre's shoes and whispered, "Love them. Manolos?"

Deidre nodded, full of regret. She had bought them last month on eBay for $349 after a heated bidding frenzy with two other buyers. She had told herself she wouldn't bid higher than $275, but as the seconds counted down, she found herself too caught up in the bidding to stop. She'd do anything to turn the clock back on that one.

Caroline continued to admire the shoes, then held up her hand to silence Deidre even though Deidre hadn't said anything. "Teddy, it's Caroline. Can you pull up Deidre's account and give me the quick rundown?" She started jotting things down in her Blackberry. "Okay, uh-huh." She cut a quick glance at Deidre, gave her a quick thumbs-up. "Okay. Yeah. Great. Okay, see you in a few." She hung up, tossed her phone in the bag, and took another drink.

Deidre waited impatiently.

Caroline cleared her throat. "Well, we put seventy-five percent of your portfolio into equities, because you said you wanted to take an aggressive approach . . ."

Deidre interrupted. "*You* said I should take an aggressive approach, because I'm single and . . ."

Caroline continued. ". . . of which fifty percent of that was that hot tech–dot com stock that crashed and burned . . ."

"That's stock you recommended I buy!"

"It was highly favored, Deidre. Everyone bought in, myself included." Caroline tapped her planner. "You've also been going through your cash account pretty quick, too. What did you do last month?"

Deidre chewed her bottom lip. "Got the Volvo SUV."

"Leather seats?"

"Yes."

"With the seat warmers?"

Deep breath. "Yes."

"Very nice. My neighbor just got that—he loves it. What color?"

Deidre willed herself not to scream. "Caroline, can you please just tell me how much money I have?"

"The value of your total accounts, not including your retirement funds, is just shy of nineteen thousand dollars."

"What? I thought I had over sixty thousand dollars!"

"Well, you did, but the stock market crashed and that tech stock tanked, and it looks like you've been doing some shopping." Caroline's eyes flickered as she scanned Deidre's Bernard Zins jacket. "Is that a new suit?"

Deidre glared at her. The suit was over six months old.

"Sorry. Look, investments are risky, I told you that. If you hold on to your stock positions for the long-term, they'll probably come back. Equities rule; they always do if you can ride it out. I think this strategy still makes good sense—you were drawing in a respectable income, you hardly pay anything in rent, and it shouldn't take you long to find another job, right?" Caroline took a long sip of her water.

"Caroline, I have no idea where to begin," Deidre said despondently. "I don't even know where my resume is. I need to live off my savings until I figure out what to do next."

Deidre saw a brief flash of compassion from her usually hard-edged cousin. "I'm sorry, Dee. What do you want me to do?"

"Can you tell me what the market's doing now?"

Caroline laughed and brushed the question away. "Now? Ha, you don't want to know."

Deidre blinked. "Yes, I do, actually," she said.

"No, trust me, you don't," Caroline said dismissively before taking another bite of her salad. The hard glint had returned.

Deidre was on the verge of hysteria. "Look, Caroline. *I need to know*. That's been the problem. I've been listening to you, and to Len, and to the stupid lawyers and accountants and everybody else all this time and I have no idea what's going on and now my entire life is screwed!"

Caroline glanced around the restaurant, embarrassed. A couple at the table next to them was whispering and looking their way. "Jesus, Deidre, take it easy! I'm not the enemy here. Calm down, will you?"

Deidre bit the inside of her cheek. "Don't tell me to calm down, Caroline. Just tell me what the market's doing, dammit!"

Caroline fixed her steely eyes on Deidre. "Fine. Right now we're in a bear market. Interest rates are high, the economy is still in a downturn, investors are still scared and trying to preserve their capital. Trading volumes are steady but low; the Dow Jones was around nine point eight zero zero when I left the office. Investors choosing to sell their positions now still have a way to go to recover where they were last year."

Calming down, Deidre readjusted her napkin, smoothed her hair, and looked back at Caroline. "Thank you. Now, tell me again, only this time, use English."

"That was in English." She shot Deidre a superior look.

"Okay, fine." Deidre pursed her lips and looked at Caroline with as neutral a face as she could manage. "What about my Roth?"

"You had the same aggressive ratio, same stocks. It's also down. Anyway, you can't touch that money until you retire, or you'll pay tax and penalties." Caroline took out her compact and began reapplying lipstick.

That was not what she wanted to hear. Deidre took a deep breath. "Okay, fine. I want to move everything except for my IRA into my money market account." Caroline looked surprised. Deidre sat up a little taller. "And yes, I know what that is."

"Deidre, I don't recommend . . ."

"I know you don't, Caroline, but it's my money and I need it."

"There are two approaches to having more money, Deidre," Caroline said haughtily, snapping her compact closed. "Earn more or spend less. Maybe you should think about cutting back your expenses." She glanced down at Deidre's heels.

Deidre didn't say anything, but crossed her legs and sat back in her chair, forcing herself to regain her composure. "Do I need to sign anything?"

"I'll have Teddy fax something to your house." Caroline slipped her purse over her shoulders and stood up. "You can pay for my salad, I hope?" There was a tinge of sarcasm in her voice.

Deflated, Deidre fell back into her chair. "Yes. Caroline, I can pay for it. Look, I'm sorry for being so snappy. It's just been a rough week."

"Welcome to my world, Deidre. See you later."

Deidre watched Caroline walk away just as the waitress placed the check on the table. "Let me know when you're ready to take care of that."

Deidre picked up her clutch and searched for her wallet. Keys, sunglasses, cell phone, Franklin Planner, tons of receipts and pens, but no wallet. Feeling on the verge of a full-blown anxiety attack, Deidre gave a polite smile to the couple sitting next to her and tried to calm herself. The couple nodded and smiled back, still whispering.

When the waitress returned, Deidre looked up, flustered. "I seem to have left my wallet at home."

"Oh." The waitress glanced uncertainly toward the maître d'.

"It might be in the car," Deidre said, knowing perfectly well that it wasn't. She recalled the hurried events of the morning. She had taken her wallet out early that morning to run downstairs and peruse the newspaper stand to see if the show cancellation had made the papers. It hadn't. And now her wallet was sitting on the counter at home. She might be able to scrounge up some change if she searched the seats in the Volvo, but it obviously wouldn't be enough to cover the bill.

The waitress looked nervous, as if she thought Deidre might bolt if given the chance. She hesitated. "I'll need to check if that would be okay."

Deidre was both embarrassed and indignant. Didn't she know who Deidre was? It wasn't as if she was going to skip town for a forty-six-dollar bill. The Uptown Bistro definitely wasn't going to get a thumbs-up for service at this rate. Then Deidre remembered that her show was canceled and the days of restaurant reviews, among other things, were over. God.

Just take me now, she thought wearily.

Just then, someone reached over from behind her and flipped a credit card square onto the tray. "I've got it."

The waitress looked relieved and hurried off. Deidre slowly turned around.

A man with dark auburn hair stood behind her. He was casually dressed, but Deidre noticed that his trousers were pressed and he wore an expensive blazer over a light sweater. *Very JFK*, Deidre instantly thought. There was something about him that was familiar, but Deidre couldn't place it.

His dark brown eyes were watching her intently, and a smile played on his lips. Embarrassed, Deidre glanced down at his feet and took in his shoes. *Marc Jacobs? No, classier. Bally? John Varvatos?* It didn't really matter; this guy could wear flip-flops and he'd look just as good.

She cleared her throat and started to gather her things. "Thank you so much," she finally said, standing up. "I was in such a rush this morning that I left my wallet . . ." Her voice trailed off as she met his gaze. Steady, attentive, intelligent. And handsome wasn't the right way to describe him; devastatingly handsome was more appropriate. Deidre pulled herself together. ". . . at home."

He didn't seem to notice. "Not a problem." He smiled and offered his hand. "I'm Kevin."

His grip was solid and warm. She didn't want to let go. "Deidre."

"I know. Deidre McIntosh, of *Live and Let Live*."

She stiffened. "It's *Live Simple, and Simply Live*, actually," she said, releasing his hand.

He was stifling a smile, which made her cross. She didn't have time for this. Deidre straightened up and looked at him coolly. "Just . . . can I get your number or address or whatever so I can send you a check?" She pretended to busy herself looking for a pen in her cluttered purse.

"Whoa, hold on." Kevin's voice was instantly apologetic. "I'm sorry, I was just trying to get a smile out of you. I know it's *Live Simple*. It's just that you've been frowning ever since you walked in here."

Deidre flushed at the thought that he had noticed her. While she did enjoy some small celebrity, it was usually among women, not men, and she knew her usually poised demeanor sometimes discouraged men from approaching her. This guy, on the other hand, hardly seemed put off.

Just breathe, Deidre told herself. *And try not to humiliate yourself any more today, okay?*

"It's been a rough couple of days," she said, but mustered up her million-dollar smile.

"That's better," Kevin said. The waitress arrived and he quickly signed the bill, tucking his card back into his wallet. "In fact, it's almost believable."

Deidre kept her smile on despite wanting to smack him. "Well, it's not going to get any better than this today, I can guarantee you that," she said, continuing to smile brightly.

Kevin cocked his head to one side. "Then I guess I'd better enjoy it while I can." He studied her face. "Even forced, I have to say that's one hell of a smile."

For the first time all day, Deidre felt like laughing.

Kevin smiled. "Now *that's* better." He glanced at his watch. "Damn, I'm late. We'll settle up some other time, okay?"

"Wait, do you have a card? Here, let me give you mine." She frantically wrote her number on the back and handed it to him. "I'm not at the studio anymore so just call my cell. Anytime. I mean, so I can figure out how to pay you back."

"Sure," he said. "Great." He took her card, studied it briefly, then was gone.

Deidre watched him leave, oblivious to the occasional glances from other diners. If she didn't know any better, it would seem that things were finally starting to look up.

STELLA HAD BEEN talking about Marla for a solid hour as Deidre was getting her hair colored. For someone who didn't seem to care for Marla, Stella sure had a lot to say.

"Stella, do you mind if we change the subject?" Deidre said at last.

"Oh, sorry, I'm just running on and on. I just can't get over it, that's all." She placed the final strip of Deidre's hair into a square of foil, brushed on color, and folded it up. "How is that cute roommate of yours doing? Still a doctor?"

"Still a doctor. Still cute."

"Still gay?"

"Still gay."

"Damn." Stella smiled and snapped her fingers. It was the same routine each time. They gave each other a smile.

Deidre added, "And, as of late, unavailable. He's got a boyfriend."

"You're kidding, that's so great!" Stella trilled. "Will deserves somebody good. Serious?"

"Seems that way." A few seconds later, Deidre realized she was holding her breath. She exhaled slowly and looked at Stella. "They're going to move in together."

William and Alain had broke the news to her sometime around dessert. Alain was older, very funny and very mature, and seemed to keep both Will and Deidre in check. He also helped make Deidre feel hopeful again, and for the first time since the show was canceled, Deidre was actually in a good mood. And even though he was gay, he had a way of making her feel very feminine and attractive. Being forty was a good thing, he told her. A *very* good thing. Deidre whispered to William, "He's definitely a keeper. In fact, I'll take him if you don't want him." She was laying out dessert plates.

William chuckled nervously then glanced at Alain. They were holding hands and Deidre saw Alain give William's hand a squeeze. Deidre instantly tensed up.

"Deidre?"

"Yes?"

William sighed. "I know the timing is terrible, and that there's so much going on, but I'll get straight to it. Alain and I have been talking about moving in together for a while."

"Oh," she said, unsure of how to respond. *Not a big deal*, she told herself. *Just go with the flow*. "Okay. Well, I won't be needing my study and that's a good-sized room, so you can have that if you like," she offered. "Or you can have the master bedroom. I've been spoiled for five years; I don't mind switching."

Alain looked back at William. "Ah . . ."

"Deidre, I'm going to be moving in with Alain," William said firmly. "In Belmont. It's closer to the hospital and Alain owns his place, so it just makes sense we do it that way. We've wanted to do it for a while and have been putting it off because the timing never seemed good. I know it seems like this is the absolute worst time, but I think if we wait any longer, it'll just be harder on all of us."

"Oh. I see." Deidre was in mid-slice. The crystallized ginger cake didn't look very appealing anymore. "Does anyone still want any?" she asked absently.

"Sure, all right," Alain said, a little too eagerly. He held out his plate.

"Deidre, are you okay?" William's hand was on her arm.

"Sure, I'm fine," she said, shrugging it off. "Cake?"

"Deidre . . ."

She plunged the cake knife into the cake. William and Alain jumped back. "You're moving out? *You're moving out?* William, what am I supposed to do in this huge apartment by myself?"

"Uh, you could not wield any sharp objects for a while," William said. "For starters."

Deidre burst into tears.

"I am forty years old," she sobbed. "I'm single, I'm out of a job, and now I'm totally alone! What am I supposed to do? What? *What?*"

They sat in silence as William handed Deidre tissues.

"I just got my license last year," Alain finally said. "I was the oldest student in medical school by about twenty years. Before that, I was an auto mechanic."

"What?" Deidre stared at him from behind a crumpled tissue. *What the hell was he talking about?*

"I was always very good with my hands. I always dreamed of being a doctor but when I was younger my family did not have enough money to send me to school, and my grades were not very good because I was always working at a job to help my family. After I started dating Celeste, she encouraged me to go to school, so I did. First university, then medical school. It took me almost fifteen years, but I did it."

Deidre clutched at her tissues and thought, *Good for you, bad for Celeste.* Unlike most American men, Alain wasn't rattled by her lack of response.

"It's never too late," he said. "To try something new, to go for something you really want."

"I really want *Live Simple* to go on forever," she said unconvincingly. Even as she said the words, Deidre knew it wasn't true, but for such a long time, it had been. "Now I don't know what I want. And even if I did, I don't have the resources to get there!" The last few words were punctuated with a wail.

"Look." Alain grabbed both her hands and looked Deidre straight in the eye. It was a little disarming. His gaze was so steady that Deidre was unable to look away. "This is an opportunity. I know it doesn't seem that way, but it is. When my marriage to Celeste was falling apart, she felt just like you."

"I feel a bit like her," Deidre admitted, not wanting to offend him and also not really caring if she did. She and Celeste had a lot in common: they both lost the man closest to them for another man.

"But you should see Celeste now. She is running an art gallery—her dream—and she is hot. Sexy. She always was, but she didn't know it. She knows it now. And she is *happy*." Alain said the last word with finality, gave Deidre's hands a squeeze, and dropped them. "Happier than she ever was in her life with me, but she didn't know it until after that life was over."

"Great. What are you two waiting for? Get out of here so my great life can begin." Deidre sniffed into her tissue.

William looked tormented and guilty as he reached for her. "Deidre . . ."

Alain pushed him aside. "Deidre, listen to me. If you're angry, get angry. If you're sad, be sad. Do it, but get it over with and don't look back. You just don't have that kind of time."

Deidre blinked rapidly, on the verge of crying or on the verge of hitting him, she couldn't decide which. "What are you saying, that I'm old?"

Alain rolled his eyes and looked at William like he wanted to give up. "American women," was all he said. He talked to William as if she weren't there. "She's good-looking, classy, incredibly competent, and incredibly insecure." He glanced at her briefly and cut a small smile. "No offense."

"Hey!" Deidre said, her anger rising, "It's not like I've been wallowing for months. It's barely been one week. *One week!* I think I'm at least entitled to one week, goddammit!"

She began pitching tissues across the living room. They fluttered and fell at her feet, making her angrier, and she rifled through the tissue box until it was empty and then threw it against the wall, not quite satisfied with the gentle thud but figured it would have to do.

"Last week, I had no idea any of this was going to happen. *No idea*. Things were great, I was happy! Then some socialite decides it would be *fun* to have a competitive show and take pot shots at me from the side of every city bus, and, oh, by the way, Deidre, your production manager is about to backstab you in exchange for job security *and* a promotion, and the station owner who hates you is gleefully getting a divorce and throwing the show out the window since his ex got to keep the summer home in Barbados. Oh, and let's not forget, your best friend in the *whole entire world* finally decides to fall in love and move in with the French doctor that *I* should be marrying. How is any of this fair? How? How? *How?*" Deidre was yelling now and both William and Alain were pressed back against the couch as Deidre leaned over them.

"Well?" she demanded, then realized she was no longer crying.

William shrunk back against Alain and glared at him. "Well, she's angry. Happy now?"

"Much better." Alain beamed at her, but he was still keeping his distance.

Deidre straightened her back and wiped her cheek with the back of her hand.

"I'd offer you a tissue, but . . ." Alain looked toward the pile of discarded tissues and the mangled box.

Deidre looked around the room, at the two men—doctors approaching middle age and nicely dressed in what seemed like matching J. Crew turtlenecks—watching her warily but with small smiles on their lips. Her beautiful crystallized ginger cake, the one that she had made special for this occasion, had a cake knife plunged into the heart of it. She closed her eyes and tried not to laugh, much less smile. It was crazy. God, *she* was crazy.

"I suppose you'll want to borrow my car for the move," she sniffed.

William pulled her to him, wrapping his arms around her before planting a heartfelt kiss on her lips. Then Alain gave her a hug and they almost rolled off the couch, barely catching themselves, and laughing.

STELLA BRUSHED OFF Deidre's shoulders before turning her back to face the mirror. "Ta-da! What do you think?"

"JESUS, STELLA!" Deidre's jaw dropped. "What did you do?"

Deidre almost didn't recognize herself. Her first thought was, *What will the station think?* Her second thought was, *What will the audience think?* Then she remembered that it didn't matter anymore.

Stella surveyed her proudly, oblivious to the shock in Deidre's voice. What she had done was taken Deidre's normal color and upped it a shade or two. Okay, maybe a little more. Okay, fine, it didn't matter. What mattered now was that Deidre was blond. *Really* blond. "Like it?"

Deidre had a thing about blondes—as a rule, she didn't like them. They lived up to their stereotype, they were ditzy, they were after men, they married rich. They took things away from women who were brunettes. You couldn't trust a blond, and now she was one.

"Do you think you could have asked me first before dying my hair platinum?" She touched her hair, expecting it to be wiry, but found it soft instead. It did make her look younger. In fact, she looked great.

"It's not platinum," Stella objected. "It's Beach Beige." Stella chewed on her lip. "You don't like it?"

"I . . ." Deidre ran her fingers through her hair, getting used to her new look. "Could you please just *ask* next time?"

"Well, you were all wrapped up in your thoughts and looking so depressed, I thought this would cheer you up. It works on all my clients."

"Thank God you're not my plastic surgeon."

"You do plastic surgery?! I always wondered . . ."

Deidre gave her an exasperated look. "No, Stella, I do *not* do plastic surgery. These are real." The one feature that hadn't let her down, literally. They weren't huge, but they were just right, enough to get cleavage if she needed it and enough to keep things demure if that was appropriate, which was usually the case. "And I do like my hair, I just have to get used to it." Deidre stared at herself for a long time in the mirror. "I don't even look like myself."

"You think?" Stella removed the smock and shook it out. "I can see your face better; it highlights your eyes. I think you should have been born a blond, it suits you. Plus it accents your . . ." She nodded toward Deidre's breasts. Deidre instantly covered her chest with her hand.

"Thank you, Stella, I think you've done enough for one day." Deidre reached for her purse and pulled out her checkbook. "What's the damage?"

"It's on the house," Stella said.

"What? That's not necessary, Stella." Deidre opened her checkbook and looked hesitantly at her dwindling balance. Still, she said, "How much?"

"It's on the house," Stella repeated firmly. She was sweeping up Deidre's hair, strands of sandy blond mixing together. Her hair looked so light, Deidre not only felt younger, but hopeful. "It's a present, from me. For five years of great television, so don't insult me by trying to pay for it. Just promise you'll come in before your roots take over—I can't be responsible for anything that happens after that."

Deidre was touched. "Thank you, Stella. I'm really . . . I don't know what to say. I think this is one of the nicest gifts anyone has given me in a long time."

Stella gave her a hug then walked her to the door. "Hey, we're all here to help one another out, you know? And give William a big kiss from me. "

Stella's receptionist was waiting for them, holding out a portable phone and looking impatient. "It's *her*," she said to Stella in an annoyed voice.

Startled, Stella glanced nervously at Deidre. "Tell her I'll call her back, Joan," she said.

"I did. But she insists on talking with you now and I've put her off for *ten minutes*. She's irate. I don't get paid enough to take her crap."

"Please tell me you've mastered the HOLD button," Stella snapped before forcing a smile at Deidre and taking the phone. "I should take this. Take care, okay? Things will be good, no, they'll be great. You'll see." She gave Deidre's arm a reassuring pat before turning and hurrying back to her station.

Deidre watched her, then looked at Joan, who was scribbling something into the appointment book. "Who was that?"

"Nobody." Joan refused to look up, confirming what

Deidre already knew. From a distance she could hear Stella's animated chatter, then a burst of accommodating laughter.

Joan glanced at her for a brief second. "Your hair looks good, by the way." Then she stood up and went to straighten the shampoo bottles on the shelf.

"Thanks," Deidre said, to no one in particular. She looked at herself in the mirror, stunned at the blond looking back at her.

Another peal of laughter came from Stella's station.

Deidre ran her fingers through her hair. It looked good but, she reminded herself, it wasn't real, it was a dye job, a fake. It was all fake.

"CHERRY GARCIA. TODAY is your lucky day." Deidre reached into her freezer and pulled out a pint of ice cream. She dragged a spatula across the top layer of ice cream and took a large, satisfied bite.

The last of the movers had gone, taking what was left of William's things. Deidre realized that other than clothes, shoes, and an inordinate amount of kitchen tools, she didn't really own anything substanital. She didn't even own a bed or any real furniture. William had left enough for Deidre to be comfortable, but still there were big gaps in the apartment, whole walls left suddenly bare.

She stared at the rust-colored wall that used to be home to several framed black-and-white photographs of the city. She and William had painted that wall together shortly after she had first moved in. Depressed, she put another larger scoop of ice cream into her mouth.

Marla's show launched to critical acclaim, but that was

also around the time that William took his television so Deidre was thankfully, blissfully, naively unaware of what was happening except for the occasional gossip at the corner newsstand and the obnoxious ads strewn across the city. Her new hair color made her incognito for a while, giving Deidre's ego a break. It was strange not being stopped on the street or being asked questions about the show. Caroline wasn't talking to her, and the station was running old episodes of *Get Smart* until it decided on what to air in place of *Live Simple*. As for Deidre, she was going to start the hunt for a new roommate as soon as she had enough energy to run an ad.

She heard a key turn in the lock. He was back! Suddenly joyful, Deidre rushed to the door. "William!"

But it was Henry Johnson, the balding and wizened superintendent, looking startled at finding Deidre in her pajamas and wielding a rather large spatula. His eyes widened at her new hair, then dropped from the top of her head and settled somewhere around her chest area. Deidre put one hand on her hip and leaned against the door.

"Uh, you're here," he said stiffly.

"Yes . . ." she said, not comprehending. "Why wouldn't I be?"

"I was told that you would be moved out by today."

"*William* was moved out by today. *I'm* staying."

Mr. Johnson met her gaze, void of any emotion. "Mr. Sen relinquished his lease. I'm showing it this afternoon at four o'clock."

"Well, I'm not relinquishing my lease."

Mr. Johnson looked her right in the eye. "You're not on the lease."

• • •

WILLIAM COULDN'T BELIEVE IT. "Oh my God, I am so sorry. I guess we never got around to adding your name to the lease."

"I know, it completely slipped my mind, too." She was lying on the floor, her legs resting on the walls with the telephone propped between her shoulder and her ear. An almost-empty bottle of vodka rested beside her.

"Can't he just draw up a new lease?"

The floor felt like it was tilting. "He says there's been a waiting list and that my credit score isn't high enough. I think he probably figured out that I'm not a safe bet anymore."

"Bastard."

"I know. So much for five years of holiday parties and cookie baskets." Deidre studied her nails, then frowned. Her eyes couldn't focus. "It's just as well. I can't really afford the rent here anyway. He's already paraded two couples, a family, and some foreign diplomat through the place. He said the best he could do was give me two more days, tops. I spent the afternoon packing." She gave a loud hiccup. "Luckily, I found an old bottle of Stoli's in the buffet."

"Oh my God. Have you been drinking?"

She drummed her feet on the wall. "A little." She picked up the bottle and squinted. "There's still some left." Suddenly heavy, the bottle tipped and smacked her on the forehead. "Ow. I should have known that was going to happen."

"Deidre, it's been a hell of a week. Why don't you crawl into bed and call it a night?"

The idea of crawling in between her bed sheets and falling asleep sounded blissful. "I will. I just have to take out the trash."

"Deidre, it's ten o'clock on a Friday night."

"It'll just take five seconds." Deidre may have been slightly inebriated, but she still believed in keeping a clean house.

Deidre took her time getting up, gathering her trash bags, and headed out the door. She walked down the hallway toward the garbage chute. She groaned when she saw the sign taped across the chute, scrawled in Mr. Johnson's surprisingly neat handwriting.

Under repair.
Please dispose of your garbage in the basement.
Thank you, The Management

Muttering under her breath, Deidre headed over to the elevators and punched the down button.

The elevator doors opened and she stepped in, still muttering under her breath. It took a couple of seconds before she realized she wasn't alone.

"Deidre?"

Deidre's mouth fell open but she quickly shut it. It was Kevin, the man from the Uptown Bistro. God, he looked good. *Really* good.

"Deidre?" he said again. "I almost didn't recognize you. You look different."

"Oh, Kevin, right?" She gave a nervous laugh as she ran her fingers through her tousled hair, praying she didn't look like a total wreck. "Oh, yeah, my hairdresser thought I could use a change."

"Well, it looks great." He gave her a broad smile as he leaned against the elevator wall, legs crossed, hands in his pockets.

"Thanks." She pressed the button for the basement and quickly glanced at him. Imported loafers, jeans, white T-shirt and suede leather jacket. And he smelled great. Deidre felt her heart beat double time but she kept her voice calm. "So do you live here? I've never seen you in the building before."

Kevin shook his head. "No. My uncle lives here. I had to drop something off on my way to a party."

"Party?"

"More like a get-together. Hey, you should come." Was it her imagination or had he moved a bit closer to her?

Deidre looked down at what she was wearing, a bag of trash in each hand. "I'm dressed in sweats and taking out my trash. Plus I've been nursing a bottle of vodka for a good part of the evening. Not exactly one of my finer moments."

"Actually, I think you look gorgeous," he said. "And you can't smell the alcohol . . . too much."

Deidre reddened and wanted to die. Reeking of vodka in front of the only man whom she would actually consider dating wasn't exactly the scenario she had hoped for.

The elevator arrived at the ground floor and Kevin stepped out, hesitant. Then he turned back to face her. "You know, I really don't feel much like going myself."

Deidre felt suddenly hopeful but tried to keep her voice cool. "Really?"

"Yeah. I've got better things to do on a Friday night." He stepped back into the elevator and took the trash bags from Deidre. "Like helping you dump your trash. Plus you owe me for saving you from abject humiliation at the Uptown Bistro."

"Actually, you were about five minutes too late, but that's okay." Deidre was smiling and trying not to swoon. She couldn't remember the last time someone helped her take out the trash.

They dumped the trash in the basement and then took the elevator to her apartment. "I should warn you, I wasn't exactly planning on having guests tonight, so my place is a mess."

"I'm ready." The expression on Kevin's face was serious.

They stepped into the sparse but spotless apartment. "Well," he finally said. "I guess you're not kidding about the *Live Simple* stuff. There's hardly anything here to make a mess."

"What?" Deidre looked around and then laughed. "No, it's just like this because I'm moving out. Besides, living simple doesn't mean sparse and empty. My show was about living authentically and having what you need or love." Her voice was wistful and then she frowned. "Anyway, that's a thing of the past."

"What do you mean?"

"Haven't you heard? My show got canceled, thanks to my lying production manager and a half-assed station owner who threw in the towel because his divorce was finalized and Marla Banks launched a competitive show on Channel Two."

Kevin looked oddly uncomfortable.

"I stunned you into silence, didn't I? Okay, I am letting it go." She took a deep breath then held up her checkbook. "First things first. How much do I owe you?"

He seemed to shake off the discomfort. "Deidre, you don't have to pay me back. It was my pleasure." He picked up the bottle of Stoli's from the ground.

"No, I insist."

"I'd really prefer if you didn't." His voice sounded determined, but Deidre ignored it.

"Too late, I'm already writing it out to 'Cash' . . ." She quickly wrote out a check before he could change his mind and handed it to him. "Thanks."

Kevin hesitated then pocketed the check reluctantly. "You're stubborn, but beautiful, you know that?"

"Well, at least I have something going for me right now." Deidre tried to hide her smile. That compliment alone was definitely worth forty-six dollars.

Kevin held up the bottle of Stoli's. "I also think we should probably break your habit of drinking alone. It's not healthy." He went into the kitchen and started opening cabinets.

"Oh, sorry. Everything's already packed," Deidre said. She walked over to him and reached around him for the small stack of paper cups.

He turned and faced her. She could feel his breath on her cheek and wondered if he was going to kiss her. Instead, he gently brushed her cheek with his lips before plucking two cups from the stack. "Thanks," he said lightly. He walked over to the refrigerator as Deidre stood there, speechless.

"Can I use this?" he asked, holding up a container of grapefruit juice. She managed to nod. He added a splash of vodka and ice, then handed a cup to her. "Cheers."

"Cheers."

He took a sip, then held up the paper cup, admiring it. "I think I'm going to get rid of all my glassware and fill my cabinets with Dixie cups instead. It really brings out the waxy flavor of the Greyhound, don't you think?"

Deidre laughed. Handsome, great dresser, *and* a sense of humor. It was almost too good to be true.

Kevin took her hand and led her into the living room. "Come on, let's at least sit down and drink like civilized people."

Deidre felt giddy. Holding hands was so fourth grade but also, God help her, so romantic.

"So, what are you going to do next?" he asked as they settled onto the couch.

"I have no idea," she said, sipping her drink.

"Where are you going to move to?"

"Again, no idea."

He leaned back, an envious look in his eyes. "You have no idea how lucky you are. I'd love to be in your shoes."

Deidre almost choked. The events of the past week flashed before her eyes. "What? You're kidding."

"Nope."

She tucked her feet under her and leaned toward him, interested. "Why? What would you do?"

"Easy. I'd pack my bags and go straight up to my place on Lake Wish." He took a long sip of his drink and looked back at her, content.

"Lake Wish? Where's that?"

"It's about four hours south, southeast of here. In Jacob's Point."

Deidre shook her head. "I've never heard of it."

"The population is forty at best." A thought occurred to him. "Hey, you're welcome to stay there anytime if you like. As my guest. You'd actually be doing me a favor: I'm hardly ever there and every now and then I think about getting someone to house-sit so it wouldn't be empty all the time."

"Wow." Deidre sat back and thought about this. "I don't know what to say. Where did you say it was again?"

Kevin put down his drink and picked up a pen from the coffee table. He checked his pockets until he found a piece of paper and began to draw a small map.

"You head southeast on I-ninety and once you cross the Columbia River, it'll start heading north and then east again. At Ritzville, catch highway three-ninety-five, heading north, and exit two-thirty-one. Follow the feeder for a couple of miles, and it will eventually become a dirt road. Continue for about eight miles, and you'll come upon a grove of evergreens." He drew a small cluster of pine trees. "Turn left at the evergreens. There's a gorgeous blue-green lake nestled in there called Skit's Wish—we call it Lake Wish—and my place is right there." He finished his drawing with a small house, studied it for a little while, then slid it over to Deidre.

"It's in the woods but Jacob's Point is only ten minutes away. It's a small town with nice people. You'll have plenty of privacy, if that's what you want."

Deidre studied the map uncertainly. "Seems a little out of the way . . ."

"It's definitely off the beaten path," Kevin agreed, picking up his drink again. "My grandfather owned some land out there, and we've just kept it in the family. He loved to camp, but I like a roof over my head, so I put something up a while back." He gave a small chuckle. "It's not the Ritz, but it'll do."

Deidre had flashes of bathrooms with wooden toilet seats and fending off bears with a rolling pin. Creepy sounds at night, a million miles away from civilization.

"I really appreciate it," Deidre said, hoping she didn't sound ungrateful. "But I'm not really an outdoorsy kind of person."

"There's a lot of ancient legend and folklore about the place. You might find it inspiring."

Deidre shook her head. "Not without a Starbucks nearby." She wasn't interested in reliving her days as a Girl Scout.

Kevin gave her a wry look. "Stubborn but beautiful," he finally said, giving an exaggerated sigh. "Well, think about it."

"I will. Thanks."

Kevin finished his drink and then put down his cup, turning to face her. "Okay, I have a confession." He cleared this throat.

"Yes?" Suddenly nervous again, she clutched her drink.

He gently eased the cup from between her fingers. "I've been thinking about you since the restaurant. That sounds like a total come-on line, doesn't it?" He brushed aside a stray lock of hair that had fallen in her face, making her shiver.

"A little," she managed to say. Then again, who cared? It was working.

He smiled at her, his fingers continuing a path down the side of her face, down her neck, down to the center of her chest. Deidre fought the urge to rip his clothes off altogether. "I have to say that I'm surprised we haven't run into each other before," he murmured.

"I guess we don't travel in the same circles," Deidre said faintly. Kevin ran the back of his hand between the gentle valley of her breasts. Maybe it was the alcohol, but Deidre was feeling bold, sexy, and tired of the small talk.

Kevin started to say, "Well, actually . . ." but didn't get to finish before Deidre pressed her lips against his in a kiss. He kissed her back, his mouth hot on hers. Her arms found their way around his neck, pulling him closer. He smelled clean, musky. His tongue caressed the inside of her mouth, then became urgent, intentional. Deidre let her hand slip down until she felt his arousal, making her instantly wet. His hands slipped under her shirt, under her bra. He cupped her breasts, molding them to his touch. Deidre sighed, arching with pleasure, then pressed against him, wanting to feel more of him.

"God, you are beautiful," he said huskily, looking down at her. He ran his hands slowly down her body as Deidre's breath became ragged. He coaxed her pants over her hips and down her legs, eventually stripping her free. He tossed them aside and brought his hands between her legs, feeling her dampness through the thin fabric of her panties. He pressed his hand against her sex and Deidre saw stars.

She pulled off his shirt and jeans, not wanting to waste any more time. His body was beautiful—broad shoulders, muscular, perfect. Deidre didn't care about anything anymore, she didn't care about losing the show or losing the apartment. The fact that she barely knew his name, much less anything else about him, made it all the easier. She was tired of trying to have it all figured out, of taking care of everyone but herself. And it had been a long time since she had been with anyone.

Kevin pressed her back into the couch and began kissing

her neck, tracing a line down to her chest, past her breasts, gently spreading her legs apart. The apartment filled with the sounds of sex.

Deidre cried out just as he slanted his mouth over hers and kissed her deeply, exploding at the same time. She held him inside of her, shaking as she came. She collapsed against him, their bodies slick with sweat, and before she knew it, she was fast asleep.

DEIDRE WOKE UP the next morning, sunlight dancing on her bedroom walls. God, her head hurt. She yawned and stretched and, in doing so, almost had a heart attack. Kevin was next to her, asleep and naked. It wasn't a dream. To make matters worse, it turned out that *she* was naked as well. Mortified, Deidre clutched the sheet around her and tried to make a dash for her closet.

"Deidre?" Kevin stirred and turned over, giving her a sleepy smile. "Good morning."

"Good morning," she stammered. The events of the past night came flooding back. "I thought we were . . ." She stared, perplexed, toward the living room. "How did I . . . we . . . get in here?"

Kevin yawned and sat up. "I carried you. After you passed out."

Deidre closed her eyes, feeling dizzy. She heard the sheets rustle.

"I'm going to run to the bathroom," Kevin said. "Unless you want to go first?"

He's probably going to come back fully dressed and I'm going to look like a complete idiot. She forced a smile, gathering the blankets around her. "There's another one down the hall. I can use that."

The minute she heard the bathroom door close, she got up and rifled through her closet, looking for clothes. She grabbed a shirt and some jeans and hurried to the other bathroom, desperately hoping she wouldn't come across as needy or clingy when she saw him next.

She washed her face and changed her clothes, taking slow meditative breaths. *It's not a big deal, it's just sex. With a perfect stranger.* Her life falls apart and she takes the moral low road. It was now official: the host of *Live Simple* was a slut.

Deidre took a frantic look at herself in the mirror. Okay, so maybe it was a bit early to look like she was heading off to work, but it was still better than running around naked. She steeled herself and headed toward the bedroom, forcing herself to look cheerful and indifferent. *Don't look like you want him to stay*, she told herself sharply. *You'll just make it harder for everyone. You're both adults, it was just great, make that amazingly great, casual sex.*

Deidre stopped at the doorway, a smile plastered on her face, and immediately felt like a fool.

Kevin was back in bed, tucked comfortably between the sheets, and still naked. He raised an eyebrow. "I take it I've overstayed my welcome?" he asked dryly.

"I . . ." Deidre was at a loss for words.

Kevin gave her a relaxed smile and shrugged. He slid out of bed and walked past her. "That's okay. I'll get my clothes."

Deidre followed him out. "I just thought . . . you probably needed to get going. I mean, not for me, for you. I've got a lot to do today, and I'm sure you weren't planning on . . . staying over."

Kevin was pulling up his jeans. He looked so good that Deidre was tempted to drag him back to bed, but clearly that window of opportunity had closed. He shrugged on his shirt and patted his pockets for his wallet and keys. He glanced around the apartment to see if he had left anything.

He ran his hand through his hair. "So, maybe I can call you sometime?"

Deidre forced another smile. *Maybe?* From sex to the remote possibility of a phone call. "Sure."

"And, by the way, the offer is still on the table for my place down by Lake Wish," Kevin said as he opened the front door. "I'll leave the map over there in case you change your mind."

Deidre had almost forgotten about that. "Thanks, but I'll figure out something in the city."

He shrugged. "Suit yourself." He bent down to pick up the newspaper on her doorstep and handed it to her. He hesitated for a moment and turned back to face her. "What do you think about grabbing some breakfast?"

Relief flooded through her body—she would love to have breakfast with him. "That would be . . ."

Kevin's cell phone rang. He glanced at the phone number and said, "Sorry, I need to get this." He walked into the hallway, flipping open his phone as he cleared his throat. His voice was low as he turned his back on Deidre. "Hey, sweetheart . . ."

He has a girlfriend, she thought, instantly panicked. *No, worse yet, he's married!* Deidre quickly opened the newspaper and pretended to flip through it, straining to hear what he was saying. She could only hear mumbling before he reappeared, shoving his phone in his back pocket and looking preoccupied.

"I'm going to have to take a rain check," he said. "I'll call you later?"

Deidre waited for a longer explanation but he didn't offer one. "Okay. Great."

He gave her a quick kiss on the cheek—*the cheek?*—then closed the door behind him.

"Yeah, great," Deidre muttered, throwing the newspaper at the door. It fluttered to the floor, pages fanning out everywhere. The Entertainment section landed at her feet.

Deidre brought her hand to her mouth. There was a high school yearbook shot of her, one at senior prom standing alone with a huge wrist corsage, and another on the set, looking completely distraught. She recognized the picture—it was taken on the day the butternut squash lasagna had caught fire because her assistant at the time, Jan, had turned on the broiler by accident. There were also two pictures of Marla Banks—a high school prom shot and a shot on the set. While Marla looked sexy and radiant, Deidre looked like early shots of Hillary Clinton having a bad day.

The headline read: "Survival of the Fittest—New Show Takes Over."

> So long, Deidre McIntosh, hello, Marla Banks. Seattle's own Marla Banks debuted her new show, *At Home with Marla Banks*, to a welcome audience this month. McIntosh, originally a Denver transplant, has reportedly ended her run of *Live Simple* on the eve of Marla's debut after holding

> Seattle housewives captive with her home and cooking show for five years . . .

Deidre grabbed the map and rushed to the window, yanking back the blinds. Kevin was just stepping out of the building, flipping up the collar of his jacket.

"Wait!" she called, waving the map. "I'll take it!"

CHAPTER 4

It is common to overlook what is near
by keeping the eye fixed on something remote.
—SAMUEL JOHNSON

"THIS," DEIDRE SAID slowly and deliberately, "is a shack."

She was staring at the small cabin in front of her from the safety of her car. She looked around slowly, seeing nothing but trees. It was dusk and in an hour or so, Deidre would lose the last of her sunlight.

Deidre sat in her car, the engine still running, unsure of what to do. It had taken her several hours to make the journey to Jacob's Point. She had gotten lost along the way, made a couple of unexpected detours, and was seduced, but only for a moment, by the whimsical rural charm of the small towns she passed through. Now that she was finally here—turning left after the grove of evergreens per Kevin's wrinkled-but-now-ironed forty-six-dollar map, which turned out to be the back of the check she had given him—it was all she could do not to turn around and head right back to the city.

"Why not?" she argued with herself. "I could make it back by nine, ten o'clock tonight. Plenty of time to grab coffee and dessert at Wild Ginger." She glanced back at the dilapidated shack. From the outside it looked like a Boy Scout's survival project, random pieces of wood nailed against the house, an old doormat, the windows covered with mud and dirt. There was no driveway to speak of and no front lawn. Debris was scattered all over the porch. Deidre could hear William clucking his tongue disapprovingly, "Weak entrance? Bad feng shui. Clutter? *Very* bad feng shui."

Kevin said there was a key under a cracked flowerpot on the east side of the house, near the doorway. Deidre squinted at the house, wondering if she should at least go in and take a look before heading back to the city. Maybe the cabin looked beat-up to discourage break-ins. Maybe it was like one of those cartoons where the exterior, a bank façade for example, would flip at the press of a button and voila!—instant contraband saloon. Okay, maybe that was a stretch, but anything was possible.

Deidre chewed on her bottom lip in indecision, and finally shook her head. Camping, the woods, and being a million miles from nowhere just wasn't her thing.

"Thanks, but no thanks," she said, and put the car in reverse. She turned to look over her shoulder when the engine sputtered and died.

Deidre turned back, startled. "Oh no," she said, looking at the dead panel in front of her. She tried to start the car, but it wouldn't catch. "No, no, no, please do not do this to me right now! You are a brand new car, I paid almost fifty-five grand for you, I sold everything but you! *You . . . do not . . . break down!*"

Deidre tried the engine a few more times before slamming the steering with her fists. "Shit!"

It was definitely starting to get dark; the sun was kissing the horizon and she could see patches of sunlight through the trees. She fumbled through the owner's manual but couldn't find anything of use. Deidre looked at the cabin, which seemed just as bleak as before, and even more foreboding.

Desperate, Deidre flipped open her cell phone to call AAA. There was a hint of signal—only one bar—but then it disappeared. No service. She got out of her car and began walking around frantically, holding her phone up like a beacon to see if she could get reception. Nothing.

"Don't panic," she told herself. She'd been in worse situations before. Of course, none of them came to mind, but she was sure there had to have been a couple, and Deidre was sure she'd soldiered through them just fine. She could try to make her way back to the road and wait for help, even though she didn't remember seeing any other cars when she had turned toward Jacob's Point. *Eventually someone will drive by*, she reasoned, but that meant potentially standing in the dark. Near the woods. With no one nearby to help her if a psycho pulled up . . .

A few seconds later, Deidre was overturning every broken flowerpot in search of the key.

She couldn't find it. It was getting darker and the sky had turned a menacing gray.

"This is not good," she muttered, looking everywhere around the exterior of the house. *Which way was east? Left or right?* Deidre wiped her hands on her jeans and heard a thunderclap. Just as she peered over the edge of the eaves to look at the sky, it started to rain. Large, fat drops of water splashed the dirt in front of the house in every direction.

"Just find the key," she commanded herself, making another pass along the exterior of the house. It was raining heavier now, bits of mud kicking up onto Deidre's shoes and jeans from the ground. She felt her shoulder get wet and looked up just as a trickle of water began to run off the edge of the roof. *So much for having a covered patio*, Deidre thought. The porch was getting wet, and so was Deidre.

She felt trapped. She could make a dash for the car, but then what? Her car headlights wouldn't work—the battery was dead. She didn't think to bring a flashlight because Kevin had made it sound as if the place had everything she would need. Maybe the car came with an emergency kit, some flares or emergency candles. Deidre remembered that she had some Illume candles in her bag, too; maybe the cigarette lighter in the car might be able to set the wick aflame . . .

A thought occurred to her. Deidre turned and studied the doorknob. Almost reluctantly, she reached out and turned the knob. The door opened with a creak.

On a small table inside the door Deidre could see the key, resting primly and patiently.

"Of course," she said, stepping into the house and picking up key. "Why wouldn't the key be *inside* the house? Makes perfect sense." Her sarcasm masked the overwhelming sense of relief she was feeling at the moment.

She felt along the wall for a light switch and flipped it on. Light filled the cabin and Deidre felt relief drain from her body, replaced by shock as she took in what was in front of her.

So you can *tell a book by its cover*, she finally sighed. The inside needed just as much work as the outside. It was musty, as if no one had lived in it for a long time. The corners had cobwebs. She could see dust particles floating in the air. It was incredibly small—the entire cabin seemed about the size of her old living room. It was definitely simple, definitely a bachelor's pad (the animal skin rugs and elk horns on the wall were the big clue), and definitely in need of a good cleaning.

Deidre could hear the rain beating down on the roof. No leaks yet, but only time would tell. She was about to go outside to her car when another loud thunderclap shook the house. Opting to stay dry, Deidre grudgingly decided to look around a little more. It certainly wouldn't take very long.

It was a small two-bedroom, one-bath cabin, maybe nine hundred square feet in total. The hardwood floors were dull and scuffed up, a layer of dust coating them. A beat-up washer and dryer were in the hallway closet, partially concealed by a folding door with rusty hinges. The kitchen faucet sputtered before spitting out brown water which eventually turned clear. Deidre noticed the stained chrome finish could have possibilities if cleaned properly. The kitchen had two large sinks and a window directly above them, with just enough counter space. The oven and stove were old but seemed to work fine. The two small bedrooms each had a full-size bed draped with outdated crocheted blankets that needed a good wash, small dressers that held an assortment of men's clothes, as well as other odds and ends. Deidre continued to walk through the house, taking inventory, shuddering when she accidentally stepped on what looked like mice pellets.

Deidre heard a funny scratching and turned. As if on cue, a mouse ran across the floor of the cabin then stopped and turned to look at her. Startled, Deidre backed away and then turned face first into a spiderweb. Wispy strands tangled in her hair. "Arghh!"

Deidre rushed back to her car, got in, and slammed the door, furiously wiping her face and hair clean of any remaining strands. As her heart rate slowly returned to normal, Deidre willed herself not to pass out or have a nervous breakdown. Who was she kidding? After all she'd been through, attempting to pull this off was a disaster waiting to happen. Discouraged and at an utter loss of what to do next, she spent the next twenty minutes sitting in the car, staring at the open door of the cabin.

The rain slowed to a lazy drizzle and then stopped completely to reveal a starless night sky. Deidre opened her door a crack to let in some fresh air, and the scent of fresh pines and clean, wet earth filled her nostrils. She took her first deep breath and felt her muscles finally begin to relax.

She had to make a decision.

Deidre tried to start her car again with no luck. *Think*, she told herself. *You can figure this out*. She was getting tired, and the only real option was becoming more and more obvious. Resigned, Deidre got out of the car and slowly walked back to the cabin.

She found a broom with a broken handle and swept the space as best she could before unloading her things, making a small pile in the corner of the cabin. With most of her clothes sitting in a consignment store in Seattle, Deidre was relieved for the first time in days that she didn't have much stuff. She had felt like a failure after ferrying her final load of clothes to the store, having kept only a few choice outfits and putting the rest up for sale. All of her hard work seemed to have been for nothing, and now she didn't even have a decent wardrobe to show for it. But at this moment, she was surprised to find that she felt lighter. Freer. Not to mention dustier and in desperate need of an eventual shower.

Once everything was inside the house, Deidre returned to the car, put down the back seat, and climbed in. She locked the doors and pulled a blanket over her. Then she lay there, aware of how intensely quiet and dark it was. Lonely.

I need a warm body, she thought gloomily. Then she shivered, but it wasn't because she was cold.

The mere memory of the other night began to generate its own heat in her body, although not quite where she needed it at the moment. When Kevin had returned to give her information about the cabin, he acted as if nothing had happened: the sex, the sleepover, the invitation to breakfast. Deidre acted just as polite, bordering almost on professional, discreetly shoving the offending newspaper into the trash while he was talking. He had told her to stay as long as she needed, and then had to leave when his cell phone rang again. It was another "*Hey, sweetheart*" call, so Deidre turned away and tried to focus on a small chip on the counter.

Kevin gave her another innocuous peck on the cheek and left. *Wham, bam, thank you ma'am*, Deidre had thought, suppressing her irritation. When she realized that she was pouting like a lovesick teenager, it made her even more upset.

"Wow," William had said when he came over to help her

pack up her car. "I can't believe you slept with a complete stranger, Deidre. That's so not you. It's so . . . pedestrian!" He grinned.

She shot him a dirty look. "Thanks, that makes me feel a *whole* lot better, William."

"I just wouldn't have dreamed it in a million years." He whistled, then studied her face, which looked wistful. "So I take it was good?"

Deidre groaned, burying her face in hands. "It was *so* good."

William leaned forward eagerly. "Details, please."

She shook her head. "I'm not one to kiss and tell." Before he could snicker, Deidre pleaded, "Will you please let me retain even some semblance of dignity?"

"Fine. So moving on to the next issue . . . you're going to stay in his place, somewhere in the boondocks?" He raised a questioning eyebrow.

"What? I don't really have much choice—I have no income, I'll barely be able to scrape by on my savings, and you and Alain really don't want me sleeping on your couch. I need a place where I can think, figure out what to do next. Everyone at *Live Simple* thinks I should revamp the show, or come up with another idea for a show. A couple of headhunters said companies would be clamoring for me, you know, anything from management to spokesperson . . ." She rolled her eyes. "Suffice it to say there have been approximately, oh, zero calls." She began to open and close drawers in rapid succession, checking that they were empty.

William ran the tape gun across the top of a box. "So you're just going to squirrel away in your secret hideaway for a while?"

"I'm not hiding from anything," Deidre said defensively. "I just need some time. I'm forty, I've been hosting my own show for years . . . it's not like I can go out and land a job tomorrow."

"Sad, but true." William twirled the tape gun. "So . . . when are you going to see him again?"

"I don't know. After I showed up fully dressed five minutes after we woke up, he was ready to bolt." Deidre was glum.

William tried to sound hopeful. "Maybe he'll call."

"He won't."

"Why?"

"Because I told him not to," Deidre said. She started to cross things off her checklist, dejected.

William's jaw dropped. "*What?* Why did you do that?"

"I don't know! It just didn't seem to make sense at the time, to get something started up and I don't know . . ." She covered her face with her hands, muffling a groan.

William looked skeptical, then shook his head. "Well, at least he knows where you'll be if he wants to see you."

"Yeah, him and his girlfriend or wife. Fun!"

He gave her an exasperated look. "You don't know he's married. You didn't see a ring."

"Married men who sleep around don't wear their wedding bands, William. Besides, even if he isn't married, he's got some girlfriend who calls all the time. It was actually quite annoying." She picked up a box and followed him out the door toward the elevator.

"I bet." He gave her a nudge until she laughed.

Now, in her car, Deidre snuggled deeper under her blanket. *Don't waste any more mental energy on that*, she reprimanded herself. *He's letting you stay at his place, just call it even and move on.* She didn't have the luxury to dwell on romances, married men, or one-night stands. Deidre had more important things on her mind. Like what she was going to do with the rest of her life.

THE MORNING SUN cast a pinkish hue in the sky. Sunlight entered the car and reflected rainbows off the small crystal hanging from Deidre's rearview mirror. A small rainbow danced on Deidre's eyelids and she woke up, a small smile on her face until she remembered where she was. She groaned.

The windows had fogged up and Deidre was a little cramped, but cozy. She rolled down the window and a cold morning breeze swept in like a splash of cold water. The air was so clear and crisp it almost hurt to breathe.

She could hear birds and the rustle of wind through the trees. The sun was sparkling through the leaves. Everything felt alive. Deidre wrapped the blanket around her tighter, not sure what to do next.

She fumbled for her cell phone and read the time: 6:00 A.M. She sighed. So much for sleeping in every morning. Deidre rubbed the window with her palm and looked at the cabin, hoping that maybe it had somehow transformed overnight.

It hadn't. She tried the car one more time before getting out and heading toward the cabin to go the bathroom. She really had to go, but after taking a long look at the bathroom, complete with the obligatory wooden toilet seat, Deidre opted to do her business in the bushes. When she was finished, she went through her things until she found a container of Clorox wipes. She took a deep breath and readied herself for dangling spider webs and wandering mice. She walked back into the cabin.

She tackled the bathroom first, not wanting to have a repeat performance of her morning toilette later in the day. By the time she was done—having used one container of Clorox wipes, a roll of paper towels, and two buckets full of an orange-infused cleanser, the bathroom actually looked—and smelled—good.

"Still missing something . . ." Deidre mused, and then got it. She found an old glass jar and went outside. She cut a few small branches from a pine tree outside and arranged them in the jar with some stones, and placed them in the bathroom. She fussed until it felt just right. "There we go. Perfect."

Deidre walked through the rest of the house. It seemed unlived in, with hardly anything of personal value. The only artwork was an exquisite collection of black-and-white photographs of scenery, including a gorgeous, shimmering lake.

That must be the lake Kevin was talking about, Deidre thought, surprised. She blew a coat of dust off the glass of one of the pictures, then began rubbing it with the sleeve of her shirt. She stepped back, sighed, then went into the kitchen. She gingerly opened the cabinets until she found, to her relief and surprise, glass cleaner, rubbing alcohol, and several rolls of paper towels and old rags. Deidre rinsed the rags, then began wiping down the photograph, taking care not to scratch the glass. When she was finished, she stood back to survey her work but she wasn't satisfied. Deidre began digging through her things until she found a box of Q-tips, then went back to work on cleaning every groove of the framed photograph.

When she was finished, the framed photograph shined.

Gleamed. Sparkled. Deidre was impressed and felt a small twinge of pride. "You do good work, McIntosh," she said quietly. Of course, it helped that the photography and frame were beautiful to begin with. Her eye caught the photograph next to it, a quiet scene with sunlight coming through the trees, dusty and disillusioned. *Me, me*, it called to her. *Clean me next. Please?*

"Damn," she muttered, knowing what came next. She sighed and went to go rinse the rags.

Deidre spent all morning cleaning the house, opening the windows, and shaking out rugs. The washer and dryer shook and seemed to want to fall to pieces but Deidre managed two loads before a funny knocking sound convinced her to finish the rest of the linens later.

Starving and finally ready for a late lunch, Deidre went through the groceries she had bought on her way into Jacob's Point, remembering that Kevin had said the town of Jacob's Point was past the property, heading in the opposite direction. She sat at the kitchen table, eating a large green salad and having a cup of tea, surprised at how well the house cleaned up even though there was much more to do.

Why bother, a voice said inside of her. *You're out of here as soon as you can figure out how to get the car started. This isn't a* Live Simple *project.*

That's right, another voice said. *It's a roof over your head. In case you've forgotten, we have no money and no place to live. Clean it up a bit, be a good houseguest, and then you can get out when something better comes along.*

Just get us the hell out of here, the first voice ordered. *How long can you last in the middle of nowhere? We can't even get groceries until we figure out how to get the car fixed.*

There's plenty of food, the second voice argued. *There are at least ten cans of chili and pork and beans in the pantry. We'll be fine.*

Put on your walking shoes and head for the road, the first voice advised. *We need to get help. Time is of the essence. We need to figure out what we're going to do next. We need to get back to the city. Think of all the fun everyone is having right now. We need culture, an income, restaurants, shopping. We need shopping!*

Deidre put down her fork, her appetite lost. She was used to having arguments with herself, but this was getting out of hand. So maybe she didn't need shopping, at least not yet, but she did need to get in touch with someone, anyone, before she was stranded.

Deidre went outside, bundling her coat around her. It would be at least a mile's walk before she hit the main road, and from there it was anybody's best guess. Deidre couldn't remember the last time she had walked a mile. Still, there was no point in complaining since there was no one around to hear her or commiserate. She'd have to take it one step at a time, literally. She locked the door, tucked the key safely under a flowerpot, and pulled up her collar. Then she began walking.

LUCK WAS WITH her, because once Deidre got to the main road, she only had to walk for a few minutes before a weathered pickup came by. The driver was surprised to see her walking along the road. "You're in the middle of nowhere," he told her as he opened the rusty passenger door.

"Trust me, I know," she said.

It took about fifteen minutes to drive into town. Deidre listened with polite interest as the driver predicted an early winter and complained about the rising cost of gasoline, all while driving at breakneck speed. The drive along the way was a flash of trees until suddenly the town appeared as if out of nowhere.

"Shoot," the driver said, slamming on the brakes. "I always just miss it."

He checked the rear window before slowly backing up and depositing Deidre on the curb. "There's supposed to be a sign telling you to go slow, fifteen miles or something, but it got knocked over in an accident and they never got another one back up."

Deidre brushed herself off, smoothing her hair and trying to look composed even though her nerves were on end. "An accident, really? Let me guess—someone was speeding?" She was still trying to calm herself.

"Something like that." He tipped his faded baseball hat, gave a friendly wave, and drove off.

Deidre turned and looked around, grateful to be on solid ground. She *was* in the middle of nowhere. The street was completely empty and if it wasn't for the occasional movement inside one of the buildings, Deidre would have assumed it was deserted. There was a general store, a hardware store and across the street, a diner. All that was left were a couple of vacant storefronts. Uneasy, Deidre checked her cell phone again. Still no service. She took one more look around before walking into the diner.

The moment she stepped inside, Deidre relaxed. It was warm, and there was the scent of cinnamon, mingled with the smells and sounds of breakfast being served. Someone was back in the kitchen, and there was a single patron, an elderly woman, who couldn't be bothered to look up from her morning paper.

Well, that's a good sign, Deidre thought. Even the slightest hint of civilization was welcome, especially when laced with the aroma of fresh coffee. She glanced around for a pay phone and spotted one in the corner.

Deidre quickly crossed the room and dialed the number for AAA.

"What city please?"

"Jacob's Point," Deidre said. "I'm at a diner . . ." She read the name off a menu. "The Wishbone." She gave the woman more details and, after unsuccessfully attempting to explain where Kevin's house was, agreed to wait for the tow truck at the diner.

"Give us two hours," the AAA woman said. "I'm not sure who I have in the area."

Deidre hung up the phone and looked around. The woman in the kitchen still hadn't come out and the elderly woman had glanced at Deidre indifferently, then returned to her coffee and cinnamon roll. Deidre hesitated, unsure of what to do next. She decided to call William.

"Deidre!" he exclaimed. "How is it? Is it everything you ever dreamed of? Alain and I have this lovely picture of you lounging around on a bucolic estate, with does and fawns in the background. Wait, are does and fawns the same thing?"

It was a relief to hear William's voice but instantly Deidre became whiny. "William, the term *rural* doesn't even come close," she grumbled. "And the place is a dump. I cleaned it up a bit but you should have seen it when I walked in. *And* my car broke down. I'm heading back later in the day."

The elderly woman glanced up, frowning. Obviously Deidre's conversation was interrupting her morning ritual. Deidre gave an awkward smile then whispered into the phone, "So is it okay if I stay with you and Alain after all? It'll just be for a while."

"Um . . ." William seemed to have difficulty clearing this throat. "Sure," he finally said. "Did you happen to see today's paper by chance?"

"What do you think?" she asked sharply. "Of course I didn't! *I'm sleeping in my car, William.* It's not exactly like I had time for a cup of coffee and the morning paper!" The elderly woman snapped her paper indignantly and Deidre managed another tight smile before whispering fiercely in the phone, "This isn't Starbucks."

He sounded dubious. "I know. But maybe you just need to give it some time. It's a new place, after all . . ."

"William, I don't want to give it some time," she said pointedly. *"I want to come back."*

"Okay, fine. Come back."

Deidre couldn't put her finger on it right away, but then sucked in her breath and said accusingly, "You don't want me to come back!"

William sounded exasperated. "Of course I want you to come back, don't be ridiculous. It's just that I don't think that you've given the place a chance. I mean, what's it been, eighteen hours?" He waited for her to answer.

"Fourteen," Deidre finally admitted, feeling somewhat foolish.

"Look, Deidre. I love you, but things are different now. I'm with Alain and I can't hang out like we used to, you know?"

She knew. In fact, she felt it in the pit of her stomach. The days of the William and Deidre show were over. She was on her own.

As if sensing this, William said gently, "I'll leave a key under the mat, okay? We can talk about it later. Hey, I'll take you to the Jacaranda. I finally tried the tiramisu and it's to die for. I'll take you there, my treat."

Deidre gave a small smile. So help her, she still loved this man. She glanced briefly at the meager selection of baked goods and doubted if anyone at Jacob's Point even knew what tiramisu was. "That sounds great. I'll see you soon."

"Okay. Drive carefully."

Deidre hung up the phone, relieved to have a plan in place but forlorn at the prospect of being a third wheel. Still, what choice did she have?

"Lindsey!" the old woman shrilled. Deidre jumped, startled. "More coffee!" Her cup rattled against the dish.

The waitress emerged from the kitchen with a pot of coffee and made her way over to the elderly woman.

"Hold your horses, Janet," she said, casting Deidre a sidelong glance.

"Is this decaf?" Janet demanded.

"Of course not," the woman said reassuringly. She tucked a lock of hair behind her ear and retreated behind the counter.

Deidre warily slid into a booth and motioned for some coffee. She spotted an abandoned newspaper at the table next to hers and reached for it, looking forward to reading the day's news. As was habit, she turned first to the Entertainment section.

The story was below the fold, but it was there.

> Marla Banks and her new show continue to sweep Seattle, but the former first lady of *Live Simple*, Deidre McIntosh, has been mysteriously subdued. Rumor has it she has since gone blond and has moved out of her posh apartment on Capitol Hill. 'It's her alter ego,' Banks explained. 'Life has thrown her a curve ball, and this other side of her emerged. Sort of like the *Many Faces of Eve*. I've been inspired to reach out and understand this better, so I'm going to devote a whole show on women and their multiple lives, multiple personalities.' Don't miss the Queen of Glam and her show, *At Home with Marla Banks*, 4:00 P.M. weekdays on Channel Two.

Aghast, Deidre closed the offending paper, barely glancing at the waitress who poured her coffee. Deidre sullenly nursed her cup of coffee, wishing there was some Kahlua to go with it.

An hour later, she was on her third cup and restlessly looking out the window when the waitress poured another refill. She had been studying Deidre for the past hour but neither of them had said more than a couple of words. The elderly woman had left, slapping a few dollars on the table and shuffling away.

The waitress approached Deidre and leisurely poured the coffee. She asked, "I haven't seen you around here before—are you lost?"

"No," Deidre said. "I was staying at a friend's . . . house, and my car broke down."

"What's wrong with it?"

Frustrated by everything that seemed to be going wrong, Deidre was tempted to say, *If I knew, I probably wouldn't be sitting here, would I?* but she bit her tongue instead. "I don't really know," she said. She gave a small smile. "It just won't start."

"I can call the garage for you," the waitress offered. "Those guys fix all the cars in Jacob's Point. Whipped my Durango into shape after the carburetor dropped out last winter." The waitress rolled her eyes in disgust. "I had just bought it used, can you believe it? Was sure I had thrown four grand down the toilet."

Deidre could picture someone tinkering with her brand new Volvo, removing random parts and not being able to put it back together again. "Thanks, but I just called AAA. They'll send someone to take care of it. I'll be heading back to Seattle pretty soon after," she said with a slight air of importance.

"Oh, you're from Seattle," the waitress replied in a smirky voice that said that explained everything, but Deidre missed it, having been starved for attention since she went blond.

"I used to have a show there," she boasted, making a feeble attempt at looking modest. "*Live Simple with Deidre McIntosh.* It ran for almost five years." The tone of her voice suggested its success.

It worked. The waitress gaped at her. "Get out. Is that you? You're Deidre?"

Deidre gave a modest nod. "I'm Deidre." Then she remembered today's paper, glancing furtively at it, wondering if the waitress had read it.

"You look different . . ." The waitress mused for a moment, then snapped her fingers. "It's your hair. I didn't know you had blond hair in real life. Do you wear a wig on the show?"

She touched her hair a little self-consciously. "No, no. I just needed a change."

"Well, Jacob's Point is a good place for that." Now that the ice was broken, the waitress slid into the booth across from her, resting the coffeepot on the table. "We get a few city folk who come here to get away."

"No, I meant . . ." Deidre started to say.

The waitress was looking at her intently, leaning forward. "Are you married?"

Deidre was taken aback. "No, I'm . . ."

"Divorced?"

"No, I'm single," Deidre said firmly.

"Any kids?"

"No."

"I have three," the waitress said. "My husband and I homeschool them. Have since the oldest was in third grade. Public school just didn't work out for them, and the drive is so far away, they spent half their time on the bus." She shook her head, then shrugged it off. "Never thought I'd be one of those people who homeschool, but sometimes you do what you have to do. It's actually working out great."

Deidre nodded in agreement, thinking about the past few weeks. "I know what you mean," she said. The waitress opened her mouth, supposedly to barrage Deidre with more questions, so Deidre quickly asked, "I'm sorry, what's your name?"

"Lindsey. Lindsey Miller. I own the Wishbone. I cook, I clean . . ." She held up the coffeepot. "I do pretty much everything."

"Really?" Deidre was impressed.

Lindsey shrugged, indifferent. "We had a rocky year last year—the bank foreclosed on us but one of our neighbors bailed us out. He's holding the note, lets me pay it down when I can. In the meantime, he lets me run the business and keep the proceeds, even if I have to miss a payment or two." She smiled, happy. "It's not much of anything, but it keeps me busy. I do a great dinner. We're doing my meatloaf special tonight. Five-thirty sharp—I'm usually sold out by seven."

Deidre tried to give a polite smile. "Thank you, but . . ."

"You're heading back up to Seattle soon?"

"*Really* soon." Deidre glanced at the clock. *Where was AAA?* "It's just where my life is," she explained, as if Lindsey expected an explanation. "I just need a place to stay and my friend thought this might work, but . . ." Her voice trailed off and she smiled apologetically. "I just need to get back."

Lindsey watched her for a moment, then gave a big exhale. "Me, too. Back to work, that is." There was no one else in the diner other than Deidre, but Deidre suspected Lindsey was getting bored with her. Then, as if it were an afterthought, Lindsey said casually, "If you have some time before you go, you might want to go see our lake."

Deidre suddenly remembered. "Lake Wish?"

Lindsey looked surprised. "You know it?"

"My . . . friend mentioned it."

There was a gleam in Lindsey's eye. "There are some legends about the lake, you know."

Deidre glanced out the window just as a tow truck drove by. She jumped up, almost knocking over Lindsey. "Oh,

I'm sorry. I need to go catch that tow truck. Here . . ." She fumbled through her wallet for a couple of dollars and handed them to Lindsey while shrugging on her coat at the same time. "Thanks."

Lindsey picked up the bills and tucked them back into Deidre's jacket pocket. "On the house. Everyone always gets their first cup of coffee free." She began to clear Deidre's coffee mug, wiping away a coffee ring. "Have a safe trip back to Seattle."

Deidre gave her a quick wave as she hurried to the door. "Thanks. I will."

"I KNEW IT just needed a jump," Deidre said unconvincingly as the AAA man unhooked the cables from her car. The Volvo was humming nicely and Deidre was giddy with relief. She was finally free to leave Jacob's Point and make her way back to Seattle.

"I'd leave it running for a while," he suggested. "Be careful not to drain your battery again."

"But I didn't," Deidre said. "It was running and it just died."

"That's strange. You should probably have the dealer check it out. Could be a problem with the electrical connection." He got into his truck and looked around, perplexed. "How do I get out of here?"

After he was gone, Deidre left the Volvo running as she went to go pack up her things. Once inside the house, she noticed her half-eaten salad still on the table. She glanced around the cabin and saw the shiny photo prints on the wall and the fresh flowers in the bathroom. The rest of the house was still a dusty mess.

Deidre forced herself to ignore the mess. *I am going back to Seattle,* she told herself resolutely as she began to clean up the table and wash the dishes. As she went to put her dishes away, she looked at the dusty plates and dishes in the cupboard, stacked patiently.

Deidre glanced at her watch. It was three o'clock. If she wanted to head back to the city, she needed to do it soon. Deidre looked at the cupboard again. It wouldn't take more than fifteen minutes to have them all washed and dried. Twenty at the most.

She bit her lip, unsure of what to do. They were just dishes, for God's sake. No one was probably going to be using them anyway. She looked around the house again. It looked back at her quietly. For a moment, Deidre felt strangely, inexplicably, peaceful.

I can't stay here, she said, breaking her reverie. She was suddenly agitated as she moved toward her boxes with the intention of putting them in her car. *I'm just wasting time. I need to figure out what I'm going to do and I can't do it here.*

She began to load up the car, ignoring the kitchen each time she came into the house. The sound of her engine was strangely reassuring. Knowing that she could now leave, if she wanted to, was a huge relief.

Deidre almost had the last box in the car when she made the mistake of looking into the kitchen. The afternoon sun was streaming in through the window over the sink, filling the kitchen with light and warmth.

No, Deidre thought wildly. *I can't. I have to get back. I have to figure things out. I don't have a chance if I don't get back. I can't change my life if I'm here.*

The sunlight was reflecting off something on the table.

Deidre walked over to it and picked it up. It was her watch, which she had taken off when she had cleared the table.

Deidre slipped it onto her wrist; it was still warm from the sun. She looked at the open cupboard once again and knew that the only person she was kidding was herself.

Deidre turned on the hot water, letting the steam rise to her face as the sink filled up. She added some soap and began to slip the dishes in, one by one. As they were soaking she began to scrub down the cupboards, removing all of the cobwebs, clearing away all of the dust. Beneath the dirt and grime, the maple cupboards shone with a brilliant luster.

There was something cathartic about cleaning, and Deidre felt a calm overtake her. When she was finished and the dishes were dried and back in the cupboard, Deidre looked at her watch. *I can still make it*, she thought. She turned off the lights in the house, locked the door, and slipped the key under the flowerpot.

Her Volvo was still humming, the hood of her car hot and ready to go. The back of her car was jammed full of boxes and suitcases. She stared at the cabin for a long time, her windows rolled down to let in the scent of fresh pine needles. It was the right thing to do, and Deidre knew it. She finally put the car in reverse, and headed out toward the road. The vibration of the engine under her feet felt good. Deidre felt good. She felt alive.

It was getting dark by the time she pulled her car to a stop. She got out, took a deep breath, and stepped into the warm aroma of the Wishbone.

The Wishbone was almost full, and the lively chatter paused for a moment as everyone looked at her, curious. It was obvious she wasn't local, and even though she was wearing an old barn jacket, she felt overdressed. Deidre stood there awkwardly, suddenly self-conscious, wondering if she had made a mistake. While she had been cleaning, her intuition had told her to stay, to try, but maybe she had been wrong. After all, where had her intuition been this past year?

Maybe she should head back for Seattle after all. Just as Deidre was about to leave, Lindsey came out of the kitchen, her arms full of plates steaming with food. She didn't seem surprised to see Deidre and nodded to an empty table.

Deidre hesitated, and Lindsey smiled reassuringly, nodding again toward the table. "Go ahead and sit down," she said, her voice comforting but firm. "I'll bring some water. One meatloaf special?"

"Yes," Deidre said, taking off her coat, giving a small smile to the old lady at the next table, who was still staring at Deidre, her mouth agape. "That would be good."

CHAPTER 5

People only see what they are prepared to see.
—RALPH WALDO EMERSON

"YOU'RE STAYING?" WILLIAM asked the next day, when Deidre drove back into town for a cup of coffee and to give him a call. "I thought you said the place was a dump. And I waited up for you, by the way. I almost called the police or the sheriff, or whoever it is you have out there. I could see you in a ravine, hysterical."

Hysterical? Deidre was mildly offended but didn't blame William for thinking that. He knew her better than she knew herself. "Well, I was thinking that you're right; I should just stick it out a bit longer, maybe stay through Halloween."

"Does this have anything to do with what was in the paper yesterday?"

"Maybe," she acquiesced. "But I need to do this for myself. I can't live with you forever. Besides, I want to have things figured out before I come back to Seattle. Everyone's going to be asking me questions about what I'm going to be doing next, and I don't have those answers."

"You don't have to have those answers," he reminded her gently.

"But I *want* to have those answers, William. I need them. I need to figure out what I'm going to do next, and I can't do it in Seattle living with you and Alain."

"Well, I'm proud of you," he said, and Deidre beamed. She felt proud of herself as well. "So are you going to be working on a pilot for a new show?"

"I've been thinking about it. I just don't know what it'll be about." Deidre glanced furtively around the diner, as if someone might hear her. "So . . ." She tried to keep her voice light, as if she didn't care. "What's the latest on Marla's show?"

William snorted. "That woman's a live wire. Talk about high maintenance. She totally has the press in her pocket, though I think you took the wind out of her sails by disappearing. I think she was looking forward to some competition."

"She seems to be slamming me just the same. I'll call you once I settle in."

Deidre walked over to a booth, sliding into the checkered upholstery. She took a sip of coffee. Not exactly French roast, but it would do.

"So what are you going to do today, now that we have you for a little while longer?" Lindsey asked, flipping a dish towel over the counter.

"A lot of cleaning and a little relaxing," Deidre said. Her eye caught something on a cake dish. "Are those scones?" she asked.

Lindsey looked over. "Yeah. I think I have a blueberry and a cherry left."

"I'll take the blueberry. Do you make them?"

"Nah. We used to have a woman in town who baked for us, but her husband got sick so she's taking care of him. This is just a mix I get from the food service. Just put the whole thing in the mixer, spoon drop them on a cookie sheet, and bake. It's pretty good, though not as good as Hannah's." Lindsey slipped the blueberry scone onto a plate and served it to Deidre.

Deidre took a bite. Definitely processed, cheap flour, too much sugar, but it had enough butter to make it flake nicely.

"I need to get a few things," Deidre said, taking a sip of her coffee to wash it down. "Is there a hardware store in town?"

Lindsey pointed with her chin. "Across the street."

"And the grocery store . . ."

"Hardware and grocery store are the same place. They can post mail there, too; the big post office is in the next town over. Connie is using the space next to us to do some sewing—she used to be a seamstress, still has some fancy clients in Spokane and Walla Walla."

Deidre waited. Lindsey looked back at her.

"What?" she asked Deidre. "That's it."

"That's it? What about medical care?"

"Dr. Hensen is our GP and he practices out of his home. Hospital is an hour and a half away."

Deidre remembered that Lindsey had mentioned kids. "Didn't that stress you out when you were pregnant?"

Lindsey shook her head. "Not really. Besides, all my kids were home births."

Curious, but not wanting to press for details, Deidre simply said, "Oh."

"Pros and cons of living in a small town," Lindsey said, unfazed. "But everything else is within a couple of hours, so it's not like we're out in the middle of nowhere." She glanced at the clock as she wiped her hands on her apron. "Dinner tonight is broiled fish with green beans. I'll have some apple crumble for dessert."

"Homemade?"

"I wish. My grandma had a great recipe but it takes too much time, I only do it on special occasions. Mix comes from the food service as well. I serve it à la mode, though. Tastes pretty good."

Deidre fished in her jacket for change for her coffee and scone. "It sounds great but I'll probably eat in tonight. I'm kind of on a budget and I have some work to do."

"Suit yourself. Ice cream's vanilla. Also from the food service, in case you were wondering." She gave Deidre a friendly wink, then ambled back to the kitchen.

At the store, Deidre bought some food and, after much thought, a no-kill mousetrap. The clerk was explaining how the trap worked, so that Deidre could release the mice in the woods after she caught them in the box.

"You use a saltine cracker and place it right over the slot," he was saying. "When the mouse eats the cracker, it sets off the trigger and the trapdoor comes down. Then you get into your car and drive a few miles to release them."

"Can't I just put them outside?" Deidre dreaded the idea of touching the rodent and was hoping she could push the trap onto the porch with a broom.

"Sure, if you want them back in your house by dinnertime."

Deidre shuddered. "Have you got anything else?"

"This is my only live bait trap. They're not really too popular around here. A little too much work for most folks and they pretty much like those critters dead." Deidre could see boxes of the traps behind the clerk. "You can think about it if you want. These traps aren't going anywhere anytime soon."

There was no way Deidre was going to share the cabin with any mice. She bought a trap and a box of saltines, and tried not to grimace when the clerk advised her to check the trap regularly.

"Shouldn't take you too long to get your first one," he said. He made it sound like she would be fishing, bound to return home with a catch that would make the front page of the local paper.

Deidre finished her shopping and headed back to the cabin. The leaves of the trees had turned into a rich palette of reds, oranges, and browns, nestled among the waxy deep green of the pines. Fall in the city never looked this good. It was a gorgeous day, and even though it was almost fifteen degrees cooler than Seattle, Deidre opted to forgo the AC and had the windows down.

Deidre spent the rest of the day cleaning the cabin, reasoning that she wouldn't be able to concentrate on work or anything else until the place was in better shape. She set the trap out tentatively, hoping that the mice would see it, turn around, and leave, sparing her the problem of having to carry a box with a live mouse out into the woods.

IT WASN'T UNTIL Deidre started really cleaning the cabin—floors *and* walls, plus all of the nooks and crannies—that she realized she hadn't needed to clean the studio or her old apartment in almost three years.

When the show first aired, Deidre did everything, with Len and William's help, because she wanted the station to think that she would make their lives easier, that her show would actually be a blessing and wouldn't cost them a cent. Len would grumble but do the work, complaining that Deidre was a neat freak with some control issues.

Len. Deidre stopped for a moment to think about him, feeling incensed but sad as well. They had so many good times on and off the set, that the fact that he had betrayed her and sacrificed the show seemed almost ridiculous. And yet, here she was in a cabin in the woods, scrubbing somebody's floor and eating tuna from a can while he was comfortably back in Seattle, enjoying a raise and job security.

Think of something cheerful, she commanded herself, and a picture of Kevin instantly came into her mind. He was so easy to talk to, funny but intelligent. And it helped that he was good-looking, that there was definite chemistry . . . Deidre sighed.

They were prey to bad timing. Clearly it wasn't the right time for her to get involved with anyone. She hardly knew him, and she didn't see how there'd be an opportunity to get to know him better. And it was clear that he was involved with someone else. Still . . . her mind shifted to thoughts of their night together before she forced herself to snap out of it. *Think of something else.*

She started to think about *Live Simple*. God, she missed it. She missed the feeling of going out in front of a studio audience, of a program script that went off without a hitch, of the sincere and enthusiastic applause at the end. She loved coming up with new ideas—whenever she or one of her staff came up with something new and original, the intense creative sessions that followed which were always accompanied by great food, compliments of Deidre. William would sometimes join them. Deidre fondly remembered those late nights, with Diana Krall singing in the background and open bottles of wine on the buffet. Experimenting in the studio kitchen was always full of surprises, the night cleaning staff taking longer than normal to mop the set, hoping to be a part of the tastings. They always were, though sometimes wished they hadn't been. The habanero pepper recipes had been a disaster, and there wasn't enough water to go around. Deidre's eyes began to water just remembering that night, and she couldn't help smiling.

Deidre stood up, brushed off her jeans, and looked at the bathroom floor, gasping with pleasure. This was something else that she loved, the discovery of a beautiful hardwood floor underneath all that dirt. If she had time, she could wax the floors. There wasn't that much floor space to cover and she knew a great homemade paste wax recipe. In the meantime, a good buffing would do the job, and Deidre set to work.

Despite her efforts to push him out of her mind, her thoughts kept returning to Kevin. She hadn't had sex like that since she was in her twenties. She complimented herself on having handled herself well, under the circumstances. Then Deidre remembered the look on his face when she appeared in the doorway, fully dressed. God, who was she kidding? What was wrong with her?

"And I wonder why I'm still single," she sighed aloud.

She looked at the open boxes in front of her, having forgotten what she was looking for. "Anyway," she said to the empty room. "He's taken."

Looking around the cabin, however, made Deidre doubtful. It just didn't seem like it had ever had the company of a woman. Ever. Then again, maybe the girlfriend/wife/lover had never been here and it was some kind of private getaway, but even that didn't quite seem to fit. He didn't seem like the kind of person who would hide things.

So who was *sweetheart*? And how could she find out?

Deidre looked up as the washing machine began groaning as the cycle started to spin. The rickety dryer wasn't doing much better. A plan started to form in Deidre's mind and, with a sudden burst of energy, she resumed buffing the floor.

AT THE WISHBONE, Deidre's fingers were shaking somewhat as she checked the number and dialed. Nervous, she started to twist the telephone cord until Lindsey walked by and frowned.

Maybe she would get an answering machine. That might give her a clue. And if a woman answered, Deidre could always hang up.

"Hello?" Kevin's deep voice sounded friendly.

Panicked, Deidre hung up the phone and instantly regretted it. It was childish and immature. She punched the return coin button angrily. How could one man reduce her to a spineless excuse for a woman? She had launched her own talk show, for God's sake. She was forty, she was talented, she was smart, she was stylish. She was making it in the big, bad woods all by herself. She was Deidre McIntosh, woman extraordinaire, queen of the . . .

The pay phone began ringing and Deidre jumped back.

Lindsey called from the counter, "Get that, will you?"

"Uh . . ."

"I'm expecting a call from my sister. Thanks, Deidre."

Mortified, Deidre slowly answered the phone.

"Hello?" Kevin asked.

"Hi," she stammered, embarrassed. "It's Deidre, and I . . ."

"I know. I have caller ID and I recognize the area code for Jacob's Point." He sounded amused. "Are you at the Wishbone?"

God, how embarrassing. "Yes. I just thought I'd call to say thanks again for letting me stay here. It's, uh . . ." She searched for the right words. "Simple and quiet." At least that much was true.

He laughed. "Like I said, it's not the Ritz but it will do. What did you think of the kitchen?"

The kitchen? Deidre tried not to make a face. "It's . . . something else all right."

Kevin gave a chuckle. "I know it's probably not what you're used to, but I'm glad someone's making use of it. I'm not much of a cook but I like spending time in there when I go. It inspires me to whip something up, even if it isn't anything fancy."

Deidre thought skeptically of the cupboard full of pork and beans. But then she thought of the sunlight streaming through the kitchen window when she washed the dishes and had to agree. It *was* inspiring.

"Are you finding everything you need?"

Lindsey walked by and flicked her dish towel at the phone cord, which Deidre had twisted into a knot.

"Yes," Deidre said, lowering her voice as she quickly untangled the cord. "And, uh, I did call for a reason. I wanted to make sure if it's okay to use the washer and dryer—it seems like they've seen better days."

"Hold on." There was muffled talking in the background and Deidre strained to hear. "I'm sorry, could you say that again?" asked Kevin, coming back to the phone.

It was such a lame excuse but Deidre persevered anyway. "The washer and dryer. Is it okay that I use them?"

"Deidre, " Kevin's voice was low and suggestive. "Use anything you want." Deidre could hear the blood rushing to her ears.

Lindsey had sidled near to where Deidre was standing and was suspiciously wiping a table *very* clean.

"Actually, I was thinking about coming down for a visit this weekend, but . . ." There was more muffled talking in the background and when Kevin continued, his voice was low, almost a whisper. "Now's not a good time."

"Oh." As quickly as she had felt her spirits rise, they came crashing down again. "Well, it's your place so whenever you want to come is fine with me."

His response was simple but adamant. "Great. I intend to do just that."

Deidre forced herself not to read into it, but she felt her body temperature spike. Lindsey was continuing to wipe the same spot on the table and pretending not to listen.

"I'll call you later," he promised. "Bye." He hung up before Deidre could tell him that her cell phone wasn't working in Jacob's Point. She replaced the phone into its cradle and leaned heavily against the wall. Despite her nagging suspicion that he was hiding something, she was elated to have heard his voice, to have had even one minute of playful banter. And, against her better judgment, she could tell she was falling for him.

Lindsey gave Deidre a smile. "Everything all right?"

Deidre smiled back. "Everything's great."

"Can I get you anything?"

"Actually I have a lot of work to do . . ." She glanced around the empty diner and then back at Lindsey, who looked like she could use some company. "Maybe a cup of coffee," Deidre said. "I could use the caffeine boost before I head back."

Lindsey went back behind the counter as Deidre settled into a booth. Wanting something to read, she picked up the menu and studied it.

"You hungry?" Lindsey asked, walking over and placing a mug of coffee in front of Deidre.

"No, thanks. I like your logo, though." A simple image of a wishbone framing a lake, it captured the essence of the Wishbone perfectly.

Lindsey glanced at the menu with a smile. "Thanks. My sister designed it for me. She lives out in Pallayup. She's pretty artistic."

"I can see. It's nice. How did you come up with the name for the diner?"

"Well, it kind of has two meanings. I named it 'The Wishbone' because of Lake Wish, but it's nice because it's also about food, about finishing a good meal down to the wishbone. My kids think it's about people, because you can't pull a wishbone by yourself, you need another person. So that's kind of like the diner. A place for people to come and get together."

"That's great," Deidre said admiringly. One of her favorite things about *Live Simple* was the chance to hear the stories behind the people and companies she profiled. She definitely missed that.

Lindsey grinned. "Yeah. That and the fact that there's nothing else for twenty miles in either direction also helps." She walked away.

Deidre turned the menu over. There was a story about Jacob's Point, about how a tribe of the Coeur d'Alene Indians passed through as they were settling along the eastern border of Washington and into Oregon State. Lake Wish was a derivation from the name *Schitsu'umsh*, or Skitswish, literally meaning, "The ones that were found here." Still, it wasn't until Sir Jacob Bostitch, a traveling apothecary, stopped here in the early 1900s and began to build the small town, which later became known as Jacob's Point.

The population of Jacob's Point was under fifty, and one local legend—either informally decreed by Sir Jacob, who later served as the town's adjunct mayor, or through the folklore that developed over the years—went that there should never be more residents than the number of trees surrounding Lake Wish.

"Lindsey?" Deidre called, her eyes still on the story.

"Hmmm?"

"How many trees are around Lake Wish?"

Lindsey was busy writing something down and didn't look up. "Have you been yet?"

"No."

"Then I'm not telling. Legend says you have to walk around it and count the trees yourself."

"What, are you kidding?" Deidre stifled a laugh, not

wanting to seem rude, but it sounded ridiculous. "That would take forever!"

Lindsey shrugged. "More like an hour or two. Most people walk the lake several times."

Deidre doubted she could cover the perimeter in an hour, even if she ran. "Have you walked around the lake?"

Lindsey busied herself with straightening things around the cash register. "Yep."

"How many times?"

"I've lost track."

"So how many trees were there?"

Lindsey gave her an exasperated look. "Like I said, I'm not telling. Go see for yourself, it won't take you very long."

"How big is the lake?"

"Big enough that you'd better have some bottled water and a sandwich nearby. And wear good shoes; it can get slippery near the water. Lots of people fall in."

Deidre studied the sketch on the back of the menu. "Well, maybe I'll just buy a postcard of it. Seems easier."

Lindsey scoffed. "Easy? This isn't about easy. Go to the lake. In fact, don't come back in until you've been there."

"What?" Deidre was about to laugh until she saw the stern look on Lindsey's face. "Come on, it can't be that good."

"Good? This isn't about good." Lindsey shook her head, disgusted with Deidre's apparent lack of respect for the legend. She snatched the menu from Deidre and stuck it back behind the napkin holder. Then she looked at Deidre expectantly, her forehead puckered in a frown.

It was an obvious cue to leave; Lindsey's small town hospitality was over. Deidre slowly handed Lindsey a dollar. "So I have to see the lake before I can come in for a sixty-seven cent cup of coffee?"

"I'll be serving dollar pancakes tomorrow morning," Lindsey answered, pocketing the money. "They're the best in town. If you want them . . ."

"I know, I know." Deidre gathered her things and scooted out of the booth. "I'll see you later."

Lindsey didn't look up but gave her a dismissive wave as she began to clear the table. Deidre pulled her coat tight around her, preparing for the blast of cold autumn air, and left.

BY THE TIME Deidre returned to the cabin, she was not in the mood for a walk. She wasn't even entirely sure she knew where the lake was. Lindsey talked about it as if Deidre already knew, and it never occurred to Deidre to ask for directions. She hadn't passed any signs or seen a turn-off that might lead to the lake.

"Forget it," she said. She would go into the Wishbone tomorrow and tell Lindsey she couldn't find it. She was new to the area, she didn't have a map . . . it was a completely legitimate excuse.

Deidre poured some white wine into a small glass and went into the living room. She put her feet up on the ottoman and relaxed into the couch. As she brought the glass to her lips, she glanced straight ahead and saw one of the silver tone, black-and-white photographs of the lake.

"Forget it," she said aloud to the photograph. "Tomorrow. I'm exhausted from doing nothing. I need my rest."

She made another attempt to sip her wine but it was

as if the photograph were beckoning her. Deidre sat up, irritated.

"I'll go tomorrow, I promise. I have to work now, I have to get started . . ." Deidre caught herself. She was talking to a photograph of a lake, for God's sake. Deidre stood up and moved to another chair, her back to the photographs. She reached for her laptop and turned it on, waiting impatiently. When she was finally able to open a new document, she typed, "Ideas for a New Show," and waited.

Ten minutes later, Deidre's wine was untouched and the same five words stared back at her from her computer screen. She tapped the keyboard impatiently, sending random letters across the screen. Finally she heaved a big sigh, downed the wine, and closed the lid of her laptop. She took her time walking to her bedroom.

She emerged minutes later dressed in jeans and a dark green cashmere sweater. She was wearing thermal underwear as well—no sense in taking any chances. One of the many things the cabin needed was a full-length mirror, but Deidre was learning to do without.

"Satisfied?" she asked as she walked past the photographs. She pulled on her sneakers, grabbed her coat, and stepped outside in search of Lake Wish.

DEIDRE WALKED CAREFULLY along the soft mossy earth, gingerly dodging the long branches in her path. Even though it hadn't rained for a couple of days, the ground was damp and the air smelled cool and moist.

"This isn't too bad," Deidre admitted, mildly surprised. She continued to push her way through the trees.

It took only a few minutes for her to realize that she had no idea where she was going. Kevin had said that the lake was in easy walking distance, and Lindsey made it sound as if it were right around the corner. But as Deidre continued to walk deeper into the woods, she realized she might not only miss the lake altogether, but get seriously lost. There was no trail, no signs, not even a hint at where the lake might be. Even in Seattle, her sense of direction was questionable at best.

She looked behind her, and thought she could see where she had walked. In fact, that was the corner of the cabin nestled back in the trees, wasn't it? Deidre turned back, uncertain, but decided to push on.

The woods seemed to be getting thicker, and it was harder to see where she was going or where she had come from. "Five more minutes," she told herself. "Then I'm turning around."

When her five minutes were up, Deidre stopped and leaned against a fallen tree. She was slightly out of breath, having picked up her pace in the last few minutes. The sun was slanting through the trees, warming the top of Deidre's head even though her nose and ears were clipped by the cool autumn air. She didn't seem any closer to being able to find Lake Wish than when she had started.

"Forget it," she finally sighed. She straightened up and prepared to head back.

She turned just as a twinkle of light caught her eye.

Deidre craned her neck to look in the direction of the twinkle, but it was gone. Had she imagined it? Deidre looked around, squinting slightly, and saw it again. She walked toward it, picking up her pace and pushing branches out of her way. She suddenly stepped into a clearing and caught her breath.

A beautiful lake shimmered orange and pink as the sun prepared to set against the sky. The lake was still, with gentle ripples from an early evening breeze brushing across the lake's surface. It wasn't as huge or intimidating as the photographs, but it was just as majestic. A small flock of swans, their long necks held straight up, glided along the water, oblivious to her.

Deidre found a rock and sat down, nestling deeper into her coat as her eyes scanned Lake Wish. There wasn't another human being to be seen, and Deidre felt almost as if she were intruding.

Being here seemed so separate from the life she had just come from. Seattle, the show, even William seemed so far away. It was surreal, almost . . . the absence of noise, the cold, crisp air, the smell of the evergreens, the tranquility of the lake . . . what *was* she doing here, anyway? Even though it had only been a few days, she didn't seem any closer to figuring out what to do next. It seemed a little late in life to be searching for what to do with the rest of it.

Deidre sighed and shook her head. As she did, she noticed a lone, two-story house across the lake. Funny she didn't notice it right away. It was the only house on Lake Wish, and on closer inspection, quite large. It was beautiful, no, handsome would be a better description. The color palette had been chosen intentionally to blend in with the surroundings. The house was a lovely pale gray with gentle white trim that seamlessly nestled among the tall evergreens. A large deck overlooked the lake. Each of the bedrooms on the second floor seemed to have their own balcony. There was a small dock on the lake, with a rowboat pulled ashore. A tarp was pulled over it.

Deidre stared at it for a while, scanning the windows for any movement. There was none. Somehow she knew it was unoccupied and felt it was a terrible waste. Sure Jacob's Point was remote and rural, but with a house like that, and on Lake Wish, anyone would be lucky to be able to live there. In the past, the show would feature a real life *Live Simple* home, one that married simplicity with beauty. Even though this house wasn't in Seattle, it was exactly the kind of house Deidre would profile.

She snuggled deeper into her coat as the sun started to fall and a cool breeze blew across the lake. It was too late to start walking around the lake, but now that she had her bearings, Deidre planned to return. Soon.

The sun was about to dip beyond the horizon when Deidre began to walk back to the cabin. She somehow knew which way to go, and when the cabin came into view, she smiled calmly, not at all surprised. Rejuvenated from the walk but happy to be back, Deidre bent down to gather some broken branches on the ground to help start a fire.

DEIDRE WAS TUCKED safely between the flannel sheets and down comforter, fast asleep after her long walk. A strange *scritch, scritch* woke her and she listened, sleepily, hoping she had been dreaming. A moment later there was the sound of a heavy bump, as if a heavy box had fallen over.

It had to be past midnight. The moon, high in the night sky, illuminated her room. Peacefully sound asleep only seconds ago, she was now wide awake with her adrenaline racing and her heart pounding. She gripped the edge of her comforter, unable to move, her body frozen. Every possible worst-case scenario flashed through her mind.

She heard it again, a clumsy bumping that took one of her worst-case scenarios to the next level. Not only was there a prowler, but he was drunk. Another bump. That, or he was totally inept.

Her mind was racing. She had no phone, no cell service, and her only exit was the paned window by the bed. Breathless, Deidre reached for her robe at the foot of the bed, her eyes never leaving the closed door of her bedroom. She shivered as she edged the warm blankets off her body and gingerly got out of bed. She edged cautiously toward the window, her fingers searching for the window lock, as the bumping continued. Deidre turned the lock, praying that it wouldn't creak. It didn't. She raised the window slowly and readied herself to run for safety.

She was halfway out of the window when she realized that her laptop, with all of her notes and years of hard work, lay on the kitchen table. It was probably the only item of value in the cabin, the easiest thing to grab, something that would be worth more than a few dollars to any dopehead who might try to pawn it off. There was also her purse, which pretty much held the last of her remaining cash after she had paid off a mountain of credit card debt, and, of course, the keys to the Volvo. Those things she could live without, but she needed her computer. Despite everyone's advice that she back up her data on a regular basis, she hadn't done it since the show ended. Her old program notes, formats, e-mails and correspondence, the random bits of research she had done half-heartedly . . . well, she would need them when the time came to buckle down. If she lost that, she wouldn't have anything left.

She had to get her laptop.

Deidre's heart rate began to race again as she tiptoed around the edge of the cabin. She peered around the corner to the front door. The front door was closed.

Deidre picked up a log of firewood and looked through the living room window. The moonlight sent a beam of light into the living room but Deidre didn't see any movement. And, strangely enough, the only car outside of the cabin was hers.

She tried the front door—it was locked. Perplexed, Deidre tried again, rattling it slightly. The key was inside of the house—she only left it under the flowerpot when she was going out, a ritual that she was going to discontinue after tonight. There was no sign of forced entry. Deidre looked through the window one more time. Nothing. Then another faint bump, coming from somewhere inside of the living room.

Curiosity piqued, Deidre hurried back to her bedroom window, climbed back into the house, and opened her bedroom door.

The bumping was coming from the kitchen. Deidre gripped the log tightly, held her breath, and flipped on the light switch.

No one was there.

Another bump, and Deidre turned to see that the mousetrap she had set out two days ago had moved from the pantry about a foot. She watched as the trap bumped against the floor, and stifled a laugh.

She had caught a mouse. The moment she had been dreading actually came as welcome relief.

There was no way she'd be able to fall back asleep. Remembering the comments from the clerk at the hardware store, as well as having read the instructions that came with the trap, Deidre bundled up and prepared to take the mousetrap for a little drive.

Deidre grimaced as she used two garbage bags as gloves to take the trap outside and into her car, where she had an old box waiting. She drove five miles and then pulled over to the side of the road. She positioned herself safely away from the opening of the trap, then lifted the trapdoor and watched as a mouse suspiciously emerged, sniffed, and then ran toward the woods. She was surprised by its small size after hearing it knock and scratch around inside of the trap like a wild cat.

You're tiny, she thought, somewhat astonished, as it scurried away.

The moonlight was brilliant as Deidre drove back, triumphant and beaming. When she walked into the warm glow of the cabin, she set about making a cup of tea, and found herself drawn to the stack of *Live Simple* program binders and her laptop computer, sitting on the small antique writing table in the corner.

Deidre smiled at the familiar hum of her computer when she turned it on. The cursor blinked patiently as she poured her tea. Then, when she was ready, she began to type.

Chapter 6

Life is a series of collisions with the future.

—JOSÉ ORTEGA Y GASSET

IT WAS ALMOST noon by the time Deidre found her way to the Wishbone. She had been working since 4:00 A.M., after releasing the mouse and resetting the trap for any remaining friends or relatives. She was starving. She didn't feel like cooking and needed to get out.

The Wishbone was half-full with tourists and truck drivers mostly. A few locals were looking at the outsiders with disgust, the elderly Janet Everett being no exception. She glared at all of them, though Deidre noticed with a twinge of pleasure that she ignored Deidre altogether. Neutrality was good. It was a start.

Lindsey came by Deidre's table. "Know what you want?"

Deidre reached for the menu. "Any specials?"

"It's all special." Lindsey grinned, nodding back to the kitchen. "Got little Mary Martin—well, she's not so little anymore—waitressing at breakfast and lunch. Sidney Peters needed a second job to help with her mortgage so she's helping with dinner. Which means I had time to make my famous beef stew. Janet Everett's been complaining for the past month that I haven't been cooking good food lately." Lindsey rolled her eyes. "Rich folk are always eccentric. Anyway, it comes with potatoes and green salad, eight dollars and ninety-five cents plus tax."

Deidre sneaked a glance at the older woman who was bent over her newspaper, muttering to herself over the din of the diner. She was dressed in clothes that reminded Deidre of mothballs, prim collars, and sensible shoes. "Thanks, but I only have five dollars." Her stomach growled loudly but Deidre pretended not to notice.

"You can pay me later."

Deidre shook her head, her eyes still on Mrs. Everett. "I'm on a pretty tight budget. I wasn't planning on eating out so much while I was here."

Lindsey raised an eyebrow, not quite believing, and her eyes glanced outside to where Deidre's new Volvo was parked.

"It's a long story," Deidre said. She tucked the menu back behind the salt and pepper shakers. "So Mrs. Everett is rich? You're kidding."

Lindsey looked offended. "One thing about me: I don't kid." She lowered her voice and leaned into Deidre. "She and her husband used to own Finnegan's Furniture chain out of Seattle. A hundred and fifteen stores from here to the Mississippi."

"Used to?"

"They sold it ten years ago for God knows how many millions of dollars. May have been hundreds of millions, I don't know. But it was a lot of money, and then her husband passed shortly after. That's when she moved here—said her kids were driving her crazy."

Maybe they succeeded, Deidre thought, watching Mrs. Everett move her lips as she read the paper. "Did her husband inherit the business?"

"What? No, it was Janet's business, actually. Her father was a carpenter turned master woodworker—I heard she's quite good as well, though I would be a little nervous to be around Janet and anything sharp. When they first opened, everything in the store was made by Janet and her father."

"What about . . ."

Lindsey was tiring of the gossip and straightened up. "So do you want to try the stew? It's good, if I do say so myself."

"I'll just have a side salad and coffee." Deidre took out her purse and put the five-dollar bill on the table.

"I can do a half order of the stew for you, if you like," Lindsey offered, taking the bill and tucking it in her apron. "You might even have enough left over for half a cup of coffee."

Deidre smiled. "That sounds great, thanks." As Lindsey prepared to walk away, Deidre remembered. "Oh, and I found Lake Wish yesterday."

Lindsey turned, eyebrows raised. "Oh, really? And what did you think?"

Deidre answered simply. "It was gorgeous."

"Did you walk around?"

"No, I didn't have time."

Lindsey gave her a funny look. "Well, maybe next time," she finally said. She turned and hollered to Mary, "Half order of the stew for Deidre here!"

Mary jerked her head, startled, and began scribbling furiously into the notepad.

Deidre rubbed her eyes, suddenly tired. In the past eight hours she had typed almost nonstop, one of her "brain dumps" as she liked to call them, getting out every possible thought or idea for a new show that had ever crossed her mind. The cabin was a mess, with almost every binder open and papers strewn everywhere. It seemed like each idea led to another, or opened a whole new series of thoughts, and Deidre couldn't type fast enough. Still, none of them grabbed her enough to commit more than two or three pages before she abandoned it and moved to the next great idea. She had pages and pages to show for the past few hours, but nothing had clicked just yet. Still, it felt good to have her creative juices flowing again, and Deidre was anxious to get back to work.

Her eyes drifted to the pay phone. Kevin had said he would call her, but he never did. She was tempted to call him and even had a good reason: the water heater had been making funny clanging sounds for the past two days. But Deidre had her pride—if he didn't have the time to call her, she sure as heck wasn't going to call him again. If the water heater broke down, she'd just have to manage with cold showers.

How appropriate, Deidre thought ruefully. She was intentionally suppressing her memory of their first night together, not wanting to go crazy with desire. She needed to stay focused now more than ever.

Mary was awkwardly carrying out trays of food and Deidre felt like it was only a matter of time before the inevitable happened. Unable to watch and anxious to get her mind off of Kevin, Deidre fished a pen from her purse and began jotting some thoughts down on a napkin.

Master carpenter, woodworker, furniture empire. Deidre thought for a moment and then added, *Organic, ground up, start to finish.* A picture was forming in her mind. More words: *Opportunity, legacy.* And then: *Seattle in the making. History.*

"Whoops," Mary said. The stew tipped precariously as she placed it in front of Deidre. Deidre helped steady the bowl as Mary unloaded the rest of her tray. There was a generous side of potatoes, a huge salad, and coffee.

"This is a half order?" Deidre asked, astonished.

"That's what Lindsey says. Can I get you anything else?" Mary brushed a lock of hair away from her face and for a moment, the frazzled teenager disappeared and in its place was a composed young woman.

"No, thank you." Deidre gave her a warm smile but it was missed as Mary turned away. Deidre eagerly started eating her lunch as she glanced at her scribbles on the napkin, thinking.

DEIDRE SLEPT THE rest of the afternoon and into the evening, waking only to finish the leftovers from lunch. Lindsey had packed up Deidre's doggie bag, but Deidre caught her sneaking in several raisin scones just the same.

"Lindsey, you don't have to do that," Deidre protested, secretly touched.

"Do what? These are a couple of days old, they're like hockey pucks. You can use it as bait for that mousetrap of yours."

Deidre finished her salad and went back to bed, her brain totally spent. She was too tired to build a fire, and the cabin was chilly. She crawled underneath the covers. She didn't have the stamina to pull off all-nighters anymore, that much was obvious.

She slept through until mid-morning and woke up feeling well rested. *It's luxurious to get this much sleep,* she thought as she showered and dressed.

Revived, she sat at the kitchen table, waiting for her coffee to steep as she bit into a raisin scone. She spit it out almost immediately. Lindsey hadn't been kidding—it *had* turned into a hockey puck and was completely inedible. She tossed all of them in the trash, disappointed.

Deidre went back to the living room and looked through her notes, including the scribbles on the napkin. She felt the stirring of something good here, but what? She chewed on her lip nervously. Her bank account was dwindling and she was going to be out of money if she didn't come up with something soon. She could sell the Volvo and get a cheaper car, a truck maybe . . . that might buy her a couple more months. But those things took time. Even if she came up with a great idea, she'd need to shop it around, someone would need to say yes, and then they would need to shoot the pilots. It would be months before it would finally air. And if nobody said yes . . .

There is something good here, Deidre told herself firmly. *I know it.*

She was drawing a blank and it didn't help that she was still hungry. Deidre finally gave up and went back into the kitchen for something to eat. She had been counting on the scones to tide her over, and it just felt like the perfect thing to eat on a day like today. Nothing else appealed to her. In an act of desperation, Deidre fished a scone from the trash and took another bite, just in case it wasn't as bad as she thought. It was. She threw it back into the trash, disgusted.

If Deidre wanted a fresh scone, there was only one way she was going to get one. She began to gather ingredients. Flour, sugar, eggs. Walnuts—sure, why not? And maple syrup. Deidre could almost taste them. She'd bake enough to get her through the week.

Deidre began mixing the ingredients, her hands moving in autopilot as she continued to muse about her notes. There was something important in there, she knew it, but she couldn't see it.

She preheated the oven, then lined a cookie sheet with parchment paper. The parchment paper was too long and hung over the side of the cookie sheet. Taking a pair of kitchen shears, Deidre carefully trimmed it. She spoon-dropped the batter onto the cookie sheet in generous heaps. She slid the sheet into the oven, set the timer for twenty-five minutes, then sat down to wait, fiddling with the scrap of parchment paper.

She folded it in half. She loved the sound of creased paper—it was crisp, precise. She had a memory of a previous *Live Simple* program when they had invited a Japanese origami master. He filled the studios with cranes, a thousand in total, a sign of good luck to come. He showed them how to make envelopes with hidden pockets, lucky hearts, blooming flowers. Deidre didn't think she remembered much—each shape consisted of a myriad of folds—but suddenly a simple envelope had formed in her hands. The flap was probably bigger than it should be and the envelope itself looked more like a cone, but Deidre liked it. She reached for the roll of parchment paper, her mind humming with ideas.

• • •

IT WAS ALMOST four o'clock by the time Deidre was finished. She was full, her appetite and her anxiety abated. The kitchen was clean and the oven had cooled, and now it was time to get back to work. Deidre poured another cup of coffee and went into the living room to sit among her papers. Still nothing. When she looked up, she found herself staring directly at the television, an old Zenith that looked anything but reliable. She hadn't turned it on since she had been in Jacob's Point. It was plugged into the wall. No remote control from what she could see. Deidre checked her watch, debated, then finally gave in.

She turned on the television and stepped back nervously, almost expecting it to crackle or explode. Instead, it hummed with static electricity and then a picture started forming. Deidre turned the dial until she found Channel Two.

"Research," Deidre told herself, settling into the couch.

Deidre hadn't seen the show in its entirety and immediately grimaced when the opening music for Marla's show began. It was Vegas pretentious, very *Lifestyles of the Rich and Famous*, and a voice-over that sounded suspiciously like a Robin Leach wannabe announced: "Coming to you from her estate in Fairfield Hills, she's *mah*velous, she's *Mah*la, and she's alllllll yours!" *At Home with Marla Banks* was officially on.

"God save us," Deidre murmured as the camera panned over Marla's estate, went through the gate, over the gardens and finally into the house where it then "searched" the many lavish rooms until it ended up in Marla's bedroom. Marla was propped up in bed, martini in one hand and her miniature chow chow in the other. She was fully made up, hair perfect, lipstick glistening, a flash of diamonds from her ears and fingers. She blew a kiss at the camera.

"Hello, everyone, and welcome to my home. Fred Astaire, say hi." She lifted the dog's paw and made it give a little wave to the camera, then tossed the dog onto the ground and took a sip of her martini. The camera panned briefly to Fred Astaire, who was walking circles on his velvety dog pillow before plopping down unceremoniously and closing his eyes.

"I'm Marla Banks, and today we have an *amazing* show in store for you! We're calling it *'Fabulous at Fifty,'* because me and a few of my friends"—here she winked—"are going to prove to all of you that life *starts* at fifty."

Deidre froze. It sounded exactly like their "Fabulous at Forty" segment.

The camera cut to a montage of different fifty-something celebrities, local and Hollywood, all of whom, Deidre had to admit despite herself, looked pretty fabulous. Marla's photos were randomly interspersed throughout—Marla with the former First Lady, Marla with Diane Keaton, Marla with Donald Trump, Marla with Yo Yo Ma.

Then, as a group shot flashed on screen, Deidre sat up, startled.

It was a picture of Marla, on a yacht, lounging with four other people. Everyone wore sunglasses and was toasting the camera. Arnold Schwarzenegger and his wife, Maria Shriver, sat in the middle. Next to Arnold was Marla, and on the other side of Marla was a man who looked suspiciously familiar. A confident smile, strong shoulders and a washboard stomach. Deidre bristled when she saw Marla's arm draped over his shoulders as she kissed up at the camera.

Kevin?

Deidre leaned forward for a closer look but it was too late, the picture had already changed to Marla and Kenny Loggins, dancing at a concert.

No, it was impossible. Deidre shook the thought from her head. Marla and Kevin? There was no way he was fifty, first of all. And Marla didn't seem at all like his type, not that Deidre would know . . .

The camera was back on Marla, who was now standing in front of the law offices of Black & Black, one of Seattle's leading law firms.

"First things first," Marla was saying. Her microphone had a white fluffy pom-pom at the end of it, with little sparklies throughout. "Ladies—gents, too, but if this pertains to you, you have bigger problems—fifty-something is usually when your mate decides the twenty-something cheerleader, receptionist, or Starbucks barista is suddenly his soul mate and you are out, or on your way out. Trust me, you know if I'm talking to you and don't kid yourself. So we're meeting with Richard Black, attorney to the rich and famous wives who have little interest in being left with a one-hundred-thousand-dollar payoff and a five-year-old Mercedes." Marla leaned into the camera confidentially. "Richard is, incidentally, also fifty-something and single." She gave a wink.

Richard gave the audience a run-down of what to ask for, along with a formula for calculating what a discarded wife should go for.

"It doesn't matter," Marla was saying, "if your husband's net worth is two-point-five million or twenty-five thousand dollars. Use this formula, and you can't go wrong. Right, Richard?"

"Right, Marla."

She then put up her own list of "Warning Signs for Straying Husbands," which flashed across the screen.

"If you notice any of these symptoms, *act now*. Richard has also made a checklist of what you can do now to protect yourself. You can find it on our Web site, *www.athome withmarla.com*. You'll also find an application if you're interested in dating this wonderful man. Don't forget to upload a picture of yourself and, ladies, make it nice."

Richard reddened but didn't say anything.

"Richard, you're a doll." Marla turned back to the camera. "He's kept me rich, and he can do the same for you. Let's move on!"

The next shot was at Grace's Bakery, where Grace shared a fifty-year-old family recipe for Morning Glory turnovers. Deidre knew Grace Farish, a shy, quiet woman with unfortunately poor camera presence. She avoided looking at the camera, talking into her mixing bowl or staring at Marla's microphone, which seemed to be shedding fluff into the Morning Glory mixture.

Grace brought out a prepared turnover and offered it to Marla, who took a small bite. Bits of frosting clung to her perfect lipstick and Marla dabbed it off while she chewed. "It's scrumptious, darling." Grace mumbled what sounded like a thank-you.

As she left the bakery, Marla rolled her eyes and whispered to the camera, "Maybe go just a *tad* lighter on the frosting, Gracey. I think we'd better take a commercial break so I can fix my lipstick and get over to our next stop, fifty-year-old Sorvino's, where Seattle's best can take a break to indulge in *adult* pleasures that can bring a bit of color to your cheeks and keep you 'Fabulous at Fifty.'"

An *ooh-la-la* sounded before they broke for commercial.

Deidre turned off the television and stared at the black screen. Either she was losing her touch or Marla was crazy. How could you possibly air something like that on TV? Didn't anybody care about quality programming anymore?

Live Simple had followed new trends in home, food, garden, personal wellness, and crafts, but they were all safe, all generic, very conservative, and very, well, boring. Still, Deidre wasn't about to get dolled up in some Victoria's Secret camisole to sell more shows.

Deidre spent the rest of the afternoon and late evening watching TV, getting acquainted with all the new shows that were on the air. Reality shows were a big hit, and in some ways *Live Simple* was just that, but somehow it wasn't enough. It was missing something, some secret ingredient, and Deidre needed to find out what it was if she wanted to survive.

AT THE WISHBONE, Lindsey stared at the large Tupperware in front of her. Stacked inside were thirty maple walnut scones, each individually wrapped in parchment pockets and tied with kitchen twine and a small sprig of pine needles. "Um . . . I take it you had some time on your hands?"

Deidre shrugged. "It's a long story."

"You've got a lot of long stories." Lindsey surveyed the Tupperware uncertainly. "I'm not sure I can sell all of them," she said truthfully. "I sell nine, maybe ten a day. And that includes one to you."

Deidre shrugged. "It doesn't matter. You can give them away for all I care."

"How much do I pay you?"

"Don't worry about it, Lindsey. I wasn't thinking about selling them, I was just a little bored."

Lindsey was all business. "I paid Hannah half of what I sell 'em for. The food service ones sell for three dollars each as you know." Lindsey hit the register and handed Deidre forty-five dollars.

Deidre took the money, surprised. Forty-five dollars. It was better than nothing, and it more than paid for the flour and sugar. After receiving fat paychecks for the past few years, it was funny to feel so elated for forty-five dollars. Despite herself, Deidre couldn't help beaming.

"Thanks," she said. The bills were crisp in her hand. She folded them carefully and tucked them into her wallet, and tried not to look like she cared much.

Lindsey opened the Tupperware and took a scone out. "They're so pretty," she said. She began arranging them on a cake plate. "If nothing else, I get to look at them and pretend I'm Martha Stewart."

Deidre took her coffee and went to her favorite booth to sit down. Just then, the door opened and a bell jingled behind them. A small group of tourists walked in, shedding coats and brushing snow off their shoulders.

Snow. Delighted, Deidre looked outside and saw fat, white flakes drifting down lazily. The first snowfall of the year, and she was going to spend it in Jacob's Point. She took another sip of coffee and snuggled into the cushion of her chair. It felt cozy being inside the Wishbone with the smell of fresh coffee and hot food.

"Sit anywhere," Lindsey said, waving them toward the empty tables.

A man nodded. "Four coffees, please," he called to her, barely giving eye contact. He glanced at the cake plate. "Are those scones?"

"Maple walnut," Lindsey said.

"We'll take four," he said. "Can you heat them up?"

Lindsey raised an eyebrow.

"Never mind," he said hastily.

Lindsey brought their coffee and scones to them and Deidre continued to sip her coffee, her back to them, ears perked.

"Oh, look," a woman said, admiring the parchment envelope. "Is this the cutest packaging ever?"

Someone took a bite and said, "They're amazing. Miss, are these homemade?"

Lindsey said, "You bet. Made fresh in Jacob's Point."

"We should take some to your mother's," the woman said definitively. She turned to Lindsey. "Do you have eight more?"

"I sure do."

"We'll take them."

Lindsey returned to the counter, eyebrow raised, and gave Deidre a wink. Deidre blushed and modestly turned her attention back to her coffee.

Lindsey walked by, the scones delivered, and casually began to punch numbers into the register. "You know, I'm no genius but I do my own color if you want to touch up . . ." She loosely gestured to the top of her head.

"Oh, I wouldn't be any good," Deidre said, not comprehending. "I've only had mine done in a salon, and I would probably mess yours up."

"*Not mine*," Lindsey said, nodding toward Deidre's head.

Deidre looked in the mirror above the register. Her blond locks were growing out, but she hadn't thought much of it. In the few weeks since she had been at Jacob's Point, she couldn't be bothered to blow dry or style her hair; usually she twisted it up or she wore a hat. Looking at herself now, with Lindsey's sympathetic eyes on her, Deidre realized she was the epitome of a bad hair day.

"Oh," Deidre said, tentatively touching her hair.

"You can drive into Pullman," Lindsey said. "There's a Supercuts that does a pretty good job for thirty-five dollars. Unless you want someone fancier. Or just ask Bobby over at the hardware store to pick up some color for you when he goes into town next. We can do it this weekend; it won't take but a second."

Hair color from the hardware store? A home coloring job? Supercuts? Deidre sighed. Where was Stella when she needed her?

"Thanks, but uh . . ." Deidre looked at herself again in the mirror. It didn't really look so bad, did it?

Lindsey read her mind. "Honey, you need to do something," she said grimly. She checked her own hair in the mirror with a look of satisfaction.

Carl Hensen, the local doctor, walked in. "Coffee to go, Lindsey," he said to her. He looked suspiciously at the cake dish. "What're those?"

"Maple walnut scones."

"Good?"

"Of course," Lindsey said indignantly.

"I'll take one. Make it two. Give one to Agnes." He glanced at Deidre. "You still here?"

"Carl!" Lindsey gave him a look.

"I'm still here," Deidre said, suddenly self-conscious. She wished she had a hat to cover her hair.

"What? I'm just asking. Thought she was supposed to be heading back to Seattle."

Deidre, who had never spoken to Dr. Hensen before, look pointedly at Lindsey, clearly the town gossip, who reddened and avoided her look. Lindsey handed Dr. Hensen his coffee and scones.

"Didn't mean anything by it," he said apologetically, taking the bag.

"That's okay," Deidre said.

"She's doing just fine," Lindsey said, giving Deidre a wink. "She has yet to walk the lake, so I suspect she'll be with us a while."

"That so?" He looked into the bag of scones. "Mmmm, these look good. Hannah's?"

Lindsey shook her head, surreptitiously gesturing toward Deidre, who was turned away and didn't notice.

"Ah," he said, nodding back conspiratorially. He smiled. "You all have a nice day." He headed for the door.

"Thanks," Lindsey said.

Deidre gave a small wave, then leaned toward Lindsey, arms crossed. "Just small-town talk, huh?"

"I'm ordering some hair color for you this afternoon," Lindsey said, ignoring her.

"Okay, okay," Deidre said. She was surprised to find herself a little relieved—worrying about hair color was not top on her list.

Lindsey flicked a dish towel after Dr. Hensen. "Don't worry about him. People are just curious. They like to know what's going on, who's coming, who's going, why they're here. That sort of thing. They find it interesting."

Dr. Hensen was holding the door open for Mrs. Everett, who came in and settled herself in a booth before taking out a newspaper.

"Morning, Janet," Lindsey said, pouring her a cup of coffee.

Mrs. Everett grunted in response, snapping her newspaper as she took a quick inventory of the diner. Her eyes came to rest on the remaining scones. "One of those," she said briskly, before burying herself in her newspaper. Lindsey brought her a scone and she stared at it before taking a bite. "Fancy," was all she said.

"Looks like you may have a fan," Lindsey said, impressed. She glanced around the diner. "Everyone's fine for now—I need to get off of my feet for a sec." She sat down across from Deidre and heaved a sigh.

Deidre remembered what Lindsey had told her already about Mrs. Everett. "So tell me, Lindsey. Why did Mrs. Everett move to Jacob's Point?"

"Ah," Lindsey said, smiling. She crooked a finger at Deidre and leaned in confidentially. "Well, let's just say that people come here for different reasons. Everyone has a history, it's part of being human, right?"

"Right," said Deidre eagerly.

"Well, some people come here to get away, some people come here to raise families. Some people come here to understand things . . ."

"Like what?"

Lindsey studied her. "Do you know why this is called Jacob's Point, even though the only body of water in the vicinity is landlocked?" She was talking about Lake Wish.

The thought had never occurred to Deidre, but now that she thought about it, it was odd. A *point* usually referred to an outcropping of land into the ocean. But they were hundreds of miles away from the Pacific. "No, why?"

"The area was named for Sir Jacob Bostitch, who came here in the late 1800s in search of a cure-all, an all-purpose medicinal root that had been talked about for centuries. Lewis and Clark supposedly documented this during their expedition, but nobody had actually ever seen it. So Sir Jacob arrived and found this root with the help of local Indians. But it turns out that he couldn't take it, once he learned about what it took to grow and cultivate this root. It grows wild, but only once every fifty years. If it's allowed to grow without disruption, it supposedly has the ability to rejuvenate the soil, the earth, for miles within its reach."

"So you're not supposed to cut it?"

"It *can* be cut, but only in a certain way, so it can continue to propagate, and with a special knife. As Sir Jacob learned more, he came to understand all the steps it took just to get this root to grow, and how if he just took it—just cut it and stuck it in his bag—how it would impact an entire ecosystem. He got the point. That understanding led him to settle here, in part to harvest the root and in part to protect it, and that's how this place became known as Jacob's Point." Lindsey straightened the salt and pepper shakers, giving Deidre a satisfied smile.

She stared at Lindsey in disbelief. "You're kidding, right?"

Lindsey was indignant. "No. Why would I be kidding?"

"*That's* how the town got its name?"

"That's what they say."

"Well, it's interesting and all, but what does that have to do with Janet Everett?"

A frown puckered on Lindsey's forehead. "Well, you wanted to know why Janet was here."

"And?"

Lindsey looked exasperated. "Do you listen to anything I tell you? I have customers." She got up and stomped off.

Deidre sighed. Obviously she didn't get it, whatever it was. She snuck another glance at Mrs. Everett, engrossed in her newspaper. Deidre could see her lips moving as she read each sentence.

God, she thought admiringly. *How totally fascinating it must be to have lived her life.*

And then, just like that, Deidre got it.

"Lindsey, I gotta go," Deidre said, grabbing her things.

"Where's the fire?"

"Long story," Deidre said. "I'll tell you later, I promise!"

Lindsey gave her a look like she didn't quite believe her, and waved a dismissive good-bye. "My house, Saturday, four o'clock. We'll get your hair right yet. And I'll be looking forward to all those long stories."

Deidre sped back to her cabin, her mind racing. "Of course, of course!" she muttered to herself, a picture already forming in her mind. She couldn't stop smiling.

"It's brilliant."

IT WAS ALMOST two weeks later before Deidre picked up the phone to call William.

"You don't call, you don't write . . ." he complained.

"Yes, I love you, too. Anyway, take it as a good sign, William. Trust me. I'm sure you have better things to do than hear me whine about my life or complain about Marla's."

"True. So how are things coming along?" William asked.

"Great. Just working on the new show." She dropped the last sentence in casually.

"Are you serious?"

"I am!" She couldn't contain her enthusiasm and started gushing. "And it's good, William. *Really* good. Do you know I hardly watched other shows in my time slot? I had no idea what other people were producing, or more appropriately, *why* they were producing certain shows. I had completely lost touch with the audience."

"*Live Simple* was a good show, Deidre," William said a little defensively.

"I know, but it was dated. I needed to keep up with how the world was changing. And I didn't get *why* they liked the show. Anyway, I just . . . *got* it."

"Well, what is it?"

"Um, I'm not saying just yet," Deidre said protectively, after a moment's pause.

"Why not?" She could hear the hurt in his voice.

It still felt a little raw and too early to share with anyone, even William. "I want to have the first six shows ready," she said, anxious to change the subject. "Anyway, I've got a lot of other things going on. I've been baking up a storm, and last week I started helping Lindsey in the kitchen. I'm only doing it to help fill in, but it's actually kind of fun. I never thought I'd be a short order cook working for eight dollars and fifty cents an hour. Plus tips!" She laughed, then realized she was laughing alone.

"That's great," he said unconvincingly. "When did you say you were coming back?"

Deidre thought about that. "I don't know," she said uncertainly. "I promised Lindsey I would help her with Thanksgiving at the Wishbone." Thanksgiving was less than three weeks away.

"Thanksgiving?! You're not going to be back for Thanksgiving?" William's voice took on a slightly hysterical baritone. "We *always* celebrate Thanksgiving together. I've been telling Alain about how great your Thanksgivings are!"

"Well, I thought you and Alain would have it all worked out, it being your first Thanksgiving together."

"Ha! Alain doesn't really like to cook, it turns out. The man is Mr. Prepackaged Junk Food. *He eats KFC*, Deidre." William's voice was ominous.

Deidre grimaced but had to force herself not to laugh. Poor William. He always seemed to attract men who loved artery-clogging food. "I thought you said he liked to cook."

"Yeah, TV dinners and takeout. He just said that to get me into bed."

"Oooh, tricky." Deidre couldn't help smiling. "I guess it worked."

"Well, no kidding, but now I have to cook Thanksgiving by myself," William fretted. "It'll completely stress me out and you've always been the one who organizes everything."

"William, you'll do great. You have the number of the Wishbone so you can call me anytime for moral support." She saw Lindsey frowning at a piece of paper, undoubtedly the shopping list for their Thanksgiving dinner. "I love you, Will. I'll talk to you soon."

"Sure, I'll bet," he said sulkily.

"Bye, sweetie."

Lindsey looked up from her notepad as Deidre hung up the phone. "I think I have the final count. Ready?"

"Ready."

"Fifteen turkeys, one hundred thirty new potatoes, three large cans of cranberry sauce, or should we make that four?"

"Four to be safe." Deidre smiled as Lindsey continued down the checklist for Thanksgiving dinner. It was almost as if the entire town were going to be eating at the Wishbone on Thanksgiving day.

When Lindsey was finished, she smiled at Deidre, shaking her head. "I can't believe it. I am actually looking forward to this! Thanksgiving dinner for sixty-three people." She pointed her notepad at Deidre. "This is your fault, you know."

"*My* fault?"

"I'm having too much fun. For the first time in a long time, the thought of a full house is exciting instead of intimidating." Lindsey shook her head again. "Connie thinks we should do a cookbook for the Wishbone. I told her that was crazy."

"No, Lindsey, that's a great idea!" Deidre was immediately inspired. "You can put in all of your favorite recipes, or maybe have everyone vote on their favorites. Instead of chicken fried steak you can say . . . is it Jerry who likes the chicken fried steak?"

Lindsey nodded, eyes wide.

"Okay, so, 'Jerry's Pick: Chicken Fried Steak.' Or arrange it by days or a month, you know, thirty recipes, one for each day. Include information about Jacob's Point, make it something the tourists will go for, too."

Lindsey's eyes were bright, and then a look passed over her face. "I can't do all that," she said darkly, and started to quickly wipe down the counters. "Thanksgiving dinner is one thing. But a cookbook? I don't know the first thing about doing something like that."

Deidre reached over and put her hand on top of Lindsey's. "I'll help. We'll work on it when we feel like it, and when it gets done, great. But we don't have to rush it and make it another job—nobody needs that, least of all you. *Keep it simple.* It's supposed to be fun. What do you say?"

"I don't know. It sounds like a good idea, but . . ." Lindsey looked skeptical but Deidre could tell she was encouraged.

"If you don't want to do it, you don't have to. I'm just saying that if you do, we can find a way."

Lindsey was silent for a while. Then she said, "You'll help?"

Deidre gave Lindsey's hand a squeeze. "Of course I'll help. It'll give me practice for my book. It can be part of the legacy of the Wishbone."

A broad smile stretched across Lindsey's face. "I never thought of it like that. It would be nice for my kids to have something they could keep, with all my recipes."

"And the rest of Jacob's Point, as well as a few tourists. Make it like a little fund-raiser. You can sell them in between the muffins and the chocolate chip cookies."

Lindsey laughed. "Okay. You're on." She gave Deidre an admiring glance. "You really have a lot of good ideas."

Deidre sighed. "Yeah. That's the problem." The last thing she needed was another good idea. "You know, I think we should have some more vegetables at Thanksgiving, some kind of leafy green, like chard. We can toss it with sweet onions and cranberries." Deidre held out her hand for the Thanksgiving list, relieved to be able to put her attention on something else for the moment.

IT WAS LATE afternoon by the time Deidre returned to the cabin. She surveyed the living room critically. Her papers were strewn everywhere, but it helped to see everything at once. The room was separated into different work stations: research, program ideas, the first six pilots, the calendar, production timetables . . . Deidre even thought about potential advertisers that would fit hand-in-glove with the shows. It was almost too easy.

What wasn't so easy was figuring out production costs and the financials. For the first time in years Deidre forced herself to look at the financial documents for *Live Simple*. She cringed when she saw exactly what Buford had been talking about—gross negligence in production areas that didn't make sense. Lavish after-show expenses that Len had assured her were part of the sponsor package or purchased at nominal cost. And a huge supplies budget, of which Deidre knew only a fraction had actually been used since many donations were made to the show in exchange for mention in the post-show credits, yet actual expenses *exceeded* the budget. How could that be? Worse yet, in the bottom left hand corner of each page were Deidre's initials, signed with flourish and now, Deidre realized, ignorance.

Deidre stared at the documents until her eyes blurred, flipping between years and supporting statements. It was a bit like cramming for a final—some of it she got and the rest made her eyes glaze over. There was no way she would be able to prepare credible financials for the new show if she couldn't understand the ones from her old one.

Deidre realized she needed help, and there was only one person she could think of who could do it. She packed up her papers and headed for the Wishbone.

The Wishbone was full of regulars and tourists, famished and happy to be out of the cold. Lindsey gave her a nod and Sidney, the nighttime waitress, gave Deidre an enthusiastic wave. Deidre managed a small wave back as she fumbled through her papers by the pay phone.

She punched in Caroline's number as a sheaf of papers fell onto the floor.

"Hello?" It was less of a greeting and more of a demand, but Deidre warmed at the sound of her cousin's voice.

Still, and as expected, Caroline was not impressed by Deidre's plea for help, despite Deidre's apologies.

"You were *rude* to me at the Uptown Bistro," Caroline said, her voice clipped. "It was *embarrassing*! I'm a professional and I had clients in that restaurant!"

"I was in the middle of a crisis, Caroline. I'm sorry I overreacted and took it out on you. Now will you please help me?"

"You questioned my advice! *My* advice! Which, if you hadn't dissolved your portfolio, would be paying off big-time right now. Except for that tech stock, but like I said, no one saw that coming. My point is, if you had held out over the long-term, which was my original advice to you, you would be doing pretty well right now."

Deidre relented. "You know, you're right. I *didn't* trust your advice." She could sense Caroline bristling on the other end, so she added, "I think I just need to have a better understanding of how it all works so I can really appreciate how good you are."

There was a small murmur of consent on the other end of the receiver. Deidre knew she had Caroline's attention now.

"Finances aren't my area of expertise, they're yours," Deidre continued. "But I need a basic understanding of how it all fits together so that when you tell me what you want to do, I actually know what you're talking about."

"My other clients trust me without question," Caroline declared. Caroline wasn't going to let her off easy, but Deidre could tell her cousin's resistance was wavering.

She admitted, "Well, I'm not as sophisticated as your other clients. I was in a bit of a hole but I'm coming out of it now, and I could really use your help. So if you can help me, I would really appreciate it, but if not, then I'll let you go. I know you're busy as well."

Caroline seemed to be thinking about this but Deidre had a feeling her cousin wanted her to sweat it out. After what seemed like forever, Caroline finally said, "Fine. Fax them over and call me later. I'll walk through them with you. But only once, I'm really busy with the end of the year coming up."

"Thank you, Caroline," Deidre said, sincerely grateful and relieved. She looked across the street at the hardware store, which had a fax machine and basic photocopier. The CLOSED sign was already turned on the door. "Uh . . ."

"Half an hour, tops," Caroline was saying. "Call me between seven and seven-thirty. After that I'll be busy. I'm really swamped right now, and as it is I'm going to be late meeting some friends for drinks."

In the past, Deidre would have battled with Caroline over whose schedule was more important, but those days were over. Deidre was learning the subtle art of relationships.

She glanced frantically around the diner. "No problem," she said cheerily. She spotted Bob Carson, owner of the hardware store, patting his stomach and laughing with Dr. Hensen. "I'll call you in a little bit."

She crossed the Wishbone to Bob Carson's table. Dr. Hensen looked up and gave Deidre a friendly smile.

"Well, if it isn't our resident baker," he said. He nodded to the remaining bite of apple pie on his plate. "This yours?"

"Yes," she said hurriedly.

He took a final bite. "It was real good."

Bob Carson looked at him enviously. "Doc here got the last piece. And he knows how much I like a flaky crust."

"Can't get a crust like that these days," Dr. Hensen agreed, leisurely wiping the corners of his mouth. "I sure did enjoy it."

"Thank you," Deidre said. "Um, Mr. Carson . . ."

"Hold on there," he said, putting a hand up. "My father is Mr. Carson. Just call me Bobby."

Deidre managed a polite smile as she glanced nervously at the clock. "Okay . . . Bobby. I know your store is closed but I have an important fax I need to send to Seattle tonight and . . ."

Bobby laughed. "Sorry, little lady, but my fax isn't working."

Deidre couldn't hide the crestfallen look on her face. Caroline probably wouldn't be sympathetic if Deidre called back, claiming she couldn't find a fax machine.

"I ran out of ink this morning. But I'm going into Pullman tomorrow for more supplies—Lindsey said you need some Clairol hair color, too . . . I don't remember what kind but I have it on the list . . . so it should be up and running by the time I get back."

A thought occurred to Deidre. "But I just need to send something, not receive something. I won't need any ink, and I have a calling card to pay for the call."

Bobby covered his mouth with one hand and started to clean his teeth with a toothpick. "That might work, I suppose. But I'm closed for the day. If I make an exception, the whole town will be wanting me to open up at all hours of the night."

Dr. Hensen said, "Come on, Bobby. Help her out."

"I'm not even finished with my meal yet," he said, even though Deidre noticed his ice cream dish was licked clean. "I don't like to be rushed. Interferes with the digestion. *You* told me I should slow down, not eat so fast." He called to Lindsey, "More coffee, Lindsey!"

Dr. Hensen gave Deidre a scheming look. "Deidre, you planning on making any more of that pie?"

"No, I was going to do a . . ." She caught his look and said, "Actually I *was* thinking about doing another apple pie. Makes my kitchen smell wonderful."

"I'd be happy to buy that from you directly," Dr. Hensen said, reaching for his wallet. "Margaret would sure enjoy it."

"Hey, now," Bobby said, indignant. "You already got your pie! What about me?"

"I could bake one for you as well," Deidre said sweetly.

"I'll say! I . . ." Bobby gave her a look, then glanced over at Dr. Hensen who was grinning. "You two are having me on." He tossed the toothpick onto his plate. "Okay, little lady. You bake me that pie and drop it off in the morning."

"I'll drop it off first thing."

Bobby sighed and reached for his coat. "Tell Lindsey I'll be back for my coffee."

"I'll do that." Dr. Hensen gave them a friendly wave as Bobby strode toward the exit with Deidre following behind him.

AT SEVEN O'CLOCK, Deidre called Caroline.

"I only have half an hour," Caroline reminded Deidre, but Deidre noticed her voice was much softer than before.

"That's fine, I appreciate whatever time you can give me," Deidre said honestly. She looked at the stack of papers in front of her and tried not to feel overwhelmed. She'd just have to start at the beginning.

When thirty minutes was up, Deidre said, "Caroline, it's seven-thirty. You probably need to go." There was still a lot to go through, but Deidre wanted to stay on Caroline's good side.

"Oh," Caroline said nonchalantly. "Well, I can talk for a bit longer. Now when I look at the balance sheet going back to 2003 . . ."

It took almost an hour and a half to go through five years' worth of the balance sheets and income statements, but Caroline seemed to be enjoying the role of teacher with Deidre as student. Deidre's mind was swimming with numbers and financial jargon, but was thrilled that everything was starting to make sense.

"So my debits and credit need to tie, and then this number carries forward into next year?" Deidre was saying.

"That becomes your opening balance. I think you're getting it," Caroline said approvingly. "God, it's almost eight-thirty. I think we got through everything."

"Thank you so much, Caroline," Deidre said. The Wishbone was closing up and both Bobby and Dr. Hensen had left, but not before reminding Deidre of the apple pies due tomorrow.

"Extra cinnamon," Dr. Hensen had whispered. Deidre gave him the thumbs-up and turned her attention back to Caroline.

"Glad I could help," Caroline said, sounding a bit smug.

"I couldn't have done it without you," Deidre said truthfully. "You're a great teacher, Caroline."

"Well . . . good luck, Deidre. And if you want me to look over the numbers for your new show, just fax them to the office and Teddy'll get them to me. Remember, if worse comes to worse, just assume payroll is twenty-five percent and expenses are another forty percent."

"Got it."

"Where did you say you were again?" For someone who wanted to get off the phone, Caroline didn't seem to be able to stop talking.

"Jacob's Point. Not far from the Idaho border."

"Never heard of it."

"I know. Most people haven't."

"And you're calling me from a pay phone?" Caroline's voice sounded incredulous, but impressed.

"I canceled my cell service a week after I got out here. No reception plus I didn't need the extra expense."

"Well, call me when you get back into town, we'll do lunch again. My treat. I'll talk to you later."

"Talk to you later."

Deidre hung up the phone. Caroline offering to pay for lunch—this was a first. There were a lot of firsts, Deidre was beginning to realize. And it was about time.

CHAPTER 7

When life kicks you, let it kick you forward.

—E. STANLEY JONES

IT WAS DAYS before Thanksgiving, and Deidre was hard at work, bent over her papers in a booth at the Wishbone. Lindsey walked by several times, surveying Deidre's papers critically, but saying nothing. Finally Deidre looked up, exasperated, and Lindsey immediately put her hand on her hip, defensive. Deidre was sitting in a booth for six and using up every inch of available table space. "You trying to make a case for a town library?" Lindsey asked. Her voice was guarded.

"I hadn't thought of it, no, but now that you mention it, that's not a bad idea." Deidre looked back at her papers. All six pilots were ready, as well as a proposal and preliminary budget. She hadn't slept much, but she didn't care. She was finally done, and the feeling was tremendous.

"Is this that secret new show you're working on?"

"It was. I mean, it is. I mean, it's finished. I just have to clean it up a bit, get it printed professionally and bound, but it's finished. Somebody will bite and if they don't . . ." Deidre looked at her work proudly as she stretched and then shrugged. Somebody would love it, she knew it. She could picture herself sitting in an office while Buford praised her, saying, "This is genius. Pure genius! I want you back, Deidre. It was a mistake to let you go. In fact, I'm firing Len if that's what it'll take to bring you back on board. Name your price, we'll give you whatever you want. Anything!"

Lindsey was talking. "I have a name for it."

"What?" Deidre was still dreaming and didn't look up.

"I have a name for the cookbook we talked about. We could call it *Wishfull Eats: Recipes from the Wishbone*. Use two *L*'s, you know, so it's like their stomachs are full. Sidney thought we should have something like, *Time-Honored Recipes from the Wishbone* but I've only had the place for fifteen years. That doesn't quite seem long enough, does it?"

Deidre circled a typo. "Sure."

"Sure what? Use the first title or the second?"

"Uh, the *Wishfull Eats* one."

Lindsey added, "Also, I checked around and almost everyone said they'd get a copy. Glen even volunteered to shuck it at his next Lions' Club meeting in Pullman."

"Great." Deidre's eyes were still on her papers. Where did she put the comps? She began to shuffle through the stacks.

"Sidney said she could help type—she does seventy words a minute. She used to be a secretary before she got married. I told her I'd check with you first, just in case you had some other ideas about what to do."

Deidre found what she was looking for. "No, that sounds good."

Lindsey shifted her weight uncomfortably. "Hey, did you bring anything in today? I sold out of those almond poppy seed muffins you brought in on Sunday."

"Oh, in the car. I was short on a lot of ingredients so the best I could do was a few orange-anise bread rings. Use the leftover for bread pudding . . . you can figure it out." Deidre slid her car keys across the table to Lindsey without looking up. "Here. I may have locked it."

Lindsey stared at her, then turned on her heel and went outside. Deidre flipped through a set of pages, lost in thought.

When Lindsey returned, her arms full, she tossed the keys onto Deidre's table without a word and retreated behind the counter.

Deidre looked up, jolted from her reverie. She was imagining dinner parties with William and Alain. She saw herself looking at new apartments, maybe getting one that overlooked the water, maybe even buying one. William had always wanted a view of Lake Washington or Elliott Bay, but it had never appealed to Deidre. Until now.

Living in the cabin showed her that she could get by on less and do just fine. She still hadn't walked around the lake, but ventured out from the cabin every couple of days to look at it, as if to make sure it was still there. The sight of it reassured her—it was calm, placid, unmovable. It was beautiful.

And Kevin. Even though she hadn't heard from him since the embarrassing telephone conversation last month, Deidre still had a nagging hope that she would see him again soon. It would probably have to be back in the city.

She relished the idea of bumping into him again at the Uptown Bistro, except this time she would pick up *his* tab and surprise him. Her reasons for returning to Seattle were growing stronger by the minute.

Lindsey was angrily slicing one of the bread rings and arranging them on a serving dish. Deidre felt guilty and knew she had missed something important.

"Lindsey?" she asked. She had seen Lindsey mad before, but never at her.

Lindsey was moving slices of the bread ring around the plate, frustrated. "How am I supposed to sell this? They're more bread than dessert. And the slices are too small—if I cut them any wider, they look funny."

"I don't know. Maybe sell two slices at a time? I thought a bread ring would be fun; I hadn't made one in ages. I guess I felt like twisting something."

"Yeah, me, too." Lindsey snapped the lid of the Tupperware shut.

"What's that supposed to mean?"

"It means that you've been in here almost every day, working on your show, which I know is important, but Thanksgiving dinner is only a few days away. It was *your* idea to do this big town dinner, but I need to get the stuffing prepared, the potatoes ready, the greens washed and chopped, and the food service didn't include the order of walnuts . . ."

"Well, I can help you with that now, I . . ."

Lindsey slammed the cover on the cake plate and made Deidre jump. "You got me and everybody else here all fired up about the cookbook and now you won't even talk to me about it! I told you I'm not good at this, but you said you would help, that it would be easy, but you've already moved on to some other bright idea . . ."

"That's not true, I . . ."

"The girls and I have been writing down the recipes and we have thirty-some already, but we don't know what to do next." Lindsey held up a binder and Deidre could see pages of handwritten recipes inside. "Everybody's pitched in, everyone but . . ."

Deidre finally interrupted. "Me. I know. I will, Lindsey, but first things first."

"You mean, *your* things first."

"Well, Lindsey, that's why I'm here," Deidre said, frustrated. "This"—she gestured to the papers in front of her—"is going to help me get my life back on track. I can't live out here forever; this is just a temporary arrangement. It's not like I came here to take in the scenery."

The minute she said the words, Deidre knew she had made a mistake. Lindsey's face had turned a bright purple.

Deidre stammered, "That didn't come out right. What I meant to say was . . ."

Lindsey's nostrils flared. "Don't bother explaining."

Deidre put her head in her hands. "I'm on a roll, Lindsey. I am so close, so close! I just need some more time to finish this and then I can give you my undivided attention . . ."

"Forget it," Lindsey said curtly. "We always knew you were going to go back to Seattle. I shouldn't have let you talk me into all of this." She shook her head, annoyed.

"Lindsey, I'm not going back for a few more weeks. We have plenty of time to get all of this done."

"Oh, really?"

"Yes, really," Deidre said. "I just need to get this out of the way and then I can work on the cookbook with you. I'll make it a priority, okay? We'll focus our energy on Thanksgiving dinner and then as soon as that's done, we'll dive into the cookbook."

"Well . . ." Lindsey was cooling down but still looked doubtful.

Deidre glanced at the calendar on the wall. "How about right after Thanksgiving, on the twenty-eighth? That's a Saturday, so we'll have a creative meeting at the diner in the evening. What do you think?"

Lindsey turned to look at the calendar as well. "Are you sure? Should I pencil it in?"

Deidre gave her a broad smile, her heart pounding. It was aggressive to try and get it all done, but it was possible if she stayed on top of it. "Absolutely." She gathered her things and got ready to go.

"I'll tell the girls. They'll be pretty excited." Lindsey looked back at the kitchen and let out a big exhale. "I should get back there," she said, giving Deidre a sheepish grin. "Sorry for flying off the handle like that. Stress."

"Don't worry, you're speaking to the Queen of Stress."

Lindsey was about to walk off when she spotted something tacked onto the message board. "Oh, you got a phone call this morning."

"Oh, from William? He's probably stressed out about Thanksgiving, too."

"Nope," said Lindsey, handing the piece of paper to Deidre before retiring to the kitchen. She gave Deidre a mischievous wink before disappearing behind the swinging doors.

Kevin. 8:55 A.M. *Please call ASAP 206-548-4443 or cell 206-949-2308.*

Deidre drew in her breath as she stared at the scrap of paper.

Lindsey came out of the kitchen holding two lunch plates. "Why are you still standing here? Aren't you going to call him?"

Deidre stared at her in surprise. "Do you know Kevin?"

Lindsey scoffed. "*Kevin Johnson*? Of course I know Kevin." She served one of the tables.

"I know Kevin," Mary chimed in from the counter. She giggled nervously.

Lindsey shot her an annoyed look and motioned for Mary to go back to the kitchen. "Table four has a ham and cheese and two bowls of soup." She looked back at Deidre. "Everyone here knows Kevin. Who do you think owns the note to the Wishbone?"

Deidre felt her mouth go dry.

"He wanted you to call him when you get a chance. He's coming down with Claire."

"Claire?" Deidre croaked.

Lindsey rolled her eyes ominously. "I know." Clearly Lindsey was not a fan of Claire.

"When?" Deidre struggled to keep her voice even.

"Thanksgiving Day. I told him about our big dinner, said they should join us." Lindsey picked up some dollar bills from a table and swept the change into her hand, then disappeared in the back. "You'd better call him or he'll think I didn't give you the message," she called from the kitchen.

Deidre walked slowly to the pay phone. Claire? So it was true, he was involved with someone. So much for her dreams of moonlit walks with Kevin around Lake Wish. She punched in the number on the piece of paper, her hands shaking.

"Hello?" At the sound of his voice, Deidre felt her knees go weak. She swallowed.

"It's Deidre. I . . . got your message."

"Deidre." He sounded almost relieved, almost happy to her from her. Or was that just wishful thinking on her part? "You're impossible to get a hold of, you know that? For a second there I thought you had disappeared off the face of the earth."

"No, just here to Jacob's Point." Deidre gave an unnatural laugh.

"Are you enjoying yourself?"

"Yes," Deidre said, wanting to dispense with the small talk. *Who was Claire? And why was he bringing her to Jacob's Point when he knew I was here?*

"I know. It's impossible not to." His voice shifted and he started to sound more business-like, as if someone had just walked into the room. "Anyway, Claire wants to get out of the city so we thought we'd come down for Thanksgiving and stay a couple of days. Lindsey said you were having a big dinner at the Wishbone, so we thought we'd join you. What do you think?"

"Yeah, come on down. It'll be fun." What else was she supposed to say?

"Great. I didn't think you'd mind sharing the place, but I figure you've had it all to yourself for a while and it was time for an invasion of your privacy."

He said the last few words seductively, and Deidre felt her heart pounding in her chest. Maybe he just had a flirtatious nature and she was misreading everything. She decided to keep it friendly and polite. "What? Don't be silly. It's your place, in fact, I should clear out so you and Claire can have enough room." If necessary, she could stay with Lindsey for a couple of days.

"Now *you're* being silly. We should all be able to manage just fine. There's no sense in you moving out just because we're coming down. We have to leave by the weekend anyway."

Deidre tried not to think about how awkward it was going to be to share such a small place with the man she had slept with and his girlfriend. God, and she had a lot of cleaning up to do. "Oh, I hope you don't mind but I rearranged some of the furniture to make the space work better. I'm happy to put it all back before you get here . . ."

Kevin chuckled. "Why am I not surprised? I'm sure it's fine, Deidre. You have excellent taste."

Deidre felt herself melt and wanted to slip through a crack in the floor. He always knew how to say just the right thing. Why did he have to be so damn perfect? "I think you'll like it," she said. His compliment made her courageous and she decided to ask him, point-blank, about Marla and Claire. "Kevin, what's your relationship with Marla Banks?"

There was a long pause on the other end. "Marla?" he asked. His voice sounded hollow.

"Yes, Marla," Deidre said, though with less confidence. Given his response, she wasn't so sure she wanted to know anymore. "You know Marla. The socialite? The woman who launched a rival show and decided to publicly aim poisoned darts at me?"

For the first time since she'd known him, Kevin was at

a loss for words. He finally managed, "Deidre, I thought you knew . . ."

Deidre felt a sense of dread. She cut him off. "You know what, Kevin? Never mind. I'm sorry I asked." She didn't want to know. She didn't want to go there.

"Wait, Deidre . . ."

"No, it's none of my business." She gave a semi-hysterical laugh on the phone and willed herself not to cry. What was she thinking, letting herself fall for a man who was clearly involved with one, maybe two, other women? "Look, it's your place and I'm really grateful for having had a place to stay these past couple of months. Really. So I'll see you on Thanksgiving, okay?" She said a quick good-bye and hung up before he could say anything.

Her eyes blurred with tears as she headed toward the door. Lindsey, her head down as she studied a list, apprehended her before she had a chance to get away.

"Okay," Lindsey said. "Here's the final count for Thanksgiving dinner. We should probably make enough extra for people who come in at the last minute or anybody who burns their turkey. Do you want to see?"

Deidre quickly wiped her eyes with the back of her hand and took the list from Lindsey. "It looks good. I just need to run back to the cabin and drop this stuff off. I'll be back later tonight to help with the menus."

"Okay. I'll have Sidney stay a little later so she can hear what we're planning. Bobby says he can do a Costco run if we need walnuts." She noticed Deidre's red eyes. "Are you all right?"

"What? Oh, just . . . dust. Allergies." Deidre fanned her eyes. "Pay phone's a bit dusty."

Lindsey looked at the pay phone doubtfully. "Dusty?"

Deidre buttoned her coat. "Look, Lindsey, if I need to crash at your place for Thanksgiving, would that be all right?"

Lindsey looked puzzled. "Well, sure, but why?"

"Long story." Deidre looked forlornly into the street. The snow had turned slushy and brown.

"So should I tell Bobby to get the walnuts?"

"Tell him to get the walnuts," Deidre said. "Halve the order, we'll improvise. Did we get the extra brown sugar?"

"Twenty-five pounds of it."

"Fine. I'll be back in a little bit." Deidre pushed the door open and stepped out into the bitter cold.

THE NEXT COUPLE of days were a blur with Deidre running between the cabin and the Wishbone, trying to get everything ready. Her days were spent prepping and cooking food for the big Thanksgiving dinner, as well as coordinating all of the decorations and table settings. Her nights were spent finishing her proposal and trying not to obsess about Kevin.

On Thanksgiving morning, Deidre staggered into the Wishbone shortly after dawn, exhausted. It had been another sleepless night after cleaning the cabin and packing the Volvo with her things. She had packed slowly, almost reluctantly. When the car was finally loaded and ready to go, Deidre had a hard time driving away, her eyes looking back at the cabin even as she made her way to the main road.

"All good things must come to an end," she muttered. It was becoming her new motto, but Deidre didn't really believe that. Maybe that's why she didn't see the writing on the wall for *Live Simple.* She naturally assumed that if things were going well, they would continue to do so, or even get better. Call her an eternal optimist or simply naive, but that philosophy of thinking had always worked for her in the past. Worked, that is, until now.

Lindsey came up behind her with a cup of coffee. "Here, the caffeine will help," she said.

Deidre accepted the cup gratefully. "How did you know I had a headache?"

"You've been rubbing your temples all morning and you look like you've got about two hours of sleep."

"Well, it's nice to know I look as good as I feel. I didn't even have time to put any makeup on." Deidre glanced critically at herself in the mirror.

"I don't think any of us are going to win any beauty pageants today," Lindsey said, brushing some flour off her arm. "But the girls almost have everything ready in the back. Hannah's burned the walnuts twice, though."

Deidre felt a surge of adrenaline. Or panic. They had less than five hours before the Wishbone would be filled with hungry diners. She gasped as she thrust the coffee cup at Lindsey. "We need those walnuts!"

She hurried to the kitchen with Lindsey on her heels. Smoke was rising from a large skillet and Hannah wrinkled her nose in defeat.

"I managed to save a couple," she said apologetically, nodding to a small plate of unburned caramelized walnuts. "I keep forgetting this is a nonstick pan. It seems to get hot faster."

"Here, may I?" Deidre asked, taking the skillet from Hannah and dumping the black sticky remains into the trashcan. "This butter has a high melting point so you've got to take it off once it starts to bubble, then mix in the brown sugar, quickly." She looked at the remaining walnuts sitting at the bottom of a ten-pound bag. "Is this all that's left?"

"Sorry." Hannah looked apologetic.

"No, that's okay, it's not easy to get right." Deidre racked her brains. Bobby had only picked up half of what they originally had planned for and there was barely a quarter of the walnuts left. "We'll just use what's left for dessert," she decided aloud. "It'll bring out the flavors of the ice cream and pies. We can toast some almonds and use that for the salad. There's plenty of food, we'll be fine." She smiled at everyone who looked worried. "Sidney, grab a cookie sheet and line it with parchment—no, that's wax paper, it'll melt; yes, that's the one—and chop up these almonds."

"How?"

"Just put them in the food processor and set it on chop."

"Sorry, I'm still using it for the cranberry salsa," Lindsey said. "I still need a few more minutes."

"We don't have a few more minutes . . . Okay, Sidney, just pour them into a Ziploc and find a hammer. Don't pulverize it, just break it up a bit. Spread them out on the sheet and sprinkle some of this on top." She quickly scanned Lindsey's shelves until she found what she was looking for. She tossed Sidney the jar of crushed anise. "Go lightly," she warned. "It'll give the salad that kick we're looking for."

Lindsey smiled broadly. "See," she told everyone. "I told you she was the expert."

A small shriek emitted from the corner of the kitchen. Mary had forgotten to stuff one of the turkeys.

"That's fine," Deidre said, glancing at the clock. She wanted to change and freshen up before Kevin and Claire arrived. "Just pull it out forty-five minutes earlier. Since there's nothing inside it'll be cooking faster and we don't want it to dry out."

"I can take it out and stuff it now, if you want." Mary's hand was on the oven handle.

"No!" Deidre crossed the kitchen quickly and made sure the oven doors stayed closed. "The temperature of the stuffing will slow down the cooking and we don't want to lose any of the heat in the ovens—it'll slow the rest of the turkeys as well. We have extra stuffing, right?"

"Plenty of it," Lindsey said. "I'm already thinking about what to do with the leftovers."

"Stuff the turkey after you take it out. If it's too dry, we'll save it for casserole. Or better yet, tomorrow's lunch special: turkey enchiladas."

"Mmmm," Sidney said. "I think I like leftovers better."

"What? No way," Mary argued.

"Okay, okay," Deidre said hastily. She mentally went through the checklist. Everything seemed to be in order. "I'm going to run to the ladies room and get changed. I'll be right back."

"What should we do until then?" Mary asked.

"What kind of question is that?" Lindsey asked, exasperated. "We have a laundry list of things to do! You can go finish setting the tables, for starters."

"I still have to cut up the crepe paper for the tablecloths," Hannah said, looking panicked. It had been Deidre's idea to create a faux runner for the tables.

"And I need to finish folding the napkins," Sidney said.

"You're all doing a wonderful job," Deidre reassured

them, worried that Lindsey and the girls were heading for a meltdown. "We'll do what we can, and what doesn't get done . . ." She shrugged. "Don't worry. There's going to be a lot of happy people out there."

Everyone beamed back at her and Deidre knew she had done her good deed for the day. With renewed energy, everyone set back to work.

Deidre took her purse and garment bag from the hat rack and headed toward the bathroom. She had chosen a simple outfit, a Michael Kors charcoal and cordovan cashmere turtleneck with a matching wool skirt, and black calf Coach loafers. The perfect hostess outfit.

She was easing on the skirt when she remembered that she forgot to tell Lindsey about the potatoes—the buttermilk needed to be added last. Lindsey was probably preparing them now and if she didn't hurry, it would be too late. Dressed in her U of W sweatshirt with her Michael Kors skirt, Deidre quickly padded out in her athletic socks after taking a quick look around to make sure the coast was clear. She was about to go back to the kitchen when she heard something drop, followed by swearing. Deidre opted to leave a note instead.

She quickly jotted down instructions and then went to stick it on the kitchen door where they wouldn't miss it. As she taped it on the door, she heard a whistle behind her.

"Hey, good-looking," a familiar voice said.

It was Kevin, looking handsome as ever, dressed in jeans and a black knit turtleneck. He was shaking snow off his duffle coat. God, he looked good. Deidre felt her mouth go dry.

He seemed to be watching her, too, keeping his distance

for a moment, a smile tugging on his lips. "I knew you'd turn around," he said, and she could tell he was trying not to laugh. He stepped up to give her a kiss on the cheek. Oh, and he smelled great, too.

Deidre tried not to swoon. "I'm the only one here," she pointed out, but she couldn't help smiling back, embarrassed.

"True." He gave her a long look. "Wow, it's good to see you, Deidre. You look great. Changed your style a bit, but still great."

God. Deidre glanced down at herself and began smoothing her sweatshirt and tucking her hair behind her ear, not that it would have made a difference. "I was in the middle of changing," she said. "I haven't had a chance to put on any makeup . . ."

"You look great, Deidre," Kevin said firmly, interrupting her. He took her hands in his.

His touch made her shiver but she reluctantly pulled away. "Thanks, you, too. Um, tan?"

"Hawaii. I had a meeting there last month." He was still looking at her. She had forgotten about those deep-set brown eyes. "You're still blond, I see?"

"Yeah, for now." Deidre reminded herself to say a special prayer of thanksgiving for Lindsey, who had colored Deidre's hair in less than an hour and still managed to get dinner on the table while helping her children with their math problems. "You know, I'm going to change. I'll be right back."

"I'll be waiting." His words were tinged with expectation.

In the bathroom, Deidre splashed her face with cold

water. "Pull yourself together, McIntosh," she said sternly. She quickly changed and emerged, resolved not to weaken again.

His hand reached out to touch her cheek but Deidre ducked, not so subtly, out of reach. Kevin looked surprised but nodded his head in understanding. "We should probably talk . . ."

Deidre didn't let him finish. "So, is Claire with you?"

He nodded to the street. "In the car. It was a long drive and I promised her we'd stop for something to eat, but I didn't want to be late. So she's hungry *and* in a bad mood. Look, there's something you need to know . . ." He looked around the empty diner.

Deidre held up a hand. "Kevin, I already know what I need to know."

"Really?" He didn't seem convinced.

She put on a brave smile even though her heart was breaking. "Really."

"Well, great." He looked relieved and gave her a quick kiss before she could protest. "Listen, can you take a quick break and go with us to the house? I thought we could work out all of the living arrangements and just relax for a bit."

"Actually," Deidre said hesitantly. "I'm going to be staying with Lindsey. I thought you and Claire should have the place to yourselves."

"That's not necessary. I'm sure we can all make do."

"Well, I should probably stay and help Lindsey and everyone in case anything goes . . ."

Lindsey emerged from the kitchen holding a deep pan of dinner rolls. "We're fine. Go. Hi, Kevin."

"Hi, Lindsey."

Lindsey left the pan on the counter and retreated back into the kitchen, taking Deidre's note off the door. "Perfect timing."

Kevin turned back to look at Deidre expectantly.

"Well, I guess I can go back to the house with you," Deidre said. "But I'm still going to stay with Lindsey."

Kevin's eyes searched Deidre's face. "Something tells me I'm not going to win this one." He pulled a small red box out of his jacket and handed it to her. "Not that I'm trying to bribe you, but . . . here."

Deidre stared at the box in surprise. "Kevin, you didn't need to get me anything."

"I know I didn't need to," he said impatiently. "Go ahead, open it up."

Deidre sighed and reluctantly opened the box. A pair of elegant rainbow drop earrings were inside, with perfect conch pearls dangling at the ends. "Oh," she said softly, taken aback. "They're exquisite."

Kevin smiled. "I was in New York for a meeting the other day. I saw them and thought they'd look good on you. Try them on."

"Are you sure?"

"Of course I'm sure."

She tried to put him off. "Maybe later."

"God help me, you are stubborn." Kevin carefully removed one from the box and put it up to Deidre's ear—she didn't have any earrings on yet. "May I?"

Deidre nodded weakly and he put an earring on one ear, then the other. When he was finished he brushed a lock of hair away from her face, his fingers gently caressing her cheek. "You know, the oysters that created these pearls had to be coaxed to maturity with the greatest of care."

"Really?" she said faintly. She couldn't resist smiling.

He continued to stroke her cheek. "Beautiful as ever. And there's that million-dollar smile . . ."

It felt so good to be touched by him again, and Deidre sighed as she leaned into his hand. There was a quickening of his breath, a smoldering look in his eyes. Deidre took a step closer, her lips brushing his chin.

"Kevin!" a voice behind them made them both jump. "What's taking so long? I want to get to the house!"

Kevin sighed and stepped aside to make the introductions. "Claire, this is Deidre."

Startled, Deidre opened her eyes and saw an eight-year-old girl with straight brown hair and glasses glaring at her.

"Deidre, this is my goddaughter, Claire."

CLAIRE MARCHED OUT of the Wishbone with a bewildered Deidre and sighing Kevin in tow. "Her mother's a bit of a jet-setter and doesn't really have time for her. Claire's father is remarried and on his second family." He slowed down his pace, keeping his voice low. "Claire goes to boarding school in California but I try to see her whenever I can. She loves coming down here. After she recovers from the drive, that is."

"It's definitely a drive," Deidre agreed. It was slowly sinking in. He was single. And available. Her fingers fluttered up to her ears. *And he likes me.*

He glanced up ahead at Claire, who was climbing into the front seat of Kevin's black Lincoln Navigator. "Hey, sweetheart, can you jump in the back and let Deidre sit up front?"

"I can follow you in my car," Deidre said, noting the displeased look on Claire's face.

"Don't be ridiculous. Come on, Claire. Scoot."

Claire gave Deidre an insolent look before sliding out of the front seat and moving to the back.

"Hey," Kevin gave Claire a warning look, then turned to Deidre apologetically. "She thought it would just be the two of us celebrating Thanksgiving. I didn't get to tell her about you until the drive down."

"You know I can hear you." Claire's voice was muffled from the backseat.

"Sorry." He started the engine.

"I'm starving," Claire announced.

Kevin turned around to look at Claire. "Can you wait ten minutes? Deidre probably has some food back home."

"No. I'm hungry now, and you had promised me we would eat before we got to Jacob's Point!"

"That's true," Kevin admitted. He looked at Deidre and mouthed the words *low blood sugar* and then turned off the ignition. "I'll run into the Wishbone and grab something to go," he said. "Are you two okay waiting here, or do you want to come in?"

"I'll wait here," both Deidre and Claire said simultaneously. Before either of them could change their mind, Kevin was already walking swiftly toward the Wishbone.

Deidre and Claire sat there for an uncomfortable few seconds, maybe thirty in all, before Claire informed her, "He's too busy to have a girlfriend. Just so you know."

"Well, thanks for the update." Deidre willed Kevin to get back as soon as possible. She flipped down the visor to take a quick look at herself in the mirror and was stunned to see how radiant she looked. And the earrings were perfect. Deidre smiled at herself in the mirror when Claire shifted behind her and suddenly her glaring face came into view. Startled, Deidre closed the mirror and flipped the visor back up.

Kevin was walking back, smiling at them both. Deidre and Claire both gave a small wave and then grimaced at each other.

"You girls getting along?" he asked playfully, a hint of concern in his voice. He handed Claire a small waxed bag from the Wishbone. "This looked good. Lindsey said she was saving one for her husband, but said you could have the other one." He started the car and pulled into the street.

Claire bit into a peach turnover and Deidre watched her in silent triumph.

"Good?" she asked innocently.

Claire ignored her until she saw Kevin's stern look in the rearview mirror. "It's all right," she said to him, but Deidre could tell she liked it by the way she was chewing.

"Let me have a bit," Kevin said. Claire broke off a small piece and handed it to him.

Kevin offered it to Deidre, who shook her head. He ate it and smiled. "Lindsey outdid herself," he said. "Pass more forward, Claire."

"No," Claire said, her mouth full. "Can we go back and get another?"

"Claire, we're almost at the house. We'll just unload our things and head back to the Wishbone."

When Claire was on the last bite, Deidre casually dropped the bomb. "You know, I made those."

Kevin turned to look at her admiringly just as Claire spit her piece out, making an elaborate show of wiping her mouth and tongue. Kevin gave her a disgusted look. "Claire, really! Where are your manners?"

"I want her far away from me," Claire said. "I don't want to be anywhere near her."

Deidre thought of the tiny cabin and was filled with dread. At this rate somebody would be sleeping in the car, and Deidre was pretty sure it would be her.

"Stop it." Kevin's voice had a ring of authority and finality. "There's plenty of space, just pick your room when we get there, Claire."

Claire crossed her arms and pouted out the window.

Kevin rubbed his eyes. "Thank God we're almost there," he said grimly.

Deidre watched as they sped past the turnoff for the cabin. "Oh, you just missed the turnoff," Deidre said, pointing behind them.

Kevin laughed. "I think I know where my house is, thank you." His voice was slightly cocky, not leaving room for much discussion. Instead, Deidre rolled her eyes. He would find out soon enough.

Kevin drove up a few hundred feet and started to slow down. He turned off the road and was shifting into four-wheel drive.

Deidre tried to stifle a smile as Kevin maneuvered through the trees, branches brushing against the car. He was going to get stuck if he didn't back out soon.

But then the road began to widen and suddenly they were in a clearing, driving along the lake, right toward the two-story house Deidre gazed at every time she took her walk out to Lake Wish.

Deidre bolted upright, almost banging her head on the ceiling. "Where are we?"

"At the house. Where did you think we were going?" Kevin cut the engine and looked at her, genuinely perplexed and a little concerned. "Is everything okay?"

The driveway was paved. *Paved!* The house loomed up in front of them, stately and handsome as Deidre remembered every last detail in architectural delight. Expansive window shutters and French flower boxes. A winding pathway marked with large, flat stones that led around the house. There was a separate three-car garage, something Deidre couldn't see from across the lake, with what looked like a guest house above it. Kevin touched a remote and one of the garage doors opened, revealing a brightly lit and clean—*clean!*—garage. The front door of the house was painted a warm brick red ("*Very good feng shui,*" Deidre could hear William murmuring in approval).

Deidre stammered, "*This* is your house?"

"Of course." Kevin's eyes grew narrow, eyebrows raised.

Claire slammed the door as she exited, running toward the boat ramp. Deidre knew she was heading for the small rowboat.

Kevin opened his door and called after her, "Wait for me, Claire. Do not get in that boat yet. I mean it!" He turned back to Deidre, whose face was pale as she pressed her forehead against the glass. "She's usually not like this . . ."

A headline flashed in her mind: Live Simple *Host in Jail for Breaking and Entering.* She had been in the wrong house for almost three months.

"Deidre, are you okay? You're starting to worry me a bit here."

"I . . . you know, it's a funny thing." What was the

likelihood she would get arrested? She would be the talk of Jacob's Point.

"What? What is?" Kevin looked genuinely concerned.

Deidre opened the door and swung her legs out, desperate for more air. The smell of evergreens was sharper, more intense.

She tried to laugh. "I, well . . . it seems I've been staying somewhere else all of this time," she finally managed.

"Where?"

Deidre made a general gesture across the lake and then squinted. "Over there." She pointed wildly in the general direction. "Small . . . cabin . . . big . . . elk . . . horns . . ."

Kevin looked across the lake and a look of recognition replaced the confusion on his face. "Oh my God," he finally said. "You've been staying in Uncle Harry's cabin?"

"I don't know who Harry is, but it's a cabin, yes."

"About the size of a shoebox, no telephone, an old TV? A total pigsty?"

The look on Deidre's face was answer enough. Kevin burst out laughing. "Oh my God," he said. "I don't believe it! You've been staying in Uncle Harry's cabin!"

Deidre watched him laugh, unsure whether or not to join him. "Who's Uncle Harry?"

"My uncle, my father's brother. You know him, he owns the building you used to live in. Remember? I was visiting him the day I bumped into you."

Deidre stared at him, not comprehending. *"What?"* The sharpness in her voice surprised her. Kevin looked at her, suddenly uneasy.

Deidre slid out of the car and marched over to Kevin, who backed up, thinking it best if he kept some distance between them. "Henry Johnson is your uncle? He *owns* the building? I thought he was just the superintendent!"

"Well, he's that, too," Kevin admitted. "He doesn't like people to know he owns it. He's just a little hands-on with his investment, that's all."

"*He's* Pacific First Management Company?" Deidre remembered writing the checks, month after month. "LLC?"

"Um, yes." Kevin looked down the ramp for Claire, then back at Deidre. "Is everything okay, Deidre?"

"No, actually, it's not! Are you telling me I've been staying in his cabin . . . *in his bed* . . ." Deidre shuddered at the thought and saw Kevin flinch a little as well. "And the entire time *this* was here?" She looked up at the house that towered above her, much larger now that she was in front of it than when she spied on it from across the lake.

Kevin looked at her steadily, matched her pointed gaze. "Seems that way," he said.

"But . . . how? I mean, I followed the directions on your map!" She gave him an accusing look before reaching into her purse and bringing out the worn piece of paper she always kept in her wallet—it was the only thing she had of his and had been a talisman of sorts.

"You still have it?" Kevin seemed touched but Deidre wasn't in the mood to reminisce.

"Don't change the subject!" she snapped.

Kevin sighed. He took the map and studied it. "No, it's right."

Deidre snatched it back. "*I don't think so*. If it was right, what would I be doing *over there* instead of over here?!"

Kevin pointed to the small grove of trees. "You turn left at the trees . . ."

"No, you told me turn left *after* the trees . . ."

"No, I said *at*. It looks like you're driving directly into the woods. We thought it would discourage tourists from driving in. I guess I should have made that more clear; I can see how you would've misread the map," he said, squinting at the small drawing.

Deidre stared at the wrinkled map, stricken. She couldn't think of a single thing to say.

Kevin tried humor to cheer her up. "Well, at least that explains why you never returned my phone calls."

"There's a phone here?!" she yelped. She looked about to charge. Kevin cringed and turned his attention to Claire, who was bounding up the path toward them.

"Hey, what's taking so long?" Claire demanded.

"I have a Thanksgiving dinner in three hours that I need to get back to, I stayed up *all night* to clean that cabin for you and Claire, I need a shower, not to mention a nap . . ." Deidre was speechless then burst out. "Henry Johnson is your *uncle*?!"

"Look, Deidre, I . . ." Kevin glanced at Claire, who was looking at Deidre as if she were crazy, which wasn't too far off the mark. "Can you give us a moment, please, sweetheart? Go unload our bags."

Claire whined. "But I don't have a key . . ."

"It's under a broken flowerpot on the east side of the house."

"Which way is east?"

"North, south, east, west," Kevin gestured impatiently. "Now go."

Deidre closed her eyes, remembering her first night in the cabin, frantically overturning every broken flowerpot within a six-foot perimeter of the cabin.

Kevin turned back to her, then reached for her, pulling

her into his arms. Deidre felt comforted by his warmth. She buried her face in his chest. "You must think I'm an idiot!"

"Of course I don't," Kevin said fondly, stroking her hair. "I'm just amazed you actually lived there for as long as you did. Even Uncle Harry doesn't stay there more than a few days at a time." He chuckled.

Deidre smiled happily into his sweater, her embarrassment waning and replaced with a feeling of contentment. So she stayed in the wrong place for a couple of months. That was nothing compared to the fact that she was finally in Kevin's arms.

Still, she had to be sure. She looked up at him. "So, just so I'm clear and there's no misunderstanding, are you single?"

"Yes."

"Single as in available?"

He smiled. "Yes."

"Not gay?"

"Definitely not gay." He bent down to give her a long, hot kiss.

"God," she said, when they came up for air. "If you knew what has been going on in my mind these past few weeks . . ." She laughed and snuggled up next to him. "I'm just so glad it's all out in the open now."

Kevin gave a small laugh. "Yeah. Well, you know, we should probably talk about one more thing."

Deidre was giddy, almost indifferent. "What's that?"

"You asked me about Marla the last time we spoke. I meant to tell you, but it was never the right time . . ."

Nothing could faze her now. "What, is she Claire's mother?"

"Marla a mother? Now that's a laugh."

"An ex-wife?"

Kevin looked appalled at the thought. "No!"

"Then what?" Deidre gave him a playful look.

Kevin straightened up and looked Deidre in the eye. "Marla's my sister. I'm her brother, Kevin Johnson."

CHAPTER 8

If you are distressed by anything external,
The pain is not due to the thing itself,
but to your estimate of it;
And this you have the power to revoke at any moment.
—MARCUS AURELIUS

THEY SAY LIFE is full of defining moments. If that was true, then this was definitely one of those moments for Deidre. She felt the color drain from her cheeks.

"But, but . . ." she stammered, her face as white as a sheet. She gestured helplessly. "Marla's last name is Banks . . ."

"Johnson is her maiden name," Kevin said gently. "She's been married three times, as you probably know. Her last husband was Stephen Banks, and she hasn't changed it since."

"Why didn't you tell me this before?!"

"When did I have the chance? At the Uptown Bistro I thought maybe you knew, and then when I ran into you in the elevator I realized you didn't. I was waiting for the right time to tell you, but then you kissed me . . ."

"*I* kissed you?" She placed her hands on her hips. "I don't think so!"

"In your apartment?" he reminded her. "On the couch?"

Oh, right. She had made the first move. Damn the Stoli's.

"The next day it didn't seem like you wanted to see me again so I let it go. And then you came down here and we talked on the phone and I was going to tell you then but then you hung up. I've been calling you at the house but you never called back . . ."

"Because I was staying in your uncle's cabin that has no phone!"

"Well, I didn't know you were staying in the wrong place, now did I? I just assumed you were hard at work."

"I was." She glared at him. "Kevin, your sister has made my life a living hell! She's one of the reasons I'm here—she practically chased me out of Seattle!"

"Deidre . . ."

She climbed into the passenger side of the car. "I need to get back to the Wishbone. *Now.*"

"Deidre, we need to finish talking about this. Marla doesn't have anything to do with us."

"Kevin, she has *everything* to do with us! I thought you were different, that there was a chance that maybe, I don't know, something might work out. Okay, fine, I was hoping, praying that something would work out. How could you not tell me you were related?"

"I was going to, Deidre. It just was never the right time."

"What? First your uncle, then your sister, and now you! I can't deal with this right now, Kevin. I just can't. Please just take me back to the Wishbone." She stared fixedly out the window.

"Deidre, you're overreacting . . ."

"You think *this* is overreacting? I haven't even gotten started. I've given you fair warning, Kevin. So, for the last time, please take me back."

Kevin sighed. "Fine, whatever." He went to get Claire, who wisely remained silent as they drove back into town.

"WHEW, I AM SO glad to see you," Lindsey said as soon as Deidre walked through the door. She was beaming, flushed with excitement. The diner was decorated, baskets filled with pinecones and oranges, adorned with dried fruits and nuts. The tables were set and the crepe runners looked lovely against the white tablecloths. "I think everything is ready, but Hannah had to go home to check on her husband and get ready, and Mary needs help whipping the cream—she just can't get it to thicken and I'm up to my arms in chard. Sidney's on turkey duty." Lindsey shook her head in amazement. "I almost don't recognize the place. People are going to be in for a big surprise."

Not as big as the one I just got, Deidre thought. She couldn't even look at Kevin when he dropped her off, afraid that she might break down or give in, and he didn't make an attempt to talk with her. As far as she was concerned, it was over. She didn't know whether to cry or scream, so she settled for grabbing an apron instead.

Deidre headed for the kitchen, anxious to get to work. "Okay, I'll take over on the chard." She took the largest butcher's knife she could find and began chopping furiously. "If there's room in the fridge, chill that large stainless steel bowl and the whisk. Throw the cream back in. It'll whip better if everything's cold. In the meantime, you all can take a break and get ready, then come back and we'll finish up. I'll keep an eye on the turkeys, too."

"This is going to be the best Thanksgiving," Mary told Sidney as they wiped their hands clean.

"You sure you can handle everything?" Lindsey asked, removing her soiled apron.

"Absolutely." Deidre reached for another handful of chard, her voice brisk. "I've got everything under control."

HER TIMING WAS impeccable. The oven timers went off the minute the first customer walked into the diner. Lindsey, Sidney, Mary, and Hannah were nicely dressed, ready for the entire town of Jacob's Point to join them for Thanksgiving.

Deidre surveyed the diner with a familiar sense of accomplishment. Then she reached for her coat.

Lindsey looked at her and laughed. "Don't tell me you're cold! It must be one hundred degrees in here!"

"I'm not staying here, Lindsey. I'm leaving. I'm heading back to Seattle."

"Leaving? What are you talking about?" Lindsey had a smile on her face but it quickly faded. She gave a half-hearted laugh. "It's Thanksgiving, Deidre. Everyone's going to be here any minute!"

Deidre wanted to get on the road before Kevin and Claire showed up. Now that they had both had time to cool down, she was sure he would want to talk. But she didn't know what to say to him, and no matter how many times she thought about it, it seemed like the impossible relationship. He was related to all the wrong people—what kind of future could they realistically have?

"I know," Deidre said. "It's just that it's time for me to head back."

"Can't you go after dinner? Everyone's expecting you."

"No, I can't." The tone of Deidre's voice was definitive. Where was her car? "How did I get here this morning?"

"You parked around back, by the service entrance, to drop off the pumpkin pies," Lindsey said slowly.

It came back to her. "Oh, right." Deidre checked her purse for her car keys.

"I guess this means you won't be back in time for the cookbook meeting tomorrow night."

Deidre had forgotten all about that. She didn't want to let Lindsey down but there was no way she was going to stay. "No. I'm sorry, Lindsey. I just . . . I have to go." The Wishbone was slowly starting to fill up with more patrons. Deidre looked nervously toward the front door.

"Well, of all the . . ." Lindsey just shook her head. "Just hold on, will you?" She disappeared into the kitchen.

Deidre waited restlessly, checking the clock on the wall. Lindsey emerged with a bag and handed it to Deidre. "Food for the road. I can't bear the thought of you driving alone on Thanksgiving, but you may as well have some turkey to keep you company. The chard, the potatoes, that cranberry salsa, the pie . . . it's all in there, and then some."

Lindsey's generous gesture, one of many Deidre had come to experience, brought Deidre to tears. She didn't know what to say, much less how to say good-bye. "Lindsey, I . . ."

"Oh, get out of here," Lindsey said, her own eyes getting misty. "I have customers to take care of."

Deidre gave her a grateful hug and the two women held each other, sniffling.

"Now go," Lindsey said, pushing her away and reaching for a tissue. "I just got my makeup on. I'll make your regrets to everyone."

Deidre gave her a thankful smile before hurrying out the back door. She got in her Volvo and began to drive.

BACK IN SEATTLE, weary and drained after six hours of driving in holiday traffic and crying, Deidre slowly walked up the steps. She could hear laughter coming from inside the house. She hesitated and then knocked. Footsteps.

The door opened and William was staring at her in surprise before rushing to give her a big hug, oblivious of Deidre's red, puffy eyes.

"It's Deidre, everybody!" he called, ushering her in. "She's back!"

IT WAS COMFORTING to be fretted upon by two gay men who were ecstatic to see her. Deidre stayed in her pajamas for days, only emerging from the guest room to watch TV and eat bowls full of microwave kettle popcorn. Alain was happy to join her, but William watched the two of them in disgust before finally unplugging the TV and hiding the remote.

"Hey!" Deidre and Alain protested in unison.

"Enough," William said firmly. "Pity party's over." He grabbed the bowl of popcorn and dumped the remains in the trash. "This doesn't even qualify as food, Deidre. You should know better."

Deidre picked at a few crumbs that had fallen on her robe. "It's good enough for me," she said, popping the last crumb into her mouth as William stomped out of the room.

Alain got up, stretched, checked his watch. "I'm on call," he said reluctantly. "I'll find the remote. Same time, same place?"

She gave him the thumbs-up. "I'm not going anywhere."

Alain went to wash up and Deidre sought out William, who was getting ready to do some laundry.

"I'm doing whites," he said, his voice distant. He tossed some socks and a couple of T-shirts into the washer.

"Why are you so grumpy?" she demanded.

He poured in the detergent and started the cycle. "If anything, I thought having you back meant that we could co-parent Mr. Junk Food out there. Instead, it's like I have two kids who sit on the couch all day eating manufactured 'food' . . ." He made quotations marks with his fingers.

"Newsflash: air quotes are out."

William shot her an annoyed look and did the air quotes again to annoy her. ". . . and arguing over who should win *Project Runway*." He banged the lid to the washer shut.

"Give me a break, William. Look at what I've gone through in the past three months! My life is totally ruined and I can't even sit on the couch and eat popcorn in peace?"

William snickered. "Ruined? Ha! You don't know how good you have it, Deidre. So Kevin didn't tell you he was Marla's brother. Big deal. It was deceitful, maybe, but he's a heterosexual man, and they screw up these things. They've got that gene that messes with common sense, you know that. I don't think he did it on purpose. You should call him, Deidre."

"And say what?" she asked. "It's not just him, it's his whole family! This relationship was doomed from the start. There's Marla, who hates me, his goddaughter, Claire, who sees me as a threat, and of course there's Mr. Johnson, who couldn't wait to evict me." She shuddered. "And I slept in his bed for almost three months!"

William grimaced. "Yeah, that's not pretty," he agreed. "But you have to admit, it's kind of ironic. He kicks you out of the apartment and you break into his cabin and live there, rent-free. He's going to walk in and it's going to reek of Deidre McIntosh. I don't have to see it to know it totally has your touch all over it."

Deidre couldn't help but give a small smile. She could see Mr. Johnson standing at the door of the now-clean and brighter cabin, mouth open in shock, his ratty dungeon a thing of the past.

"*Call him.*"

She shook her head. "I'm focused on other things now."

"Really? Like what? All you've done is sit around. What happened to that new show you were raving about? You haven't worked on it at all since you've been back, have you? Do you have any appointments scheduled?" He headed for the kitchen.

Deidre trailed after him. "No, but I will. When I'm ready."

"You've got to get in front of them, Deidre. There's no time to lose: aren't most of the stations planning their summer lineup right about now?"

Deidre tried not to fret. All of the editorial meetings were happening now, and some stations probably had their calendar already set for the next year. "Yes," she said, brooding. If she wanted to get in, she didn't have a moment to lose.

Alain poked his head in. "Shall I pick up KFC for dinner?"

William threw a dish towel at him. "You'll need to double your time on the StairMaster, mister."

Alain shrugged. "It'll be worth it. Shall I get a bucket?"

"No," Deidre said, catching the dish towel as Alain flung it back at William. She folded it and hung it on the oven door. "I'll cook tonight. But late. I need to make a few phone calls and visit an old friend first."

STELLA WAS TRILLING with excitement when Deidre stepped into the salon. "I can't believe it's you!" she exclaimed, enveloping Deidre in a hug. She looked at the top of Deidre's head and frowned. "Now I know I didn't touch up your color . . ."

"I was desperate," Deidre said. "And about three hundred miles away. Forgive me?"

Stella made a face as she searched through Deidre's roots. "Well, it could be worse, I suppose. Let's get you started." She patted the chair in front of her. "Now sit down and tell me everything!"

"Well . . ." Deidre hesitated, remembering the suspicious phone call Stella had taken during her last visit. She decided to be up front about it. "Is Marla Banks a client now?"

Stella gave an uneven laugh as she started rinsing Deidre's hair. "Oh. *Her*. Well, she hired me to work on a couple of shows, part of that Marla Makeover thing, but she was driving me crazy. Driving all of us crazy. And she made Joan cry . . ." Stella nodded toward the receptionist. "So that was the end of that." She paused and gave Deidre a nervous smile. "Forgive me?"

Deidre laughed, relieved. "Let's call it even."

"Great." Stella breathed a sigh of relief. "I was so sure you were angry with me! I figured that's why I hadn't seen you all these months. I actually got myself worked up into a frenzy about it."

Deidre felt a twinge of discomfort and thought remorsefully about Kevin. "Yeah, it's funny what the mind can do."

Stella finished shampooing and ushered Deidre back to her station. "What do you want to do today? Go blonder? Redhead? Jet black?"

"Actually, I want to go back to my natural color," Deidre said. "Minus the gray, of course."

Stella was nodding and selecting the color bottles. "Good choice. We're going to do a cut and color . . . I'm going to make you look like a million bucks. Marla won't even know what hit her!"

"Actually, I'm not planning to go up against Marla," Deidre said. "I have a new show planned."

"You do?" Stella rested her hands on Deidre's shoulders. "What's it called?"

Deidre hesitated and then decided to spill the beans. "It's called *Seattle Revealed*."

"*Seattle Revealed?*"

"It's about the people of Seattle. Not as pretty as a biography but not quite as nasty as an exposé. It would just show real life, such as what people have to do to make things work in their life, in their vocation. The trials and tribulations, like when everything seems to be saying, 'Give up,' and pushing on nevertheless. And it won't focus on just one person, but a chain of people, key individuals that make an event happen and how their lives intertwine, knowingly and unknowingly. I have one pilot that focuses on the Seattle Zoo, from the zookeepers to major donors and philanthropists. I guess part of the message is that every person along the way is important, and yet we're all human, too. We'll see what everyone has to do to make things work."

Interest piqued, Stella stopped working for a moment to listen to her, intent.

"Of course it will end with everyone happy and contributing to the diverse mix of Seattle. Mix celebrities and businesspeople with everyday people. I was just thinking that life can seem so hard sometimes, that if people saw that they weren't alone, it might help . . . with the loneliness, with finding inspiration in the strangest places, that sort of thing." Deidre stopped and took a breath, looking at Stella shyly. "It looks great on paper, but it sounds kind of silly as I'm explaining it out loud. I need to work on my presentation a bit."

Stella smiled and resumed running a comb through Deidre's hair. "Well, I think it sounds fabulous and I can't wait to see it!"

"Thanks," Deidre said. "What I especially like is that you can take the model and use it in other cities, *Los Angeles Revealed*, or expand it across the state—*Washington Revealed*. I have a short list of people—I thought each segment could have a theme, either around an industry, like, say, the floral industry, and each segment would have five subject stories from the industry. So you could have someone who grows flowers, someone who sells them, someone who designs and arranges them, and so on. Each person would have a different socioeconomic background, a different measure of success, and we get to go in and get to know the people behind it all." Deidre was feeling inspired, and straightened up in her chair. "Who knows, maybe we'll all start treating each other better as well."

"We should definitely send Marla a copy," Stella said, reaching for the color bowl and brush. "What I can't figure out is if she's really just spoiled or if it's all an act. Maybe it was the way she was brought up. Who knows."

"I doubt it has anything to do with the way she was brought up," Deidre said, thinking of Kevin. He was the complete antithesis to Marla.

"Well, I have a feeling you're going to turn everything upside down for her," Stella predicted. "Now just sit back and relax."

DEIDRE SPENT THE next day at the nearest Kinko's, running off duplicate copies of her proposal and getting it typeset and bound. As she waited, she realized the Uptown Bistro, where she had lunched with Caroline and met Kevin, was across the street.

Deidre checked the time—it was 11:15. The last thing she needed was to spend money on eating out, but she was starving. When her copies were finished, she crossed the street and entered the lobby. She decided against the elevator and walked the one flight up to the restaurant. An intoxicating aroma was wafting from the restaurant, and Deidre was ready to eat.

I'll limit myself to ten dollars, she told herself as she neared the maître d'. *Whatever I can get for ten dollars, including tax and tip.* The proposals were heavy in her arms. *This is cause for a celebration of sorts, anyway.*

The maître d' straightened as she approached. "Hello," he said. "Party of one?"

Deidre looked at the menu displayed by the door. For eight dollars she could get a cup of their soup of the day. That was the only single-digit item available; even a side salad started at eleven dollars.

"What's your soup of the day?" she asked. *Anything tomato-based*, she prayed. *Or in a bouillon base. French onion would be perfect.* Deidre's mouth was watering.

"Split pea with bacon."

Deidre smiled at the maitre d' but groaned inside. Most restaurants masticated split pea soup until it was only a slightly more glamorous version of baby food. But it was better than nothing.

"Wonderful," she said, giving him a smile. He raised an eyebrow—clearly he didn't think too much of the soup of the day, either. She followed him in.

"I'll tell your waitress. Have a nice lunch." He cleared the remaining place settings.

Deidre's eyes fell onto the tablecloth in front of her. A clean, creamy Damask, a little overstarched, but it still draped nicely over the table. The flatware was masculine and oversized, the finish a little too matte, but with no spots and hardly any scratches. The restaurant was slowly filling up and Deidre reached for one of the Kinko's bags, wanting to take another look at her finished proposals.

"Ah, I'd recognize that million-dollar smile anywhere."

Deidre knew that voice. She sucked in her breath, not wanting to turn around.

He came around and stood by the table, looking down at her.

Len.

"Deidre," he said, then bent down and kissed her cheek. Deidre stiffened.

She looked out the window, staring fixedly at the Kinko's across the street. She watched pedestrians walking up and down the street, hunched inside of their winter jackets.

"Aw, come on, Deidre, love, don't be mad," he said. "Can I sit?" He gestured to the empty chair in front of her.

"No."

"You haven't seen me in ages, and you won't even let me sit for a moment?"

"I'll be seeing you tomorrow with Buford, Len. I can see you then." Deidre sipped her water again.

"You're not being civil."

"I was wondering when you'd catch on."

"Ow." He pretended to look wounded as he settled himself at the table next to hers. He stared at her admiringly. "You look fabulous, love. Really fabulous. I heard you had gone blond, but I guess it was just a rumor." He waited for some confirmation.

Let him wonder, she thought, sipping her water. Len hated being left out of a secret.

He nodded toward her bulky paper bags. "I saw you coming out of Kinko's. Is that for our meeting tomorrow?"

"As a matter of fact, it is." She pulled them closer to her and made it clear she wasn't going to show him anything.

"I thought so." When he realized Deidre wasn't going to share, he changed the subject. "Hey, you know there have been quite a few people who have been trying to get in touch with you."

"Is that so?"

"Yes. We have a couple boxes of mail and some messages for you. I'll have it ready tomorrow. We didn't know where to forward them since you moved. Manuela Jamison in particular seems *very intent* on getting a hold of you . . . wants some more of that orgasmic corn fritter, I imagine." He gave a small chuckle, hoping to get a smile from Deidre for old-time's sake, but she didn't respond. Len sighed and settled back in his chair, playing with his silverware.

Deidre snuck a quick peek at him. He hadn't changed much, but there was a relaxed assuredness in the way he was carrying himself. He had the same tousled brown hair, the same nose with a slightly crooked bridge, and he still sported his ever-popular five o'clock shadow. Deidre had actually given him a top-of-the-line shaving kit one year from Burberry's, but she would still catch him dry shaving over the soundboard with a disposable Schick. Len looked up and caught her staring at him, and smiled. Deidre scowled.

"Stop pouting," he said. "I know I fucked up, okay? And that it will take some time for you to trust me again, but you took off so quickly I never had a chance to make it up to you."

"I really doubt there is anything you can do to make up for it."

"I'll be there tomorrow. And Buford listens to me."

"What are you saying? That if I don't forgive you, you'll tell him not to listen?"

Len scoffed and looked away, as if insulted. "The man has ears, Deidre. It's not as if I can keep him from hearing what you have to say. And I'm curious myself. I'm just saying that it might be nice to have a friend in your corner."

"I agree. Except that you're not a friend." Deidre made her dissatisfaction with him clear.

Len's expression changed as he quickly glanced around the restaurant. "Look, Deidre, whether you like it or not, the show had been struggling before Buford pulled the plug. Everyone knew it was coming except for you. I did what I could to keep you on the air for as long as possible, thinking that it could turn around and we'd be square. But it didn't happen."

Deidre didn't say anything. She remembered the night with Caroline, going through the *Live Simple* financials by phone. "Len, I reviewed the financials for the show. You were padding; we both know it."

Len dismissed the accusation with a wave of the hand. "It wouldn't have made much of a difference, Deidre. You like the finer things of life—you didn't notice them when you had them but trust me, you'd have noticed them if you hadn't had them. I was doing you a favor; I kept you comfortable. I helped put your name in the ring for daytime television."

"Yeah, that has really been a *huge* help in my current situation."

The waitress came by and handed Len a menu. "I can take your order whenever you're ready."

"I'll have whatever she's having," Len said impatiently, waving the waitress away, anxious to get back to his conversation with Deidre.

"Give him a bowl," Deidre said. "A BIG one. I'll be taking mine to go." She started to gather her things.

Len was starting to get irritated. "Look, Deidre, business is business. *It's not personal*. It was really awkward for me but I didn't have a choice."

"Wrong. You always have a choice, Len," Deidre said. "And you made yours." She stood up, fumbling through her purse for ten dollars to leave on the table. She only had a couple of bills, and the first one was a one. For a second she panicked. *Please don't make me go through that again*, she begged silently. The next bill was a ten.

Relieved, Deidre placed it on the table and looked around impatiently for the waitress. The restaurant was slowly beginning to fill up. Len was frowning at the table.

"Look, Len," she finally said, softening a bit. "I'll see you tomorrow. You and Buford can take a look at what I have and if it works for you, great. If not"—she shrugged—"I have other appointments lined up."

"Ha, you're bluffing," he said. The waitress came out with a bowl of soup that she placed in front of Len. He made a face; Deidre knew he hated soup. He peered at it closely, unable to recognize it. Len looked back at Deidre, a little less confident this time. "You're bluffing," he said again. He reluctantly accepted a soup spoon from the waitress. "What *is* this?"

"Split pea," the waitress said. "With bacon." Len's face fell.

"See you tomorrow, Len," Deidre said coolly, standing up.

"Hey," the waitress said suddenly as she began to clear Deidre's table. "You're Deidre McIntosh from that show, *Live Simple*, right?"

Deidre gave the waitress a smile reserved for her favorite fans. "Yes. And you are?"

"Evelyn."

"It's nice to meet you, Evelyn," Deidre said, flashing another smile at Evelyn and Len, who was starting to scowl. "I'm sorry, but I have to run. Bye."

"Bye," Evelyn said, still surprised. She turned to Len. "That was Deidre McIntosh from *Live Simple*!"

"Yes," Deidre heard him say sullenly, or maybe it was from the soup. "I know."

AFTER MONTHS OF being in denim and flannel, it felt strange to step into one of her old form-fitting suits and zip it up around her body. She had lost weight and her arms were shapely and stronger. She chose a dark navy Ann Taylor pantsuit, wool, and wore a cream-colored sweater beneath it. She studied herself in the mirror then walked into the living room and stood in front of William and Alain.

"What do you think?" she asked, turning once.

"Very nice," they said, throwing in a few catcalls for good measure.

William added, "You look just like before. Ready to take on the world."

Deidre looked at herself critically in the hallway mirror. That was the problem, she looked the same as before. And she wasn't interested in taking on the world, just Channel Five.

"Hold on," she said, and went back into the guest room to look through her things. She spotted a 70s polka dot scarf she had found at a garage sale in Jacob's Point, and tied it around her neck. Then she chucked the small gold hoops and chose instead the earrings Kevin had given her.

She fingered them gently, feeling that she shouldn't wear them if she wasn't speaking to him, but . . .

"Oh, what the hell," she said. She smiled at herself in the mirror. She looked good.

She reappeared and Alain clapped as William raised an eyebrow. "New look?"

Deidre dramatically fanned herself. "I feel the need for a little color. I expect everyone else will be dolled up in blue."

"And probably lacking in the polka dot area."

"Probably." She took a deep breath. "And, after I meet with them, I'm going apartment hunting." She held up her hand as they started to politely protest. "I called my old assistant, Anne, and she set me up with a property manager who has a couple of good leads. If I'm going to stay in Seattle, I'll need my own place. I'm going to rent, but eventually I'm going to look for a small condo or loft to buy."

William said, "Just call us after the meeting with an update. We want to hear what happens."

"Yes, yes!" Alain said. "We want to hear how you blow them away."

"Oh, sure," she said, pretending to be offended. "I'm finally on the path of personal freedom and independence, and you just want to know what's going to happen with the show."

"We just want to know before the rest of Seattle," William said innocently.

"You'll be the first to know. Wish me luck."

"Good luck." They gave her kisses and walked her to the door.

"*Deidre Revealed*," Alain said as they watched her walk away. "This should be good."

DEIDRE EXPECTED TO feel something when she walked through the familiar doors of Channel Five, but she didn't. She was surprised to still see her picture on the wall, with the *Live Simple* studio signage behind her. For some reason she thought they would have taken it down. Seeing it there made her feel proud; she was now part of Channel Five history, a permanent blip on their screen.

"Len was right," she admitted to herself, surprised at the thought. He had helped put her on the map for daytime television.

There was a bit of a hush as she stood in the lobby and waited to be buzzed to the back offices. She smiled and remembered people by name. When Jenny, the receptionist, handed Deidre a guest pass, she gave Deidre an apologetic smile.

"Sorry," she said, as Deidre clipped the pass onto her suit. "It's just policy."

"Don't worry about it, Jenny," Deidre said reassuringly. "It's not a big deal. May I?" She motioned to the security door.

Jenny looked relieved. "Oh, sure. I'll buzz you through. It's really good to see you, Deidre. They're waiting for you in the conference room, which is . . ."

"I remember. Thanks, Jenny." Deidre pushed the heavy door and walked through.

The buzz in the back of the station was familiar, but it wasn't quite as thrilling as she remembered. Production assistants were rushing around and people were talking a mile a minute, though most of them stopped to look at Deidre as she smiled and walked by.

Someone whispered, "Maybe she's back," and Deidre wanted to turn to them and say, "I am!" but instead just gave a Cheshire cat smile as she continued to the conference room.

She knocked once, took a deep breath, and opened the door. The look on Buford's face was grim, as if he didn't really have time for this. Len's face looked tight, and he quickly put away the small stack of papers in front of him.

"Deidre, come in," Buford said tiredly.

"Deidre," Len said. He was all business.

"Len, Mr. Buford," Deidre acknowledged.

"Here's some mail and messages for you," Len said, pushing two full boxes toward her. Deidre tried to hide her surprise. There had to be at least two hundred letters or packages, along with a stack of phone messages bound by a thick rubber band. She glanced quickly at Buford, but he looked gruff and uninterested as usual.

"Let's get right to it; I only have half an hour. You have some ideas you want to discuss?" Buford sat down across from her and waited expectantly.

"Just one, actually," Deidre said, handing a proposal to each of them. "I've included most of what might interest you in the executive summary; the other pages are backup and sample pilot manifests. I also ran some projections on viewership and advertising. It's in the back. I think you'll see that it has the potential to be much more successful than *Live Simple* ever was."

Len was first to flip to the back and gave Deidre a quick glance. "I'm impressed, Deidre."

"*Seattle Revealed.*" The look on Buford's face revealed that he didn't care for the name.

"It's just a working title; I'm not attached to it," Deidre said evenly.

"Same time slot as *Live Simple?*" There was skepticism in Len's voice.

"Actually, I was thinking early evening, right after the evening news but before you go to the network for the nighttime lineup. It could also air later, before the ten o'clock news. Each show is only twenty-three minutes, unlike *Live Simple's* forty-eight."

Buford had flipped through the proposal, looking more at Deidre than at the proposal. "Why do you want to come back to Channel Five? After all that's happened?" Buford looked her right in the eye.

Deidre felt a moment's hesitation but knew he was waiting for an immediate response. "I learned a lot from the show," she said honestly. "What worked and what didn't. I took some time off to get clear on a lot of things. I think *Seattle Revealed* is a strong concept and, as I told Len yesterday, I'm confident it will get picked up. It's only natural that I'd want to come here first."

"You would host the show?"

Deidre had written herself in as the host, but suddenly she wasn't sure. "I haven't decided," she said. Then added, "There are a few other people I'm thinking of who could present the program well."

"A brand new show with a brand new host will be harder to sell," Len said.

"Oh, I don't know," Deidre said lightly, pulling out her trump card. "Channel Two seems to have a made a hit with it."

Buford didn't say anything and continued to glance through the proposal. Finally, he put it down.

"Yes," he said. Len was watching them both closely. Buford pushed the proposal back toward Deidre. "So maybe you should talk to them. I'm sorry, Ms. McIntosh. I admire your tenacity and I can see that you've learned a lot, but it's just not a show I'm interested in taking on right now. Thanks for stopping by."

CHAPTER 9

Life is a play. We're unrehearsed.

—MEL BROOKS

ALAIN WAS PASSING large amounts of chocolate toward Deidre as William rubbed her shoulders.

"I know I said it wouldn't matter, but it does. It's over!" She buried her head in her hands. "I am totally screwed."

"You are not screwed," William assured her. "You're just going to do exactly what you said you were going to do. Take it to the other stations until you find the right home for it."

"It was my scarf, wasn't it?"

"Er . . ." Alain exchanged a look with William then fished through his box of chocolates. "Here . . . this one has almonds. Extra protein."

"I was so sure he was going to say yes, and this would all be over by now. All this time I thought it was petty revenge for Rosalind, or that he didn't think I was competent . . ."

". . . or that maybe he doesn't know a good thing when he sees it," William finished for her. "Stop your moaning and pick up the phone to call Channel Two."

"I am *not* calling Channel Two. That's Marla's station." Deidre took another bite of chocolate.

"So call the other stations. Someone will bite, Deidre, but you need to call them. They don't have ESP."

"You can't score unless you shoot," Alain agreed, popping another chocolate in his mouth.

William just rolled his eyes and whispered to Deidre, "He's been reading a lot of self-help books. He's fascinated by them." He called to Alain, "Easy on the chocolates, turbo."

Deidre was removing her earrings, tossing them in the candy dish. "It's these earrings. They're jinxed."

"Where'd you get them from?"

Deidre sighed. "Kevin."

"Ah." The boys exchanged a knowing look.

"God, do I really have to go through with this?"

William hefted the *Yellow Pages* and pushed the telephone toward her. "I'm afraid so. It's time for you to turn on the McIntosh charm and pull your connections at the other stations. This is it, baby."

Reticent, Deidre took the phone. "There's no other way?"

William looked at her slyly. "Not unless you want to marry Kevin and all his money and live happily ever after."

As if that were going to happen. Deidre began flipping through the *Yellow Pages*. "Say no more."

THE RESPONSES WERE pretty much the same.

". . . Deidre, it's so good to hear from you but the station isn't looking for any new programming right now . . ."

". . . We're still reeling from a massive budget cut and we can't afford to bring on another show right now . . . ."

". . . It sounds great but it doesn't really fit into our program matrix right now. Maybe next year . . ."

". . . We're actually in the process of developing something in-house that has a similar profile nature to it . . ."

And so on.

Deidre lay in bed, papers strewn about her, every name and number crossed off her list. William came in and perched next to her after moving a pile of papers to the side.

"Not looking good, huh?"

"Not really, no. Even the ones I thought would bite, didn't."

"What about going after one of the cable stations?"

Deidre shook her head. "Forget it. That's a year in the making, at best." She rolled to her side, plumping a pillow under her head. "I give up. It's just not meant to be. I'm washed up. It's over."

William sat with her in silence, commiserating. She hit his arm. "You could at least disagree!"

"Yeah, but what would be the point?" William looked at the yellow pad with writing and scribbles all over it. He picked it up. "You called everyone?"

"Everyone."

"Everyone?"

"Everyone."

"I don't see Channel Two on the list."

"I already told you, William, it's Marla's station and I'm not knocking on that door. They would love that. *She* would love that. It'll be such a kick to tell me no."

William persisted. "But what if they say yes? You were always saying that Channel Two was the risk-taker, that they were the only ones in the business willing to think out of the box, whereas Channel Five was always so difficult to work with, and given what's happened . . ." William stood up and walked to the door. "Sounds like a marriage made in heaven."

Deidre sighed and stared absently at the ceiling. She needed to unwind, to create some inspirational ambiance. She sat up and reached for a matchbook to light the patchouli candle by her bedside.

She turned the matchbook over in her hand. It was from the Wishbone, and she smiled as she gazed at the logo. She lit the candle, then picked up the phone.

"Wishbone." Lindsey's voice sounded busy.

Deidre instantly warmed at the sound of her voice. "Lindsey, it's Deidre."

"She lives!" Lindsey shouted, presumably to the others in the diner. She came back on. "We were all wondering about you. Is everything okay?"

Deidre felt an intense longing for Jacob's Point. "Everything's fine, thanks."

"That new show working out?"

Deidre tried not to sound too discouraged. "Actually, no. No one's interested."

Lindsey let out a low whistle. "That's a damn shame. It seemed like such a good idea."

"Yeah, well, like you said: I'm never short of good ideas."

"No, but this was a good one. I'm sorry it won't have a chance to prove itself out there. *Mary, I told you, you have to wipe those knives to get rid of the spots before you put them in the tray.*"

"Well, you sound busy," Deidre said.

"Oh, just the same old, same old. Except that we're swamped. The *Adams Country Tribune* covered our Thanksgiving dinner, thanks to you. We even made the front page."

"No kidding?"

"I saved a clipping for you. Where is it? . . . Here we go: 'The Wishbone's secret ingredient, master baker Deidre McIntosh, former host of the popular lifestyle show, *Live Simple*, has transformed this traditional holiday fare into a symphony busting with flavor, a meal soon not to be forgotten.'" Deidre knew Lindsey was grinning over the phone. "Isn't that something?"

"It is."

"Well, I would love to chat but I have to get going on tonight's dinner special: chopped steak with a side of green beans and those buttermilk mashed potatoes you taught me how to make. Give me a call sometime next week and we'll talk more. We sure do miss having you around here."

"I miss being there."

"Well, then, there's an easy answer to that, isn't there?" It was more of a statement than a question, and Deidre smiled. "You take care of yourself, Deidre."

"I will. Bye."

Deidre hung up the phone and lay back down on her bed, breathing in the earthy combination of patchouli and amber. *I'm sorry it won't have a chance to prove itself out there.* The words echoed in her head.

THE NEXT MORNING, Deidre appeared in the kitchen fully dressed in a beige suede suit, adorned with the polka dot scarf and Kevin's earnings. She poured a glass of orange juice as Alain and William eyed her suspiciously.

"Going somewhere?" William asked.

"As it so happens, I have a meeting with Juliette Farquahar, the station manager over at Channel Two," Deidre said smugly.

"Oh." The boys exchanged a knowing look.

"What about Marla?" William asked.

"What about her? They air at least sixty productions a week, of which six are produced in-house, like *Live Simple* was."

"And that would include *At Home with Marla Banks*."

"Yes." Deidre refused to blink.

William sipped his latté, satisfied. "Okay, just checking."

Alain gestured to his neck, nodding at hers. "You're going to wear the . . ."

Deidre gave it a little toss. "I just wanted to make sure the scarf wasn't what blew the deal before."

The boys exchanged a doubtful look.

"I'm kidding," Deidre said. "I *like* it. So I'm going to wear it."

"The earrings look good, too," Alain said.

"Well, I'm learning to work with what I got. So, are you going to wish me luck or just look at me like I'm the *Titanic* preparing for my final voyage?"

"Good luck, good luck," William said, getting up to give her kiss.

Alain pecked the other cheek. "*Bon chance.*"

Deidre tucked the proposals for *Seattle Revealed* under her arm, gave them a little wave, and headed out the door, tripping over one of large cardboard boxes that rested beside it. "Ow!"

"I was meaning to ask you, what is that?"

Deidre leaned against the door frame and rubbed her foot. "Some fan mail and messages from the station. I haven't had time to go through them yet. I'll move it to my room, I promise." She slipped her foot back into her shoe and straightened herself up. "Let's just do that again," she said. "Bye, wish me luck!" She gave them another airy wave.

"Good luck," William and Alain said, exchanging a nervous look as Deidre walked out the door.

"NICE CONCEPT," JULIETTE Farquahar, the station manager at Channel Two, told Deidre. She had perused Deidre's proposal with interest and Deidre had already been in her office for forty-five minutes, a good sign.

Deidre felt a flood of relief. She liked it, she liked it, *she liked it*, thank God. No one else had blinked twice.

Juliette took off her reading glasses and studied Deidre. "Not something I would have expected from a Channel Five alumni, no offense."

"No offense taken," Deidre said. "I know it doesn't seem to fit our typical programming."

"Yeah. It's pretty diverse in concept." Juliette considered Deidre some more. "I'll be honest with you. My spring and summer lineup are set. Barring any unforeseen surprises—"she laughed—"which is pretty much everything around here, I don't know if I can commit to your project, much less fund it."

Deidre felt her heart sink.

"But I think it's good, really good, and with the trend toward biographical profiles and memoirs, it's timely. If you could bring me the pilots, already shot and edited and ready to go, I could have it ready if one of our classic Channel Two emergencies comes up."

Deidre grimaced. "I can't self-finance this project," she admitted.

Juliette frowned. "That's too bad. I think if we could just get it out there, advertising and sponsors will fall into place. What about private investors?"

"I . . . don't know anybody offhand that I feel comfortable approaching."

"You have a solid following. Surely someone would consider backing you."

Deidre pushed the thought from her mind. "I don't think so."

"You may be able to go after some of the big money—banks and so on—and, of course, there's always grants, but it's not always worth the headache. I'll leave it to you to decide what to do, Deidre. If you want to make this happen, I'm sure you'll find a way. Like I said, if the pilots are good, I'm willing to trial it." She stood up to shake Deidre's hand.

Deidre knew she should be happy—Juliette was practically saying she would take the show if Deidre could provide the pilots. But the thought of finding someone to underwrite the project felt overwhelming. And Deidre was back to square one.

The look of disappointment on Deidre's face wasn't easily masked. Juliette cocked her head to one side and asked, "Have you ever seen the studio?"

"No."

"Come on. If you have a minute, I'll show you around. I'm sure the staff will get a kick out of seeing you here.

The rumors will be flying." Juliette gave her a mischievous smile. "Let's do it."

Deidre followed Juliette around Channel Two, a much smaller building than Channel Five. But everything inside was colorful, hip, full of plants, and very much alive.

"I have to admit," Juliette was saying, "that I never thought we'd be seeing you over here, especially after this past season's PR and ad campaign for Marla's show. It was all in good fun, I hope you didn't mind."

"Well," Deidre said, feeling like all was lost anyway. "It wasn't particularly fun for me, actually."

"We heard a lot of rumors about you over the past couple of months," Juliette said, taking out an ID card and running it through the scanner. It unlocked the security door and she pushed it open. "Let's see: you were a blond, a redhead, you shaved your head . . ."

Deidre laughed. Juliette continued, "You moved to Los Angeles, you moved to Denver, you took a job in New York, you were living on a ranch in Texas . . ."

Deidre was glancing around the backstage of the studio. It was similar to Channel Five, but the energy was different. People actually seemed to enjoy their work.

Juliette looked at her. "So, any of it true?"

Deidre looked back at her. She genuinely didn't know, and she was genuinely very interested in finding out.

"I'll put it this way, Juliette," Deidre said, leaning toward her confidentially. "You wouldn't *believe* where I've been the past three months."

Juliette raised an eyebrow. "Is that so?"

Deidre gave her a slight nod while pretending to be interested in the backstage of the studio.

"Hmmm." Juliette seemed lost in thought. People were whispering and looking at them, curious expressions on their faces.

Deidre whispered to Juliette, "I have to admit, this is kind of fun. I seem to have fallen off everyone's radar. Yesterday's news, I guess."

"No. You didn't feed into it like we had hoped, so the media lost interest even though it went pretty well for us. Marla has the art of the potshot pretty well mastered—it was like child's play. But you two are different birds—I would kill for the kind of loyalty you get from your fans. It wouldn't take long for you to get back into the limelight."

They continued walking and then stopped in front of a set. It was elaborately made up, loud and extravagant. It didn't take Deidre long to realize where they were.

"I take it this isn't the stage for *My Life with Animals*?" she said, half-joking.

Juliette walked into the middle of the set and picked up an overstuffed fuschia pillow, heavily fringed and sequined. "This is our *At Home with Marla Banks* studio bedroom," she said. "We shoot most of the show at her house in Fairfield Hills, but every now and then we have a studio guest or want to have an audience so we'll use it."

Deidre glanced around apprehensively, but tried to keep her voice casual. "Is she here often?"

"Often enough." There was a hint of annoyance in Juliette's voice. "Anyway, she's here today, and I thought you should meet. She's probably in her dressing room."

But right as Juliette turned to lead Deidre down a hallway, a loud, irritated voice snapped, "I said *no autopen*—it looks cheap and artificial. How hard can it be to find a calligraphist to do the signatures on the cards? Jesus!" Then Marla, flanked by a nervous assistant, turned the corner and was facing them.

Marla was dressed in high-heeled, fur-trimmed boots that matched her outfit. Except for the scowl on her face, she looked very festive. There was a look of surprise on her face to see Deidre, but the scowl quickly returned. Marla's searching eyes were strangely familiar to Deidre, and then she remembered why. Kevin.

"Marla, it's almost Christmas, and Hanukkah, and Kwanzaa, and New Year's. No one is available right now." Her assistant looked very nervous.

"Just find somebody, Tommy, before I serve your balls on a plate for Christmas dinner."

Juliette smiled as Tommy scurried away. "You're going to give that poor boy a heart attack, Marla."

"I pay him enough," she answered haughtily. She crossed her arms in front of her chest and pursed her lips.

"Hello, Marla," Deidre said, feigning politeness.

"I mentioned to Marla that you were coming by the studio to talk about some potential programming, so, in case you two haven't officially met, Marla, this is Deidre, Deidre, this is . . ."

"I know who she is," Marla said flatly, tossing her hair. Deidre had to admit that Marla looked even better in person. Marla was ten years older than Deidre, and she looked great.

Juliette said, "Well, I have to get back to my office . . ."

Deidre turned to her, eyes wide. *Do not leave me alone with her!* she implored, but Juliette seemed intentionally oblivious.

". . . so I'll see you two later. Deidre, we'll be in touch about the show, okay?" Juliette gave them a wave and disappeared.

God, she's the devil in disguise, I knew it! Deidre had to force herself to look back at Marla, who was looking at her impatiently.

"Do you smoke?" Marla asked.

"No, I don't." Deidre tried to keep her voice steady.

"Well, I do and I need a cigarette." Marla marched over to her studio bedroom and began rummaging around the side tables, banging drawers and swearing until she found a pack of Dunhill Lights and a lighter. She lit a cigarette, took a deep inhale of smoke, then blew it out slowly, a look of satisfaction on her face.

"Juliette says you have a show. Are you going to do it here?"

"Doesn't seem that way. She liked it, but the spring and summer lineups are full."

"Ha! If she really wanted it, she would take it." Marla shrugged. "So take it somewhere else."

Deidre bit her tongue and then said, "I did. No one's interested."

Marla blew a smoke ring. "That must suck for you."

"It's less than ideal, but I'll manage."

"Of course you will." Marla toyed with a beaded lamp on the desk. "Tell me, did you enjoy your show?"

Deidre was beginning to get uncomfortable. "You know, Marla, I think I'd better go."

"Oh. Well, then, good-bye." Marla took another draw off her cigarette and gave Deidre a condescending wave. She leaned against the desk and crossed her legs.

Deidre turned to leave but on a second thought turned back to face Marla. "To answer your question, I did enjoy my show."

"Really?" Marla looked like she didn't believe her.

"Yes, really."

Marla blew out some smoke. "I think running a show is a major pain in the ass. I've never met more incompetent people in my life." She ground out her cigarette and reached for the pack again.

"You didn't ask me if I thought it was a pain in the ass, you asked me if I enjoyed it."

Marla shook out another cigarette and lit it, offering one to Deidre.

"I already told you, I don't smoke," Deidre said. Her body was completely tense and she felt agitated.

Marla pointed the cigarette at Deidre before lighting it. "I know. You should, it would relax you."

"Like you?"

Marla laughed. "Darling, you don't know the first thing about me."

"And you know everything about me?"

Marla gave her a coy look. "I know where you were these past three months." She took a long drag off her cigarette.

Deidre was startled. "How . . ."

"Claire. Girl is *eight*. Can't keep her mouth shut about anything."

Deidre reddened.

Marla was slowly pacing the stage, as if slowly inspecting each item. "What I find so interesting is how Kevin didn't mention this to me once. Now why is that? And then

I got to thinking, how do they even know each other? How does Deidre McIntosh suddenly find herself in my brother's home out in the boondocks?" Marla was dangerously close and her voice was threatening. For a second, Deidre felt like running.

Instead, she said, "I actually didn't stay in Kevin's place. I didn't quite understand his directions, and it turns out I was in your uncle's cabin instead."

Marla looked incredulous. "What? You're joking!"

If she told Marla the truth, she could expect to hear about it on the next show. But, Deidre shrugged, it would only be a matter of time before she found out anyway. Deidre didn't put it past Marla to exploit her family to further her career. She pictured cameras descending on Jacob's Point, a full house at the Wishbone.

Deidre looked Marla in the eye and said again, "I didn't understand the directions and I broke into Mr. Johnson's—your uncle's—cabin and was staying there."

"I don't believe it. That place is a dump!"

"Trust me, I know. I had to clean it up a bit. I spent the first night in my car."

"Oh my God!" Marla was actually laughing. "I don't fucking believe it!" She was laughing so hard that the ash from her cigarette fell to the ground. "Does Uncle Harry know?"

"I have no idea."

"Ha!" Marla was still laughing and looking at Deidre with a hint of admiration. Even Deidre felt a smile tug at the corners of her mouth. This was probably the high watermark of their relationship—Deidre couldn't expect much more.

"Well, Marla, it was nice meeting you. It's been a pleasure in a sort of self-punishing, masochistic way. I'll show myself out."

She walked past Marla who suddenly grabbed Deidre's arm and leaned forward suspiciously. "Wait a minute . . . where did you get those earrings?" she demanded.

Deidre was certain Marla knew perfectly well where she got them. She touched them lightly. "From an admiring fan." She shook Marla's hand off and began to walk away.

Marla called after her slyly, "My audience is going to *love* that we met and had a little visit."

Deidre stopped and froze. She could already see how Marla would twist everything, find some way to make Deidre look ridiculous. In an instant she thought of a hundred clever retorts but then her brain froze up and she had only one thought: *Marla's going to do what Marla's going to do.* Deidre sighed. Why fight it?

She turned to face her. "Frankly, Marla, I don't give a damn what you tell your audience."

Deidre left a gaping Marla on the stage, and felt, for the first time in a long time, free.

CHAPTER 10

The rare moment is not the moment when
there is something worth looking at
but the moment when we are capable of seeing.

—JOSEPH WOOD KRUTCH

"HOLY KRIS KRINGLE," Lindsey said, a look of delight on her face when Deidre walked into the Wishbone a week before Christmas. She came out from behind the counter to give Deidre a hug. "Are you here for the holidays?" she asked. Mary, Sidney, and Hannah emerged from the kitchen to give Deidre a hug and admire her hair, which was back to her signature color.

The Wishbone was packed and decked out for the holidays. Deidre instantly felt at home as the familiar patrons greeted her and even Janet Everett raised her coffee cup in a semi-salute before returning to her paper. "I am."

Alain's sister was visiting from France for the holidays, and the boys had no problem kicking Deidre out of the guest room and relegating her to the living room couch. Since she still hadn't found a place to live, it only took Deidre one night on the lumpy sofa bed to realize that she needed to make other arrangements.

"And she's bearing cupcakes. I like that in a woman." Bobby nodded approvingly, rubbing his stomach.

"White sponge cake with broken candy canes inside and peppermint frosting," Deidre said, taking one out of the Tupperware and giving it to Lindsey. "There's even little silver balls on top. Baked fresh this morning. They made it through a four-hour drive and not a single one got damaged."

Lindsey accepted the cupcake and licked the frosting. "I'm going to tip the scales at Weight Watchers this week." She reached behind the counter and brought out a newspaper clipping, mounted and laminated on a piece of cardboard. "Here's that article about Thanksgiving dinner. I had Bobby laminate it for you. Have a seat and I'll get you some coffee. I just made a fresh pot."

Deidre sat at the counter as she read the article. While it mentioned Deidre, the article also praised Lindsey. It briefly covered the history of the Wishbone, even mentioning that it had been saved from bankruptcy by a Seattle venture capitalist who frequented Jacob's Point. Lindsey even made a pitch toward the end about the Wishbone's cookbook, *Wishfull Eats*: "The perfect Christmas gift for everyone on your list."

Deidre looked up, surprised. "You finished the cookbook?" She assumed they had abandoned the project due to Deidre's abrupt return to Seattle.

Lindsey laughed. "Well, not when they did the story, but they didn't know that. See there, we gave them that recipe for meatloaf and they printed it alongside the article. After you left we figured we should try to have it ready for the Christmas crowd. It took us a few days to get the recipes down and typed, and then we drove into Pullman to have copies made. They did a nice cover, bound it up . . ." Lindsey reached for a stack of cookbooks on display by the register and handed one to Deidre.

Wishfull Eats: The Best Recipes from Jacob's Point and the Wishbone. Deidre thumbed through it slowly. It was definitely a low-cost production, but it had a nice homey feel to it, with Lindsey's scribbled notes alongside the typed text. It was a bit like inheriting your grandma's old recipe book, with all her notes and improvisations. For Hardware Bobby's Oven-Baked, Old Fashioned Fries (the recipes all had long names), there were notes scribbled like "*Keep in water*" and "*Toss midway through.*" Deidre couldn't tell if they were added as an afterthought or if it was clever marketing. She looked at Lindsey, who was humming to herself and straightening up around the cash register. *Probably an afterthought*, Deidre thought with a chuckle. Lindsey told it like it was, plain and simple.

On the page before the table of contents, Deidre read through what seemed like a rather lengthy list of thank-yous before coming upon her name, last on the list.

And finally, the authors would like to thank Miss Deidre McIntosh for her inspiration and friendship, not to mention her wonderful walnut maple scones. Without her, Wishfull Eats *would just be a dream and not a reality. Our love and thanks!*

"There's a couple of typos that we didn't catch in time, but no matter. People here are sending it off to their friends and family. Cost is eight dollars and ninety-five cents plus tax, buy three for twenty-five dollars. Bobby's getting some more printed up the next time he goes in. We've already sold sixty-three . . ."

"Sixty-four," Sidney said, as she rang up a customer and handed him his copy of the cookbook.

"Thank you!" Lindsey told him before turning back to Deidre, beaming.

Deidre smiled, slightly envious. "I think it's amazing that you did it. In fact, I can't believe you got it done so quickly; I was only gone for three weeks."

"Three weeks is enough time to get a lot of things done," Lindsey pointed out. "Besides, once I told the paper we'd have it, I couldn't back out. We're going to do it again next year, too. The girls found all these other recipes we couldn't fit in, and some of the customers complained that their favorites weren't included. So we're thinking of making it an annual thing, maybe send some of our proceeds to that Make-A-Wish Foundation. Wouldn't that be perfect? The Wishbone, *Wishfull Eats*, Make-A-Wish . . ."

Deidre wished she'd thought of that. "That's a great idea."

Lindsey had arranged the cupcakes and was writing the price on the whiteboard. "Three dollars and fifty cents for one, six dollars for two."

"That seems a bit steep," Deidre said. "They're just cupcakes, after all."

Lindsey waved her away. "I don't tell you how to do your shows; you don't get tell me how to run my business." Lindsey placed the sign in front of the cupcakes, satisfied, and looked back to Deidre. "By the way, whatever happened with that?"

Deidre tried to sound nonchalant. "I got a nibble, but they're not ready to bite. I have to do a lot more work before it'll air."

"So what are you going to be doing while you're here?"

"I don't know . . ." She shot Lindsey a surreptitious look. "I figured I'd finally make the walk around Lake Wish."

Lindsey raised an eyebrow. "Are you here alone?" Her glance looked beyond Deidre, as if she may have missed someone.

"Yes," Deidre said. "Why wouldn't I be?"

"Oh, no reason. So you're going to walk the lake! That should take about an hour, maybe two. Then what? Back to Seattle? You'll be back by nightfall." Lindsey gave Deidre a friendly pat on the hand. "Hey, it was great seeing you." She disappeared into the kitchen.

Deidre followed her. "Lindsey, cut it out. I'm not going anywhere for a while—I was hoping to stay here through New Year's, at least. I can help out at the Wishbone."

Lindsey was breading some flank steak, her arms already covered with flour. She didn't look up. "You're a city girl, Deidre. Jacob's Point may be a fun place for you to visit, but don't kid yourself—this isn't the right place for you. Sounds like you still have things to do back in Seattle."

"Lindsey, I love it here. I *wanted* to come back."

"Deidre, I'm sure that's true. But I got to thinking after you left and I realized that you're a city girl. A working girl. You're smart, you've made a name for yourself, you're successful and independent. You're going to settle for working at the Wishbone for minimum wage and spending your afternoons walking around Lake Wish?" She shook her head and dragged another strip of beef through the flour.

"Okay, fine. The truth is I don't have anything else going on. Nobody seems interested in the show unless I can raise enough money to shoot the first few pilots."

"Well, something tells me you're not going to raise that kind of money bussing tables and serving pie." Lindsey shook off the extra flour from her hands before wiping them on her apron. "Deidre, I have the Wishbone because I love it. Most days, at least. It helps me pay down my mortgage. I get a tax deduction. Overall, I'm pretty happy. Wouldn't mind working a little less and spending more time with my kids, but I'm not complaining. In general I have what I want."

"Well, we can't all be that lucky," Deidre muttered.

"Luck?" Lindsey's eyes narrowed into slits. "This isn't luck. This is hard work. Now don't get me wrong, Deidre. If you want to help me out through the holidays, maybe bake a few things here and there, I'm not going to complain. But at some point you need to decide what it is you need to do, and do it."

"I'm trying to, but no one will give me a chance . . ."

Lindsey held up her hand, uninterested in excuses. "If life's taught me anything, it's that you've got to set your mind on something and do it. Once you believe in yourself, the right people show up to help you. The Wishbone is an example of that."

Deidre knew Lindsey was referring to Kevin saving the diner from bankruptcy. But Deidre didn't see anybody lining up to help her.

Lindsey shooed her out of the kitchen. "Now go on—I've got to get started on dinner. Call me after you get some rest."

DEIDRE SAT IN her car, the engine running. She looked at the house, uncertain as the first day she had arrived in Jacob's Point. And, like that first day, dusk was approaching, and dark storm clouds were gathering. She would need to make a decision soon.

"It's not breaking and entering," she tried to convince herself. "I had an invitation, I know where the key is. It's obviously not being used, and I'm actually doing him a favor because I'm discouraging any break-ins." The fact that there was virtually no crime in Jacob's Point was irrelevant.

"I just need a place to stay until after New Year's," she continued. "I'm sure he would consider this the perfect resolution to all that's happened. He didn't tell me what's going on, I'm not going to tell him. Sounds fair to me."

Deidre heard a rumble in the clouds. A possible snowstorm was on its way.

Suddenly, the engine of her car sputtered and died.

Deidre's mouth dropped open, flabbergasted. She felt a chill run up her spine. It was one thing for her brand-new car to have broken down once in Jacob's Point, but twice? Convinced it was a sign that she was supposed to stay at the house, Deidre tried to start her car again.

To her disappointment, the car started up on the first try, humming and ready to go on a moment's notice.

"Oh," Deidre said, somewhat crestfallen.

She sat for a few more minutes, and thought about what Lindsey said to her at the Wishbone. Then Deidre made a decision, reached for her car keys, and cut the engine. She slipped out of the car, found the east side of the house, and located the spare key. She unlocked the door and let it fall open, her eyes taking in the place for the first time. Then she returned to the car and began unloading her things into Kevin Johnson's house on Lake Wish.

KEVIN'S HOUSE WAS a huge step up from Uncle Harry's cabin. Enormous. It was certainly nothing to complain about, and Deidre was quickly getting over her initial preference of the cabin; there was really no comparison.

The house had teak hardwood floors, with soft Oriental rugs running in between the hallways and covering most of the available floor space. There were two stories, and the stairs and entire upstairs were fully carpeted. The living room sported a huge stone fireplace that also opened into the kitchen. Kevin obviously had an interior decorator or really, really great taste. Deidre drew back the curtains to a huge bay window that opened onto a deck and a spectacular view of Lake Wish.

"Hello," Deidre said softly. The lake looked still and murky, reflecting the dark clouds, but a shimmer of light danced on the tips of the water. Two large birds flew across the lake, toward Deidre, then turned and landed near the edge of the water. Deidre watched them, and then realized after a minute that they seemed to be watching her.

"Sorry," she said, stepping away from the window to give them some privacy. She turned back to the house, and walked into the kitchen. Deidre fell in love immediately. It was the kind of kitchen an executive chef would have in his home. Then she remembered her telephone conversation with Kevin at the Wishbone, when he was waxing on about the kitchen and how he rarely used it.

"That," Deidre said aloud, as she opened the fridge and found a bottle of chardonnay, "can be taken care of easily." After promising to replace the wine on her next trip into town, Deidre opened the bottle, poured herself a glass, and set about moving her things in before it got too dark.

• • •

AFTER UNCLE HARRY'S cabin and the small guest room in Alain and William's house, having seven bedrooms and five and a half baths, as well as a gourmet kitchen, dining room, two living rooms, a home office, and, bless Kevin, a working Jacuzzi, was absolute heaven. Deidre remembered reading about a woman who had so many rooms in her house that she had one room dedicated exclusively for wrapping gifts. In this house, Deidre thought admiringly, she could actually pull that off.

Then the memory sharpened in her mind, and Deidre remembered that the woman was Marla.

There was nothing Deidre could do to improve the interior of the house, short of adding fresh flowers or fragrant evergreen sprigs. Unlike the cabin, Kevin's house already had pictures on all the walls, including black-and-white photographs of Lake Wish and Jacob's Point like the ones in the cabin. But there were also family pictures, including ones with Marla and Henry Johnson, and it was surreal to see them in such a different context. Deidre found herself lingering around the pictures that had Kevin in them, studying his face, tracing his outline in the photograph. She saw pictures of Claire, her arms around Kevin and beaming, the Magic Kingdom behind them.

She passed a telephone in the hallway, hesitated, then steeled herself and continued upstairs. She just wanted to take a hot bath and crawl into bed. Deidre couldn't bring herself to stay in the master suite, which had a fireplace as well and would have been her first choice. She still felt very much like a guest and didn't want to get too comfortable. She just needed a place to stay for a little while, and any of the other six rooms would do just fine. She found herself choosing the room farthest away from the master suite and got ready for bed. When she finally nestled in between the feather bed and down comforter, she let out a happy sigh and fell asleep.

THE NEXT MORNING, Deidre plugged in her laptop, made a cup of tea, and sat down, ready to brainstorm and figure out what to do next. She had a view of the lake, a fire was roaring, and classical music piped in from the living room. Fresh snowfall was on the ground, about three inches thick, pure and white. It was perfect. She was ready.

Her mind drew a blank.

"Come on, McIntosh," she finally muttered after fifteen minutes, getting up to stretch. An hour later, she still had nothing.

Deidre paced, then changed the music to something more contemporary and tried to dance and shake it out of her body. Still nothing.

"I need brain food," she finally concluded, and began rummaging through the box of staples she had brought in with her. She decided on baking gingerbread. The house needed to be filled with the aroma of gingerbread.

As she worked, sifting cups of flour with baking soda, salt, nutmeg, cinnamon, and cloves, Deidre's mind started to relax. She combined the honey and molasses in a small bowl, beating it by hand and scraping down the sides.

Seattle Revealed needed a chance to be born, and Deidre needed to stop acting like an overprotective mother afraid to let her child play in the sandbox with the other kids. That much was clear. But how? And in the meantime, how could she make a living?

Deidre whisked oil, applesauce, brown sugar, and eggs. She chopped the crystallized ginger into small pieces and a warm, sweet smell filled the room.

An idea started to form in her mind.

She stirred the dry ingredients into the applesauce mixture, then poured the finished batter into several small baking pans.

By the time Deidre slid them into the ovens, she knew what she could do. She cleaned up then went to the phone and called Lindsey.

"Can you escape for an hour or so? I have an idea that I need some feedback on, but I have something baking in the oven."

"Good. Those cupcakes are gone."

"I'm baking gingerbread—you can have half of it for the Wishbone. So what do you say—can you come over for a cup of tea? Or I can come by the Wishbone later . . ."

"Nah, I'd love to get out. Where are you?"

Deidre hesitated, then said, "Kevin Johnson's place on the lake. Do you know where it is?"

Lindsey chuckled. "Everyone knows where it is. I cook dinner for the family whenever he has them all visiting."

It was all falling into place. Deidre was smiling inside; she couldn't wait to tell Lindsey her idea. "Great. Okay, see you soon."

WHEN LINDSEY ARRIVED, her eyes got wide. "Each time I see this place, I am more amazed, but of course I never get the chance to really gawk. What is this, a million-dollar house?"

"At least," Deidre said, leading her into the kitchen.

"So I take it you and he are . . ." Lindsey waited for Deidre to finish the sentence.

"No, we're not," Deidre said. "He offered his place to me a few months ago when I was looking for a place to stay."

Lindsey looked impressed as she peered into the fireplace, and then walked into the kitchen. "You must be pretty good friends for him to let you do that. I could live in this kitchen, I tell you!"

"You and me both." Deidre cleared her throat. "But, uh, this thing with Kevin and me is . . . a little complicated, so I'd appreciate it if you wouldn't let everyone know where I was staying."

"No problem," Lindsey said. "I'll just tell them that you're still staying at old Harry's place."

Deidre gasped and spun around. "How did you know I was staying there?"

"Like I said, everyone knows what's going on. This is a small town, you know." The gingerbread was cooling on the wire racks and Lindsey sniffed the air appreciatively.

Deidre poured Lindsey a cup of tea. Lindsey chose a chair by the window, and looked out onto the lake. "That is the view," she said, whistling.

"It sure is."

Lindsey took a sip of tea. "Did you walk around it yet?"

"No, but I will."

Lindsey rolled her eyes. "Sure you will. So, what's your great idea?"

Deidre turned to face her, suddenly energized. "Are

you ready? *Catering*. We could have a catering company! Here, in Jacob's Point!"

"We?"

"Sure, why not? We'd have to do a little research to see how many caterers are in the area, but there are plenty of events—weddings, holiday parties, birthdays—that could keep us busy. You have the commercial kitchen, and now that you have all the extra help at the Wishbone, the catering would be more like a complement to the business—*Wishfull Eats Catering Co.* I mean, you're doing it anyway, like for the Johnsons . . . why not make a business out of it?"

Lindsey shook her head decisively. "Thanks, Deidre, but I'm not interested." She took a sip of her tea.

God, why was everybody saying that to her these days?

"I do it every now and then, but truth be known, it's too much stress. Especially for the Johnsons. Harry and Kevin are all right, but the rest of them . . ." Lindsey shook her head again. "I need that like I need a bullet in my head. I like the pace of the Wishbone and the cookbook is so new that I don't think I could really take anything else on."

"But you'd make more money, be able to pay down your mortgage faster."

Lindsey reached for some honey and stirred it into her tea. "Well, of course, but everything has its price and that's just not worth it to me."

"Okay. Well, what about a bakery? This town needs a good bakery. Look at how quickly you sell everything I give you."

"That's because you're baking it and because I don't feed them enough. I don't know if you would ever get your money back if you had to build a bakery in this town. I just want to pay off my note and own it free and clear—I don't want to start all over with a new business and new mortgage. Plus I don't care for the early hours."

"Fine," Deidre said. She didn't give up. "Okay, what about if we just did meal replacement? Have a menu for every day of the week, a dinner-in-a-box sort of thing? It's huge in the city."

Lindsey laughed. "I already do that. It's called *to go*."

"What about . . ."

Lindsey put up a hand to stop her. "Deidre, like I said before, you've got a lot of good ideas. I'll probably regret it someday that I didn't listen to some of them. But I have to tell you, I think you're grasping at straws here."

"What? What do you mean?"

"You don't need any more good ideas. You got a great one already, that show you've been working on. Just raise the money or whatever it is they said you need to do."

"Lindsey, I have no idea how to ask people for money. I wouldn't know where to start."

"I'm no expert, but when it looked like we were going to lose the Wishbone, we told everybody we knew. So my guess is that you just start telling people about what it is you want to do, and if they're interested, you ask them to support it financially."

"Show me the money?"

"That's my motto. No need to make it more complicated than it already is." Lindsey checked her watch. "I've got to be getting back to the Wishbone. Hannah and Sidney are going to be on their own tonight and I just want to make sure they're all set. Then I need to see if Bobby has any new videos in. I promised to bring one home for my kids. It's movie night tonight." Lindsey put her teacup in the sink.

"Here, take these loaves with you for the Wishbone," Deidre said, busily wrapping the gingerbread. "And take one home for your family."

Lindsey accepted the gingerbread from Deidre. "I'm going to do a spinach and mushroom quiche tomorrow, so stop by, it should be good. I figure everyone's going to be eating heavy at Christmas, I'd better start serving them something light."

"Sounds good." They walked to the door.

"And Deidre?" Lindsey called to her, before getting into her car.

"Yes?"

"Get a tree. 'Tis the season, you know." She waved and got into her car, and drove away.

Deidre glanced at the undecorated front door, then went back to the kitchen, thoroughly discouraged and disenchanted.

As usual, Lindsey was right: Deidre didn't need to come up with another good idea, she already had one. And the content for *Seattle Revealed* was done, as was the initial proposal.

But since none of the stations were willing to take it on, Deidre needed a Plan B. She needed to come up with a way to attract investors so that she could produce the first six pilots herself. Caroline had already done her part by helping prepare the financials, but Deidre needed someone who could tell her what potential investors would be looking for. Somebody who knew how to raise money. Somebody who was in the business and could give her a few pointers.

Somebody like Kevin.

There had to be somebody else, she argued with herself. But there wasn't. And if she wanted to make *Seattle Revealed* a reality, she was going to need his help.

Deidre flip-flopped a few more times before finally dialing his number. He answered on the second ring. "Hello?"

"Hi, Kevin. It's Deidre."

There was a long pause. "I'm glad you called," he said simply.

She cleared her throat, trying not to think about how comforting it was to hear his voice. *This relationship has no future*, she told herself. "I don't know if now is a good time . . ."

"No, it's good," he said. "I was hoping you'd call. I'm sorry I couldn't talk about things more over Thanksgiving, but I didn't want to get into it with Claire around. Then I had to fly to Germany . . ."

"Really, Kevin, it's fine. I . . . don't want to talk about it. That's actually not why I'm calling."

"It's not?"

"No. I need some advice about how to raise money for this new show I'm hoping to launch."

"Let me see if I have this straight: you're calling me for financial advice but you don't want to talk about our relationship or what happened?" His voice was incredulous.

Even Deidre could see how ridiculous that was. What was she thinking? "Maybe this wasn't such a good idea."

"No, wait." Kevin sighed. "Tell me what you need."

"I need you to educate me about angel investors and venture capital financing. Nobody picked up my new show, *Seattle Revealed,* so I need to shoot the pilots myself."

"That's ambitious."

"Well, that's my goal and I'm not giving up until I can give *Seattle Revealed* a decent chance. It's a great concept but nobody wants to take a chance without seeing what the finished product looks like."

"This isn't going to be a ten-minute conversation, Deidre. It would be much easier in person. Are you in the city? I can come by and pick you up and we can get a drink at the W."

"Ah, no," she said quickly, glancing around the living room as if he might know she was there. "I'm, uh, in my pajamas and don't feel like going out. Plus it would just make things harder if we saw each other again."

"What are you saying? That if we saw each other again you wouldn't be able to resist me?" His voice was teasing.

He nailed it right on the head, but that wasn't the point. It was a dead-end relationship that would only hurt Deidre in the end. Reluctantly, she said, "Never mind. I'm going to hang up now."

"Fine, fine, I'll stop," he said hastily, the playfulness gone. He took a deep breath. "What would you like to know?"

CHRISTMAS WAS THREE days away. Deidre had been working nonstop for over a week. She hardly had time to bake enough for the Wishbone, but when Lindsey finally called to complain, Deidre whipped up a triple batch of chocolate cherry crackle cookies and promised to bring them in before noon.

She was a few minutes late, but hurried in with the Tupperware tucked under her arm, managing a quick "Hello, everyone," before turning around and heading back out.

"Whoa, slow down there, missy," Lindsey said, stepping in front of Deidre to block her from leaving. "Where's the fire?"

"Sorry, Lindsey, I'm in a rush. What's up?"

"What's up is that you need to slow down there a bit." Lindsey steered her back into the restaurant. "Come on, have a cup of coffee with me. Fill me in on what's been going on with you. Have you walked around the lake yet?"

Deidre glanced at the clock. "You know, I really need to get back. I'm kind of on a roll . . ."

"You've been on a roll for eight days now. Things going well with your show?"

"Great. Excellent, actually."

"Well, I'm sure a few minutes won't kill you. This is Jacob's Point, not Seattle—get the point?"

Deidre got it. Lindsey slid into a booth and Deidre sat down opposite of her.

"Mary, bring us some of those cookies and two coffees, please." Lindsey gave Deidre a broad smile. "So, you didn't answer my question. Walk around the lake yet?"

"Actually, no. Not yet. I sit on the dock a lot, but I haven't walked around it yet. I will."

Lindsey rolled her eyes. "Did you at least get a tree?" she asked.

"No," Deidre said. She would have loved a tree, but she didn't want to risk having one at Kevin's house. As good of a cleaner as she was, she was sure to lose a few pine needles here and there.

"Oh, good," Lindsey said, then quickly took a bite of the cookie. "These really are delicious; we should definitely include them in the cookbook next year. Are they easy to make? I'm thinking about having some kind of a rating system, you know, ease of preparation . . ."

A thought occurred to Deidre and she clutched at Lindsey's hand. "Lindsey, *do not get me a tree*. I do *not* want a tree." Deidre felt desperate as Lindsey continued to finish the cookie and take a sip of coffee.

"I won't, I won't. What's the big fuss for anyway?"

"Um, I just don't think Kevin would appreciate me bringing a tree into his house, you know?"

"Don't worry so much," Lindsey told her. "You worry too much, you know?"

"Yeah, well, I'm getting even more worried as we speak. What's going on?"

"Nothing. Hey, that blueberry cobbler you did the other day was heaven. What was the stuff on top? I didn't recognize it."

"Vanilla hard sauce." Lindsey wrote it down on her order pad as Deidre started to panic. Something was definitely up, but small town hospitality could get her in serious trouble with Kevin if he found out she was there. "Lindsey, please, please, *please* tell me you are not getting me a tree," she begged.

"I already told you, *I'm not getting you a tree*. Relax. I just thought it would help put you in the holiday mood, that's all."

"I'm in the mood just fine," Deidre said. She pointed to the Wishbone's evergreen in the corner, overloaded with tinsel and mismatched ornaments. "I can just come here and enjoy your tree, right? So can we drop it? Please?"

Lindsey covered her ears. "I'm not talking about it anymore. Enjoy the tree here and let's leave it at that."

"Thank you."

"You're welcome." Lindsey glanced at her watch. "Look at the time! I should get back into the kitchen. I still need to get some more wrapping paper from Bobby—my kids want to finish wrapping all the presents tonight. You have any plans for Christmas?"

Deidre perked up at the question, thinking Lindsey would invite her over. "No."

"Oh. Well, maybe we'll get some fresh snow for a white Christmas and you can curl up in front of that huge fireplace and play some Bing Crosby. That'll be nice."

Christmas for one in a huge, empty house didn't sound quite so nice to Deidre, Bing Crosby or no Bing Crosby. She was tempted to go back to Seattle just for a couple of days to be with Alain and William, but Alain's sister was in town and from the sound of things, they had made some big plans for the holidays.

Lindsey looked at Deidre's body disapprovingly as they stood up. "Did you have lunch yet?"

"No. I actually haven't been eating much lately."

"No kidding. You look like a rail. Hold on." Lindsey disappeared into the kitchen and returned a few minutes later with a full grocery bag. "Here. This will tide you over until tomorrow."

Deidre peered inside, astounded. "This is too much food, Lindsey."

"So you'll have leftovers. I don't have time to split it up and put it in smaller containers. Just take it. It can be a partial trade for the cookies, I'll pay you the rest when I see you next."

"Deal."

Deidre drove back to the house, anxious to get back to work. But when she pulled up to the house and grabbed the bag of food, the smell of Lindsey's homemade chicken potpie made her hungry. She walked toward the house, debating whether or not to bother heating it up, when she realized something was different.

Really different. Deidre stared at the house, not comprehending, and then it dawned on her.

There were Christmas lights on the front of the house and a wreath on the door.

She was going to kill Lindsey, but Deidre couldn't help smiling. Bob Carson or Dr. Hensen must have come by while she was at the Wishbone. It was a total setup, which made perfect sense: Lindsey never had time to sit around, drink a cup of coffee, and gab, at least not for more than two or three minutes. It just wasn't her style.

Deidre walked up the path. She went to unlock the door, but the door fell open when she touched the key to the lock.

That's funny, Deidre thought with trepidation. *I'm sure I locked it.*

She stepped inside and heard Christmas music wafting in from the living room. Bing Crosby. And the house was warm, as if a fire were burning. The smile disappeared from Deidre's face as she stepped into the living room and almost dropped the bag on the floor.

Kevin Johnson was sitting on the couch, relaxed, and sipping a drink from a mug.

"Hi, honey," he said. "I'm home." His smile was lean and even, and he acted as if nothing was out of the ordinary. He looked as handsome as ever. A Christmas tree decorated with lights blinked behind him.

It took Deidre a moment to get over her shock and find her voice. "Kevin," she finally managed. "I, uh . . ."

"Eggnog?" He nodded toward the kitchen. "I made a batch to get us through the night. Don't worry, it's heavily spiked. We seem to get along better under the influence."

"I can explain . . ." She looked around, amazed. "How did you get this up so quickly?"

"I had help."

"Who?"

"Little elves." He stood up and strode across the room, brushing past her. She got a whiff of his aftershave, crisp notes of birch leaf and vetiver. It was the same Kevin that she remembered, but something about him was different. He was just as handsome, just as strong, just as confident, but there was something else.

He was in the kitchen, ladling a generous serving of eggnog. He came back to the living room, took the bag of food from her, and handed her the eggnog.

"I'll take your coat," he said, his hands already on the lapels of her jacket.

Determined. That was it. Deidre licked her lips, curious and nervous.

"Kevin, I know this looks bad," Deidre began, as he unwound the scarf from around her neck. "I just needed a place to stay and I . . ."

"I got a tree; do you like it? I forgot to get decorations, but I have plenty of lights." He motioned over to the window, where Deidre saw boxes and boxes of Christmas lights. His lip curled ruefully. "I may have gotten a bit carried away."

Deidre took a sip of eggnog, which was one step away from rocket fuel. Kevin seemed to read her mind.

"One quart bourbon whiskey, one pint brandy, one cup rum. Plus milk, eggs, sugar, and all that other fun stuff. It's a Johnson family recipe." He held up his glass. "Cheers."

Deidre placed her cup to the side. "I'm assuming it's not a random coincidence that you came down here and happened to discover that I was staying here," she ventured.

"That would be a valid assumption."

"So how did you know?"

Kevin stepped up close to her until his warm breath tickled her ear. "I have caller ID, remember?"

Deidre reddened. How could she have forgotten?

His body leaned into hers, his lips brushing her cheek. "Nice earrings," he murmured, nipping at her earlobe before turning and walking to the couch. He sat down, crossed his legs and took a leisurely sip of his eggnog. He looked comfortable and relaxed, with a king-of-the-castle air about him. The house was definitely designed to suit Kevin; he looked picture-perfect in it.

Deidre's hand inadvertently touched her earlobe, fingering the silver drop earrings that he had given her over Thanksgiving. She knew how this looked: staying in his place, wearing the earrings he gave her, calling him to ask for advice . . .

Wait a minute. She suddenly didn't care about how it looked to him; she realized how it looked to *her*. It was obvious that she definitely wasn't over Kevin. How could she be? She was crazy about him, and it was apparent to everybody but her.

Still, this wasn't exactly the Kevin she had dealt with in the past. And that made her nervous.

"When I realized you were staying at my place, I decided to give Lindsey a call. She tried to play dumb at first, but when I told her that you and I had spoken, and that I knew you were here, she couldn't stop talking. She told me how great the place looked, and how comfortable you were, and that you didn't have a tree." He was assured, confident, and Deidre could hear the cockiness in his voice.

Out of the corner of her eye, Deidre saw her laptop and papers spread out all over the kitchen table, and she couldn't remember if she had made the bed this morning. In any case, it was clear that she had made herself at home.

"So I got you a tree." He gave her a smile, but there was something slightly impetuous about the way he was looking at her. "*Us*, a tree," he corrected.

She struggled to keep her voice calm, not sure what that meant. "When did you call her?"

He shrugged. "Sometime last week."

"You knew for a week that I was here but you didn't come down earlier or call?"

He stretched out his long legs. "I was working. I figured you probably weren't going anywhere anytime soon. I also figured that Lindsey had no idea that you were staying here without my knowledge."

Deidre pressed her lips together. "Well, um, I can get my things together and head back to Seattle."

"Why? I canceled my trip to Bermuda so I could help you with your proposal. You know what you have that most entrepreneurs or new ventures do not? Buyability."

Her nose wrinkled. "What's that?"

"My point exactly." He put down his eggnog. "I figured you would need me to explain it to you, so here I am."

"Kevin, you didn't have to cancel your trip just to come down and tell me that," she said faintly. He was walking toward her slowly and she was backing up, nervous again.

"Well, I figure it'll take us a few days to sort through things, for me to apologize and for you to forgive me, for you to apologize and me to forgive you. And then we can get down to business."

"Well, I . . ."

He was in front of her. "Deidre, honey?"

"Yes?"

"Give it a rest."

He pulled her to him and wrapped his arms around her, almost a bit too tight, as if he were expecting her to wrestle away. But Deidre's body was already softening, molding itself into the solidness of his body. He touched her lips gently with the tips of his fingers.

"Okay, so maybe this will take a bit longer than I thought." He brushed his lips across her forehead.

"I don't think this is a good idea," she murmured unconvincingly, eyes closed. Her hands rediscovered his broad chest, his arms, his neck.

"Of course you don't." He laced his fingers through her hair.

"What about your family?"

He pulled her into him even tighter. "Deidre, did it ever occur to you that you might actually be the only woman who would even stand a chance of surviving in my family? In case you haven't noticed, you fit right in. You're not exactly short of personality, either."

In an odd way, it almost made sense. "But . . ."

He had enough and was suddenly kissing her, his mouth slanted over hers as he pulled her tight against him.

His mouth was hot in her mouth, his tongue stroking her, wanting more of her.

Deidre felt his hardness against her, and she held her breath as she felt the heat through his jeans. She pulled out his shirt, slipping her hands under his clothes to touch his body. He was warm. She loved the feel of his skin, his flat stomach.

"Still don't think this is a good idea?" he asked, breaking their kiss and looking at her.

Deidre loved those eyes, too. "Actually, I think this is a great idea," she said, trying to look mad, her hands continuing to roam over his body.

Kevin's hands were roaming deliberately under her sweater, his touch sending shivers up her spine. He traced a line up and down her back.

"You are an impossible woman to pin down," he said. His hands slid to the front of her chest, brushing right below the heaviness of her breasts, lingering along the cup of her bra, making her nipples erect at the mere suggestion that they would be next.

"Try," Deidre said, and he lowered her onto the floor, his weight pressing against her as he slowly edged himself between her legs. He rained kisses on her face, her neck, the sensitive clefts below her ears. Deidre hooked her leg against his and rubbed herself against him, a soft moan escaping her lips.

"When you left on Thanksgiving, I had no idea where you were going or how to get ahold of you. Then, when I was in Germany, I heard you had been at the station. And then you disappeared again." His hands slid down her leg, then settled in between her thighs to rest at the warm place between her legs, making Deidre wet with desire. She strained against his hand and was rewarded with a gentle, teasing squeeze. "Then, suddenly, I get a phone call. And here you were, under my very nose, staying in my home. Without my permission, of course, but I figured it had to be a sign."

"You told me I was welcome here anytime," she reminded him, breathing heavily. She pulled off his sweater and impatiently unbuttoned his shirt. His broad shoulders were muscular and tan, and Deidre ran her hands over them with great appreciation.

Kevin had begun to unzip her jeans and was slowly sliding them down her legs. His breath got heavy and ragged when he saw her panties: black, silky, skimpy, incredibly comfortable and intensely sexy. He stopped, for a second, and just looked at her, eyes smoldering, and then proceeded to impatiently peel off her jeans and throw them across the room.

"Tell me you came prepared," she panted.

"Like a Boy Scout," he said. He nipped her ear. "And you should know that I have plenty more in the suitcase as well. I have every intention of using every last one before the new year."

Kevin brought her hands behind her, and as he did, he brushed the bare cheeks of her buttocks. Her panties, skimpy, sexy thong bikinis, had only a trace of fabric holding them together. The look in Kevin's eyes was unmistakable. His dark brown eyes were smoldering as his hands followed the curve of her buttocks, gently releasing her wrists. He cupped a cheek in each hand and pulled her to him once again.

"Is there anything else you want to talk about?" he said huskily.

Deidre shook her head, speechless, her own eyes heavy and lidded with desire as he continued to mold her in his hands. "I . . . think I'm good."

Permission granted, Kevin removed her sweater in one deft move so that she was standing in front of him wearing only her bra and panties. Kevin was shirtless but still had on his jeans, which Deidre began to undo. She hooked her fingers in his boxers and pulled them down with the jeans, freeing him. Deidre wet her lips with the tip of her tongue, eyeing him hungrily as he led her to the couch.

The fire was beginning to burn down as Kevin hovered over Deidre, poised and ready to enter her, taking one last look at her spread out beneath him. Deidre raised her hips to meet him, arching when he plunged deeply into her, gasping out his name as he began slow, rhythmic thrusts, his eyes closed, his fingers digging into her hips as he pulled her to him. Deidre, her long legs wrapped around him and her arms holding onto the edge of the couch above her head, stayed with him as long as she could and then she came, so deeply and intensely that her entire body shook, every inch of her body at full attention, her cries so passionate that Kevin followed quickly after, his back arched, every muscle strained, as he gave one final thrust and joined Deidre.

Later, when Kevin had stoked the fire and wrapped them both in a blanket, Deidre's hands began to dance over his body and he rolled onto his back so she could sit astride him. He took her again, cupping a breast in each hand, beneath the blanket, their cries muffled. And when Deidre had gotten up to shower and change, Kevin stepped into the steamy stream of water and they joined together again, Deidre on her tiptoes and grasping the showerhead as Kevin thrust into her from behind, kissing her neck and shoulders, the water streaming down over their bodies.

In the master suite, exhausted and fully satiated, they curled up into each other's arms and fell asleep.

Chapter 11

Life shrinks or expands in proportion to one's courage.
—ANAÏS NIN

THE LAKE LOOKED magnificent from the master suite, a very different view from the small guest room down the hall. Deidre awoke, a small smile tugging at the corners of her mouth as she stretched, then burrowed deeper under the covers. The bed was still warm from where Kevin had been, and she was about to call his name when he appeared in the doorway, clad in a navy monogrammed bathrobe, a breakfast tray in hand.

"Good morning," he said, and crossed the room to put the tray in Deidre's lap. He leaned over and gave her a long, luxurious kiss. God, she loved his kisses. "I thought I would beat you to the punch this time and be the first one up. Just in case you had any ideas about chasing me out of my own home."

"Very funny," Deidre said, kissing him back. She stared at the overwhelming amount of food in front of her, impressed. Orange juice, coffee, four eggs, toast, two of Deidre's cranberry orange scones, and six links of sausage.

"I didn't know what you liked," Kevin said, shedding the bathrobe and crawling back into bed with her.

Deidre bit into a slice of toast when she realized she was starving. Kevin watched her, smiling.

"You're not going to eat?" Deidre asked, taking a bite of the sausage while spreading butter on a scone.

"I was nibbling as I cooked," he said. "Plus it took me several tries before I got it to look this nice, so I had to eat the evidence. I've been up for . . ." He glanced at the clock. ". . . almost an hour trying to get this damn breakfast done."

Deidre leaned over and gave him a greasy kiss. "It's wonderful. Thank you."

"I couldn't find any fruit—are you out?"

"I used it up for a fruit tart for Dr. Hensen. I'm surprised you didn't see it and put that on here as well."

The guilty look on his face revealed that there probably wasn't any fruit tart left.

Deidre smiled. "I'll come up with something else, no worries." She took another bite—everything tasted so good. She wiped the corners of her mouth and took a sip of coffee.

Kevin was propped up on one arm, watching her eat. "I didn't have a chance to tell you, but Juliette told me she thought your program had some merit." His hands were roaming under the blankets again and finally rested between her thighs. He gave her a mischievous grin.

Deidre snorted. "*Merit*? It has more than merit. It's in line to pick up an Emmy." She started in surprise as Kevin did a little exploration. "I've contacted everyone I want to help with the first six pilots. Almost everyone said yes."

"That's a lot of first pilots."

"Well, I'm calling them pilots but the truth is, I know the program will get picked up the moment someone sees it. I want to be ready to go with it. All I have to do now is get some money to produce the segments and, thanks to your excellent tutelage, I'm ready to hit the pavement."

Kevin began stroking her, his eyes never leaving her face. "I can help," he said, looking innocent.

She knew that was coming. "Forget it."

"Deidre . . ."

"Kevin, I don't want your money."

He looked at her dryly. "You're going to have to work on your pitch a bit. That's not exactly what most investors expect to hear."

She smiled. "Look, I've done my homework and I have a strong list of potential investors, sponsors, foundations. It'll get done." Her thoughts were becoming incoherent as Kevin continued to watch and touch her. "I . . . I . . . just don't want to mix . . . I mean, I . . . I'm just . . . not . . ." Her sentence ended in a moan.

"Let me help," Kevin said again, moving the breakfast tray and pulling her closer, his hands working her into a fevered pitch.

"Not . . . with . . . this."

The tray safely put away, a small smile played on his lips as he slipped one, then two fingers inside of her.

"Oh, God," Deidre gasped, bucking against his hand. Kevin moved between her legs, hovering above her, kissing her. Then he began his descent down her body.

"Say you'll let me help," he said, his tongue grazing a nipple and tugging it gently with his teeth.

"No." Deidre's hands pulled at his thick hair.

He continued to plant kisses down to her stomach, teasing her as she writhed in anticipation of what was to come.

"I'd really . . . rather not talk . . . about that . . . right now." She was practically panting.

"So say yes, and we can focus on . . . other things." He dipped his head below her soft curls, withdrawing his fingers and replacing them with his tongue, spreading her legs apart. His mouth seemed to cover her completely, warm and wet, and the erotic sensation rocketed throughout her body.

He had her where he wanted her, and he knew it. Deidre was practically coming off the bed, her hips and back arched, her fingers entwined in his hair and she pulled his head closer to her. She was close, very close, and it wouldn't take much more.

"Are you going to let me help, Deidre?" he demanded.

Deidre opened her heavy-lidded eyes and looked down at him through her thick lashes. She was on the verge of coming. Her lips were wet and she was breathing heavily, her face flush, her chest heaving unevenly. Despite all of this, she managed to whisper, "No."

"No?"

"No." Deidre held up his chin and looked him straight in the eye, her breath still erratic and uneven. "Not with this. And I don't want to talk about it anymore." Her fingers ran along his shoulders and she gently raked his back, her voice low and sultry, "I think we should focus on those . . . other things you were talking about instead." She started suggesting what some of those "other things" might be.

She knew she had won when his eyes were ablaze once again and she could feel him against her, harder than ever. It looked like he was having a difficult time concentrating.

"You're impossible," he finally rasped, dipping his head to taste her some more, his tongue probing with a vengeance that sent her screaming over the edge a minute later.

Impossible. He had no idea.

THEY MANAGED TO get out of the bedroom by early afternoon, and Deidre insisted on returning the favor of breakfast by making a late lunch of leftover homemade vegetable soup and bread.

"You made this bread?" Kevin looked incredulous as he tore off another chunk.

"*And* the soup," she said, in case he had forgotten.

"The soup is great, but the bread is amazing!"

"Baking has always been my first love," she said. "And, by the way, you have a great oven. Your whole kitchen is like . . . Disneyland for me. And in saying that, I do not mean to imply that your uncle's kitchen was . . . insufficient." They looked at each other and burst out laughing.

Kevin shook his head in disbelief. "What you did to his cabin is pretty amazing. Claire loved it: it was such a rat trap before that I wouldn't even let her go in it. Now she wants to make it her secret hideaway, like a little clubhouse."

"*A clubhouse?*" Deidre shook her head. "She's *eight*, Kevin. An eight-year-old doesn't need a two-bedroom cabin with appliances. God, *I* can't even find a place to live, and you want to give her a nine-hundred-square-foot clubhouse?"

"Uncle Harry's not going to let her have the cabin, so I wouldn't get too worked up about it."

"I'm not worked up," Deidre said, clearly worked up. "I don't know her very well, and I know she's important to you, but I think she's just a little . . . demanding."

He looked amused.

"Okay, what? *I'm* demanding? Is that what you want me to say?" Deidre busied herself by clearing the table.

"I didn't say that. *You* said that. What's the matter, don't you like kids?"

"I love kids! It's just that . . . I don't think she likes me."

"Well, maybe not yet, but then again, she hasn't exactly seen you at your best."

Deidre flung a dish towel at him. "I can throw a tantrum with the best of them."

"Yes, I know that well," Kevin said, coming up behind her. "Actually, I thought that you of all people would understand her better than most."

"Me? Why would you think that?"

"I don't know. You're both feisty, independent, tough on the outside, fragile on the inside. You're both too smart for your own good, not to mention stubborn beyond belief . . ."

She put a hand over his mouth to get him to stop talking. "Stop, stop. I get it."

He pulled her to him and wrapped his arms around her, kissing her neck. Deidre sighed. She loved being in his arms.

"I will try to be more compassionate when I see her again," she said.

"I'm not asking you to," he said. He kissed a trail down her shoulder.

"I know," she said simply. "I'm not making any promises, I'm just saying I'll check my ego at the door and give her a break. I mean, she is *eight* . . ."

Kevin gave her a kiss and looked deeply into her eyes. "Want to go for a walk?"

Deidre gazed back at him. God help her, she was falling hard for this man. "All right."

THERE WAS, DEIDRE discovered, a well-worn path around Lake Wish. It wasn't obvious until you began walking on it; from a distance it looked rocky and precarious, one of the reasons Deidre had not felt confident enough to do it. But standing on the muddy path now, Deidre saw that the path was actually flat and even. They walked in silence, hand in hand, stepping over stray branches and rocks, careful not to slip on wet or icy patches.

About halfway around, they came upon a small clearing and rested. There was some debris on the ground—an empty water bottle, the foil wrapper from an energy bar. Kevin picked them up in disgust.

"Tourists," was all he said, shoving them into the pocket of his jacket.

"How do they get here if they don't have access from your place or the cabin?"

"There's a trail from the road that leads to this clearing—it's in all the guidebooks so we occasionally get people who are on their way out of state. Birders like to come here in the summer as well. But as you can see, there's no picnic tables or public trash cans so some of them leave their garbage behind for me to pick up."

Deidre nestled in his arms as they looked over the lake.

"Ever count how many trees are around Lake Wish?" Deidre asked.

"Not for a while, but I don't think we've lost too many since I counted last." His breath was warm on her ear.

Deidre turned to look at him expectantly. "How many?"

"Six hundred and seventy-four. Fortunately the population of Jacob's Point is a fraction of that, so we're in good shape."

"Are you superstitious?" Deidre teased.

"No, but I have a certain reverence for customs and beliefs that have been around longer than you or me." They sat on a tree stump for a while longer and then got up to continue their walk.

"You know, I have to say I was intimidated about doing this walk," Deidre admitted. "But it's really not so bad."

"Things never are."

"Never bad?"

"No. Never as bad as we think they are."

The walk, with their occasional stops to rest, took them less than forty-five minutes.

"Should we do it again tomorrow? Same time, same place?"

Deidre gave him a kiss. "It's a date."

They walked into the house and Kevin started to pull off his shoes, scarf, and jacket. "I'm going to build us a fire," he said, "and then I have a few ideas on how we can spend the rest of the afternoon."

"Sorry, I can't," Deidre said. She picked up her purse.

"What?"

"*Some* of us have to work. I need to go in to town to get a few things, then come back and send some faxes. And since *somebody* polished off Dr. Hensen's fruit tart, I need to stock up on more flour, sugar, and fruit. Bobby's not planning any runs into Pullman until after Christmas and since tomorrow's Christmas Eve he probably won't be getting any deliveries for a couple of days. I need to get there before the last-minute shoppers come in."

Kevin laughed and blew on his hands to warm them up. "Somehow I wouldn't worry about that."

Deidre pretended to be offended as she headed toward the front door. "Jacob's Point isn't that sleepy little town you remember. It may be a little drowsy still, but people are coming through. The Wishbone's getting famous."

Kevin reached for his coat. "Somehow sitting in front of a fire waiting for you to come home doesn't seem all that appealing. I'll go with you."

THEY TOOK THEIR time in the general store, holding hands and filling up the wicker shopping baskets with food, last-minute presents, and bags of flour and sugar.

"Do you really need this much flour?" Kevin grunted, heaving the twenty-pound bags of flour onto the counter.

Deidre gave him a dismissive look. "You obviously have no idea what it takes to bake for this town."

"You're kind of bossy," Kevin said, pretending to read the label of a can of cocoa. "And a little snappy. Are you always like this?"

"No. Yes. Okay, usually." She gave a sheepish grin. "Is the honeymoon over?"

He laughed and put a can of cocoa, along with a bag of marshmallows, into his basket. He nipped her ear, which made Deidre blush. "I like bossy and snappy," he whispered confidentially. "It's a weakness I have."

"Well, then, I think you're in luck." Deidre tossed in a bag of dried cranberries. She grabbed a handful of walnuts, still in the shell, and filled a large mesh bag. "You've been seeing me at about a four, but I can take it up a few notches to a seven or eight," she said. Kevin raised a wary eyebrow—he obviously liked smaller amounts of snappy and bossy.

"Or we can keep it at a four," Deidre offered.

"That would be good, I think," Kevin said.

Deidre surveyed their groceries piled up on the counter. "I think that's everything . . ."

"I hope so—you pretty much bought everything in the store."

Deidre made a face as they paid for their groceries and helped bag everything up. "Let's stop by the Wishbone," she said.

"You're the boss. Lead the way."

The Wishbone was filled with tourists and locals; several customers were leaning against the wall, waiting for a table.

Lindsey gave them a cheerful but flustered wave and had a harried look on her face.

"I've never seen the place so full," Kevin said. "This should be good for business."

Deidre handed Kevin her things. "Yeah, but it looks like Lindsey's on her own. I'd better go see what's going on."

"I'll finish loading up the car," Kevin said.

Deidre made her way through the crowds to the counter. "This is amazing!" she whispered excitedly to Lindsey. "I can't believe how busy you are!"

"Sidney is out sick and Mary has to leave early for a church Christmas pageant," Lindsey said, a little breathless. "Hannah's in the back but she's having massive anxiety attacks and I can't get back there to help her much. I think I'm going to have to close early—everyone's waiting half an hour to an hour for their food, and I'm beat." She handed Deidre two plates of food and nodded to the corner table. "He has the meatloaf, she has the salad."

Deidre served the food and then returned to Lindsey. "I'll help," she volunteered, reaching for an apron. "You don't want to close on a day like today, Lindsey. Days like this pay for your retirement." People were laughing and looking relaxed. Even the people waiting along the wall of the diner were joking and at ease. If anyone was unhappy with the delays, Deidre couldn't tell.

Lindsey shook her head. "Thanks, Deidre, but it's not enough. I need at least two people in the front and two people in the back to make this work."

Kevin walked in, brushing snow off his shoulders. A small smile played on Deidre's lips. "We'll make it work," she reassured Lindsey. "You go back into the kitchen and help Hannah fill the orders; I'll take care of the customers." She motioned for Kevin to join her as Lindsey hurried back into the kitchen.

"What's up?" he asked, still bewildered.

"Lindsey needs help. Put this on." Deidre handed him an apron and an order pad.

Kevin looked stunned. "I . . . I've never . . ."

"I know. It'll be good for you. Show us how down-to-earth you can be."

"But I don't know what . . ."

"It's easy. Just count the tables from left to right, beginning in the far left corner. We'll split them down the middle but I'll help with your side when I can. That's table one, that's table two . . . you *can* count, right?"

"Very funny." He put on the apron.

"The menus are here, just write down what they want on the pad, then come over here and stick them on the roundabout and ring the bell." She gave him a devious look. "In fact, you should probably call out, 'Order up!' just to make sure Lindsey knows she has an incoming order."

Mrs. Everett hollered over the din, "Coffee! I need more coffee!"

"Oh, decaf only for Mrs. Everett. Do not let her manipulate you into giving her regular coffee."

Kevin was beginning to look flustered when a table near him waved a check in the air.

"I'll handle the checks and getting the food out," Deidre said. "Just bring them up to the front. You just take orders and bus the tables." She gave his hand a squeeze and pushed him toward the table to collect the check. "Don't worry, you'll be fine. It's just until the rush passes."

"I have no idea what bussing the tables is."

"Just refill beverages, clear dirty dishes, put silverware and napkins down."

Lindsey emerged from the kitchen, her arms laden with lunch plates. She froze when she saw Kevin as he attempted to clumsily clear a table. "Am I seeing what I think I'm seeing?" she asked, a slightly horrified look on her face.

"What? You said yourself that we need the help."

"But Kevin? Mr. Big Bucks? Deidre, he *owns* the note to the Wishbone! What am I supposed to do, put him on payroll for eight-fifty an hour?!"

Deidre scoffed, "Don't be so dramatic. Just pay us in dinner since I won't have time to cook tonight. And look on the bright side, Lindsey. This way he knows that it's a good investment."

Lindsey's look was doubtful as she watched him from afar, trying to take an order and referring to the menu himself. "Has he ever waited on tables before?"

Deidre raised an eyebrow. "I think we both know the answer to that. Don't worry, Lindsey. He'll be fine. Now go back there and cook—we need to feed some of these people and move them out of here."

Kevin looked over toward them and gave Lindsey a friendly wave while winking at Deidre.

"I have this *down*," he said. He held up an order. "Now where am I supposed to put this?"

Lindsey raised an eyebrow and whispered, "I guess this means that you and he . . ."

"Lindsey, *go*." They both looked at Kevin and waved.

"You can't use your 'it's a long story' card on this one," Lindsey warned, before retreating into the kitchen. Deidre collected the check from the table and picked up some dirty dishes as she glanced nervously in Kevin's direction. He was talking to a customer and laughing.

"Miss, can we get some more water? And rolls?"

Deidre turned to a customer and smiled. "Sure. I'll be right back."

IT WAS ALMOST eight o'clock by the time Kevin and Deidre finally made it home. They collapsed on the living room couch and kicked off their shoes. Kevin picked up

Deidre's foot and began rubbing it. Deidre sighed in relief. After a few minutes he tried to get up.

"No, no, don't stop," Deidre moaned, trying to pull him back down. "Where are you going?"

"I still have to unload the car," Kevin said.

"Do it tomorrow. It'll keep. Flour doesn't freeze."

"Are you sure?"

"Do you really have to ask?"

Kevin grinned and sat back down, massaging the soles of her feet again. "The restaurant business is hard work," Kevin said. "I don't know how Lindsey does it."

"I think she broke a record tonight. But she loves what she does and being able to keep up with her loan payments for the Wishbone makes her very happy, and I guess you as well."

"Me?"

"Don't you own the note to the Wishbone?"

"Well, yes, but . . ." He regarded her suspiciously. "How did you know that?"

Deidre shrugged. "It's a small town." She was surprised at how good it felt to be a part of Jacob's Point. "Why, does it matter?"

"No. Everyone knew she was in trouble when the bank foreclosed. I don't remember who I heard it from, but I went in to talk to Lindsey and Sid and we got something worked out."

Deidre looked at him. "It was a nice thing for you to do."

"Oh, it was a purely selfish motive," Kevin said. "I'll be the first to admit it. When I come here, the last thing I want to do is cook. If we didn't have the Wishbone, I'd be in big trouble."

"So she spared you from TV dinners every night?"

"That qualifies as cooking in my book. She saved me from three meals a day consisting of trail mix and water."

"Well, I'm glad she had you," Deidre said honestly.

Kevin gave her a sly smile. "You can have me, too."

Deidre shook her head. "No, thanks. At least, not in the way that you're implying. But I'll take it the other way." She began to unbutton his shirt.

He clutched his shirt in his hand, fending her off. "Why? You said yourself that you need an investor. *I'm* an investor."

"That's right. *You're* an investor. But I don't want *you* investing in *Seattle Revealed.*" Deidre stood up and walked toward the kitchen.

"Why not?"

"Because it's you. And I don't want everyone saying that I got it because of you."

"Who's going to say that?"

"Everyone."

"Who's everyone?"

Deidre poked her head out of the kitchen. "I don't know, just everyone. And I need to do this for myself. It's not that I don't want your help, it's just that I want the project to stand on its own two feet. I don't want you giving money to the project just because of me."

Kevin sighed. "Deidre, one thing you're going to learn in the world of finance is that people don't lend to projects, or buildings, or potential blockbuster TV shows. They lend to *people*. I guarantee you that the people who will give you the most money will be the people who like and believe in you. In fact, they may not even care what the show is about, they may never even watch it, but they'll put their money where *your* mouth is because they trust and believe in you."

"*Seattle Revealed* is not about me," Deidre argued. "It's about showing how important . . ."

"Yes, I know, you told me. And I'm telling you, when it comes to investors, that's the small part, not the big part. You're the big part. They're backing you. I want to back you. Why is that a problem?"

"Because if we weren't . . . I mean if it was just about . . ." Deidre didn't know what to call it. What *were* they doing? Dating? Sleeping together? "I mean, if we weren't . . . involved, and if you didn't know me like you know me, would you consider funding the show?"

Kevin groaned. "Don't you listen to anything I say? It would depend on how well I knew you, how much I trusted your past history to perform, the project's buyability . . . but the bottom line is that people invest because of who you are. If I didn't know who you are, why would I bother to invest?"

"Because it's a great project."

"There are lots of great projects out there. Why wouldn't I choose one that was being run by someone I liked, respected, and trusted?"

Deidre pursed her lips. "It just seems so unfair. What about those great projects that do a great service but are run by people with no personality or people skills?"

Kevin gave her an amused look. "I'll let you answer that question."

When Deidre remained silent, he said, "Personally, I would question how far someone can take something, regardless of how great the project is, if they don't have the skills to push it to its full potential. I think people skills play a big role in that. A PhD or Harvard Business School diploma is useless if you're not able to build, maintain, and nurture relationships. You need to be able to inspire the ranks and the people you provide this great service for. All the bleeding hearts in the world can cry about the environment or cruelty to animals but if they really want to make some changes, they need to master the art of relationships. If they can do that, then look out."

Deidre still didn't look convinced.

"Okay. Let's do a little pretend scenario here. One day, you get a knock on the door and there's a Girl Scout who lives down the street selling cookies. You can tell that she doesn't want to ask you to buy her cookies; in fact, she doesn't look particularly enthusiastic or interested when she tries to talk them up. She doesn't give you eye contact and she doesn't smile. She may even mumble when she talks. The next day, another Girl Scout from another neighborhood comes to your door, but this one is beaming, smiling from cheek-to-cheek and it feels sincere. She looks you straight in the eye and asks you to please consider buying some Girl Scout cookies. She may even know your name and address you directly. Now which of the two girls would you buy cookies from?"

"Well, both."

"Why?"

"I'd buy from the first girl because it's for a good cause and because I know she'd probably have a hard time selling a lot of cookies. I'd feel sorry for her. Maybe this would help her self-esteem, then she'd go on to win the national Girl Scout cookie award, and then remember that there was one person out there who believed in her first . . ."

He was looking at her in disbelief. "You have a real tendency to overthink things, you know that?"

"Well, I just think someone should buy from her."

He held up his hands in surrender. "Okay, fine. The sympathy buy. Now what about the second girl?"

"Well, the second girl because she likes what she does. So I guess since I would buy from both, your theory doesn't really work."

"Then let me ask you this: would you rather somebody buy from you out of sympathy or because they like you and your enthusiasm?"

"Well, the latter of course. But . . ."

"I'm not finished. Who do you ultimately think has a better chance to having more cookie sales? And before you answer that, fast forward: both these girls grow up and they both want a job from you. Who do you pick?"

Deidre sighed.

"You can answer now," Kevin said.

"Okay, fine. You've made your point. So if that's all true, why are there people out there who are successful even though nobody likes them?"

"Maybe they have money or they're really good at what they do. But I promise you, Deidre: when push comes to shove, if these people haven't built good, solid relationships around them, it's just a matter of time before the whole thing goes up in flames. Trust me, I see it all the time." Kevin leaned back, speech over.

"Well, then let me ask you this: why does it seem to work for Marla?"

"Who says it works for Marla?"

"Her show's doing great, she's rich, she's got a loyal following . . ."

Kevin shook his head. "Marla is entertainment. Everybody knows it, even the women who are in denial and think they want to be like her. She can be downright mean at times, and people know that. She can be difficult, incredibly high maintenance, and rude, but she knows how to work people. Not the sort of model I'd recommend for you to follow, but her success is definitely a function of the relationships in her life. Do you think the station would have put her on the air if she didn't have some relationships she could draw upon? And do you think I would have financed her show if she didn't have a relationship with me?"

"*You* financed her show?"

"Yes."

"Why?"

He shrugged. "In part for the same reason you would buy cookies from the first Girl Scout. The *should* category. I *should* give to a good cause, I *should* help out this poor Girl Scout, I *should* give money to my sister. The other part is because I do have a relationship with her, and even though it was a gamble from the start, I did it because I believed she could pull it off."

"What about that whole story about things going up in flames? I've seen the way she treats people around her and it isn't pretty. I've seen the way she treated me when the show first aired."

"Deidre, Marla is my sister and I love her. She's flawed, she can be intensely bitchy at times, but we also have a lot of fun together and she is a very smart woman. In short, we have a good relationship, and because of that, I'm willing to take a chance on her. Like I am with you."

"But she's your sister. I'm just . . ." Deidre struggled to find the right words. "I'm . . ." What was she to him? She retreated into the kitchen, blinking back tears.

"Deidre?" Kevin called from the living room. She heard him get up and she threw open the door to the fridge, blocking her view of him as he entered the kitchen. "What is it?"

Deidre slammed the fridge door shut. "We need to unload the car," she said vehemently. "There's nothing to eat or drink in this house." She stormed past him, looking for her shoes, when Kevin grabbed her wrist gently.

"You're what?" he asked.

Deidre shook her arm free. ""What am I to you, Kevin? Your lover? Your one-night stand? What would you call it?" Deidre pulled on her boots and jacket, then headed to the front door.

Kevin came after her, shrugging on his coat and stepping into his shoes. "How about someone very special to me?"

"Great. I sound like a great-aunt." Deidre opened the trunk of the car and brought in a box of groceries, pushing past Kevin.

"Okay," Kevin said slowly. He followed her in, holding the bags of flour. "Well, what would you call it?"

"I told you. Nothing." She brushed past him, heading back to the car. He followed her back outside.

"Fine. How about this: what am I to you?"

She grabbed a box full of canned goods.

"That's heavy, let me carry that," Kevin said, taking it away from her. "I've got it."

"No, *I've* got it." Deidre took it back and marched toward the house.

"God, are you always this stubborn and pigheaded? You're going to hurt yourself carrying something that heavy." He wrestled the box from her and went inside.

Deidre followed him, hands on her hips. "I told you I had it!"

"Deidre, it's not a big deal. I'm bigger, it's easier for me to bring in the heavier boxes."

Deidre turned her back on him and headed back out to the car. He called after her, "And don't go looking for another heavy box just to prove you can do it. I'll just take it from you again."

Deidre stomped back into the house. "You know, I carried heavy boxes before you showed up, and I did just fine."

"I'm sure you did. But I did show up, so I can help you. You don't have to carry all the heavy boxes around, Deidre. Not anymore. Can't you just accept this as a good thing and stop looking at me like I'm depriving you of your favorite pastime?"

Deidre was silent as Kevin finished bringing in the boxes and closed the front door, turning the bolt lock until it clicked. The heavy sound of the bolt somehow made Deidre feel more secure and she relaxed a bit as she watched Kevin get out of his coat.

"Use it as a learning experience and it won't be wasted," Kevin told her. "God knows I've been preaching to the choir on that one."

"What do you mean?"

"Marla." He started unloading the groceries. "She wanted the show but not the responsibility. Where are you putting the pasta? I told her if she was going to do it, she'd have to do all of it, and even if she surrounded herself with good, smart people, she would still have to know exactly what was going on and be aware of what she was signing off on." He shrugged. "She's impressed me, but she's wearing down. The day-to-day business is tedious for her, and she's used to things happening quicker." He glanced at Deidre. "Did you meet her on the set at Channel Two?"

"Briefly." Deidre slipped off her coat and shoes and started to help him.

"That's what Juliette said, but when I brought it up with Marla, she couldn't remember."

She stacked the canned tomatoes in the pantry, turning the labels facing out. "I don't tend to be someone Marla has a memory for," Deidre said wryly.

"Don't be ridiculous," Kevin said. They started sorting out the contents of the boxes and putting them away. "Of course she knows who you are. She's as aware of you as you are of her. You're a Seattle icon—it's not as if she could *miss* seeing you."

Deidre liked that he said that in the present tense and not the past. "Well, let's just say that I don't think she cares much for me."

"That might be true," Kevin conceded. "But it doesn't really matter, does it?"

"No, except that I'm . . . with her brother, and that seems a little awkward, don't you think?"

"No, not for me." He studied her. "Is it awkward for you?"

Deidre thought about it. "It was, but I'm getting used to it. I mean, at this rate it can't get any worse. I just don't know what we're doing."

Kevin feigned an exasperated smile. "Ah. We're back to where we started. Do you want some tea? I sense this is going to take a while." He opened a drawer and perused through the boxes and tins of teas. "I have no idea which one to use."

"Like *that*. What *is* that? Are we playing house? I need to find my own place and make my own money." She looked through the drawer with him and chose a tin of loose leaf green tea.

"So find your own place and make your own money if it's so important to you."

"I intend to. What else am I going to do? Live here with you?" It was meant to be a joke, but her laugh didn't sound natural.

"Here, or Seattle, or New York, or London."

"I'm joking."

"Well, I'm not."

Deidre stared at him, incredulous. "What, are you serious?"

"Well, you asked. I'm just answering the question." He filled the tea kettle with water and put it on the stove.

"I'm *not* staying with you!"

Kevin sighed and rolled his eyes. "Here we go again." He gave her an exasperated look. "Haven't you done the independent woman thing already?"

"Don't talk about it like it's some kind of phase, Kevin. And that burner's not working—you'll have to use one of the other ones."

He moved the teapot to another burner. "Well, what is it then?"

"I just don't want you—or anybody else, for that matter—to think that I can't do it on my own."

Kevin burst out laughing. "I don't think there's a single person out there who thinks that." He was still laughing as he scooped the loose tea leaves into the strainer. "This is very nice, by the way," he said, referring to the loose tea canisters which were neatly labeled and stacked neatly in the spice drawer. They were Deidre's but seemed to fit in well with the house.

A smile tugged at the edges of Deidre's mouth. "Thank you. I mixed the tea blends myself."

Kevin peered into the strainer. "Oh, right. I see little dried flowers and things."

"Some are medicinal, and some I put in for color. We had a supplier who grew edible flowers and had a variety of tea plants. They have a beautiful little store on Valley and Boren . . ." Deidre stopped and then scowled. "Don't distract me. What were we talking about?"

Kevin paused, pretending to think, and then said, "Oh, right. I was about to tell you to get over it."

Deidre was taking down the tea cups when she stopped and turned to stare at him in disbelief. "*What?*"

"GET OVER IT." Kevin looked through the pantry and then came out. "Do you have anything that we can eat with the tea, some kind of cookie or something . . ." He opened a Tupperware. "Is this gingerbread okay to eat?"

"Of course it's okay to eat," she snapped. "I just can't believe you would be so insensitive as to tell me to get over . . . whatever it is I'm supposed to get over."

"Well, if you don't know what you're supposed to get over, that's probably the first big clue. But you've got a bit of a chip on your shoulder, Deidre. You need to get over what other people think. Just do what you want to do. And if part of what you want to do includes spending time with me, then do it."

"It's so easy for you to say. You're rich."

"I may be rich, Deidre, but it's not any easier for me, believe me." The tea kettle was whistling and Kevin slowly poured the hot water over the strainers into their tea cups, then handed one to her. Even though she was still angry, Deidre accepted it, blowing gently on the tea leaves. "If you want to succeed, you're going to have to not let these little bumps in the road throw you for such a loop."

"It wasn't a little bump."

Kevin took a bite of the gingerbread. "Fine. Anthill, mountain. Mountain, anthill? You win, it was a tragic injustice, so let's all just roll over and die with it."

"What are you talking about?"

"It's all perception. If you think it's not a little bump, you're right, it won't be. But, big picture here, Deidre. So your show got canceled. So your show's producer padded the books. So you lost your great apartment and a great roommate."

"And I'm broke. Don't forget that one."

"And you're broke. What else?"

"Isn't that enough?"

"It's pretty good. So you get to choose if, because of these bumps in the road, you're going to stop the car altogether and lament the bumps in the road, or if you're going to keep on driving."

"*That's* what you've been trying to tell me?"

"Something like that."

"Keep on truckin'?"

"Hey, Trump got his millions back because he kept on truckin'. I'm telling you, Deidre, it was looking pretty bad for him for a while, but . . ."

"He kept on truckin'. Okay, I get it."

"Personally, I think it's pretty nice the way things worked out. You need a place to stay, I just so happen to have a place for you to stay. So stay here."

Deidre sighed. "I already told you, I can't."

"You seemed to be doing it just fine until I showed up the other day."

Deidre turned scarlet. "Well, that's different."

"Oh, right. *That's* breaking and entering." He sipped his tea.

"Well, technically you invited me," she pointed out.

"That's true." Kevin sighed tiredly—it had been a long day. "If conversations like this are going to be the norm, I need to get some more sleep. I am completely beat. I've said all I can say, so whatever you decide to do is fine with me. I'm not going to force you to stay here. I like to think I'm not *that* desperate." That got a small smile from Deidre. "So what's it going to be, Deidre? Should I help you start packing so you can look for another place to stay in Jacob's Point or Seattle, or do you think you can force yourself to stay here a little while longer?"

"I . . . could probably force myself, if I had to." She took his hand. "I would love to stay here a little while longer, actually." It was a huge relief to finally say it.

"Good." Kevin finished his tea and yawned. "I want to take a shower and go to sleep. And I really think you should take a shower, too. You'll feel much better afterward."

Deidre rinsed their plates and teacups. "Oh, you think?"

"Let's just say I feel pretty confident—in a word, yes."

"Well, when you put it that way, how can I resist?"

"You can't. At least, that's what I'm hoping." He came up from behind her and wrapped her in his arms and began kissing her neck. A teacup almost slipped from Deidre's hold.

He was right.

Chapter 12

Everything is connected . . . no one thing can change by itself.

—PAUL HAWKEN

THE PHONE RANG early on Christmas Day when Kevin and Deidre were still asleep. Deidre had never heard the phone ring in the house, so she was startled awake, the unfamiliar ring disorienting her for a moment.

She shook Kevin awake. "Phone," she said.

He yawned and rubbed his eyes, then reached for her. "Let the machine get it." He nuzzled against her and fell back asleep. The phone continued to ring.

Deidre shook him awake again. "I haven't seen an answering machine in the house. Do you even have one?"

Kevin let out a heavy sigh. "Apparently not. Are you expecting a phone call?"

"No. No one knows I'm here."

"Hmm." The phone continued to ring, echoing throughout the house.

"Does anyone know you're here?"

Kevin checked his watch and said, ruefully, "Everyone knows I'm here. But I did leave instructions not to bother me unless it was very important." He reached over to answer the phone. "Hello? Oh, hi. No, no, you're welcome. Anytime. Yeah, she's right here. Hold on." He held the phone out to Deidre. "It's for you."

"Me?" Deidre accepted the phone gingerly. Kevin groaned and rolled out of bed, heading to the bathroom. Deidre heard him turn on the shower. "Hello?"

"I don't mean any disrespect on this day of all days," started Lindsey, "but is that who I think it is?"

"Well, of course," Deidre said, a little impatiently. "Who else would it be?"

"I didn't think he'd still be here! He's usually so busy he never stays for more than a day or so. Are you two . . ."

Deidre yawned. "Lindsey, can we talk about this another time? What time is it, anyway?"

"Eight-thirty. You're not up yet?"

"Do I sound up yet?"

"Okay, okay. No need to get huffy. I was just calling to wish you a Merry Christmas and to see if you wanted to come over while we open presents, because I thought you'd be all alone, but obviously you're not." She chuckled gleefully.

"I appreciate the invitation; I'll check with Kevin when he gets out of the shower. I'm going back to bed. Merry Christmas and good-bye."

Lindsey didn't want to hang up—she was having too much fun. "You sure are a sleepyhead."

What a leading statement. Deidre knew what Lindsey was thinking—that woman had a racy, albeit perceptive, mind. "Well, we've been doing lots of walks around the lake, which brought my physical activity up from nonexistent, so I'm a little wiped out."

"What?" Lindsey stopped jeering for a moment to take it in. "You walked Lake Wish? With Kevin?"

"Yes."

"How many times?"

"God, I don't know, Lindsey. Can I call you later?"

"Just tell me how many times and I'll let you go."

Deidre sighed and counted. "He showed up three days before Christmas, we went out twice yesterday, so . . . three times. We'll probably go out again today."

"Sid!" Lindsey hollered. Deidre winced and held the phone away from her ear. *"She walked the lake twice! With Kevin Johnson!"* Deidre could hear them holding an animated conversation in the background.

"Lindsey," Deidre finally said, bringing the phone back to her ear. Her voice was firm. "I am going back to sleep. I am going to hang up now. I will call you later. Good-bye."

"Wait, there's one more thing . . ."

Deidre hung up the phone and fell back against the pillows, ready to go back to sleep. The shower stopped running, and Deidre heard the shower door open.

He appeared in the doorway, beads of water still on his chest and shoulders, completely naked.

"Oh good," he said, striding to the bed. He lifted the comforter to take a peek at Deidre. "Just checking."

"Checking what?"

"That you're not fully dressed and ready to bolt." There was a twinkle in his eye.

"You cannot hold that moment against me," Deidre said defensively. "I thought *you* were going to take off on me. I was trying to make it easier for you to leave."

"As always, so thoughtful." He crawled back between the covers and reached for her. "Shall we . . ."

The phone rang again, causing them both to jump.

"Okay, so Lindsey was the one person who knew that I was staying here," Deidre admitted. "But I told her I'd call her back later, so it's probably not her."

Kevin reached for the phone. "Hello? Yes, she is. May I ask who's calling?" His eyes crinkled and he frowned. "*William?*"

Deidre turned scarlet. She motioned for Kevin to give her the phone. He handed it to her, then started to run his hands up and down Deidre's body. She tried to fend him off, giggling.

"William, how did you get this number?"

"I called Lindsey. But my question is, *What is he doing there?* I thought I had the wrong number."

"I'll give you the details later," Deidre said quickly, before William could start asking questions.

"Is he there right now? Say yes or no."

"Yes. But, Will, that's not necessary . . ."

"Did you sleep with him? Say yes or no."

"Yes, yes, yes, yes. And yes. And there are probably a few more that I've forgotten."

"Oh my God!" Deidre could hear William calling to Alain in the background. *Here we go again*, she sighed.

"Okay, okay. Alain is going to pick up the other line . . ."

By now Kevin's hands had found a warm resting place, and Deidre gasped and squirmed. "You know, this really isn't a good time right now, Will. Can I call you back in a couple of hours?"

"No, hold on, hold on. The reason I'm calling is because . . ."

"*Joyeux Noël*, Deidre!" Alain said, picking up the other line. "I want *every* steamy detail, beginning with . . ."

"Alain, I was *talking*," William said. "I was going to tell her about that woman so Deidre can get her to stop calling us."

"Yes, yes! Deidre, she is driving us out of our minds, you must call her *right away* and tell her . . ."

Kevin was tracing a line of kisses up Deidre's arm. "Guys, guys, can we pick this up in a little bit?"

"No, really, Deidre, you have to get in touch with this woman, she is calling us every day and I swear we are on the verge of changing our number. She really wants to talk with you."

"Who is it?" Deidre asked, hoping it was Juliette from Channel Two.

"I think it was the woman from one of your shows. The one who had the orgasmic experience?"

"Oh. Manuela Jamison." She let out a yelp as Kevin found the soft spot in the nape of her neck. "She left a bunch of messages at the station as well. I've been so focused on the new show I haven't bothered to call her back. I think she's trying to organize a tryst with me while her husband is gone." Kevin raised an interested eye but Deidre gave a definitive no and tried not to laugh.

"I knew it!" Alain cried out. "I told Will that she has that Rosie O'Donnell quality. Very belligerent and sassy when she doesn't get her way."

"I was just kidding. I don't think she's a lesbian even though she did make that pass at me . . ." Deidre curled her lip in uncertainty. "She probably just wants to find out what happened to the show."

"Well, whatever the case, please, please, please call her and tell her to stop calling us," William said. "The woman is relentless. She's left us six different numbers you can reach her at. I practically have them memorized."

"Okay, okay," Deidre said, nudging Kevin to get a pen and paper.

"You've got to be kidding," Kevin said. He rolled his eyes and searched in the bedside table for a pen and paper.

"All right, what are the numbers?" She wrote them down. "Okay. I'll call her."

"*Soon.* Call her soon," William implored.

"If you have to sleep with her to get her to leave us alone, so be it," Alain said.

"I get the picture. I'll call her tomorrow. It's Christmas, she's probably celebrating with her family."

There were disappointed sounds on the other end of the phone.

"Well, I don't know how you expect us to celebrate Christmas without knowing exactly what is happening in the backwoods of Jacob's Point," William said dramatically.

"I'm sure you'll find a way. I love you, Merry Christmas, good-bye."

Kevin watched her as she hung up, a smile on her face. "Should I be jealous?" he asked.

"Green's not really your color," Deidre said, pulling the comforter back over her. "That was my ex-roommate, William."

Kevin raised an eyebrow. "As in, live-in?"

"As in my oldest friend in the world. I have a vendor who was on one of my shows who's been trying to get in touch with me. I'll call her tomorrow." Deidre gave an impish smile. "I suppose I should find a way to make up for all these interruptions."

"Yes . . . that would be the polite thing to do . . ."

Deidre laughed and rolled on top of Kevin, straddling him, the comforter wrapped around her like a teepee. She reached over to the bedside drawer.

"*Ladies and gentlemen,*" Deidre said, straightening back up and pretending to be an airline stewardess. "*We have been cleared for takeoff. Please sit back and prepare to enjoy the ride . . . please note that we will be reviewing the safety procedures before takeoff.*" She held up the condom and Kevin laughed.

The phone rang. Deidre was getting used to the sound of the ring by now. Kevin shook his head and reached for the phone.

"Don't answer that phone," she begged, and then assumed her stewardess persona again. "*All electronic equipment must be turned off and stowed away for takeoff . . .*"

"I'm sure it's another one of your admirers," Kevin said. "You may as well answer it."

"Let it ring," she said. She shifted her position until she got it just right, and when she did, both she and Kevin let out a small sigh of pleasure.

The phone continued to ring as Deidre lowered herself onto Kevin, slowly, every inch made her moan. The look in Kevin's eyes was unmistakable—he was completely at her mercy, and he pushed up to meet her, eyes smoldering.

By the time he was fully inside of her, Deidre's breath was ragged and she started to circle her hips, languidly, teasing him while each movement pushed her closer to the brink. She lowered her head to give him a deep kiss.

When he couldn't take it anymore, Kevin reached up and grabbed her hips, moving her with more urgency. Deidre threw her head back and cried out, seeing stars, the comforter falling around her. They came together in a shuddering climax, and Deidre collapsed on top of him.

"God, that was amazing," Kevin said, still out of breath.

Deidre could only nod her head in agreement.

As her mind slowly cleared and her breathing returned to normal, she opened one eye and realized that the phone was still ringing.

"Maybe it's an emergency," she said, hesitating.

Kevin said, "It's up to you. *I'm* not answering it."

She let the phone ring a little while longer and then reached over Kevin and grabbed the phone. "Hello?"

"Finally!" It was an older woman's edgy voice and Deidre thought it might be Manuela Jamison. But it had a sniffly sound to it, and Deidre's second thought almost paralyzed her. Was it Marla? "Who is this?"

"Um . . ." Deidre bit her lip. She glanced at Kevin, who had his eyes closed and a smile on his lips. She decided to throw caution to the wind. "Deidre McIntosh. Who's this?"

"*This* is Kevin's mother, Mrs. Edward Johnson."

Oh, shit.

"One moment, please." Deidre closed her eyes and held the phone out to Kevin, her hand covering the mouthpiece, and nudged him.

"For me?" He opened one eye.

"Oh, yes." Deidre eased herself off the bed and headed toward the bathroom to wash up, still apprehensive but wanting to give Kevin some privacy.

"Mother?" Kevin said in surprise. He glanced in Deidre's direction and laughed. "Oh, well, that's the woman

I was telling you about . . ." Deidre's heart started pounding. He told his mother about her? Deidre was planning on taking a shower but wouldn't be able to hear if she did. Kevin kept giving her little winks so it wasn't as if he needed the privacy. She decided to brush her teeth. "Yes, it's Deidre McIntosh . . . yes, except that I think you scared her away. No, don't. No, it's fine, really . . . she's a big girl, I doubt she even noticed . . . right. I'm sorry I couldn't join you, too. I wanted to spend some time with Deidre." Deidre swooned and tried not to swallow her toothpaste.

"Oh, it is. Gorgeous, actually. I don't know why I don't come down more often . . . I know, I know. We got fresh snow yesterday . . . no, not too deep. Oh, really? Oh, really?" He gave Deidre a questionable glance. "Sure. No, no, that would be great. Right . . . right . . . right, okay. I'll see you then. I love you, too. Merry Christmas." He hung up the phone and gave Deidre a half smile.

"Uh-oh. I haven't seen that smile before and I'm not so sure I like it." Deidre finished brushing her teeth.

"What?" Kevin played innocent. "They just wanted to wish me a Merry Christmas and say how sorry they were that I wasn't going to join them in Bermuda for the holidays."

Oh, that. Deidre looked apologetic. "Sorry to ruin your plans with your family."

"Are you kidding? I love them, but I wouldn't have traded the past few days for anything."

He was definitely a keeper. Deidre came back to bed and gave him a kiss.

He kissed her back and then asked, casually, "So, any interest in meeting my family someday?"

"Well, I don't really . . ."

"Great, because they're flying back and want to come up to Jacob's Point for New Year's Eve."

"What?!"

"It's not every day that I tell them about a woman I'm crazy about. Plus they want everyone together for the holidays. We're all over the place for most of the year, so this is sort of our family tradition."

"Hold on." Deidre was slow to process and dreaded the answer to the question she was about to ask. "Who's everyone?"

"You, me. My mother, my father, Uncle Harry . . ."

Deidre's face went pale. "Oh God . . ."

"You said you wanted to see the look on his face when he sees his cabin," Kevin pointed out. "You're in luck."

Deidre stammered, "I . . ."

"Claire's going to come as well. Her, and Marla, and that's about it." Kevin gave her a quick smile. "Now who wants lunch?"

Deidre bolted upright. "*Marla* is coming? Here?"

"Yes. She *is* my sister and when we have family get-togethers, she tends to be included. Pancakes sound good?" He reached for his robe.

"Oh, I don't know, Kevin. I really don't know if this is such a good idea."

He tossed her another robe. "I will talk to her first; don't worry. Her bark is worse than her bite."

"Why does that not make me feel any better?" Deidre asked. *Especially since I'll be in biting distance.*

Deidre followed Kevin down the stairs. "You know, this sounds like a time for your family to be together, and I don't want to get in the way. I can meet them some other time. I'll go call Lindsey and see if I can stay with her for a couple of days." She reached for the hallway phone.

Kevin grabbed her wrist. "Not so fast there, speedy."

"What? I just think that it's the holiday, and you should spend it with the people you love . . ."

He interrupted her impatiently. "I want to spend it with you, Deidre. That's why I'm here—I seriously hope you don't think I'm here just to take in the view. And if things keep going the way I hope they'll be going, you're going to meet my family at some point so why not do it now? Trust me: this will be as relaxed as you'll ever see them. I can't make any promises about the rest of the year."

"Kevin, that is not very helpful *or* persuasive."

"Okay. If you don't want to meet my family right now, then that's fine. It's totally up to you; it's your choice. You can stay with Lindsey or go back to Seattle and I'll catch up with you after my family and I have had a couple of days together." That was sounding like the smarter plan, and Deidre was about to agree when Kevin said, "Or . . ."

Deidre sighed. "Or . . . ?"

"You choose what's behind door number two."

"The all-expenses-paid trip to Hawaii or the man-eating tiger?"

Kevin said mockingly, "What's a man-eating tiger or two?"

"I thought you said I had a choice."

"You do. I'm just *suggesting* which choice to make, saving us from the otherwise inevitable headache down the road." He said it with a smile but Deidre knew he was serious.

She studied him for a long time. "You're sure about this?" she finally asked.

He shrugged. "I'm not a fortune-teller—I can't see into the future. But I'm as sure as I can be, given what I know and what I hope for."

What I hope for. Deidre felt her heart pound in her ears but she tried to keep her voice even. "Well, then," she said carefully. "I guess I'll be ringing in the new year with your family."

A broad grin crossed his face. "I'll call Lindsey tomorrow to see if she can cook for us that night," he said.

This time, Deidre was genuinely offended. "Now I *know* you're kidding," she said. "If we're going to do this, we're going to do it right. *I'm* cooking New Year's Eve dinner and I don't want to hear any argument about it."

Kevin gave her a long kiss. "I'll help," he said.

"I know," she said, and kissed him back.

CHAPTER 13

When riches begin to come, they come so quickly,
in such great abundance,
that one wonders where they have been hiding.
—NAPOLEON HILL

"I'M ALMOST DONE." Kevin was layering the thin slices of potatoes and leeks in the casserole dish under Deidre's watchful eye. "Is there anything else?"

Deidre surveyed the kitchen and living room. "No, I think that's it." She had decided to use the island to set up the buffet—she didn't want the responsibility or formality of a sit-down dinner, and thought it would relax everyone if they were up getting their own food. She had three entrées, seven side dishes, a big green salad, rolls, and six desserts plus a white champagne sorbet.

"Well, at least we'll have leftovers for lunch tomorrow," Kevin said cheerfully. He looked at his watch. "They should be here any minute. Are you nervous?"

"No," Deidre lied, reaching for her glass of wine. "Why should I be nervous?"

"Because that's your second glass of wine since they called us to say they were half an hour away."

Deidre put her glass back down. "Oh."

Kevin walked around the island and gathered her in his arms. "You have nothing to worry about."

"Who said I was worried about anything?" Deidre gave a nervous laugh and reached for her glass of wine again. Kevin pushed it out of her reach and handed her a Pellegrino instead.

"Drink this. I'm going to run upstairs and change my shirt, slip on something more festive." He was wearing a white T-shirt and jeans.

"Don't go," Deidre said suddenly as he headed toward the stairs. "You look great. Very . . . Gap."

He glanced down at what he was wearing and then looked at her, already decked out in a classy black skirt with a cream cashmere ballet-neck sweater. "Deidre, it'll take me one second. Don't worry, they're not going to show up during that one second." Kevin smiled, gave her a wink and headed up the stairs.

Deidre clutched the Pellegrino, unsure of what to do next. Her eyes rested on her glass of wine and, after listening to hear if Kevin was upstairs, she reached out and picked up the wineglass.

"Please get me through this night and I promise I won't give up until the show is on the air," she prayed, downing the remaining wine. She dabbed her mouth with a napkin just as the doorbell rang.

Deidre took off her apron and stuffed it into a drawer, then went into the hallway, looking up the stairs to the bedroom. She couldn't see any movement; Kevin was probably in the bathroom.

I'll just wait until he comes down, Deidre thought, staring warily at the front door. *We can say we were cooking and . . .*

The door opened and a woman's head poked in. "Hello?"

Deidre froze.

A man's voice behind her said, "What are we standing out here for? For God's sake, get inside, it's freezing."

Before Deidre could say anything, they were suddenly all standing in the foyer, brushing snow off their jackets and looking at her expectantly.

Kevin's mother was a dead ringer for Marla, flawless and in amazing shape. Kevin's father was gray and handsome and had the look of someone who was always very busy and never changed his mind. Next to him and considerably shorter was Henry Johnson, Deidre's old landlord, who was looking at her irritably, his lips pursed. Claire had her hair pulled back into braided pigtails and looked, at the moment, like a very sweet girl.

Deidre strolled forward. "Hello, I'm Deidre McIntosh," she said, holding out her hand. "Kevin was helping me in the kitchen and just went upstairs to change his clothes. He should be right down. Please come in."

"We *are* in," Claire said, shaking the snow off her scarf.

"Right. So good to see you again, Claire."

Kevin's mother gave Deidre an air kiss, then led her over to Kevin's father. "I'm Beverly Johnson, and this is my husband, Edward, and my brother-in-law, Henry. And this is Claire, who tells me you've already met." Deidre could tell that Beverly knew how to be a gracious hostess as well as a gracious guest. Deidre could also tell that Beverly had given Deidre the quick once-over, from head to toe, but by the time Deidre made eye contact with her, Beverly was smiling as if nothing were amiss. "That's a lovely color on you," she said, nodding to Deidre's sweater.

"Thank you. Can I get anyone something to drink?" Deidre asked. They walked toward the living room.

"Bourbon," Edward said. He walked straight over to Kevin's favorite chair, made from a smooth dark brown leather that was hand-stitched and sat slightly higher than the other matching pieces in the living room. For some reason it reminded Deidre of a throne.

"I'll have a glass of white wine," said Beverly. She settled herself next to Edward on the couch and crossed her legs.

"Sprite," said Claire, looking around. "Two cherries, no ice."

"Sorry, Claire. We don't have any cherries."

Claire gave her a terrible look, a what-kind-of-person-doesn't-have-cherries-in-their-house look.

"What about some lemon?" Deidre asked.

"I don't like lemon."

"Orange slices? Might give it a sort of orangeade kind of flavor?"

Claire considered this reluctantly. "Okay," she said grudgingly. "Where's Kevin?"

"Upstairs, he'll be right down once . . ."

Claire bounded up the stairs before Deidre could say anything, and she opted to keep her mouth shut. Deidre turned back to Uncle Harry who was still standing, hunched over and looking dour.

"Uh, Mr. Johnson?" Deidre wasn't sure how to address him given their new set of circumstances. "What can I get you?"

"Nothing," he said flatly.

"Sit down, Harry. Don't be such a killjoy," Edward said. When Uncle Harry refused to budge, Edward said to Deidre, "He's in a bad mood because we stopped by his cabin on the way over so he could drop off his bags . . ."

"Someone was in my cabin," Uncle Harry declared. "I'm going to call the police."

"You don't call the police when someone moves the furniture around and cleans everything up. Not to mention locking the door on the way out." This time Beverly was shaking her head impatiently. She accepted a glass of wine from Deidre and as she did so, leaned forward as if to tell her confidentially, "He leaves that place unlocked, if you can believe it."

Edward finished his bourbon in one gulp. "It would be Harry's dumb luck to have someone stumble in and leave it better than they found it. Not that there was anything to rob in the first place."

"Claire said that you would know what had happened," Beverly said. All three sets of eyes turned to look at Deidre, and Deidre's mouth went dry.

"Uh, yes, as a matter of fact, I do . . ."

At that moment, Kevin came downstairs. Claire was holding his hand tightly and beaming. The attention shifted to Kevin, to Deidre's relief, and she couldn't help but smile to herself when she saw him.

"Hi, son," Edward said. He stood up and gave Kevin a manly handshake and pat on the back.

"Kevin." Beverly gave her son a kiss and removed some invisible lint from his sweater.

"Deidre, did you meet everyone?" He walked over and gave her a kiss, which both embarrassed Deidre and put her at ease.

"Yes," she said. "Your parents and, uh, Mr. Johnson . . ."

"Call him Harry," Edward instructed. Kevin's parents were watching the couple with interest. Uncle Harry was still scowling. "Or Uncle Harry. I don't know who you're talking to when you say 'Mr. Johnson.'"

Kevin walked over to Uncle Harry. "Uncle Harry, how are things?" Kevin shook his hand and clapped his shoulder. "Can I get you something to drink?"

Uncle Harry continued to glower. "I want to know what happened to my cabin. Someone went in there and moved everything around. I can't find anything."

Kevin glanced at Deidre who was pretending to be busy slicing oranges.

"Well, Uncle Harry, you see, there was a mix-up a few months ago . . ." Kevin began.

Deidre looked up from the cutting board and sighed. ". . . and I stayed there. I thought it was Kevin's place, and I didn't mean to touch your things. It's my fault—I'm sorry. It was a complete misunderstanding."

"*I* think it looks wonderful," Beverly said. "Anything is an improvement on that place. I could actually step inside without getting my hair full of cobwebs."

"She did you a favor," Edward pointed out to Uncle Harry, who still looked mad.

"I can help you move everything back," Deidre offered tentatively.

"You'll do nothing of the sort," Beverly said. Deidre was getting the distinct impression that Edward and Beverly enjoyed treating Uncle Harry as if he were another child. She wondered why he was even there. "Harry's lucky to have you. Aren't you?"

Uncle Harry didn't say anything, but instead looked at Deidre and said sullenly, "I think I'll have that drink now. No alcohol." Apparently he was realizing that Deidre was a lesser evil.

Deidre was giving Claire her orangeade and quickly made another one for Uncle Harry. "Here you go."

Kevin gave his parents an exasperated look. Edward just chuckled and patted his belly.

"I'm starving; that trip down made me hungry. When can we eat?"

"Anytime," Deidre said.

"Is Marla coming?" Kevin asked. At the mention of Marla's name, Deidre felt her body tense. She walked quickly to the buffet and busied herself by lighting the candles, her hands slightly shaking. She was dreading Marla's arrival.

"Oh, she called to say she would be late and to start without her," Beverly said, standing up and following Deidre toward the buffet. "She had some event to go to so she wouldn't be leaving Seattle until almost three. I told her not to bother to come down, she's always so busy with one thing or another, but she said she wouldn't miss it."

Deidre felt the hairs on her neck stand up.

"Where's Lindsey? This looks wonderful," Beverly said, picking up a plate. "Is that eggplant?"

"Deidre prepared dinner tonight, Mother."

"Really?" Beverly laughed. "I knew it!" She hit Edward's arm. "I win!"

"Win what?" Deidre asked, interested.

Beverly exchanged guilty glances with Edward, who avoided Beverly's look and was focusing on the food. "Oh, nothing. It's silly."

Kevin looked mildly exasperated. "Mother, come on. Out with it. What is it?"

Edward, his eyes on the buffet, was shaking his head as if to suggest he did not approve and had nothing to do with whatever was going on.

Beverly gave a nervous smile and tried to play it off as Deidre, Kevin, and Uncle Harry looked on with interest. "It's just that Marla and I . . . really, it's just so silly . . . we just didn't know how much of what you did was . . . you know . . . real versus for TV. *I* said that you probably knew how to do most of the things you had on your show, otherwise how else would you know what your audience would like, right?"

"Well, I did have a lot of help," Deidre said honestly, a little stung. "But I did have a very good sense for what the audience wanted. Also, I love to cook and to bake." She nodded to the large selection of desserts on the table. "That's actually what got me started with the show."

"Now *this* is a spread worth coming down for," Edward declared, hovering over the desserts exultant, eyes wide.

"No dessert!" Beverly said severely, giving him a stern look that Edward was ignoring. She explained, "The doctor said he needed to cut down on sweets."

"Oh, I know, Kevin told me," Deidre said, moving toward the dessert section. "So I have a couple of desserts here that are pretty heart healthy. This is a carob fudge torte that doesn't have any sugar—it's sweetened with applesauce and vanilla—and the apple port cheese pie has the port and a touch of honey but no refined sugar. And of course there's the fruit salad—I have the dark brown sugar, rum, and spices on the side and he can just skip those."

Both Edward and Beverly were clearly impressed. For the first time since they walked in, Deidre felt that things were starting to look up. Kevin gave her a wink.

"Did you do all this, too?" Beverly asked, nodding at the beautifully set table and holiday decorations throughout the house. She straightened a runner and Deidre resisted the temptation to tell her that crumpled runners were actually the style. Instead she said, "I did the table, but actually Kevin did the tree and all the lights."

"Really?" Beverly looked impressed.

"Yes, really," Kevin said. "I'm actually quite handy. I even know how to bus tables."

The joke was lost on his parents; they already had their attention on other things. "Oh, I *love* this, where did you get it?" Beverly was admiring an arrangement of conifer, tree tomatoes, limes, and white eggplants that Deidre had put together in the shape of a Christmas tree.

"Oh, that," Deidre tried not to look embarrassed. "I did that a couple of days ago. It's actually quite easy."

"I'll bet," Beverly said, looking at her approvingly. Edward was already at the table eating.

The doorbell rang and Kevin gave Deidre's shoulders a squeeze. "I'll get it," he said.

"I'll go, too," Claire said. They disappeared into the hallway.

"Where's Uncle Harry?" Deidre asked.

Edward shrugged. "Probably having a moment somewhere." He took another mouthful of food.

"Edward, can you *please* wait until we are all seated at the table? Really!" Beverly gave him a disapproving look and Edward put his fork down reluctantly.

"Bring me some more of that bread then," he said.

Beverly snapped, "Oh, for . . ."

Deidre went into the living room and found Uncle Harry staring at some of the black-and-white photographs on the wall.

"We're eating, if you'd like to join us," she offered.

He didn't say anything so Deidre stepped a little closer and noticed that he seemed captivated by the photographs.

"They're beautiful, aren't they?" she commented.

He grunted in agreement and took a noisy sip of his drink.

"You had some in your cabin as well, didn't you?"

He cut a quick glance at her. "Yes."

"I cleaned them off. I hope you didn't mind too much. It just seemed a shame to have them hidden under so much dust." Deidre looked at one of Lake Wish that must have been taken early in the morning. A light mist hovered over the lake and there were two birds in flight. "I never found out who the photographer was. Do you know?"

"Yes." Uncle Harry took another sip of his orangeade. "It's me," he said, then turned his back and headed toward the kitchen.

Deidre looked after him, stunned, when Kevin walked into the room with Marla trailing behind him. She was dressed up and pulling her gloves off, her lips twisted in a smile as she surveyed Deidre.

"Look, she made it," Kevin said.

Damn! "Hi," Deidre said.

"Marla, you remember Deidre?"

Deidre saw Kevin give Marla a warning look but she ignored it as she flipped her hair back, revealing large diamond studs in each ear. "Sorry I'm late," she said, looking at Deidre but addressing Kevin. "The weather was treacherous and I almost killed myself driving down here." She turned to him. "Where's everybody else?"

"Already eating." He nodded to the kitchen.

"I'm going to make my plate," Claire said.

"Go for it," Kevin said. Claire skipped ahead, jubilant.

Marla brushed past Deidre and followed Claire into the kitchen. Deidre could hear her exchange exuberant greetings with her parents. Kevin shrugged and came over to Deidre. "Well, she's here, and that's a start."

Deidre gave him a skeptical look as they headed into the kitchen.

"Deidre, you've met my daughter Marla?" Beverly said, her arm looped through her daughter's. "How wonderful we can all be here together like this! Don't you think, Marla?"

"Oh, absolutely," Marla said with a tinge of sarcasm.

"Marla, can I get you a drink?" Deidre asked. *Don't try so hard*, she told herself. *Pretend you're on the air.* She gave Marla her million-dollar smile, and their eyes locked for a moment. Deidre knew her smile was inscrutable. Marla looked away, slightly taken aback, and Deidre was smiling for real, now.

"Vodka martini, straight up, two olives." Marla pretended to study her nails.

"I'll get it," Kevin said.

Marla filled her plate with salad greens. "Can't go wrong with a salad," she said to everyone. Then, as if just noticing Deidre, she added apologetically, "Watching my weight. It all looks so wonderful and . . . filling."

"Marla, darling, I was right." Beverly waved a fork. "Deidre did do this by herself."

Uncle Harry had impressively filled his plate, as if it were the only chance he'd have to eat, and sat at the end of the table. Kevin gave Marla her martini then went over to pick up Uncle Harry's empty glass for a refill. "I'll take some more of that orangeade drink," he told his nephew.

"Harry, always the heavyweight," Edward said, picking at his teeth.

Beverly gave him a swat before turning to Kevin. "I just love this china," she said admiringly.

"Well, of course," Marla said, sitting next to her. "You helped him pick it out with your interior designer when you redid this place."

"Hans did do an excellent job," Beverly said. "Kevin, remember that awful statue that used to be out front?"

"Oh my God," Marla said, rolling her eyes. "And you wonder why it took six years for this property to sell."

Beverly and Kevin laughed. "Whatever happened to that, did Hans have it demolished?" Beverly asked.

"No," Kevin said, giving Claire a wink before turning his attention back to his mother. "He bought it for one of his other clients who was into art deco. He actually gave us a credit, not that it made any sort of dent on that bill he sent me."

"Well, good interior decorators are hard to find," Beverly said, a little defensively.

As they continued to talk about old times, times that Deidre had no knowledge of or means to participate, she felt her stomach start to knot. She was clearly the outsider here, and suddenly felt very lonely and separate. She filled her plate slowly, her appetite lost.

Kevin, who was filling his plate behind her, leaned over and touched the small of her back. He whispered, "Breathe."

She didn't realize she had been holding her breath. Deidre slowly exhaled. Kevin gave her a quick kiss.

Deidre felt Edward and Beverly exchange a glance and a smile. Marla's eyes had gone wide and then narrowed into slits. Claire ignored them and continued to eat. Deidre blushed and made her way to the table, sitting next to Uncle Harry who said to her, his mouth full, "It's good."

When they were all around the table, Kevin held up his glass and made a toast. "I'd like to thank everyone for coming to Jacob's Point to celebrate the New Year with us, and to Deidre for preparing this amazing dinner."

"Hear, hear," Edward said. His plate was empty and he was eyeing the desserts.

Marla held up her glass dutifully, looking bored. Glasses clinked and the conversation resumed, this time about a property Edward owned on Saint Kitts that Kevin was helping to negotiate a sale to a prospective buyer. Excluded again, Deidre turned to Uncle Harry who was looking equally excluded.

"Those photographs are really spectacular. I could have sworn they were professionally done."

Uncle Harry didn't say anything, but Deidre thought she saw a little color come to his cheeks.

"Uncle Harry is a professional," Kevin said, overhearing the conversation and leaning toward them. "He's the only true artist in the family. He used to be a photojournalist with *Time*, *Life*, and *National Geographic.* But then when Grandpa left him all those apartment buildings, he decided to stay in one place and manage them."

"Couldn't afford a place any other way," Edward chimed in between bites. He had gone back for seconds and had another full plate of food.

"Dad!" Kevin gave him an annoyed look.

"So, Deidre," Beverly said, changing the subject. "What are you doing with yourself these days? Are you going to do another show?"

Deidre glanced at Kevin and he shrugged. She knew he was leaving it up to her if she wanted to share anything. "Actually, yes," Deidre said. "It's ready to go and I have a station—Marla's station—that is interested but I need to fund the pilots. I'm planning on raising money to do that."

"Where are you going to get the money?" Edward asked, interested.

"I'm going to start approaching some investors, sponsors, foundations . . . I have a list of about seventy-five strong possibilities, and I'll just go through them until someone says yes."

"How much do you need to raise?"

"Somewhere in the neighborhood of three hundred thousand. It can be done for less, but that would be the magic number, no holds barred. I figure if I'm going to do it, I may as well do it right."

"Is it going to be like *Live Simple*?" Beverly asked.

"No, it's actually completely different. It's called *Seattle Revealed*, and it's nothing like *Live Simple*. The whole concept is based on the people that build a business, or a community, or a city. It's similar to the biographical profiles you see on TV, except that there are four to six profiles per segment, and the profiles are all connected, some obviously so, others not so obviously so."

"What do you mean?"

Deidre took a bite of her food and chewed slowly. The roast turkey tasted wonderful. Her own food was giving her confidence.

"One of the segments starts with a family-owned chocolate business, Rainier Chocolate Company." Edward's and Beverly's heads nodded in acknowledgment: of course they knew Rainier Chocolate Company—who didn't? "They've had it in the family for over a hundred years, their headquarters have always been in Seattle. They have a factory where visitors can go and see them at work—everything is done by hand, it's a real work of art. Anyway, we go behind the scenes. Ordinarily I would include all the important links in the chain, in this case something like the cacao growers would be perfect, but they're out of state and I want to keep the content Seattle-specific.

"RCC doesn't just do pure chocolate—they do nuts, dried fruit, syrups, and other chocolate-covered snacks like pretzels. Milton Fries supplies RCC with all of the dried cherries that they use. So we'll interview him, too, see his property and the cherries when they actually get shipped from Milton's orchards to RCC. We'll talk, too, about their relationship together, what works and what doesn't. It'll be scripted from an interview point of view, but we don't know what they're going to say, so it's got that reality TV element to it."

"I'm finished," Claire announced to the table. Kevin put his finger to his lips and nodded for her to come and sit on his lap.

"In this segment we also interview their advertising exec—they use an outside firm to create and place their ads—as well as a retail store that carries their candy and a customer that actually buys and eats it. The customer will be someone loyal, but who probably buys from the retailer rather than the company directly."

"That sounds fascinating," Beverly said, nodding her head. "So it's sort of like what goes into making a chocolate-covered cherry, right?"

Deidre noticed that Edward and Uncle Harry hadn't said anything, Edward with a grim look on his face and Uncle Harry with his eyes down, eating. Deidre tried not to read into it. "On one level, yes," she replied, trying to keep her attention on Beverly. "But on another level, the human level, it's about the people behind it, their trials and tribulations, failures and successes, and how what one person does impacts another. The *human* quality is what I'm intrigued by. Often we feel alone, or that nobody understands what we're going through. By revealing how every link of the chain is important and interconnected, I hope to show how we need each other and how understanding one another can help us do what we do individually better."

"Well, *I* certainly believe that," Beverly said. The men still hadn't said anything and Marla was back at the buffet, looking purposely uninterested in the conversation. Deidre looked at Kevin and thought she saw—could it be?—a hint of pride, and it made her smile.

"Yes. So do I."

"I'll keep my eye out for it. When did you say it would air?"

"Oh, well, I still have to get some financing to fund the pilots before I can even get any air time," Deidre said. "So it may be a while before anything happens." She cast a sidelong glance at Marla who sat down and, Deidre noticed with interest, added a lot of non-salad items to her plate. "The long-term vision is to take it to other cities or states. *Los Angeles Revealed, Chicago Revealed* . . . that sort of thing."

"I had a segment like that," Marla said in her indifferent way, slathering her roll with Deidre's homemade apple butter. "Focusing on the jewelry business. Followed the diamond from the De Beers mines in Africa all the way to Tiffany's in downtown Seattle. Gave it to a young couple that got engaged . . ." She pursed her lips, squinting slightly as she tried to remember. "The Andersons . . . no, the Albertsons . . . something like that."

"The Avershams?" offered Deidre. She remembered the show well, and suddenly had an awful realization.

"Yes, that's it. I think it was the only piece of jewelry she owned that didn't turn green when she wore it. They were in tears—he manufactured rain gear or something like that—outfitted the whole studio with rain slickers." She rolled her eyes. "Tacky, but he was trying to show his appreciation, so it was sweet."

Deidre's palms grew clammy as Marla continued to divulge more information from that show. Deidre thought hard. When did the idea for *Seattle Revealed* first come together? She paled as the memory became clear.

The vision for *Seattle Revealed* was born right after Marla's segment. Deidre wanted to crawl under the table and disappear. Not only was she an idea stealer, but she stole it from Marla. *I would be a good subject for the show*, Deidre thought wryly. *It seems like I haven't really done anything without the help of others.* And suddenly, a small smile played on Deidre's lips.

"Are you okay?" Kevin asked, a look of concern on his face. Everyone at the table turned to look at her.

"Well," Deidre said. "You know, it's kind of funny . . . but I'm just realizing that I got my idea for *Seattle Revealed* from that segment so I guess"—Deidre knew what she was about to say but couldn't believe the words were coming out of her mouth—"I should really be thanking you. So . . ." Deidre had to pause to clear her throat. "Thank you, Marla."

The entire table was caught off guard, Marla in particular. A look of astonishment was on her face. For the first time since Deidre had seen her, on TV or in person, Marla was stunned into silence. Deidre felt giddy, free. *Marla.* Who would have guessed? Deidre looked at Kevin, who had the same look of amazement on his face, and they burst out laughing.

Edward was looking at them like they were crazy, and Uncle Harry was looking for another drink. Beverly had a satisfied look on her face. Claire was listening to the conversation with wide eyes, glancing back and forth between Deidre and Marla, enthralled.

Marla still hadn't said anything, but Beverly raised her eyebrows and her wineglass to them both. "Well," she said. "Isn't that ironic? Don't you think, Marla?" It was clearly a pointed question.

Marla gave a nervous laugh. "No, I don't think so."

Beverly sipped her wine. "Yes, dear, remember? It was . . . gosh, almost a year ago when I was in my room, resting from my hip surgery, and Deidre's show was on. You said . . . what did you say?" Beverly pretended to think.

"I don't remember." The smile seemed frozen on Marla's face.

"It was the show you were doing, Deidre, that had a woman who had recently divorced and was starting her life over again. She was a nurse?"

"Audrey Stoddard," Deidre said, remembering. She knew all of her shows by heart. "She actually worked with my old roommate at King County General. Her husband had left her for a younger woman and she was pretty much left with nothing. She had two little girls, too. I brought her on the show because he really wanted to help her out and thought it would be like therapy. The segment was called Second Chances and focused on making things new again. We had a great response from it—letters and all sorts of support flooded the studio."

"Yes, that's it! Marla, do you remember?"

"No," Marla said shortly, standing up, her plate empty. "I'm getting more salad."

"Get me some more of the Beef Wellington," Edward said. "With that Yorkshire pudding." He turned to Kevin. "I love Yorkshire pudding."

"Well, *I* remember. We watched the show and Marla said, 'All this woman needs is a good makeover and a new apartment. Not to mention a good lawyer.'" Beverly laughed. Marla got her idea for *At Home with Marla Banks* from Deidre, and Deidre got her idea for *Seattle Revealed* from Marla? It was too good to be true, the kind of thing that only happened in the movies.

Marla was in the kitchen at the buffet, her back to them, and Deidre could tell she was seething. "Come on, Marla, you remember," her mother called to her. "And then that night at dinner, when we had Juliette Farquahar over for dinner and she was telling us about how they had that open spot at the station . . ." She looked at Deidre. "It's just so funny how things work out, isn't it?"

"Yes, it certainly is," Deidre said, feeling exuberant. Things couldn't get any better than this. *This* was the something she had been looking for, or close to it.

Marla had returned and was dishing food onto her father's plate from hers.

"Thank you, dear," Edward said, his fork already en route.

"You're welcome, Daddy," Marla said. Her voice smug, as if to say that being her father's daughter was all that mattered at the moment.

Edward took a bite. "Looks like everyone's even now. Oh, you forgot the Yorkshire pudding."

Marla's ears turned red and she glared at him with a look of betrayal. Edward sighed and got up to get the Yorkshire pudding on his own.

Beverly ignored them and looked at Deidre. "So, what I don't understand is, if you're looking for funding . . ." She gave Kevin a silent look.

Kevin held up his hands in surrender. "I offered, she refused."

"I don't want Kevin funding the pilots," Deidre said. "I prefer somebody neutral who's doing it because they believe in the programming and in me." Kevin was about to protest when she said, "You're biased. You don't count."

"That's a bit romantic," Edward said, giving his two cents from the buffet. "Sounds like a risky investment to me. Three hundred grand sounds steep—I assume you'll be drawing a salary from that amount?"

"Actually, no. I didn't know at the time how involved I would be, if I would ultimately end up hosting or just producing the show, so I thought I would see how things went first and then put in my salary once things started rolling and the show got sold."

Kevin's entire family burst out laughing, except for Claire and Uncle Harry. Even Kevin had a small smile tugging at the corners of his mouth.

"What?" Deidre asked, feeling a bit humiliated. Obviously she had missed something.

"You're a bit more naive than I gave you credit for," Edward said, chuckling. Beverly swatted him with her napkin.

"Darling, you *always* pay yourself first, and you *always* pay yourself well," Marla said, glad to have Deidre back in the hot seat. She looked around the table as if to say, *Can you believe it?* Even Beverly was looking at Deidre with pity.

"My family has a . . . strong opinion about how to do business," Kevin explained.

"Opinion nothing," Edward declared. "Know what you're worth. That's what it's all about."

"I know what I'm worth," Deidre argued. "But it's not just about the money. I actually believe in *Seattle Revealed*, just like I did in *Live Simple*, and I'm willing to do what it takes to help get it off the ground."

"I don't want to discourage you," Edward said. "But while it sounds like a nice idea, I'm not so sure it'll take off."

Beverly and Kevin shot him an exasperated look. "Really, Edward," Beverly said, disgust in her voice.

"What?" he asked, startled. "I'm just trying to give Deidre here a reality check. She's a nice woman with some good ideas, but three hundred thousand dollars for six pilots for a local station? Come on."

From sixty to zero in five seconds flat. *Well, at least I got to sixty*, Deidre thought. She had it, and now it was gone. Deidre was ready for another drink. Kevin, sensing that she was discouraged, rubbed her shoulders supportively. Claire was yawning, too tired to care.

"I'm sure you won't have any problem finding the right investor," Beverly said reassuringly, giving her family eye contact as if to say, *Enough*. "Here's to you, Deidre. We wish you the best of luck." She held her glass up and the rest of the family followed suit, though somewhat half-heartedly. Deidre noticed that Marla was eating with more enthusiasm, while Deidre had lost her appetite once again.

"I'll do it," Uncle Harry said. They all looked at him in surprise. He took another bite of food, then stared back at them. "What?" he asked sullenly.

"Why, Harry," Beverly said, impressed. "I had no idea you were interested in television."

He shrugged and continued eating. Clearly explaining things to his brother or sister-in-law was low on his list of priorities.

"Well!" Edward looked genuinely surprised, even a little taken aback. He gave Deidre another glance, as if seeing her for the first time. "Think you got another winning horse, Harry?"

"Stuff it, Edward," was the muffled response. He stood up. "I'm getting more food."

Kevin and Deidre exchanged glances. Kevin also looked surprised, but there was a broad smile on his face. He whispered, "Congratulations."

Deidre shook her head, "I can't take his money."

"Trust me, getting money from Uncle Harry is like squeezing water from a stone. If he's offering, it's not out of charity. You said you wanted a neutral investor—it doesn't get any more neutral than Uncle Harry. He's done this maybe, what, two other times in his life. And both were huge successes."

Beverly whispered, "It's true, Deidre."

"Take his money," Edward advised in a low voice. He glanced at his brother who was hovering near the desserts. "In fact, I might want to play a little as well. Send some information to my office on Monday."

Claire said, "Why are we whispering?"

Uncle Harry returned, laden with dessert, and they all straightened up.

"Hey, I didn't know we could move on to dessert," Edward said, standing up rapidly. Beverly followed him, and slapped his hand as he reached for one of the oversized dark and white chocolate chunk cookies.

"Draw up the papers and I'll sign them," Uncle Harry said, sitting back down.

"Um, don't you want to see the full proposal? I have an executive summary . . ."

He shook his head with annoyance. "I have enough paper in my apartment. Just send me whatever it is I need to sign. And I'm only doing it on the condition that you're producing it and taking responsibility for what happens to the show, so you'd better write in your salary now because I don't want to have this conversation later."

Kevin squeezed her hand. "People invest in people," he whispered.

"I can't thank you enough," Deidre said gratefully.

"Then don't," Uncle Harry said and started eating again.

"So it looks like you'll be working out of the same station after all," Kevin said to Marla, an impish look on his face.

"I'm hardly there," she said, making a face back at him.

"I can't believe this," Beverly was saying, considering all of the desserts as she restricted Edward's choices. "I won't be able to fit into any of my clothes tomorrow! This is quite impressive, Deidre."

"Oh, the desserts were the easy part," Deidre said, trying keep her voice steady. *Seattle Revealed* was funded. Funded! It was really going to happen. Remembering her manners, she jumped up to make a pot of coffee.

"Well, this little lady looks like she's about to fall asleep," Edward said, nodding at Claire, whose eyes were half-closed.

"No, no," she mumbled, opening her eyes wide. "Firecrackers."

"We got her some firecrackers on the way down," Edward said. "I think I'm in the mood for a cigar after that meal." He patted his breast pocket.

"I need a cigarette," Marla said. "I'll join you."

"Not in here," Kevin said sternly, pointing to the deck.

Uncle Harry put his napkin down as if on cue. "Well, I'm going to go to the cabin," he said, standing up abruptly. "I'll drive myself. Good night."

"You're not going to stay for coffee?" Beverly asked.

Uncle Harry was already heading toward the hallway.

"I'll get your coat," Deidre said, getting up and following him.

She helped him into his coat. She felt like she needed to thank him again.

"Again, I really appreciate your offer to fund *Seattle Revealed*," she said, walking him to the door. Kevin came up behind her.

Uncle Harry turned to face them both, diminutive in his huge winter jacket. He pulled the furry hood onto his head and Deidre stifled a laugh. He didn't notice. "Well, I think it's a good idea and we need better programming given the garbage that's running these days." He bobbed his head toward the living room where Marla was laughing loudly at one of Edward's jokes. "Good night." His footsteps crunched in the snow as he trudged toward the car and climbed in.

"Wow," Kevin said, closing the door. "How does it feel?" He gave her a tight squeeze and Deidre melted in his arms, relishing the hug. He kissed her.

"Actually, I don't think it's totally sunk in yet, it still feels like a dream. Your family jumps so quickly from one conversation to the next that it's a bit like being on a roller coaster. Emotionally, at least." She gave him a smile. "But I think it's good for me. Toughens me up a bit."

"Ah, yes. The Johnson High-Impact Workout. You'll build muscles you never knew you had." They started walking back toward the living room. "Ready for some more?"

Claire met them in the hallway, her arms full of fireworks, awake and eager with anticipation. "I'm ready," she announced.

Deidre gave Kevin a smile. "I am, too."

CHAPTER 14

When love and skill work together,
expect a masterpiece.

—JOHN RUSKIN

KEVIN HAD TO go to Seattle for a meeting but promised to be back before nightfall. "I do love it here," he said. "But the commute is killer. Worth it, but a killer."

"Well, you can always come back tomorrow," Deidre teased.

"What? Not a chance. But at some point I'm going to have to live back in the city again." He gave her a sarcastic smile. "*Some* of us have to work, you know."

"Yes, some of us do," Deidre said, nudging him playfully before he gathered her in his arms and planted a long, lingering kiss on her lips.

"We'll talk when I get back tonight—think you're ready to return to civilization?"

"Jacob's Point is civilization," Deidre said loyally.

"Well, figure out where you're going to be so I can decide whether or not I need to get a car with better gas mileage." He gave her another kiss and was gone.

The day after New Year's the house was finally quiet again, the Johnsons having returned to their busy lives and Deidre to hers. Deidre closed her eyes and dreamed happy thoughts for all of five minutes before the telephone rang.

It was Lindsey. "Have you dropped off the face of the earth or what?"

Deidre laughed. "I'll come in a little while; Kevin had to go back to Seattle for the day. I have a big delivery for you, too."

"Good. Because we're packed again today. Must be holiday travelers."

Deidre changed her clothes and loaded the car with scones, muffins, cookies, and cakes. Deidre baked best when she was happy, and Lindsey gave a low whistle when Deidre walked in, her arms full, navigating the crowded diner.

"I take it was a good week with Kevin and the family," Lindsey said, helping her.

"It was, and I have more in the car. If it's too much you can take some of it home or give it to the girls."

"Are you kidding? There won't be anything left. Everyone's still got their sweet tooth." Lindsey glanced around the Wishbone until her eyes landed on Mary, who was flirting with a tourist. "Finish unloading Deidre's car when you get a chance," Lindsey called to her. "I'm going to get off my feet for five minutes."

"I can come back later," Deidre offered.

"You'll do no such thing. I want to know what's been going on. Come on, we'll go to the back and help Hannah prep for the lunch crowd."

Deidre followed Lindsey to the kitchen, stopping to wish Mrs. Everett and Dr. Hensen a Happy New Year. Bobby also stopped her when she passed by, commissioning a birthday cake for his wife next week.

"She likes coconut and cheesecake," he said, grimacing at the combination. Deidre knew he was more of a chocolate man.

"I'll come up with something," Deidre promised.

They greeted Hannah and the new dishwasher, Mel. Lindsey and Deidre then washed their hands and sat down in a couple of chairs in the back of the kitchen, flouring their hands. Lindsey brought out several large bowls of dough that had been rising, warm and light to the touch. Lindsey's lunch special for the day was chicken 'n dumplings but first they needed to make the dumplings.

"Okay, so first things first," Lindsey said. "You and Kevin walked around the lake how many times now?"

Deidre counted. "Seven."

Hannah, overhearing them, turned with a look of astonishment on her face. Mary, who had just walked in, clasped her hands together. Lindsey held up a hand, motioning them to be quiet.

"Seven?" she asked

"Yes." Deidre looked at the two of them. "What?" she asked.

"Girl," Mary said. "You're gonna get *married*!" She started to chant, "Deidre and Kevin, sittin' in a tree, K-I-S-S-I-N-G. First comes love, then comes marriage, then comes Deidre with a . . ."

"What?!"

"Hold on a minute," Lindsey said, calming Deidre. She pointed to the dough in front of Deidre. "Start kneading; these need to go in the pot in fifteen minutes."

"Will somebody please tell me what's going on?"

Lindsey said, "There's a saying about ol' Lake Wish. Legend has it that if you walk around the lake once, you'll find something you've lost. Twice, you'll find good luck. Three times, a wish will come true. Four times, you'll connect with an old friend. Five times . . ." She stopped, and looked quizzically at Hannah. "Five times . . ."

". . . you'll receive an unexpected gift. Six times . . ."

". . . you'll experience unequaled generosity," Mary chimed in, as she walked back into the dining room, her arms full of food.

"Seven times, you'll find your true purpose. And eight times . . ." Lindsey hesitated and Hannah looked back at her, waiting.

"Eight times . . . what happens at eight times?"

Lindsey and Hannah grinned at each other, then looked at Deidre. "Eight times, you find true love."

Deidre stared at them, stunned. "Eight times is . . ."

"True love," Lindsey said. "You're not kneading, Deidre."

Deidre turned her attention to the dough and began kneading, vigorously. It wasn't completely out in left field—if anyone was going to be the man of her dreams, Kevin Johnson headed the list. He did tell his mother about her; that had to be a good sign. And she did love being with him. Being with him felt like, well, home.

"Deidre?" Lindsey interrupted her reverie and gingerly removed the dough from her. "Take it easy there," she said.

"We want to eat it, eventually, not create a new kind of plastic."

"So, just so I'm clear about this—you're saying if I walk around the lake one more time with Kevin, he's the one?"

"I didn't say that. Did you hear me say that?" Lindsey asked Hannah innocently. Hannah grinned and shook her head, turning back to the chicken. "I said you'll find true love. I don't know, maybe Kevin's not the one and some guy will walk into your life tomorrow who'll sweep you off your feet. I've seen it happen."

"No way," Deidre said confidently.

"I'm just saying, anything is possible."

"No," Deidre said simply, shaking her head and smiling to herself as she thought about Kevin. She rolled the dough into long strips and began cutting small wedges. "That's not possible. It's not even an option."

"Sure it is," Lindsey said, arguing with her. "We've seen oblivious brides take a walk before their wedding, and bam! Wedding's off, bride's run off with the garbage man."

"I don't think so."

"Why not?"

"Because Kevin's the one and I lov . . ." Deidre caught herself and turned red.

A small smile tugged at the corner of Lindsey's mouth as she tossed a handful of dumplings into a bowl, satisfied. Hannah was chuckling.

"That's not fair, you tricked me," Deidre protested.

"So you two haven't said the *L* word yet," Lindsey said.

"Of course not! I mean, up to last week, we weren't even speaking, and now you're asking me if we've used the *L* word?"

"Well, all I'm saying is, local legend doesn't lie. Maybe you should walk that lake before he gets back, see what happens, cover your bases just in case." Lindsey nodded to the crowded diner. "Lots of nice-looking young men out there. The lucky guy could be sitting there, drinking his coffee, eating one of your scones . . ."

"I'm not going to fall for it a second time," Deidre said, tossing her dumpling wedges into the bowl. "Kevin and I are seeing each other and I have no interest in meeting anybody else."

"Okay, okay," Lindsey said. Hannah started to hum, "Here Comes the Bride," just as Mary stuck her head into the kitchen.

"Deidre, you have a call," she said. "It's a guy. I couldn't quite make out what he was saying, it's kind of crazy out there, but he said it was important."

Deidre wiped her floured hands on a towel and ignored the look the other two women exchanged. "He probably wanted to check about dinner," Deidre said hastily, trying to subdue the pleased look on her face.

"Or dessert," Hannah said, and both women began to crack up. Deidre gave them an exasperated look as she left the kitchen.

She picked up the receiver on the pay phone. "Hello?" she said, making her voice sound slow and sexy.

"You didn't call her, did you?" It was William, sounding genuinely annoyed.

"Happy New Year to you, too. Did you get my message about *Seattle Revealed*?" Deidre had a hand clapped over one ear and was shouting to him over the din.

"I did, congratulations, it's fantastic news and we are very happy for you."

Alain was also on the line. "Yes. *Trés bien, c'est fantastique!*"

William's voice crescendoed to an agitated whine. "But you *promised* you would call her!"

"Who?"

"The crazy lady from your show!" he said. Deidre could tell he was scowling.

"The lesbian," Alain added ruefully.

"She and Alain had a huge fight this morning," William said. "She doesn't believe that we're passing on the message that she's trying to call you."

"She is insane," Alain said.

"Okay, okay," Deidre said. "I'm sorry, it just got really crazy here and Kevin's whole family was here and then he just left . . ."

"I don't care," William said. "Just call her. Now. Here are the numbers."

Deidre wrote it hastily on her hand.

"We will ring back in fifteen minutes," Alain warned. "We will call every hour, on the hour, until you . . ."

"Yes, Alain, I get it. William, I will call her right now and if she's not there I'll leave a message."

"She's *always* there, Deidre. Don't you get it? The woman is obsessed."

"Sleep with her if you must," Alain said.

"Yes, Alain, you've told me that before. Thank you. Okay, if you want me to call her, you're going to have to hang up . . ."

The phone went dead.

Deidre smiled as she punched in Manuela's number and waited for it to ring.

It rang several times before someone answered. "Manuela Jamison's office," a voice said.

"This is Deidre McIntosh. I'm returning . . ."

"One moment, Ms. McIntosh. I'll put you right through."

"Deidre!" Manuela clucked excitedly into the phone. "I've been trying to get ahold of you for months. Where have you been?"

"It's a long story. What can I help you with?"

"Did you have a good holiday?"

"Wonderful, thank you." *Uh-oh, small talk.* Deidre sensed a nervous energy from Manuela. "How are you and Frank?"

"Things couldn't be better," Manuela said. "Our holiday party was the largest yet—almost one hundred and fifty employees—and it was so much fun. I would have invited you so you could meet some of our people, but I had an awful time trying to reach you. There were those two men in particular—the French one really needs a lesson in manners," Manuela declared.

Deidre squirmed. Where was this going? "What can I do for you, Manuela? I don't mean to be rude, but I need to get back into the kitchen in a few minutes."

"That's what I like about you, Deidre. You get right to the point and you're one hundred percent committed to what you do. I was very sad to hear about the cancellation of *Live Simple*, but as they say, all things happen for a reason, and I realized the opportunity I was waiting for was presenting itself. The truth is I've had my eye on you for some time, even before I was on your show."

Is she hitting on me? Deidre wondered, thinking back to the show when Manuela had been a guest.

"That pretty much clinched it for me. I was so impressed that I got to thinking. And it turns out you catered my nephew's wedding a few years back and they loved your food, especially the hors d'oeuvres and the wedding cake. I didn't really recall the food, but I remember the cake with great affection. It was a rich dark chocolate with buttercream frosting . . ."

Deidre remembered. ". . . five tiers since they had been together for five years prior to getting married . . ."

". . . with mint roses and a light mint filling." Manuela sighed provocatively.

"Well, your nephew said they loved Peppermint Patties so I tried to accommodate without going overboard," Deidre said proudly. That cake was a true work of art, inside and out.

"So let me get straight to the point. You may have heard that my father passed not too long ago . . ."

"Oh, I'm sorry to hear that."

"Thank you. It was actually a good thing; he had been in pain for a long time and held in there until he eventually had to let go. With his passing, I inherited the company outright, even though I've been handling the business development side of things since I was in my twenties and, Deidre honey, I don't have to tell you how long ago *that* was.

"Anyhow, we've been looking for a new product line for Jamison's Cookies and Confections. My husband, Frank, who worked for my father for years before he and I were ever married, would like to see us develop the candy side of the business more but Frank knows manufacturing, not business development. I'm telling you, I've done the numbers and it doesn't make sense. Market's too small, there's a higher spoilage rate and all sort of other problems that we still have yet to resolve with our current candy line. So I got to thinking: what else could we do that was new and fresh, but still in alignment with our business? Something that would have immediate credibility and could enter the gourmet marketplace easily, with panache. And, Deidre honey, it was like a dream. I instantly saw a line of cookies packaged under your name. The marketing people can figure out the branding, but it would be your recipes, manufactured and distributed by us."

"You want my recipes?" Deidre asked, not quite comprehending. Was Manuela proposing what Deidre thought she was proposing? A branded cookie line of her own?

Manuela mistook Deidre's question as a hardball negotiation tactic. "We would pay you for them, of course, and you would still own them but they would be used exclusively with your own brand. And I would expect, of course, that you would have the final say in tweaking any new recipes. We would pay you a handsome royalty, of course, provided you met your obligations in co-promoting the brand and introducing new cookies every season."

Of course. Deidre staggered, leaning against the pay phone for support. "Are you serious?" she asked.

Manuela sighed impatiently, thinking they were still negotiating. "Well, the advantage to going with us is that our production facility is already in place, we have a great distribution model, and we have the marketing dollars to support the launch of a new product. You would preapprove the entire line, the packaging and marketing. We would otherwise do all the work. I had my team run some numbers and, especially with the trend in gourmet and mail-order foods, I think it would do quite well, grossing in the low millions in the first twenty-four months. I figured by now you've been approached by other food companies, but we are really the best poised for growth."

Oh my God, Deidre realized *She's trying to sell me on doing this!* She wanted to burst out laughing.

Manuela added furtively, "Of course, there's been talk of you writing a cookbook, and that would be just the sort of thing that would ensure the success of your gourmet cookie line and we would of course be very open to collaborating with you on that project."

"Of course," Deidre said, her head spinning.

"I don't mean to pressure you, but I just didn't think it would take this long to get in touch with you, and Frank is breathing down my neck since I've been putting him off on expanding our candy segment. So if you're interested, let's meet and I can go through the proposal in detail and then you can have your lawyers look at it and we'll make any last minute changes and finalize it. That is," Manuela drawled, "if you're interested."

There was a pause as Deidre tried to catch her breath and Manuela waited apprehensively on the other line.

"I'm interested," Deidre said at last. "I am definitely interested."

There was a huge sigh of relief and then Manuela was boisterously chatty again. "Wonderful! When are you in Seattle next?"

"I can come up in the next week."

"Let me check with Frank and our marketing director and we can find a time to meet. Can you call my office tomorrow to set it up once you know you'll be in town?"

"Absolutely." They were about to hang up when Deidre asked, "Manuela, I have to ask. You've been on so many other shows as well as the Food Network. Any particular reason you're choosing to partner with me?"

Manuela chuckled and Deidre was sure that if she were standing in front of her, Deidre would have ended up with another big kiss on the cheek.

"Honey, I know a good thing when I see one. I'll see you soon."

In a daze, Deidre hung up the phone and staggered back to the kitchen. The chicken and dumplings were already on the stove, and Lindsey was stirring the large stock pot.

"How's lover boy?" Lindsey asked. She and Hannah cracked up once again.

"It wasn't him," Deidre said, faintly. She collapsed into a chair and looked up at Lindsey. "Are those legends really true?"

"Of course they're true," Lindsey said, slightly horrified. "This is sacred country out here. Why, did something happen?"

"Something did. And I can't believe it."

"Well," Lindsey said. "You gotta believe. That's the first step."

Deidre glanced at the clock. Kevin would be back in six hours. "I have to go," she said, jumping up and giving Lindsey a kiss. She waved to Hannah and rushed out the door.

IT WAS ALMOST seven o'clock by the time a weary Kevin walked through the door. "Traffic," he said grimly. "I'm ready to crawl into bed. Which is lucky for you."

Deidre was already dressed in warm clothes and her hiking boots. She had laid out a similar outfit for Kevin on the bed. He looked at her, curious. "What's this?"

"I thought maybe we could take a quick walk," she said. "It'll help your circulation."

"True. But now? Where? Around the lake?"

Deidre hesitated. "If you're up for it."

"Are you?"

"I am. I have some things I want to talk with you about tonight. Good things."

He was watching her intently. "Give me a minute to change my clothes."

They grabbed flashlights before bundling up and stepping out into the dark night.

"I've actually never walked this at night," Kevin said.

"How many times have you walked the lake?"

"A few times, maybe four or five. I usually never have more than a day or two out here at a time, so I would do shorter walks, you know—to the clearing, or over to Uncle Harry's cabin. But of course, with you, I think I've doubled my record, at least."

"Hmmm." Deidre didn't say anything, just held his hand tightly as they walked. They walked much of the path in silence, the moonlight casting a bright light onto Lake Wish. Deidre had never seen a night so clear.

Kevin finally sighed. "I'm going to miss it here," he said. "But I'm going to have to go back to Seattle in a couple of days, and then I have a barrage of meetings and business trips. Have you decided what you'd like to do?"

"I'm going back with you," Deidre said. "I'm going to miss Jacob's Point, but, as you so subtly pointed out, some of us have to work. I have to get things finalized with Uncle Harry for the show. I also have some other important meetings as well." She took a deep breath. "Jamison Cookies and Confections wants to partner with me to co-brand a line of cookies with my name on them."

Kevin stopped abruptly and turned to face her. "Are you serious?"

"I am." She laughed.

"Deidre McIntosh's Cookies?"

"Well, I don't know what we'll end up calling it, but something like that."

"Decadent Deidre's Cookies?"

Deidre laughed. "That sounds like R-rated cookies. I think you'd better leave the naming to me. I'm thinking something simple that would leave the door open for other products in addition to cookies. Of course, they don't know that yet."

"It's amazing," Kevin said, stopping to give her a kiss. "You're amazing."

"I feel so lucky," Deidre said. The she remembered what Lindsey once told her. It wasn't about luck, it was about hard work. Deidre had worked hard for five years to make *Live Simple* a good show, and now it was paying off.

They were approaching the house. Deidre thought, *That makes eight. Eight times around the lake. Eight times, you find true love.*

"You know, Lindsey was telling me a legend about walking around the lake," Deidre said carefully.

"Really?" Kevin sounded genuinely interested.

"I don't remember all of them, but it's something like seven times around the lake, you'll find your true purpose. And eight times around the lake . . ." Deidre hesitated.

Kevin waited, a smile on his lips, his hands holding Deidre's, tight.

"Eight times around the lake, you find your true love." Deidre held her breath.

Kevin didn't seem surprised. "Was this your eighth time?"

"Yes."

"And?"

Deidre said, "I think the legend must be true, because I've fallen in love with you." Relief poured from her body and there were tears in her eyes. "I know it's early, and that we hardly know each other . . ."

Kevin gathered her in his arms, kissed the top of her forehead. "Sweet Deidre," he said. "It was my eighth time around days ago. I was waiting for that moment—that was the day I made us walk it twice. I love you." He wiped the tears that spilled from her eyes.

"You know the legend about walking around the lake?" she asked.

"Of course," he said. "I know about all nine of them."

She looked up at him, astonished, eyes bright. "Nine? There's one more? What is it?"

Kevin smiled as he glanced toward the house, toward the bedroom, and then back at Deidre, taking in her slender frame, picturing her belly round and perfect, growing. He chuckled. "Tomorrow's another day, Deidre love. You'll have to wait and see."

The Recipes

Orgasmic Corn Fritters

with Chinese Peppercorn, Crème Fraîche, and Sherry

Serves 4

William uses fresh Chinese peppercorn from China, but you can substitute red chili flakes or experiment with other local peppercorn varieties. This orgasmic response helped Deidre shape her future—imagine what it can do for you!

1 cup plus 2 teaspoons all-purpose flour
1/4 teaspoon baking powder
1 egg
1 cup fresh corn kernels, off the cob
2 tablespoons red bell pepper, finely chopped
1/4 cup sherry
1/8 teaspoon Chinese peppercorn, crushed (or substitute dried red chili flakes)
1/4 cup crème fraîche
1 tablespoon extra virgin olive oil

1. In a large bowl, mix flour, baking powder, egg, corn, bell pepper, sherry, Chinese peppercorn, and crème fraîche.
2. Bring a skillet to medium high heat; add olive oil.
3. Drop spoonfuls of batter, forming four fritters, cooking until bottoms are lightly browned, about 3 minutes.
4. Flip carefully and cook an additional 2 minutes. Drain any excess oil and serve.

Linguine with Rose Petal Sauce

Serves 6

A last-minute scramble and surf on the web found this delicate yet hearty recipe for Live Simple*'s "Coming Up Roses" segment. The sauce is actually a pesto. If you choose to use rose petals from your garden, be sure that they are well-washed and free from pesticides or other chemicals.*

2 cups fresh basil, finely shredded
4 large garlic cloves, chopped
1/3 cup pine nuts
1 cup extra virgin olive oil
1 1/2 teaspoons rosewater
1 cup Parmigiano Reggiano cheese, grated
1/2 cup Romano cheese, grated
1 pound linguini
1 1/2 tablespoons salt
4 quarts water
1/2 cup heavy cream
salt and freshly ground pepper to taste
1 cup rose petals

1. To make the rose petal pesto, combine the basil, garlic, and pine nuts in a food processor or blender until chunky but not puréed.
2. Add olive oil and rose water slowly.
3. Add the Parmigiano Reggiano and Romano, salt and pepper, continue to blend lightly.

4. Cover and reserve half for future use.
5. Boil the linguine and drain (reserve 2 tablespoons of pasta water—see below). Place linguine back into hot pot.
6. Add 2 tablespoons of the pasta water and the cream into the pesto and toss with pasta.
7. Place in large serving bowl immediately, and garnish with slivered rose petals.

Uptown Bistro's Spinach Salad

with Light Roquefort Dressing

Serves 8

The Uptown Bistro didn't get a lot of things right, but this one was a winner. Try it, and you'll see why Caroline cleaned her plate before sticking Deidre with the bill.

SPINACH SALAD

4 hard-boiled egg whites, coarsely chopped

8 mushrooms, sliced

1 1/2 pounds spinach, stems removed, washed

2 tablespoons slivered almonds

1. Toast slivered almonds for 3 to 5 minutes in a preheated 300°F oven.
2. Wash and pat dry spinach leaves and tear into bite-size pieces.
3. Toss with Light Roquefort Dressing (see below) and serve on individual plates. Top with almonds, egg whites, and sliced mushrooms.

Making Yogurt Cheese

Yogurt cheese is a healthy alternative to sour cream, cream cheese, or mayonnaise. It requires some advance preparation but can be stored for up to the life of the yogurt. To make 1 cup of yogurt cheese, place 2 to 3 cups nonfat yogurt in a yogurt strainer or cheese cloth. This will remove any excess water, thickening the yogurt. Let drain 12 to 24 hours in the refrigerator, checking occasionally until desired thickness is achieved. Refrigerate any unused portion.

LIGHT ROQUEFORT DRESSING

6 ounces Roquefort cheese (the better the cheese, the better the dressing)
1 cup thick, nonfat yogurt cheese (made from 3 cups nonfat yogurt—see above)
2 tablespoons low-fat mayonnaise
freshly ground pepper to taste

1. Mix Roquefort, yogurt cheese, and mayonnaise together. Season with pepper.

Lindsey's Meatloaf Special

Serves 6

Instead of driving back to Seattle, Deidre found herself driving to the Wishbone for Lindsey's dinner special, her first official meal in Jacob's Point.

MEATLOAF

2 eggs, beaten

2/3 cup milk

3 slices bread

1/2 cup white or yellow onion, chopped

1/2 cup Parmigiano Reggiano cheese, grated

1 teaspoon salt

1/4 teaspoon black pepper

1 1/2 pounds lean ground beef

TOPPING

1/2 cup tomato sauce

1/2 cup brown sugar

1 teaspoon mustard

1. Preheat the oven to 350°F.
2. Combine eggs, milk, and bread. Let stand until bread absorbs liquid.
3. Stir in onion and cheese.
4. Add ground beef. Mix well. Shape into a loaf.
5. Bake for 50 minutes.
6. Combine topping ingredients and spoon over meatloaf after 30 minutes. Spoon topping over meatloaf every 10 minutes while meatloaf is cooking.

Maple Walnut Scones in Origami Parchment Pockets

Yields 16 large scones

"If Deidre wanted a fresh scone, there was only one way she was going to get one." A great way to keep yourself occupied for an afternoon. Tuck them in simple parchment wrap and embellish with raffia or kitchen twine. Add a sprig of pine needles and you'll be a dead ringer for Live Simple*'s popular host.*

$3\frac{1}{2}$ cups all-purpose flour

1 cup walnuts, finely chopped and toasted

4 teaspoons baking powder

1 teaspoon salt

$\frac{2}{3}$ cup unsalted butter

1 cup milk

$\frac{3}{4}$ cup maple syrup

1. Preheat the oven to 425°F.
2. In a large bowl, combine flour, walnuts, baking powder, and salt. Cut in the butter until the mixture resembles coarse crumbs.
3. In a separate bowl, combine the milk with $\frac{1}{3}$ cup of the maple syrup. Add the wet ingredients to the dry ingredients and mix until you've formed a very soft dough.
4. Flour your work surface generously. Scrape the dough out of the mixing bowl onto the floured surface. Divide the dough in half.
5. Working with half of the dough at a time, gently pat the dough into a 7-inch circle about $\frac{7}{8}$-inch thick.

Tip

To keep your scones tender, place your mixing bowl in the freezer for a few minutes before starting, and keep the butter and milk chilled. Work quickly and avoid overmixing.

Toasting Walnuts

Toast the walnuts before chopping them. Place walnut pieces in a single layer in a flat pan and toast them in a preheated 350°F oven for 7 to 9 minutes, or until they smell toasty and are beginning to brown. Remove promptly and let cool.

Transfer the circle to a parchment-lined or lightly greased cookie sheet or other flat pan. Repeat with the remaining half of the dough, placing it on a separate pan.

6. Using a knife or rolling pizza wheel, divide each dough circle into eight wedges. Gently separate the wedges so that they're almost touching in the center, but are spaced about an inch apart at the edges. Pierce the tops of the scones with the tines of a fork, and brush them with the remaining maple syrup.
7. Bake the scones for 15 to 18 minutes, or until golden brown. Wait a couple of minutes, then gently separate the scones with a knife and carefully transfer them to a cooling rack. Serve warm or at room temperature.

Hardware Bobby's Oven-Baked, Old-Fashioned Fries

Serves 10

With the deep fryer on the fritz, Lindsey has no choice but to serve her patrons Deidre's oven-baked alternative. Serve with malt vinegar for a flavorful snack or side.

2 pounds unpeeled baking potatoes (Russet or Idado), scrubbed

1 teaspoon Hungarian paprika

1/2 teaspoon freshly ground black pepper

1 teaspoon fine sea salt

2 tablespoons extra virgin olive oil

1. Preheat the oven to 425°F.
2. Cut potatoes into 1/4-inch-thick fries, leaving the skin on. If you won't be baking the potatoes right away, refrigerate in a bowl of water to prevent browning and then drain and pat dry when ready to season and bake.
3. In a large bowl, combine remaining ingredients and toss thoroughly.
4. Arrange the potatoes in a single layer on a baking sheet lined with parchment paper. Bake for 20 minutes, tossing midway through, until potatoes are soft and lightly browned. Serve immediately.

Chocolate Cherry Crackle Cookies

Yields 2 dozen

One of Deidre's confections that won the hearts—and appetites—of chocoholic locals and tourists alike!

1 1/2 cups sugar

1/2 cup prunes, puréed with 3 tablespoons of water

1/2 cup nonfat yogurt

1/4 cup canola oil

2 egg whites

1/2 teaspoon instant espresso powder

1/2 cup dried cherries, chopped

1 1/2 cups cake flour

1 cup cocoa powder

1/2 teaspoon salt

1/2 teaspoon baking soda

1 cup powdered sugar, sifted

1. Preheat the oven to 350°F.
2. In a large mixing bowl, whisk together the sugar, prune purée, yogurt, oil, egg whites, espresso powder, and cherries (the liquid mixture).
3. Sift the flour, cocoa, salt, and baking soda together in another bowl (the flour mixture).
4. Slowly stir the flour mixture into the liquid mixture until blended well.
5. Chill the dough in the refrigerator for 30 minutes.
6. Roll the chilled dough with your hands into balls the

size of ping-pong balls. Roll in powdered sugar and place on a parchment-lined baking sheet. Bake for 12–15 minutes or until firm.

Old-Fashioned Mashed Potatoes

Serves 8

Lindsey has no interest in Deidre's healthier version of the time-honored classic. Both versions are included below—you tell us which one you think should be served next to the turkey! This dish can be prepared up to 3 hours in advance. Reheat prior to serving.

LINDSEY'S RECIPE

2 pounds baking potatoes (Russet or Idaho), scrubbed
1 cup heavy cream
3 tablespoons butter
1/2 cup buttermilk
1/2 teaspoon ground white pepper
Hungarian paprika to taste
salt and freshly ground pepper to taste

1. In a large stock pot, bring water to boil.
2. Cut potatoes into pieces. When the water is boiling, drop the pieces in and cook for about 30 minutes, or until tender. Drain the potatoes, then mash using a fork or potato masher. Transfer into a large saucepan.
3. Stir in the remaining ingredients, adding the buttermilk last, and combine until well mixed. Season to taste.

DEIDRE'S RECIPE

2 pounds baking potatoes (Russet or Idaho), scrubbed
1 cup nonfat yogurt cheese (see recipe on p. 326)
2 tablespoons margarine spread
1/2 cup skim milk
1/2 teaspoon ground white pepper
Hungarian paprika to taste
salt and freshly ground pepper to taste

1. In a large stock pot, bring water to boil.
2. Cut potatoes into pieces. When the water is boiling, drop the pieces in and cook for about 30 minutes, or until tender. Drain the potatoes, then mash using a fork or potato masher. Transfer into a large saucepan.
3. Stir in the remaining ingredients, adding the skim milk last, and combine until well mixed. Season to taste.

Deidre's Aromatic Gingerbread

Serves 12

Who needs potpourri? To get your home smelling like the season, whip up a pan of Deidre's gingerbread. This is a breadier gingerbread that uses three different forms of ginger: fresh, ground, and crystallized. The applesauce is in lieu of butter, which significantly reduces the fat in the recipe.

2 tablespoons rice bran oil
6 tablespoons applesauce
1 cup dark brown sugar

Preventing Brown Sugar Clumps

Does your brown sugar clump together? Try adding a piece of bread into your brown sugar container.

1 egg
1 egg white
2 teaspoons crystallized ginger, finely chopped
1 teaspoon fresh ginger, grated
1 teaspoon lemon zest, finely chopped
1/4 cup buttermilk
3/4 cup molasses
1/2 cup boiling water
2 3/4 cups all-purpose flour
1/2 cup cake flour
2 teaspoons baking soda
1/2 teaspoon fine sea salt
2 teaspoons ground ginger
2 cloves, ground

1. Preheat the oven to 350°F.
2. In a large mixing bowl, whisk together the oil, applesauce, brown sugar, egg, egg white, crystallized and fresh ginger, lemon zest , buttermilk, molasses, and boiling water.
3. Sift the flours, baking soda, salt, ground ginger, and cloves. When ready, stir the dry ingredients into the applesauce mixture.
4. In a buttered and floured 9 x 12-inch baking pan, pour the batter and bake for 25–30 minutes, until toothpick comes out clean.

5. Cool for 5 minutes, then remove from pan and let cool for 30 minutes. Cut into squares or slices and serve.

Johnson Family Eggnog

Yields approximately 1 1/2 gallons

Kevin prepared this high-octane eggnog recipe to help usher in the holiday spirit. Like Kevin, slow and gentle does the job and will keep the eggnog fluffy. It takes forever to prepare (as most good things do), but you won't regret it.

12 eggs
1 cup powdered sugar
4 cups bourbon whiskey
2 cups brandy
2 cups rum
2 cups milk (use whole milk for better results)
4 cups whipping cream
ground nutmeg to taste, optional

1. Separate the egg yolks and whites into separate bowls.
2. Beat egg yolks until very light and frothy.
3. Beat egg whites until very stiff.
4. Beat powdered sugar into the yolks, a little at a time.
5. Stir in the whiskey slowly, then do likewise with the brandy, and then the rum.
6. Add the milk.
7. Fold in the egg whites.
8. Whip the cream until it is as light as eggs.

9. Fold in whipped cream. For best results, use a rubber spatula.
10. Sprinkle freshly ground nutmeg on top (optional) and serve at room temperature.

Fresh Salmon and Penne Salad

With Creamy Light Dill Dressing

Serves 10

Serve this healthy salad at room temperature—it's perfect on the buffet. Deidre scored points with Kevin's parents with this one.

FRESH SALMON AND PENNE SALAD

1/2 pound snow peas

1 pound penne

1 tablespoon rice bran oil

12 ounces salmon filet, poached and crumbled

1 tablespoon onion, finely chopped

2 stalks celery, peeled and sliced

2 red bell peppers, roasted and chopped

8 radishes, sliced

Creamy Light Dill Dressing (see below)

1. Blanch snow peas for one minute; put aside.
2. Boil the penne and drain. Transfer to a large bowl and toss well with rice bran oil.
3. Add the poached salmon, onion, celery, snow peas, bell peppers, and radishes to the pasta and toss well.
4. Drizzle 1 cup of Creamy Light Dill Dressing; toss well and serve.

CREAMY LIGHT DILL DRESSING

1 1/2 cups yogurt cheese (see recipe on p. 326)
5 tablespoons balsamic vinegar
5 tablespoons concentrated beef or vegetable stock
1 1/2 teaspoons honey balsamic mustard
1/3 teaspoon hot pepper sauce
5 tablespoons fresh dill, finely chopped
salt to taste

1. In a blender or food processor, combine the yogurt cheese, vinegar, stock, mustard, hot pepper sauce, salt, and dill.
2. Blend until mixture is smooth and creamy. Refrigerate until ready to serve.

Potato and Leek Gratin

Serves 8

Even Marla went back for seconds with this one when no one was looking. You can prepare this dish up to two hours in advance through step 4. Refrigerate and, when you are ready, proceed with step 5.

1 1/2 cups chicken or vegetable stock
3 large leeks, cleaned and sliced, white part only
5 cloves of garlic, sliced thin
1 tablespoon extra virgin olive oil
1 1/2 pounds baking potatoes (Russet or Idado), peeled
1/2 cup Parmigiano Reggiano cheese, grated
2 tablespoons flat-leaf parsley, finely chopped
salt and freshly ground pepper to taste

Preparing the Leeks

To prepare the leeks, remove the green stems where they naturally bend, as the green stems can be bitter. Cut off and discard. Slice each leek lengthwise, leaving the bottom inch intact, then turn 90 degrees and slice lengthwise again. Rinse well as leeks often retain dirt and sand.

1. Preheat the oven to 375°F.
2. In a medium skillet, combine 1/2 cup of the stock with the leeks and simmer until softened, about 2 minutes. Add garlic and simmer until most of the liquid has evaporated, about 10 minutes. Add salt and pepper to taste and set aside.
3. Lightly brush a stoneware baking dish with olive oil. Slice the potatoes thin, laying 1/3 of them on the bottom of the dish. Sprinkle with salt and pepper.
4. Drain the leeks and add half of the leeks. Make another layer of potatoes, salt, and pepper, adding the remaining leeks. Top with a final layer of potatoes and pour the remaining cup of stock over the potato and leek mixture.
5. Cover with foil and bake for 40 minutes. After 40 minutes, remove the foil and sprinkle cheese on top, and continue baking until golden and crisp, about 10–15 minutes.
6. Remove from the oven and let stand for 2 minutes. Garnish with parsley and serve.

Deidre's Peace of Mind Tea

Yields approximately 16 cups

Following is Deidre's favorite tea blend to help her stay relaxed regardless of how hectic things might be, on or off the set. This recipe is naturally caffeine-free, but adding 1/4 cup (about 2 oz) of loose green or black tea leaves will give caffeine lovers that extra kick.

3 teaspoons dried chamomile
3 teaspoons dried rosehips
3 teaspoons dried lemongrass
3 teaspoons dried mint
3 teaspoons dried hibiscus
1 orange
1 lemon
Note: If using fresh leaves or flowers, use 1 tablespoon instead of 1 teaspoon.

1. Preheat oven to 250°F.
2. Wash and dry orange and lemon. With a vegetable peeler, remove only outer peel, not white pith. Cut peels into very small pieces; arrange on parchment-lined baking sheet. Dry in oven 20 minutes.
3. Add dried citrus peel pieces to dried herbs; toss to combine. Transfer mixture to airtight container.
4. Add 1 teaspoon of blend to a tea ball and tea strainer.
5. Pour boiling water over tea leaves and let steep for five minutes. Discard or compost used tea leaves.

How to Make the Perfect Pot of Tea

- For best results, use a glass or china pot; metal is not recommended.
- Warm the teakettle by filling it with hot water and letting it stand for a few minutes, then drain.
- Fill the teapot with fresh cold water (this helps to bring out the full character of the tea).
- Bring the water to a rolling boil. Avoid boiling too long or the tea will taste flat.
- Use 1 teaspoon loose tea for every 5-ounce cup. Place the loose tea in an infuser into the warmed pot. Pour in the boiling water and cover the pot. Let steep 3 to 5 minutes. Careful not to let it brew too long, which will result in a bitter tasting tea.